THE WEDDING PARTY

What's not to love about a wedding?
Well, except for the I'll-never-wear-this-again
bridesmaid dress, going solo to the ceremony
when your date deserts you and those awkward
encounters with bridezilla...not to mention
the silly group dances. It's almost enough
to deliver a "no, thanks" on the RSVP!

But in this 2-in-1 collection, these women
know how to get the most out of every
wedding occasion. And once they meet that
really hot guy—just right for a sexy night of
fun—the party really begins.

So sit back and enjoy the celebrations as
these stories show that the wedding is the
perfect place to get something started!

ALLY BLAKE

In her previous life, Australian author Ally Blake was at times a cheerleader, a math tutor, a dental assistant and a shop assistant. In this life, Ally is a bestselling, multi-award-winning novelist who has been published in over twenty languages with more than two million books sold worldwide. She married her gorgeous husband in Las Vegas—no Elvis in sight, though Tony Curtis did put in a special appearance—and now Ally and her family, including three rambunctious toddlers, share a property in the leafy western suburbs of Brisbane with kookaburras, cockatoos, rainbow lorikeets and the occasional creepy-crawly. When not writing, she makes coffees that never get drunk, eats too many M&M's, attempts yoga, devours reruns of *The West Wing*, reads every spare minute she can and barracks ardently for the Collingwood Magpies footy team. You can find out more at her website, www.allyblake.com.

ALLY BLAKE

AND

AIMEE CARSON

The Dance-Off

and

Don't Tell the Wedding Planner

HARLEQUIN® THE WEDDING PARTY

Recycling programs
for this product may
not exist in your area.

ISBN-13: 978-0-373-60634-4

THE DANCE-OFF AND DON'T TELL THE WEDDING PLANNER

Copyright © 2014 by Harlequin Books S.A.

The publisher acknowledges the copyright holders
of the individual works as follows:

THE DANCE-OFF
Copyright © 2014 by Ally Blake

DON'T TELL THE WEDDING PLANNER
Copyright © 2014 by Aimee Carson

This edition published by arrangement with Harlequin Books S.A.

For questions and comments about the quality of this book,
please contact us at CustomerService@Harlequin.com.

® and TM are trademarks of the publisher. Trademarks indicated with ® are registered in the United States Patent and Trademark Office, the Canadian Intellectual Property Office and in other countries.

Printed in U.S.A.

CONTENTS

THE DANCE-OFF   7

DON'T TELL THE WEDDING PLANNER   211

THE DANCE-OFF

Ally Blake

For my Dom, whose snuggly hugs, gracious affability and eternal wonder make my heart go pitter-pat each and every day.

Love you, baby boy.

Chapter One

Loose gravel coursing through the gutter slid and crackled beneath Ryder Fitzgerald's shoes as he slammed shut his car door.

Through the darkness of late night his narrowed eyes flickered over the uneven footpath, the barred windows of the abandoned ground-floor shopfronts, past big red doors in need of a lick of paint, up a mass of mottled red brick, over deadened windows of the second floor. The soft golden light in the row of big arched windows on the third floor was the only sign of life on the otherwise desolate street.

He glanced back at his car, its vintage curves gleaming in the wet night, the thoroughbred engine ticking comfortingly as it cooled. Since the closest street lamp was non-operational—tiny shards of broken glass pooled around its base, evidence that was no accident—only moonlight glinted off the black paint.

And he silently cursed his sister.

Glowering, Ryder pressed the remote to double-check the car alarm was set, then he glanced at the pink notepaper upon which Sam's happy scrawl gave up a business name and a street address, hoping he might have read the thing wrong. But no.

This run-down structure in one of the backstreets

of Richmond housed the Amelia Brandt Dance Academy. Inside he would find the woman hired by his sister, Sam, to teach her wedding party to dance. And considering in two months' time he'd be the lucky man giving her away, apparently that included him.

A wedding, he thought, the concept lodging itself uncomfortably in the back of his throat. When he'd pointed out to Sam the number of times she'd done her daughterly duty in attending their own father's embarrassment of weddings, she'd just shoved the address into his palm.

"The instructor is awesome!" she'd gushed. *Better be*, he thought, considering the price of the lessons he was bankrolling. "You'll love her! If anyone can get you to dance like Patrick Swayze it's her!"

Ryder, who'd had no idea who Sam was talking about, had said, "Life-changing as that sounds, there's no way I can guarantee my attendance every Thursday at seven for the foreseeable future so you'll have to have your dance lessons without me."

Lucky for him, Sam had gleefully explained, the dance teacher had agreed to private lessons, any time that suited him. Of course she had. Sam had probably offered the doyenne enough to lash out on a six-month cruise.

"Your own fault she's so damned spoiled," he grumbled out loud.

A piece of newspaper picked up by a gust of hot summer wind fluttered dejectedly down the cracked grey footpath in response.

Ryder scrunched up the pink note and lobbed it into an overflowing garbage bin.

He tugged at his cufflinks as he sauntered up the

front steps. It was a muggy night, oppressive in a way Melbourne rarely saw, and he was more than ready to be rid of his suit. It had been a long day. And the very last thing he wanted to do right now was cha-cha with some grand dame in pancake make-up, a tight bun and breathing heavily of the bottle of Crème de Menthe hidden in the record player. But Sam was getting antsy. And he'd spent enough years keeping the *antsy* at bay to know revisiting the high-school waltz would be less complicated than dealing with one of his sister's frantic phone calls.

"One lesson," he said, wrenching open the heavy red door and stepping inside.

A Do Not Enter sign hung askew from the front of an old-fashioned lift with lattice casing. His eyes followed the cables to their origins, but all he saw were shadows, dust, and cobwebs so old they drifted lazily by way of a draught coming from somewhere it structurally ought not to.

Less impressed by the second, Ryder trudged up the steep narrow staircase that wound its way around the lift shaft, the space lit by a string of lamps with green-tinged glass so pocked and dust-riddled the weak glare made his eyes water.

And the heat only grew, thickened, pressing into him as he made his way up three floors—the ground floor apparently untenanted, the second floor wallpapered with ragged posters advertising student plays from years past. As it tended to do, the hottest air collected at the top where a faint light shone through the gap at the bottom of the door, and a small sign mirroring the one downstairs announced that the big black door with the gaudy gold hinges led into the Amelia Brandt Dance Academy.

Ryder turned the wooden knob, its mechanism soft with age. Stifling heat washed against his face as he stepped inside. He loosened his tie, popped the top button of his dress shirt and made a mental note to throttle Sam the very next moment he saw her.

The place appeared uninhabited but for the scent of something rustic and foreign, and the incongruously funky beat of some familiar R&B song complete with breathy sighs and French lyrics.

His eyes roved over the space—habitually calculating floor space, ceiling height, concrete cubic metres, brick palettes, glazier costs. The tall wall of arched windows looking out over the street appeared to be original and mostly in working order—he only just stopped himself from heading that way to check his car was still in situ. From above industrial-size fans hung still. A string of old glass chandeliers poured pools of golden light into the arcs of silvery moonlight streaming across a scuffed wooden floor.

Speckled mirrors lined the near wall, and to his right, in front of ceiling-to-floor curtains that made his nose itch, reclined a sad-looking row of old school lockers with half the doors hanging open, a piano, a half-dozen hula hoops in a haphazard pile on the floor, a row of bookshelves filled with records and sheet music in piles so haphazard and high they seemed in imminent danger of toppling, and lastly a pink velvet lounge—the kind a woman would drape herself over in order to be painted by some lucky artist.

Ryder took another step, his weight bringing forth a groan from the creaky old floor.

The music shut off a moment before a feminine voice called from behind the curtains, "Mr Fitzgerald?"

He turned to the voice as his earlier prediction shimmered to dust. In place of a grand dame past her prime, Scheherazade strolled his way.

Long shaggy dark hair, even darker eyes rimmed in lashings of kohl, skin so pale it seemed to soak in the moonlight. A brown tank top knotted at her waist, showing off a glimpse of taut tummy. An ankle-length skirt made of a million earthen colours swayed hypnotically as she walked. Feet as bare as the day she was born.

Ryder straightened, squared his shoulders and said, "I take it you're the woman whose job it is to turn me into Patrick Swayze."

She blinked, a smile tugging briefly at one corner of her lush mouth before disappearing as if it had never been. "Nadia Kent," she said, holding out a hand.

He took it. Finding it soft, warm, unexpectedly strong. And so strikingly pale he could make out veins beneath the surface. Warmth hummed through him, like an electrical current, from the point where their skin touched and then she slid from his grip and the sensation was gone as if it had never been.

"You're early," she said, her voice rich with accusation, and, if he wasn't wrong, shot with a faint American accent.

"A good thing, I would have thought, considering the late hour." He caught the spicy scent again, stronger this time, as she swayed past.

"And whose idea was that?"

Touché.

Light as a bird, she perched on the edge of the long

pink chair, her dark hair tumbling over her shoulders in dishevelled waves, her exotic skirt settling about her in a slow sway. And Ryder wondered how a woman who looked as if she'd been born right out of the earth had ended up in a gloomy corner of the world such as this.

With a flick of the wrist, she hiked her skirt to her knee, revealing smooth calves wrapped in lean muscle. She slid a pair of beige shoes with small heels from under the couch and buckled herself in. And without looking up she said, "You look hot."

"Why, thank you." His instinctive response echoed through the big room. The only evidence she'd even heard him was the brief pause of her fingers at the last buckle before she slid her hands up her calves to swish the skirt back to the floor.

Was he flirting? Of course he was. The woman was…something else. She was *riveting*.

While she didn't even spare him a glance as she pressed herself to standing, poked a small remote into the waist of her skirt, and, shoes clacking on the floor, walked his way. "If I were you I'd lose the jacket, Mr Fitzgerald. It gets hot in here, hotter still once we get moving, and I don't fancy having to catch you if you faint."

He baulked at the thought, and for a split second thought he saw a flare of triumph in her eyes, before it was swallowed by the eyes so dark he struggled to make out their centres.

Calling her bluff, he slid his jacket from his shoulders, and, finding nowhere better, laid it neatly over the back of the velvet chair. Moth holes. Great. He tugged his loosened tie from his neck and tossed it the same way. Then rid himself of his cufflinks, and rolled his shirtsleeves to his elbows. Moves more fit for a bedroom than a dance hall. Her gaze was so direct as she watched him losing layers it only added to the impression.

Then with no apparent regret, she looked away, leaving him to breathe out long and slow. She pulled her hair off her face and into a low ponytail, lifted her chin, knocked her heels and Scheherazade was no more. In her place stood Dance Teacher.

Which was when Ryder remembered why he was there, and *really* began to sweat.

"Can we make this quick?" he said, recalling the reams of architectural plans curled up in the shelves by his bespoke drafting table at home. More awaited his attention inside the state-of-the-art computer programs back in his offices in the city. Projects of his and projects headed up by his team. Not that he had his father's trouble in settling on one thing; he simply liked to work. And he'd rather pull an all-nighter than spend the next hour entertaining this extravagance.

Nadia Kent's hands slid to her lean hips, the fingers at the top of her skirt dragging the fabric a mite lower. The faint American twang added a lilt to her voice as she said, "You have somewhere else to be at ten o'clock on a Tuesday night, Mr Fitzgerald?"

"There are other things I could be doing, yes."

"So it's not that you're simply too chicken to take dance lessons."

His eyes narrowed, yet his smile grew. "What can I say? I'm a wanted man."

"I'll take your word for it. Now," she said, clapping her hands together in such a way that the sound echoed around the space and thundered back at them. "Where are your tights?"

"Excuse me?"

"Your dancing tights. Sam told you, I hope. If we are going to get any kind of indication of your aptitude you need to have the freedom of movement that tights allow."

He knew she was kidding. Okay, so he was ninety per cent sure. But that didn't stop hairs on his arms from standing on end. "Miss Kent, do I look like the kind of man who would have come within ten kilometres of this place if tights were required?"

He'd given her the invitation after all, yet when those sultry dark eyes gave him a slow once-over, pausing on the top button of his crisp white shirt, the high shine of his belt buckle, the precise crease of his suit trousers, his gut clenched right down low. Then her answer came by way of a smile that slid slowly onto a mouth that was wide, pink, soft, and as sensuous as the rest of her and the clench curled into a tight fist.

His voice hit low as he said, "If this is how you play with clients who are early, Miss Kent, I'd like to see how you treat those who are late."

"No," she said, "you wouldn't."

She slid the remote from her skirt, flicked it over her shoulder, and pressed. The sound of a piano tripped from hidden speakers, filling the lofty space; a husky feminine voice followed. "Now, Mr Fitzgerald, you're paying premium to have me here tonight, so let's give you your money's worth."

When she beckoned him with a finger, moving towards him all the same, saliva pooled beneath his tongue.

He held up both hands. "There is another option."

There, he thought as a flash of anticipation fired in

the depths of her eyes before she blinked and it was gone. But now he knew he wasn't the only one sensing…awareness? Attraction? Definitely *something*…

"What do you say I pay you the full complement of lessons, and we call it a day? Sam needn't ever have to know."

"Great. Fine with me. But when you hit the dance floor on Sam's wedding day, and all eyes are on you as you trip over Sam's feet, what shall we tell her then?"

He wondered for a fanciful fleeting second if the woman might well be a witch. Less than five minutes and she'd struck him right in his Achilles' heel.

"You done, Mr Fitzgerald? Because honestly, I teach two-year-olds who put up less of a fuss. You're a big boy. You can do this."

She lifted her arms into a graceful half-circle in front of her, an invitation for him to do the same. But when he did little more than twitch a muscle in his cheek, she swore—and rather colourfully—before she walked the final few paces, took his hands, and, with a strength that belied her lean frame, lifted them into a matching arc.

Up close he caught glints of auburn in her dark hair. A smattering of tiny freckles dusted the bridge of her nose.

Though his thoughts dried up as she fitted herself into the space between his arms and dropped his right hand to her hip. His palm found fabric, his fingers found skin. Smooth skin. Hot skin. Her skin.

She slid her right hand into his left and the heat of the night became trapped between them.

"Nadia."

"Yes, Ryder," she said, mirroring his serious tone.

"It's been a while for me."

The teeth that flashed within her smile were sharp enough to have his skin tighten all over.

"I'll go easy," she said. "I promise. You just have to trust me. Do you trust me, Ryder?"

"Not a bit."

The smile became a grin, and then her tongue swished slowly across the edge of her top teeth before she tucked it back away.

Maybe not a witch, but definitely a sadist, if how much she was enjoying this was anything to go by. "Nadia—"

"Oh, for heaven's sake! One last question. *One*. And then you shut up and dance."

Stunning, sadistic, and bossy to boot. An audacious combination. And, as it turned out, dead sexy. Which was why he made sure she was looking right at him, those eyes dark with frustration, before asking, "Who on earth is Patrick Swayze?"

At that she laughed, threw back her head and let rip. Her hips rocked against his, sending a wave of lust rolling through him. *Holy hell*.

Her hand landed firmly against his chest. "Let's not set the bar quite so high, hey, twinkle toes? My aim is to get you through three minutes of spinning on a parquet floor without embarrassing the bride." Curling her fingers slightly, she said, "Deal?"

While his blood thundered through his veins at her scent, her nearness, the press of her hips, her hand at his heart, Ryder's voice was rough as dry gravel as he uttered the fateful words, "Where do we start?"

"Where all great dance partnerships start: at the beginning."

As the music continued to swell through the huge

room she told him to listen to the beat. To sway with it. To let his hips guide him.

Gritting his teeth, he wished Sam had never been born. That helped for about five seconds before he gave himself a mental slug. While the kid might well be the one disruption in his otherwise structured life, she was also the best thing that had ever happened to him.

Eleven years old he'd been, only a few months beyond losing his own mother, when his father had remarried. A baby already on the way. Even as a kid, Ryder had understood what that meant—that Fitz hadn't been true to his mother; a woman with such strength, such heart, such insight. Worst of all she must have known it too, even as she'd been sick and dying.

When he felt the familiar sense of loathing rise like poison in his gut, Ryder shoved the memories back into the deep dark vault from which they'd bled. And instead hauled his mind to the day Sam was born. The first time he'd looked into his little sister's big grey eyes had changed everything. He'd vowed to never let her down, knowing already, even so young, that her father—*his* father—would disappoint, would deprive, would step over her to get ahead every chance he got.

And still, with that man as her paternal example, the sweet, clueless little kid was out there right now preparing to get married. *Married—*

"Concentrate!"

Ryder came to with a grimace as Nadia pinched the soft skin between his forefinger and thumb. He glared at her and she glared right on back. For a woman who felt like a wisp of air in his arms, she had strength to spare. "Honestly, Nadia, I don't need this. Show me how to get into and out of a Hollywood dip without pulling a muscle and we're done."

"First," she said, "it's Miss Nadia. Dance protocol. And secondly, the sooner you stop bitching and pay attention, the faster the time will go. Cross my heart." The scoop of her top tugged across her breasts as she crossed herself, the material dipping to expose the bones of her clavicle, the pale skin, the layer of perspiration covering the lot.

"Yes, Miss Nadia."

She liked that, clearly, breaking out in a soft laugh. "That wasn't so hard, was it?"

"You have no idea."

She might have brushed against him, or maybe he'd imagined it. Either way, hard was suddenly an understatement.

And as the hour wore on it didn't get any less so. Her hands seemed to be everywhere. Resting on his hips as she nudged them where she wanted them to go. Sliding slowly along his arms as she lifted them into the right position. Resting on his shoulders as she leant in behind him, pressing her knees into the backs of his to move his feet in time.

It was agony.

And not only because he wasn't used to being on the receiving end of such terse instructions. Though there was that too. Several years in charge of his own multimillion-dollar architectural firm, a guy got used to being in charge.

There was also the occasional waft of heady scent from that cascade of dark hair to contend with. The temptation of that sliver of tight skin above her skirt.

And those *Arabian Nights* eyes tempting, beckoning, inviting him beyond the dance to places dark and sultry.

And then a knowing smile would shift across her lush mouth just before she counted loud and slow as if he were three damn years old.

When she finally turned off the music, he asked, "We're done?"

"For tonight."

Then, as if they hadn't just spent the better part of an hour about as close as a man and a woman could be without their lowlier natures taking over, she simply walked away.

At the pink chair she pulled the band from her hair and shook it out, running her hands through it until it was a tumble of shaggy waves. As if she'd sensed him watching she looked over her shoulder as she bound herself in a wrap-around cardigan, and looped a long silver scarf around her neck. "Next time dress in loose pants, a T-shirt, and bring something warm for after. Even though it's crazy hot outside, your body will cool down dramatically after a workout like this."

Ryder didn't make any promises—he figured a fast cool-down was exactly what he needed. "I'll walk you down."

Her eyebrows disappeared beneath a wave of her hair. "Not necessary. I can handle myself. I'm a child of the mean streets."

Richmond was hardly mean, but, growing up with a little sister with a knack for climbing out of bedroom windows, Ryder had a protective instinct that was well honed. "It's eleven at night. I'm walking you down."

She gave him a level stare from those gypsy eyes of

hers, then with a smile and a shrug she said, "A man's gotta do what a man's gotta do."

"There's that too."

He nabbed his jacket and tie and held them over his elbow rather than rugging up. She noticed, but said nothing, clearly considering herself off the clock.

She moved to an ancient bank of light switches and flipped the place into darkness, leaving only patches of cloud-shrouded moonlight teeming through the big arched windows, and Ryder's gaze was once again drawn to the soaring ceilings, the dusty chandeliers, the obnoxious industrial fans, and last but not least the fantastic criss-cross of exposed beams above, the kind people paid top dollar to reproduce.

Nadia cleared her throat and motioned him out, then with a yank of the door, a bump of the hip and a kick to the skirting board, locked up behind them.

He followed her down the stairs, the green glow of the old lights creating sickly shadows on the wallpaper peeling from the walls. But from topside looking down, the way the stairs curled around the shaft was actually great design. If the lift actually worked—

Irrelevant, he thought, with a flare of irritation. In fact the place should probably be condemned.

But Ryder didn't need a team of crack psychologists to tell him why the building continued to charm. It was just the kind of place his creative mother would have adored. Her legacy to the world was her wonderful sculptures made from things found, abandoned, forgotten, lost. Her legacy to her son was the knowledge that following your heart led only to heartache.

Pressing the memories far deeper, he redirected his gaze to the exit.

"Will I see you next week?" Nadia asked as they spilled out of the door.

"I fear you will," said Ryder as he turned on the cracked grey footpath to face her.

A step higher than he, she swayed sensually, hypnotically, from one foot to the other, as if moving to a rhythm only she could hear. Then she tipped up onto her toes bringing her face level with his. "Sam really has you wrapped around her little finger, doesn't she? I liked her before, but now I have a new-found respect for the woman."

Ryder sniffed out a laugh.

Then when she moved past him, jogging lightly down the stairs, he shoved his hands in his trouser pockets to keep himself from doing anything dangerous, like finding that slice of hot skin at her hips again and using it to drag her against him. Like losing his fingers in those crazy waves. Like ravaging that smart, soft, tilting mouth till she stopped smiling at him as if she were one up on the scoreboard.

But Ryder held fast.

Because, delightful as she was, his only objective for the next few weeks was to survive until Sam's wedding without hiding her away in the top of a large tower where no man could hurt her. Getting all twisted up with the wilful and wily dance teacher, who he was fast gathering had become his sister's friend, would not help his cause one bit.

So instead of drowning in her dark eyes, her lush lips, all that dark sensuality so close within reach, he looked up at the building, past the big red door and up to the big sleeping windows on the third floor. "Do you know who owns this place?"

"Why?" she asked.

Because he was changing the subject.

"Something about the beams," he said, then glanced back to find Nadia halfway down the block.

"Don't ask me," she said over her shoulder. "I just work here."

Ryder watched her until she was swallowed by darkness, leaving him alone on the cracked pavement with his car, his skin cooling quickly in the night air.

Nadia fell into bed a few minutes before midnight. Literally. Standing at the end she let herself flop, fully clothed, face first onto the crumple of unmade sheets.

And the darkness behind her eyelids became a blank canvas as her memories began to play.

She could hear the creak of the stairs cutting through the song she'd been free-styling to. Could feel the disorientation of being caught out, leaving her breathless, sweaty, off kilter. Back on solid ground, wiping away the worst of her glow—*men sweat, women perspire, ladies glow*, her austere grandmother had always said— she'd peeked through the curtains.

Expecting a male version of Sam—tall, big grin, two left feet, handsome, sure, but slightly goofy with it—she'd been critically mistaken.

Ryder Fitzgerald was tall but that was where the similarities ended. Handsome had nothing on the guy—he was simply stunning. In that midnight suit, snowy white shirt, not a hair out of place, not a scuff on his beautiful shoes, he was big, dark, sleek, and razor-sharp. And to top it off, shimmering at the edges of all that relentless perfection was an aura of rough and raw sex appeal, as if the guy left behind an unapologetic testosterone wake.

When she'd ducked back behind the curtain her hands had been shaking. Shaking! Her breaths had shortened. Her stomach had curled tight and hot while her blood had thwacked against the walls of her veins. And all she had been able to think was, *Oh, no.*

With the grace of hindsight she could hardly blame herself. It had been over a year since she'd broken up with her ex after all. And if she was honest, longer again since she'd felt anything near that kind of all out, sweet, sinful, wonderful, carnal reaction to a man. For a woman whose entire life had been spent learning her body, knowing her body, celebrating her body, the fact that her body had become some sort of neutral zone had been damn near unnatural.

So much so, in her more wavery moments she'd wondered if something more than a two-year relationship had been damaged during the whole sordid mess. Even more than a bruised ego and a crumpled career.

But no, she was a Kent, and Kent women didn't cry over broken relationships—or broken bones for that matter. They got over it. Which she had admirably, thank you very much.

And then—right when she was doing so great, when she was dancing better than she had in her entire life, when she was mere weeks away from having the chance to reclaim all that she'd given up—right *then* was when the old flame had to flicker back to life?

Groaning, she rolled over and pulled a pillow tight over the thumping in her chest. It didn't help. Even with her eyes wide open she could still *feel* the play of muscle beneath the man's prosaic white shirt—hard, strong, a surprise. As had been his latent heat. All she'd had to do was touch him and she'd felt it pulsing beneath his skin. The exact same heat that had thudded incessantly through her for the entire hour straight.

Let it go, she thought. *The man's immaterial.* And heard her mother's voice.

Her mother who'd taken one look at Nadia when she'd turned up on her doorstep a year before with nothing but a suitcase and a sad story…and smiled. Not because she was glad to see her only child, oh, no. Claudia Kent's own ballet career had been ruined over a guy, and, seeing the product of that mistake in the same sorry position, she'd found herself looking down the blissful barrel of karmic payback.

Nadia gripped the pillow tighter, this time to stifle the woozy sensation in her belly.

Her mother might be completely devoid of any maternal genes, but at least Nadia had learnt early on how to cope with rejection, which for a jobbing hoofer was pure gold. One couldn't be precious and be a dancer. It was the tough and the damned. Ethel Barrymore had once said to be a success as an actress a woman had to have the face of Venus, the brains of Minerva, the grace of Terpsichore, the memory of Macaulay, the figure of Juno, and the hide of a rhinoceros. Working dancers needed all that *and* to be able to do the splits on cue.

Nadia had all that going for her and more. Yet if she didn't nail the fast-approaching chance to get her life back in a few weeks' time, she'd have deserved that contempt as she'd made the same mistake her mother did before her.

Well, not the *exact* same mistake—at least Nadia hadn't fallen pregnant.

With that wicked little kick of ascendancy fuelling her, she reached into her bedside table and found her notebook. For the next few minutes she pushed every-thing else from her mind and sketched out the moves she'd added to her routine that night before Ryder Fitzgerald had arrived.

In her early twenties she'd lived on natural talent, on chutzpah, and maybe even on her mother's name. A year out of the spotlight and that momentum was gone, and every day away younger, fitter, hungrier dancers were pouring into the void, eager and ready to take her spot. But what those hungry little dancers didn't know was that this time Nadia had an edge—she didn't sim-ply want their jobs; this time she *really* had something to prove.

Sketches done, she slumped back to the bed. She'd shower in the morning. And since she didn't start work till two the next day, she'd have time to attend a couple of classes of her own—maybe a contemporary class in South Yarra, or trapeze in that converted warehouse in Notting Hill. Either way she'd kill it. Because look out, world, Nadia Kent was back, baby.

Despite the late hour, the last whispers of adrenalin still pulsed through her system, so she grabbed her TV remote and scrolled through the movies on her hard drive till she found what she was looking for.

The strains of *Be My Baby* buzzed from the dodgy speakers in her second-hand TV, and grainy black and white dancers writhed on the screen. When Patrick Swayze's name loomed in that sexy pink font, Nadia tucked herself under her covers and sighed.

Yep, things were still on track. So long as she didn't do anything stupid. *Again.*

Sliding into sleep, she couldn't be sure if it was her mother's voice she'd heard at the last, or her own.

Chapter Two

"So how was it? Was it amazing? Aren't you glad I made you go?"

Ryder pressed the phone harder to one ear to better hear Sam, and plugged a finger in his other ear to ward off the sounds of the construction site. "It was…" *Excruciating. Hot. A lesson in extreme—patience.* He tugged his hard hat lower over his forehead, and growled, "It was fine."

"Told you. And how cool is the studio? And the ceilings. I knew you'd love the ceilings."

No need to fudge the truth there. The beams were stunning. Old school. The exact kind of feature he'd once upon a time have sold his soul to study. He glanced about the modern web of metal spikes and cold concrete slabs around him, the foundations of what would in many months be a sleek, silver, skyscraping tower— as far from the slumped thick red-brick building as architecturally possible.

His foreman waved a torch in his direction, letting him know the group he was there to meet—and who were about to make his day go from long to interminable—had arrived. Ryder tilted his chin in acknowledgement, holding up his finger to say he'd be a minute.

"She was a dancer," Sam was saying. "A real one. A Sky High one."

Struggling to picture sultry Nadia Kent in a pink tutu and a bun, Ryder asked, "Nadia's a ballerina?"

A pause, then, "No-o-o. I told you. *Sky High.*"

"Sam, just for a moment, treat me as if I am an Australian human male and speak plain English."

"Man, you need to get out more. Sky High is huge. A dance extravaganza. A kind of burlesque meets Burn the Floor meets Cirque du Soleil; all superb special effects and crazy-talented dancers. In Vegas!"

Ryder's focus converged until it was entirely on his sister's voice. "Sam, do you have a *showgirl* teaching your wedding party how to dance?"

"Oh, calm down. She wasn't working some dive bar off the strip."

And yet, picturing Nadia in fishnets, towering high heels and cleverly positioned peacock feathers wasn't difficult at all. Her pale skin glowing in the dim light, dishevelled waves trailing down her bare back, those lean calves kicking, twirling, hooking… Ryder closed his eyes and pressed his thumb into his temple.

"She's so graceful. And flexible," Sam continued, clearly oblivious to his internal struggle. "She was warming up the other night when we came in and she can pull her leg up so far behind her she can touch her nose!"

Ryder's eyes snapped open to search for a speedy exit from the conversation at hand. He had every intention of shrugging off the spark between them for Sam's sake, but the kid sure wasn't helping any.

Sam sighed down the line. "If I had half her talent, half her confidence, half her sex appeal—"

"Okay then," Ryder said, loud enough to turn heads. A few of his tradies laughed before getting back to nailing, laying pipe, measuring, chatting about the previous night's TV. "You like her. That's great. I'm taking lessons, as you wanted. Let's leave it there."

Sam might have missed his earlier silence, but he read Sam's loud and clear. He swore beneath his breath as the hairs on the back of his neck sprang up in self-defence.

Sam's voice was an octave lower as she said, "She's single, you know."

"Got to go," Ryder growled. "My foreman's jabbing a finger at his watch so vigorously he's going to pull a muscle."

With that he rang off. And stared at his phone as if he couldn't for the life of him remember which pocket he kept it in.

There was no misreading what had just happened there. The kid was trying to set him up. That wasn't the way things were meant to go.

He was Sam's rock. Her cornerstone. Which was why he'd been so careful to keep his private life separate from his life with her; so she didn't go through life thinking all men were self-centred brutes like the father who'd failed them both.

Damn. Things were changing. Faster than he was keeping up. Faster than he liked.

For if he was Sam's cornerstone, she was his touchstone. His earth. As the raw ingenuity he'd inherited from his mother had been progressively engulfed by his own well-honed single-mindedness, and the crushing need to succeed that his father had roused in him, being there for Sam, no matter what, had been his saving grace. It had proven he was different from the old man in the way that mattered most.

Without Sam to look out for what would his measuring stick be?

To ground himself, he glanced up at the twenty-feet-high rock-and-dirt walls surrounding him, and imagined what would one day be a soaring tower; a work of art with clean lines, perfect symmetry, and a hint to the fantastical that pierced the Melbourne sky. It was the exact kind of project he'd spent more than a decade aiming towards.

Not that it had always been his aim to draw buildings that split the clouds. His first internship had been a fantastical summer spent in beachside Sorrento with a renovation specialist by the name of Tom Campbell, bringing the grand homes of the Peninsula back to their former glories. The gig had been hard, backbreaking labour, but the heady scents of reclaimed materials had also made him dream more of his mother, and her sculpting of lost things, than he had since he'd been a kid.

Until the day his father sauntered in with the owner of the home Campbell was working on at the time. Fitz couldn't even pretend it was accidental; the sneer was already on his face before he'd spied the hammer in Ryder's hand.

No ambition, he'd muttered to his friend, not bothering to say hello to the son he hadn't seen in two years. *Kid's always been a soft touch. Idealistic. Artistic mother, so what chance did I have?*

Damn those bloody beams for stirring this all up again. Because no matter how he'd come to it, the very different work Ryder did now was vital and important.

And as for the woman who'd stirred other parts of him, hooking into his darker nature, begging it be allowed out to play? All elements of the same slippery path.

No. No matter how his life might be changing, his crusade had not. So he'd have to be more vigilant in harnessing his baser nature than ever.

With that firmly fixed at the front of his mind, he went off in search of the project manager, foreman, head engineer, the council rep, union rep, and the jolly band of clients, perversely hoping for a problem he could really sink his teeth into.

It was nearing the end of a long day—Tiny Tots lessons all morning, Seniors Acrobatics after lunch, Intermediate Salsa in the evening, so Nadia happily took the chance for a break.

She sat in the window seat of the dance studio, absent-mindedly running a heavy-duty hula hoop through her fingers. Rain sluiced down the window making the dark street below look prettier than usual, like something out of an old French film.

Unfortunately, the day's constant downpour hadn't taken the edge off the lingering heat. Nadia's clothes stuck to her skin, perspiration dripped down her back, and she could feel her hair curling at her neck.

And it wasn't doing much for her joints either. She stretched out her ankle, which had started giving her problems during her earlier weights training at the gym. It got the aches at times—when it was too hot, or too cold, or sometimes just because. As did her knees, her wrists, her hips. Not that it had ever stopped her. Her mother had famously been quoted as saying, "If a dancer doesn't go home limping she hasn't worked hard enough."

But it wasn't her body that had spun her out of the dance world. That would have been way more impressive, tragic even—a sparkling young dancer cut down before her time by a body pushed to the edge...

Looking back, she wished she'd handled things differently. That, after discovering her dance partner boyfriend had dumped her, hooked up with another dancer in the show and moved the girl into his apartment—leaving Nadia without an act, without a guy, and without a home all in one rough hit—she'd acted with grace and aplomb and simply gone on. Perhaps after kicking him where it hurt most. But whether it was embarrassment, or shock, or just plain mental and physical exhaustion, she'd fled.

The only *right* decision she'd made was in going straight to her mother. Oh, Claudia's gratification at finding her only kid tearful and dejected on her doorstep had been its usual version of total rubbish, but when her mother had told her to get over it and get back to work, it was *exactly* what Nadia had needed to hear.

Nadia went to work on the other ankle with a groan that was half pleasure, half pain. It meant she was dancing again. Meant she was getting closer to rekindling her life's dream.

But for now, she had one more class to go before she could ice up—her duet with Ryder Fitzgerald. She figured it was about fifty-fifty he'd show up at all.

And then, with a minute to spare, his curvaceous black car eased around the corner and into her rain-soaked view to pull to a neat stop a tidy foot from the gutter. Ryder stepped from the car, decked out once again in a debonair suit. *Nice*, she thought. He'd ignored her advice completely.

And then he looked up.

Nadia sank into the shadows. Dammit. Had she been quick enough? Last thing she needed was for Mr Testosterone to think she'd been waiting for him, all bated breath and trembling anticipation. She nudged forward an inch, then another, till through the rain-slicked window she saw he'd already disappeared inside.

With a sigh she slid from the window seat and padded over to the door. She twirled the hoop away and back, caught it in one finger and tossed it in the air before turning a simple pirouette and catching the ring on the way down.

She tossed it lazily onto the pile on the floor, plucked dance heels and a long black skirt from the back of the pink velvet chaise, and stepped into it so as to make the slinky black leotard and fishnet tights with the feet chopped off more befitting of the job ahead. Wouldn't want the guy to get the wrong idea.

Though if there was any man she'd met since coming home who she'd like to give the wrong idea... A week on and she could still remember exactly how good it had felt having the heavy weight of his hands on her hips. How lovely the strength in those arms, the hardness of his chest, the sure, slow, sardonic curl of his smile that made her lady parts wake up and sigh—

"Gak!" she said, shaking her head. Her hands. Stamping her feet. Anything to rid herself of the ominous cravings skittering through her veins. It didn't matter that she was a worshipper of the brilliance of the human body and all it could achieve *en pointe*, upside down, and most definitely horizontal; she'd be playing with fire if she went down that path. Her entire career hinged on what she did the next couple of months and that was not a gamble she was willing to take.

The beat of another set of stomping shoes syncopated against her own as the sound of a man's footsteps on the stairs echoed through the studio.

With a deep breath, she pulled herself upright, shoulders back, feet in first. She ran a quick hand over her ponytail, and then plastered an innocuous smile on her face as the door creaked open and the man of the hour stomped inside.

"Why if it isn't Mr Fitzgerald. I'd made a bet with myself you'd not show. Seems I won."

He glanced up, skin gleaming, wet hair the colour of night, the rain and heat having added a kink. A drop of rainwater slid from a dark curl on his forehead then slowly, sensuously down the length of his straight nose.

She swallowed before saying, "Get a tad wet, did we?"

He shook his hair like a wet dog, rainwater flying all over place. "This is Melbourne, for Pete's sake. It's tropical out there."

When Nadia was hit with a splat she called out, "Whoa, there! Ever tried dancing on a wet floor? Doable, but chances are high you'll come off second best."

She moved a ways around him, doing her all to avoid the puddles littering the floor, to grab a towel from the cupboard by the front door. Then turned and draped it from the crook of her finger.

His smile was wry as he realised he had to come and get it. Only he didn't look down as he took the three steps to take it, before rubbing the thing over his face and hair, all rough and random, in that way men did.

When he moved the towel to the back of his neck, eyes closed, muscles in his throat straining, Nadia gripped her hands together in front of her and pinched the soft skin at the base of her thumb to stop herself from moaning.

She must have made a noise anyway, as Ryder stopped rubbing and looked at her, hazel eyes dark over the white towel. Knowing eyes, hot and hard. Then he slowly, deliberately, held out the towel, meaning this time *she* had to go to him.

Eyebrow cocked, she barely got close enough to whip the thing out of his hand, only to be hit with a waft of his natural scent. Hot and spicy, it curled over Nadia's tongue until her mouth actually began to water. She dropped the towel to the ground and used her shoe to vigorously wipe the floor.

As if he knew exactly what was going on inside her head, Ryder laughed softly.

Nadia blamed the rain. Rain made people crazy. The last of the Tiny Tots that morning had literally gone wild, hanging from the barre like monkeys.

She hooked the towel over the heel of her shoe and flicked it up into her hands. "Now that's sorted, I think we need to take a step back."

"Back from where exactly?" he asked, his deep voice tripping luxuriously over her bare skin.

"Learn to stand before we start to move. Tonight we'll work on your posture."

"What's wrong with my posture?"

Not a single thing. "It's a process, Ryder. A journey we are going on together. A journey in which I impart my wisdom and you do as you're told."

"So what are you telling me to do, exactly?"

She looked at him—hands in pockets, legs locked, suit jacket as good as a straightjacket for all the movement it offered him—and then, before she could stop herself, she said, "Strip."

Quick as a flash, he came back with "After you."

She hid her reaction—instant, hot, chemical—and, with a flick of her hand, she spun on her toes till she was standing side on. "Unlike you, I came wearing appropriate attire. Can you not see my spine, the equilibrium in my hips, the tension in my belly?"

So much for not playing with fire. The gleam in the guy's eyes turned so flinty it was amazing they hadn't sent up sparks.

Then, right when Nadia was on the brink of recanting her rash invitation, a muscle twitched in Ryder's jaw and his dark eyes began to rove. Over her neck, her collarbone, her breasts, her ribs, her belly, not lingering at any one spot longer than any other. Which only heightened the tension pulling at every place his eyes touched.

Point made—and points lost too, she rued—she slowly turned to face him, hands on hips as she waited till his gaze lifted to meet hers. "Take off your jacket, Mr Fitzgerald. And your tie. Dress shirt too, if you're game. You can leave on your singlet. I just need to figure out where your stiffness comes from."

He opened his mouth to say something, and then closed it. Instead merely leaving his gaze on hers as the double entendre remained, lingering on the air between them, all the hotter for not being touched.

Gaze snagged on hers, Ryder lifted his hands to his jacket, sliding it from his shoulders. Next came his tie. She had no idea where the things landed as she couldn't take her eyes from his. For then she'd have to look somewhere else. Somewhere lower.

But when his long brown fingers went to the buttons of his shirt, her disobedient eyes followed as he slid them through the neat holes of his perfect white button-down one by one.

He tugged his dress shirt from his suit trousers, slid it from his arms and laid it neatly over the chaise with the rest of his gear. As it turned out, the guy wasn't wearing a singlet after all. And when she looked up again, it was to find his eyes still on hers, daring, challenging, till defiance hummed between them, filling the dimly lit room so that the windows near vibrated.

"This what you were after?" he asked, the roping muscles of his long arms bunching as he held them out to the sides.

But Nadia couldn't answer; by that stage her mouth had gone bone dry. All she could do was nod, then busy herself with getting rid of the dirty towel. She somehow made it to the corner of the room and tossed it into the plastic bin. Curling her fingers around the edge a moment, she attempted to calm her thundering heart.

Okay, so asking him to strip had been a reflex action. The curse of a quick tongue. She was her mother's daughter after all. But she'd hardly thought he'd acquiesce. And how…

The men in her life had been lean. Not an ounce of fat on their undernourished bodies. Their faces on the edge of gaunt, the rest of them covered with the kind of muscle that clung in desperation to the bones. And waxed to within an inch of their lives.

Ryder Fitzgerald, with his hulking shoulders, big rolling muscles, thick thatches of hair beneath his underarms and whirls of dark curls all over his chest that dared not mar the taut, rolling muscles of his stomach before reforming in a flagrant V that disappeared beneath his trousers, might as well have been an entirely different species. Everything about him was bigger. Stronger. Lustier. Every inch of him gleamed with robust health.

And with one glance something primal had roared to life deep within her.

She glanced back over her shoulder to check if he was for real, and found he wasn't even watching her. While she was deep in the grips of a wave of impossible lust, hands on hips, back to her, he was staring up at the damn rafters!

"Right," she said, gathering her scattered wits and forcing herself to get a grip. "Clock's ticking. Let's do this thing."

Ryder turned; silvery moonlight and golden light of the old chandeliers pouring over him till his skin glowed, making the absolute most of the hills and valleys of his musculature. If the guy could actually dance he'd have given Patrick Swayze himself a run for his money.

With each clack of her heels on the old wooden floor, Nadia's tension ramped up and up. But this was a dance class. A close-hold dance class. Not touching him would only draw attention to her folly. At least that was what she told herself as her hand went to his shoulder.

His naked skin was silken, hot, it twitched at her touch, and the spark between them morphed into some living thing, twisting and shooting around them, filling the huge space with a crackling energy that struggled to be contained.

Nadia barely had time to take it all in, as Ryder didn't wait for instructions. He curled his fingers around her right hand, placed his other hand in the small of her back and moved deep into her personal space.

Her gaze was level with his collarbone, the scent of his skin so near she was lost within the mix of rain, heat and spice, her eyes so heavy she couldn't seem to lift them to his.

"Music?" he asked, his voice deep, low, intimate.

And it took half a second for Nadia to realise she'd yet to turn the damn CD player on. Snapped out of her haze, she swore under her breath and yanked the remote from the overturned waistline of her tights, and poked the thing in the direction of the stereo.

Norah Jones oozed from the speakers, warm and sultry. As she made to change it Ryder's hand came down over hers.

"Seems as good as any," he said, his gaze as good as saying, *Now you've got me where you want me, what are you going to do with me?*

What she wasn't going to do was tell the guy the song was too damn intimate for her liking, making her think of smoky jazz bars, and dark corners, and roving hands, and hot lips, and hot skin...

She lifted her chin, clamped her hand hard over his. "Start at your feet. Press them into the floor. Your leg muscles will switch on. Now soften your knees. Like you're about to bend them, without bending them. Press your inner thighs together—"

At that his hips pressed into hers and Nadia prayed for mercy.

"Lift your torso away from your hips, like there's a string coming out the top of your head and somebody's stretching you to the rafters. Now chin up, shoulder blades back and down and—"

"Breathe?" he asked, his voice strained.

The laughter that shot from her was unexpected, and he rewarded her with a small smile.

"Can only help."

Only when she felt in her bones, in that place inside her that knew dance better than it knew life itself, that they were positioned just so, she began to sway. Pressing his hand with hers, his thighs with hers, she tilted her hips to his until his movement matched hers. And even while every point of contact thrummed with awareness, dance-wise, compared to the week before, it was actually better.

"Feel that?" she asked several bars later.

"I feel something," he murmured.

"Not so stiff tonight," she said, and felt him turn to stone beneath her touch. "Oh, relax. I meant in the hips," she added, giving his arm a shake to get him moving again. "Been practising, have we?"

A muscle clenched in his jaw as he grumbled something about the better he knew the steps, the fewer lessons he'd have to endure.

"Really?" she said, honestly surprised. "Good for you."

He grunted. "I feel like I'm in one of those movies were you're about to ask if I could be your partner in some dancing contest."

She laughed again; this time it slid more readily through her. "Don't get ahead of yourself, sunshine. You couldn't keep up with me if you tried."

"No?" Without warning, he took her by the hand and twirled her out to the ends of his fingers. Years of training kicked in and she went with it, using her weight to hit the end and swing back where he swept her into a dip that left her breathless.

It wasn't the most graceful move she'd ever executed, and yet her breath thundered through her body as his dark shadow loomed over her, as his strong arm braced her back, as his striking eyes stared hard and deep into hers.

Her hands curled against his bare pecs, and for the first time she wondered about Mr Testosterone's life beyond the hour they spent together Tuesday nights. Did he lift cars for a living? Chop down hardwoods? No, not a bump in that perfect nose, not a single scar on that dauntingly flawless face…

Then, far more gently than she expected, he eased her back upright until they stood hip to hip, thigh to thigh, in a loose ballroom hold.

"How was that?" he asked, shifting so that she fitted closer still. Close enough to see flecks of gold in his hazel eyes. Close enough that every breath in was filled with his scent.

"Needs work."

"That's what I'm paying you for."

Well reminded, she pulled away and jabbed the remote until she found something less…Norah. A basic foxtrot, pure muzak, the least sexy sound on the planet.

"Your posture's closer," she said. "Now we'll work on your feet. Because, my friend, they suck."

Soon the hour was over. Sweat had added a sheen to Ryder's skin, a muskiness to his scent.

"Okay," she said, running her hands over her damp

hair. "Work on your feet this week. Give me something else to pick on next time."

As she went to walk to the chaise to gather her stuff his hand clasped her wrist, stopping her. She looked back, hoping he couldn't feel the sudden flurry of her pulse.

"I thought it was something in the air, but it's you, isn't it?"

"I'm sorry?"

"That scent?" He leant into her, his nose brushing the edge of her hair as his eyes closed and he breathed her in. "I caught it last week too. Thought it was coming through the windows."

She opened her mouth to say…who knew what. Her throat locked up as her entire body stood stock still, riveted by the sensation of his intense attention, and all that intoxicating male body heat intermingling with her own.

"What scent might that be?" she finally managed, her words thick, as if she were speaking through a mouthful of marshmallows.

"It's spicy yet sweet. Like brandy."

She breathed in and figured it out. "Ah, my hairspray. Industrial strength."

His eyes moved to her hair, which was in its usual dishevelled array after a day's worth of dancing.

"I don't use it on my hair. Not unless I'm performing."

His eyebrows all but disappeared into his hairline. "Then where?"

"It keeps the leotard from rising."

"Rising?"

"Up," she said with a swish of her hand towards

the offending area. And then she walked away, completely unable to help from looking back to find his eyes had zeroed in on her backside with enough intensity he might as well have been using X-ray vision to see beneath her skirt. And if she added a little extra va va voom to her walk? She was only human.

She grabbed her lucky black wrap cardigan, crisscrossing the cord around her ribs.

She turned everything off while her student made himself decent. Pity. It had been fun while it lasted. Heady, hazardous, but worth every agonising second. While it was imperative she keep her hands to herself outside the one hour a week, at least her fantasies now had something to live off for months to come.

As he had the week before, Ryder waited for her as she locked up, walking behind her as she headed down the rickety old staircase. It was kind of endearing, actually, or it would have been if the feel of him a step behind her didn't make her knees give out on the already precarious staircase.

When they got outside, he motioned to his slumbering car, all vintage curves and glossy gleam, its swanky dash glinting through the heavily tinted windows. "Can I drop you somewhere?"

She looped her big soft bag over one shoulder and gripped the strap in front of her. "Thanks, but no. I live just around the corner. And I'll be fine walking. I have a mean right hook." She lifted her hands in a boxing move, then backed away from the temptation of the cool luxury of the car, and the man who owned it.

His eyes remained steadfastly on hers. "Then would you like to get a coffee?"

Damn. Nadia nibbled her bottom lip and struggled

to dampen the distinct tightening in her belly. "Thanks, but no. Hate the stuff. Stunts your growth, don't you know. See you next week."

Without another word, she turned and headed home, knowing he was watching as she walked away. She could feel it as surely as if his big hands were sliding down her back, over her backside, down her calves, deep into the arches of her sore feet.

Her pulse beat hard in her neck, her breaths coming tight and hard. And she was forced to ask herself, again, if she'd done the right thing saying no. A fling needn't be completely out of the question—

No, it needn't. Just not with Ryder.

The man had proven himself far too capable of wrong-footing her. And with the biggest audition of her life looming, she needed complete control of her feet. And the rest of her.

Yet, as she hit the corner, she looked back.

But Ryder was gone.

The heaviness that settled low in her belly had nothing to do with being alone in the dark. Living out half her teen years in New York, then Dallas, then Vegas meant it was nothing for her to walk through the shadows as easily as the pools of light.

No, it wasn't human company she craved; it was one very particular human.

She scuffed her shoe against a crack in the footpath and swore beneath her breath. Trouble lurked down that path, and, as was the fate of a Kent, she'd be the one who'd pay.

Chapter Three

Lights flashed through the darkness and music through speakers too old to handle the beat as bodies bumped and ground across the dance floor.

Nadia lifted her bare arms over her head, eyes closed, hips swaying, feet burning, as deep in her bliss she tripped the light fantastic. For her that was *exactly* how it felt; when the killer groove of the song met the rhythm in her bones, filling her muscles with liquid heat, and sparkling across her senses. It was approaching divine.

Add a fall of silk, a length of rope, better yet a sparkling silver hula hoop suspended thirty feet above the stage, adding danger, suspense, and an audience hushed with a mix of hope for a touch of magic and fear that something might go wrong... Now *that* was nothing short of orgasmic.

Feet well and truly on the ground—unless you counted three-inch spikes a prop—the vertical-drop strands of her fringed silver sparkly top swished over her belly, sensual, sexual, lifting the experience a nudge higher. Especially when she could so easily imagine the stroke of the strands belonged to the sure, sensual fingers of a man with dark hair and dark eyes and a dark voice that settled like a purr in her very core. Since she couldn't have him, she had to ease the sexual tension somehow, and dancing the hours away in a hip club deep within Prahran was the best way she knew how.

A sudden wave of dehydration swelled over her, condensing her vision to a pinprick. Knowing when she'd overdone it, Nadia wiped her hands over her face, slipped through the surge of sweaty bodies, and headed for the stairs that led down to the bar. And iced water. A jug of it for starters.

She skipped lightly down the stairs, doing a little twirl as the song upstairs hit its crescendo.

"Kiss me, Dancing Queen!"

Nadia felt herself grabbed. With a "Whoa!" she held onto a strong male arm, using momentum as much as the strength of his arm at her waist to haul herself upright. Then she looked up to find herself in the grip of a random guy. With golden curls and a wonky grin, he was cute as a button.

"What's in it for me?"

"My mates bet me a twenty you wouldn't. Too gorgeous, they said. Way out of my league. Do a guy a favour and show them different. I'll split it, fifty-fifty." The guy flashed his adorable dimple, proving no woman on the planet was out of his league.

When the dancing was as good as it got, it might even be better than sex, but sex sure had its place. And the guy was a serious honey. If she wanted a fling, a chance to scratch the itch that had been bothering her all week, this was it. Unfortunately the kick in her belly, the tension making her ache, wasn't his to erase.

"I'll have to pass." She grabbed his hand, ducked under his arm and twirled away, leaving behind a "Hey!" as she threaded through the lighter crowd to find the bar.

Instead she found that while she'd been dancing Sam and her friends had made their way downstairs too, taking up a group of soft velvet couches in a warm little alcove in the corner of the busy bar. Nadia walked that way in time with the smooth song crooning gently below the sweet murmur of conversation.

Sam stood and waved her over. Tall, skinny, knobbly; like a newborn colt. With her long straight dark hair and fey grey eyes Sam was quietly beautiful. Though, perhaps that was only compared with her brother's terrible masculine beauty, which was like a smack between the eyes.

Nadia nudged Sam's fiancé, Ben, to scoot over.

"Don't you go sweating on me, Miss Nadia," said Ben as he made space. "This jacket is suede."

Nadia eyed it, and raised an eyebrow. "That jacket is a travesty."

"See!" Sam called across the couch. She grinned past the straw between her teeth, the other end of which was deep in a tall glass of something poison green.

Nadia spied the jug of the stuff, mist wafting from the ice sprinkled across the top—at least she hoped it was mist—and poured herself a glass. Dancing hadn't erased the tight craving in her belly, and, since she'd stupidly given up a chance at a cute guy, poison-green cocktails might be her last resort.

She took a sip, shook her head at the beautiful bitterness, and settled into the lounge and the conversation swirling around her. The first real friends she'd made since moving home. Being able to talk about other things, fun things, silly things, serious things, things that had nothing to do with dance, was unexpectedly nice. Rare times she might even admit it was a relief. She'd miss them when she left.

Sam's eyes suddenly widened to comical proportions as she spied something over Nadia's shoulder. Enough that Nadia lifted herself from her slump and turned. And found herself looking into the hot hazel eyes of the man who'd sent her to drink.

"Ryder," she and Sam said at the same time.

Nadia clamped her teeth around the straw so as not to say anything else incriminating.

"The big man!" called Ben, pulling himself to half standing to extend a handshake to his future brother-in-law.

Ryder moved in to take Ben's hand, his shadow flowing over Nadia in the process.

He acknowledged the chorus of greetings with a smile in his eyes. Though when he finally looked down at Nadia, lifting his chin in acknowledgement, the glints hardened. Nadia crossed her legs to hold in the sensation that poured unbidden through her.

Belatedly, she noticed he'd changed. Gone was the ubiquitous pristine suit and in its place dark jeans and a dark sports coat. Beneath that an olive-green T-shirt that hugged the curves and definitions of his chest and made the very most of the flecks of green in his eyes. Nadia shoved the straw deeper in her mouth and took a hearty gulp.

"I'm so glad you came!" Sam called across the couch. "Was it the begging that did it? Or the promise of dancing? Ooh, you should dance with Nadia. Nothing like doing it for real to pick up some pointers."

Nadia bit down on her straw so hard her jaw hurt. Oh, Lordy, Sam was playing matchmaker. Nadia would have to put a stop to that. Meaning she'd probably have to explain why.

She'd managed not to tell a soul here her plans as yet. Not at the studio. Not her mother. And not Sam and her friends.

Not that she had any concerns of jinxing things. She'd never been superstitious though she knew many dancers who were: lucky shoes, miracle lipstick, turning three times on the spot while chanting "Isadora Duncan" over and over. It was a little more selfish than that—she'd moved on a lot in her life and knew how people began to pull away when a job was near the end. She wanted *this*—the ease, the acceptance—a little while longer.

"I just remembered!" Ben jumped in. "The Big Man's taking lessons too. I hear she told you you'd have to wear tights. Classic!"

Nadia opened her eyes wide at Ben but he just looked at her in sweet ignorance.

"Told you that, did she?" said Ryder.

"*She's* sitting right in front of you," Nadia muttered into her straw.

"How is he going, Nadia?" Sam asked. "I bet he tries to lead all the time."

Nadia smiled at Sam. "He's got potential, especially if he keeps applying himself."

"*Applying* himself to dance?" Sam repeated, eyes wide and suggestive as she grinned at her brother. "Well, I never."

Nadia made the mistake of looking up at the man in question to find his eyes glinting in warning. Unfortunately he didn't know her well enough to know that he'd just tossed fuel on her fire.

She blinked up at him. "Turns out he has excellent posture too. Quite the form."

Another beat went by in which the gleam in his eyes deepened, and the pulse in her wrist began to kick like a wild thing.

"In fact," she continued, evidently unstoppable, "I have a few amateur ballroom enthusiasts on my books who are desperate for a male partner. If I let slip about your brother here, there'll be blood in the water."

The muscle twitched in Ryder's jaw and he shoved his hands in the front pockets of his trousers, drawing her eyes down to what he'd framed all too nicely. Accident? Who knew? The man was an ocean of enigmas. Either way, by the time her eyes rose back to his, the pulse in her wrist had begun to beat loud and proud behind her ears.

Which was when the strains of a Kylie song filtered down the stairs and as one Sam's friends shot to their feet, babbling about the song and the school formal and somebody falling off the stage, before they were all gone up the stairs in the search of the dance floor.

Ben remained, stoic in his charge of the bags and chairs, and not about to get his new suede jacket anywhere near the sweaty dancers upstairs. Then with the couch all to himself he shuffled deeper, and spread out with a sigh.

"Want to get some air?" Ryder asked, not having moved an inch.

She looked back up at him, and up, and up. *Did she? Hell, yeah.* "You okay, Ben?"

"As a lark."

"Then air it is." Nadia put her cocktail back on the

table and stood, running her damp hands down the thighs of her jeans.

She pointed the way to a balcony populated with beer drinkers and followed as Ryder made a way through the throng and to a quiet patch of railing. Music pulsed through the windows above. Soft chatter spread from the star-gazers outside. While Nadia breathed deep of the cool night air, the busy street below, the Prahran railway station peeking between the nearby buildings.

Then, without preface, Ryder asked, "When I asked you out for coffee, why didn't you tell me you had plans with Sam?" and with a darkness in his voice that Nadia hadn't seen coming.

Completely foxed by the direction of his conversation, her incredulity was ripe as she blurted, "Why? Do you have a problem with that?"

He stayed silent, but the twitch in his cheek gave her the answer.

"You do!" She jabbed his forearm with a finger; when it hit solid muscle it bounced right back. "What do you think I'm going to do, corrupt her? Buddy, that venomous green potion masquerading as a drink back there was all hers."

Ryder's hands curled around the railing, the frown marring his forehead easing some. "She's...open-hearted. She's never been very good at protecting herself. That's long since fallen to me."

Okay, then. Not so much an indictment on her. This was about him. Nadia lowered her mental dukes. "I'd say Ben back there has you covered on that score."

Ryder scoffed, his frown back with a vengeance.

"What? Ben's smart, solid, and he's clearly smitten with her. I'm totally jealous."

"Jealous?" Well, that wiped the frown from his face. He turned to lean his elbows against the railing as he stared through the crowd at the young man scooched low in the soft seat, the collar of his jacket bunched up about his ears.

Nadia rolled her eyes. "Not of Sam, you goose. Of how much Ben adores her. I've never even been *close* to so adored."

Ryder's eyes slid back to hers, an eyebrow raised in raging disbelief.

"Admired by audiences, sure," she said, floating a *who cares* hand between them. "Envied by other dancers, oh yeah. Enjoyed by men, you can count on it. But adored?" She shook her head as Ryder continued to stare at her as if she'd grown an extra head. "Don't panic, Ryder. I'm not about to huddle in a corner and cry. A dancer's life is an endless series of rejections with just enough triumphs thrown in to keep us hungry. We're a tough breed, Kent women and dancers both. And it's hard to be tough and adorable at the same time."

"Puppies are adorable," said Ryder, his eyes now roving over her face, her hair, her shimmering silver top that she'd not all that long ago imagined slid over her skin with his touch. When his eyes roved back to hers she felt a good degree hotter. "Baby bunnies too."

"And your sister."

"Alas, my sister has a tendency to be that, to my constant disadvantage. As for you…" Nadia fought the urge to twist and turn under his heady gaze. "Adorable you may not be. But only because you're something else entirely."

The urge to ask what he thought was so acute she

only just managed to swallow it down. If she went there, there'd be no going back.

Instead she leant on the railing and looked out into the night.

"My adorable sister is really marrying the twerp, isn't she?" Ryder asked at long last.

"Yeah," Nadia said on a relieved laugh. "Did you think it was all pretend?"

"No. Maybe." He ran a hand over his face, then through his hair, leaving it in spikes. And upon witnessing the first spark of vulnerability she'd ever seen in the man, Nadia felt her heart kick hard against her ribs.

In punishment, she bumped her hip against the railing hard enough to leave a bruise, and said, "I see what's going on here. It's like something out of a Jane Austen novel. The big sister—or in this case brother—overlooked, left on the shelf, while the younger sister shines."

As hoped, the ridiculousness smacked the vulnerability from his eyes. Then he grinned, his teeth flashing white in the moonlight. "Alas, I am a confirmed bachelor."

"Confirmed by whom?"

"Every woman I've ever been with."

Not dated. Not known. *Been with*. Nadia breathed deep.

"I'm a determined man when motivated, Miss Kent. And my motivations lead me to work eighty hours a week in a job I take seriously. I am less motivated to give up my standing holiday in Belize every Australian winter, one ticket return. Or full rights to the remote control. And at the end of the day I go home to the bachelor pad to end all bachelor pads."

"Posters of women in bikinis straddling large…mo-torbikes all over your walls?"

Guy didn't even blink. "No. But it's a damn fine idea."

"Yeeeahhh," she drawled, letting her grin out to play. "That's what I thought. And yet even with such a fine example of determined independence to steer her to rights, your sister has succumbed to the dark side. Give in, big brother. It's happened. Your little sister's all grown up. Time's nearing where you'll have to find someone else to boss around."

When Ryder stilled, Nadia wondered if she'd said something wrong. Pressed too far. But then his face creased into a rueful smile; his hazel eyes crinkled, attractive arcs bracketed his mouth, drawing attention to his fine lips.

Stern and formal, the man was breathtaking. Smiling, the guy could stop hearts.

Not quite able to catch her breath, Nadia turned away, enough to squint into the bar. Then, thankful she'd found a subject changer, she clicked her fingers. "I forgot to tell you earlier—I found out who owns the building."

He raised an eyebrow in query.

"It's in my bag, inside. Name and number. Remind me later. Or next week. If tonight's lesson didn't scare you off for good."

"First lesson I was asked to take off my jacket. The second you talked me out of my shirt. I couldn't possibly miss the third."

"Funny man."

"I try."

Nadia smiled. Then she shivered, realising belatedly how much the night air had cooled her down.

Without a word, Ryder shucked his jacket from his back and slid it over her shoulders. She curled herself into it, goose bumps springing up all over when she found it near scorching from the man's body heat.

"Ta," she said.

"Any time." And through the darkness he smiled.

Just like that something dislodged inside her.

It hadn't happened often in her life that someone had offered her much in the way of warmth, much less *any time*.

Her mum had left when she was two, she'd never known her father, and the grandmother who'd raised her could have played indifference for Australia. Looking back over the past months she'd come to see that her ex had treated her more like an enchanting sidekick than something necessary, something precious, and she'd stayed with him for two years.

Now some guy had given her a damn jacket, hardly the first time it had happened anywhere in the world, and yet Nadia held it tight about herself to keep ahold of the kindness as long as she possibly could.

Her voice sounded as if it were coming from miles away as she heard herself say, "Was it really just dumb luck that you and I both happened to end up here to-night, Ryder?"

Ryder watched her a moment, his dark eyes flicking between hers. Then he shook his head.

Her next breath in was shaky. "Sam told you I'd be here, didn't she?"

A nod that time.

"So you came to warn me off being her friend? Or was there another reason?"

Ryder swore, the word tearing from him as if he'd been holding it in all night. Then, without preamble, without waiting for permission, he slid his hand behind her neck and kissed her.

Light splintered behind Nadia's eyes at the touch of Ryder's mouth on hers, the sparks settling over her like a dream. She came out the other end, back to reality, to find herself melting. Her limbs liquid, her resistance stripped bare.

And Ryder fed her long, hot, wet, slow kisses. His fingers shifting through her hair, his body leaning slowly into hers.

She turned into him, sliding a hand over his shoulder, the other around his waist, over his backside, beneath the hem of his shirt till she found his scorching-hot skin. He groaned into her mouth. And she took it, opening herself to him, to his heat, his skill, his need that quickly ratcheted to meet her own.

"Ryder! Oh, sorry."

Nadia heard the words, but Ryder pulled away long before she would have found it in her to stop.

"Sam," he said, his voice gruff as it rumbled through Nadia's bones. "What is it?"

"We were about to head off, and I was going to ask… Never mind."

Nadia shook her hair from her face and lifted her head to look at her friend, who was steadfastly looking anywhere but at the two of them.

"Spit it out."

"For a lift. But you're busy. So I'll get a cab. Don't worry. Have fun and I'll catch you later!"

"You going to Ben's?"

"Well…no. Mine," said Sam. "He has an early flight to Sydney for work, so I'm going home alone. He doesn't trust me not to keep him up all night!"

At that Ryder turned to rock. "I'll take you."

And Nadia felt it like a loss. In direct proportional response, she instantly stepped away, ridding herself of his jacket, and holding it out on one finger, forcing Ryder to look her in the eyes. To apologise. Or at least look chagrined.

She felt as if she'd been winded when his eyes said something else entirely—he wanted her. Still. More. They weren't done here. And heat pooled in Nadia's belly with a ferocity even she didn't see coming.

"Take it," she said, her voice gravelly. "Give me five minutes upstairs again and I'll be hot to trot."

His eyes narrowed, and his mouth opened as if he was about to say something, something she would have paid a lot of money to hear, but, needing to steel herself against the sensations stampeding through her before they got the better of her, she threw the jacket at him, forcing him to break eye contact as he caught it.

Then he seemed to remember himself, and his sister, and with a nod he and his warm jacket and hot kisses walked away.

So sorry! Sam mouthed as she backed into the bar.

Nadia waved a "don't worry" hand, before shoving it in the back pocket of her jeans so she didn't have to see how much it shook. But Sam's third-wheel moment was the best thing that could have happened. Nadia'd been in danger of jumping into the guy's arms, wrapping her legs around him and not letting go.

When she could no longer see either Fitzgerald,

Nadia made her way through the bar and to the bottom of the staircase.

She took one step up, the *doof doof doof* of the beat and the play of light at the top calling to her. But there she stopped, a finger pressed to her lips to find them swollen and tender. And she realised, for the first time in memory, she wouldn't find what she needed up there.

Instead, she turned on her heel and headed out into the night.

"So."

Ryder glanced in his rear-view mirror, changed down a gear as he neared a red light, and ignored Sam.

"You and Nadia, hey."

"Sam," he warned, when ignoring her seemed not to be working.

"Oh, come on. Anyone could see that you two have the hots for each other, even before I found you snogging on the patio." Sam shivered for good measure, while Ryder fought the urge to stick the car in Neutral and leap out of the door.

What the hell had he been thinking? He hadn't kissed a girl in a club in years. He knew privacy served a man better in that regard every time. And yet Nadia Kent slid under his skin and tapped right into his darkest instincts, making him forget all he knew. He ran a hand up the back of his neck and wondered how far things might have gone if they hadn't been interrupted. Till even the damn wondering made him ache.

"She is fabulous, though, don't you think?" asked Sam, settling deeper into the seat with a sigh.

Engaged though Sam might be, and clearly not the innocent little girl in plaits and frilly dresses she'd once been, he was not about to share with his twenty-four-year-old sister his thoughts on Nadia Kent.

Thankfully the light turned green, so Ryder could instead concentrate on grinding the gears and pressing his frustration into the accelerator. His car leapt from the starting gate with bravura and a gratifying press of backs to seats.

"And she's been brilliant for Ben and me," Sam continued regardless. "All this wedding stuff is stressful. We tried keeping it small but every time I look around it seems to have spread till I can't see to the end of it any more." Her voice trailed away with a soft sigh. "But as soon as we get to dance class it all just falls away. It's just Ben, and me. Nadia knows how to be unobtrusive, while at the same time setting the most romantic mood."

Nadia *unobtrusive*? Ryder couldn't think of a term that described her less. Stick her in any room, and she'd be the most obvious thing in it.

"We call it Thursday Night Foreplay."

Ryder slammed on the brakes so hard the car shuddered beneath them. He eased off, caught traction and drove the rest of the way home five kilometres under the speed limit.

When Sam didn't say anything for a while, Ryder risked a glance sideways to find her smiling at him. Then she raised an eyebrow in question. With her big grey eyes and sweet face she might look as if she ought to be frolicking in a field of daisies, but she was his half-sister and had more than half his stubborn streak.

Gritting his teeth against an urge to tell her to mind her own damn business, he said, "She's your friend."

"So what? I'm a big girl. I can handle it. So don't let that be your excuse this time."

"This time?" he asked, then wished he'd kept his damn mouth shut.

Sam turned, gripping the seat belt. "You're eleven years older than me, man. You should be married with three kids by now! Don't think I don't know it's me who stopped you."

Ryder shuffled on his seat, never good at this part of it all. "Don't get yourself in a knot, kid. I don't do anything I don't want to do."

"Sure about that?"

Ryder's cheek twitched. Okay, so he'd been more circumspect than other men might have been. But he'd never seen it as a sacrifice. It had benefited him that the women in his life had taken his discretion as reticence for anything long term. A reticence that was entirely genuine, only for less altruistic reasons than Sam had put on him.

"I need you to know it's never been about you," he said, his voice steady.

"It's about Dad," she said with a bigger sigh. "You can't let him rule your life. You've told *me* so enough times."

He glanced at his sister then, and in her eyes saw prudence and wisdom. When had that happened? *Since Ben,* a little voice told him. Open-hearted she might be, but she was also twenty-four. He'd started his own company at twenty-four. "I own every decision I've ever made, Sam. Every one of them was ultimately all about me. About what I want my life to be."

She tilted her head towards him, the street lights flickering over her face. "Okay, then. And while we're on that subject…"

Ryder held his breath, sure Sam was about to hit him

about Nadia again, and worried that in his wound-up
state he wouldn't be able to convince her it didn't mean
anything. Because that kiss had been…indescribable.
Seconds, minutes? He had absolutely no idea how long
it lasted, only that the micro-second he decided to go
there his world went up in flames.

He felt himself unfold all over when she said, "Let's
talk about me. I know that you've only ever wanted to
protect me. To make sure I feel happy, and safe. And for
that I love you more than you will ever know."

Ryder spared her a glance. "Right back at ya, kid."

"But I have Ben for that now. He's my knight-in-
shining-armour, my prince, leaving you to finally just
be my brother. Not my keeper, my minder, my shield."
Sam put her hand on Ryder's on the steering wheel.
"So in case you actually need to hear me say it, my big
stubborn mountain of a brother, I hereby set you free."

The fact that she'd come to him for a ride an hour
earlier seemed to contradict that, but when he looked
at her he found she was serious.

"Free to date, to have lady friends—"

"Okay. Fine. I get it. I have your blessing to…"

"Shtup."

"For the love of…" he muttered as the gate to Sam's
apartment complex opened noisily at the press of a remote, before he rolled down the drive to the under-
ground garage. "How about this—you and Ben can go
right ahead and repopulate the planet all on your lone-
some, so long as I don't have to hear about it."

She cocked her head, a frown marring her smooth
forehead. "Ryder—"

"Didn't you just set me free?"

Her mouth twisted, then with a sigh and a nod she

unhooked her seat belt, kissed his cheek, then leapt out of the door, and jogged to the lift. Ryder waited till she swiped the security card and was inside the lift up to her secure apartment before he turned the car around and headed for home.

By the time he threw his keys into a cut-glass bowl on the heavy table by the front door of his own split-level, waterfront residence it was well after midnight with more than half the working week ahead of him.

When restlessness began to flicker through him, he shook it off. He loved his job. It was extremely rewarding. Only at times, of late, he'd found himself wanting…more.

He glanced at the vintage drafting board in the corner. It had been his mother's. He'd been about three or four when she'd found it somewhere or other, cleaned it up, and placed it in a brightly lit corner of the family home. Over the years she would gravitate there to sketch out ideas. Ryder had drawn his first pictures of houses on that table, boxes with triangles for roofs. Multiple chimneys. Wings. Not tall buildings. Not back then.

He'd crammed the board into his bedroom after she'd died, and brought it with him to every place he'd lived since. He'd created the perfect corner for it when he'd built his own home—gorgeous down-lighting, a fantastic modern ergonomic chair, a wall of ten-foot-high shelves in which to keep old plans. And yet he'd never actually used the thing since she'd died.

Not about to change that, he ran his hands over his face and headed to his bar, where he poured himself a Scotch. Straight. He drank enough for it to burn its way down his throat, then sucked in a stream of cold air as a chaser.

His eyes glazed over the moonlit view of Brighton Beach and he thought of Sam's earnest face as she'd *set him free*, again struggling to picture what his life would look like without her as his responsibility any more.

But he had to ease off. To begin to let her go. She was ready. Or trying to be at least. *All grown up*, Nadia had said.

He emptied the glass, the burn not near strong enough second time around. At least, not enough to burn out thoughts of Nadia Kent. A woman who drew him in only to twirl out of his grasp. Infuriating. Intriguing. As for their attraction—it was wild, hot, barely in either of their control. It was like no other connection he'd ever felt.

But it didn't matter.

Sam was the reason he could look at himself in the mirror every morning and not cringe when he saw his father's jawline looking back at him. But even if the day came when she was no longer his number one focus, even with time on his hands and a hole in his life, he was not looking to fill it with a woman. Even one as enthralling as Nadia Kent.

He glanced again at his barren drafting table. Felt the restlessness rise, and struggled harder to press it down. Because the older he got, the harder he worked, the more successful he became, the less he was satisfied. And the more he wondered if, despite every effort to the contrary, he was beginning to experience the germination of his father's identical inability to endure. With work, with family, with relationships of any kind…

Ryder closed his eyes.

Of all his father had done in his life, it was the women the man had hurt who stuck deepest. His mother. Sam's mother. Hell, even when Fitz had been married to Sam's mother there had been so many others they'd long since morphed into a blur of false laughter and real tears. So many, even now Ryder found himself catching certain perfumes in a crowd and feeling nauseous.

In fact it was probably the smart move to remember. To shine a big bright light on their pain. Because he couldn't be sure he wasn't more like his father than he'd ever admit. Which was why he'd never risk committing to someone only to find out one day that it wasn't enough.

And even while he knew it was counterproductive, that he'd regret it in the morning, he purged the ugly memories as well as the cavernous blankness that was his future the only way he saw how.

Nadia.

He eased himself deep into an armchair, closed his eyes, breathed deep and found the scent he was looking for. Exotic, spicy, hot. Her taste erasing all others. The memory of her skin warming his ice-cold hand. The memory of her smart mouth easing the knot in his belly. Her red-blooded response to his touch, the burning pleasure, the aching tension, filling him up.

As he sank into every nuance of that kiss he wondered how hard the week would be, waiting to see her again. Wondered if he could. Wondered what it was about her that made him wonder at all.

Chapter Four

Nadia paced, trying to diffuse the surfeit of energy coursing through her body, while out of the corner of her eye she watched the old clock on the wall as it ticked down the minutes to ten o'clock.

Rehearsing her audition piece hadn't taken the edge off; in fact her concentration was so shot she'd damn near killed herself! A friend had once broken a wrist rehearsing after a couple of champagnes. With the bumps and bruises now covering her body, Nadia was going to add Don't Fly Frustrated to the list of aerial acrobatic no-nos.

It had been a week since she'd seen Ryder. Since he'd kissed her till her bones had turned to syrup. And since then she'd spent every one of those nights writhing under the influence of the hottest sex dreams of her life.

Even the kids in her Tiny Tots class that morning had picked up on her dark mood, if the higher than average number of them clinging to their mothers' legs was anything to go by. Nadia had breathed deep and blamed the incessant heat of the past couple of weeks.

Sam hadn't helped either, making little comments through the entire lesson the Thursday before, laughing as she'd asked what Nadia's intentions towards her brother were.

Argh! She didn't need this. With her pedigree she could have taken her pick of classes populated with an embarrassment of hot young things with dancers' vigour, endurance, and sex drive, which was *why* she'd taken a job that put her in the path of senior citizens and two-year-olds in tutus.

Because she was *so* close. Less than two months now till the producers were coming to Australia. To see her. To give her a second chance. And she was ready. Pride mended, body more supple and stronger than it had ever been, ambition rekindled and honed to ferocity.

And then Ryder Fitzgerald had gone and kissed her and turned her into a walking livewire with the attention span of a fruit fly.

She was going to make him pay; it was the only way. She was going to work the man so hard before the end of the night he'd be begging for mercy. If he turned up, that was.

A minute ticked by. Nadia dragged her fingers through her shaggy hair before throwing her hands in the air and growling at the walls, her voice echoing in the lofty space.

"Should I come back later?"

Nadia spun to find Ryder standing in the doorway, the arch framing him like a painting. When her eyes rose to meet his it was to find his gaze was focused intently on her stomach, which was bare except for a silver Lycra bra-top over which she'd thrown a button-down shirt so she wouldn't cool down too fast.

Sensation feathered across her belly as she remembered all too clearly how those same eyes had looked the second before he'd kissed her senseless. All hot, and dark, and fierce. As if he'd wanted to eat her alive.

Frustrated to the point of pain, she wrapped the two sides of the shirt across her torso and near snarled as she said, "Honestly, would it kill you to take five minutes to change into something more comfortable?"

Just to make her feel more foolish, from behind his back he brought forth a gym bag. And it wasn't even new. It was pretty bruised and beat up in fact, with grass stains and sweat marks, as if the guy wasn't always immaculate, as if he knew how to get down and dirty if the situation called for it.

Nadia jerked her head towards the only bathroom at the far end of the hall. With a nod Ryder strolled away, one hand in his suit trouser pocket, pulling the fabric tight across his most excellent derriere.

Nadia whipped a couple of buttons through the holes of her shirt before yanking the tails into a tight knot above her belly button. She glanced at the clock. She couldn't even growl at him for being late. She'd find a reason soon enough.

She wouldn't be her mother's daughter if she didn't have a steel spine and a smart mouth. Both of which might have got them into trouble during their lives, but at least they always landed on their feet. Well, her mother had anyway; now retired and married to a mining magnate and living in an awful mansion in uber-posh Toorak.

Nadia, on the other hand, had spent her life climbing, reaching, happy to take her mother's scraps if it meant getting a lick of attention from the woman. But now all the climbing was done, and she was perched on the highest, thinnest branch, waiting for her moment to take the big leap into her own life. Nobody's scraps, no more. And nothing was going to stop her!

The far door creaked and she glared at Ryder as he walked her way, his suit now hung from a hanger in perfect straight lines. But as for the rest of him…

His feet were encased in battered trainers. Above them the calves of a runner, golden brown and covered in a smattering of dark hair. Knees lost beneath cut-off cobalt-blue track pants, the edges frayed from where they'd been hacked away. A long navy tank-top hung low and loose from shoulders gleaming with muscle.

Nadia swallowed right as her gaze hit his mouth, meaning she didn't miss the moment it kicked into a knowing smile.

"Lose the shoes," she spat, turning and walking the hell away, ostensibly to find the remote for the stereo. "We're not playing hoops here, Ryder. This is dance class. Which means you need to be grounded. Connected to the music, to your partner, to the floor. And with the heat cooking this place tonight—" *and the mood she was in* "—you're gonna sweat more than you have in your entire life."

"Sweat I can handle."

"Yeah?" she threw over her shoulder. "Tell me so again in an hour."

His smile cocked higher, sending the pulse thudding through her straight to her belly.

He dumped the bag at the base of the chaise, hung his suit from a nail on the wall, and nudged his shoes off by their heels.

Oh, yeah, she thought with a secret smile of her own. A decade and a half of yoga had taught her the kind of pain that felt good when you were doing it, but kicked in with a screaming vengeance when your muscles came out of their trance thirty-six hours later. And he was going to feel each and every one.

That'd teach him to kiss and run. That'd teach him to mess with a Kent.

She pressed the requisite buttons. No more soft and swishy Norah Jones to make it easy on him. The hard thrash metal song chosen by a firm of accountants who'd hired her to choreograph a flash mob for their CFO's birthday thundered through the speakers, and for good measure she cranked it up.

As if the music wasn't making the building shake, Ryder ambled to their usual spot, near the centre of the room, beneath the soft glow of an ancient chandelier, and then held a hand to her.

As if that kiss had actually changed things. As if in giving her his jacket the other night he had shifted the balance of power his way.

Screw yoga, she thought, ignoring the temptation of that hand. Maybe she'd just stamp on his toes.

She was going to wipe that sexy smile off his sexy face, whatever it took. Because if the past few days proved anything, it was that if she didn't take control of this thing it would take control of her. And if she wasn't *completely* on her game come audition day, before she could say "Cyd Charisse" her reliability, her determination, her reputation as a serious dancer would be in question and any chance of a first-class professional dance career would be in ruins.

Nadia cranked the music up louder still, and, hands on hips, sauntered his way. Her eyes slid over him, as if she was trying to decide which part of him to hurt first as she worked him over and good.

Ryder stood stock still, his eyes on hers, until they

weren't. They were on her hips. On her bare stomach. Sliding past her breasts. Before they landed on her mouth. And there they stayed, long enough the urge to lick her lips was overwhelming. When, despite herself, she gave in, he breathed in so long and slow his chest expanded till his top lifted, revealing a sliver of taut stomach, and a glimpse of the dark trail that disappeared into his shorts.

Nadia jabbed at the remote, shutting the music down. The silence that followed felt louder still. Stifling. Pressing in on her until she felt as if she were going to explode.

And explode she did. "Why on earth did you kiss me the other night?"

At that, the sexy smile finally disappeared, which gave Nadia about half a second's respite before Ryder's hot eyes cut right to hers. "Why do you think?"

"Argh!"

"Yeah," he said. "I figured by all the hand-wringing that'd be about your answer. How about you answer me this: Why did you kiss me back?"

"I'm polite that way."

At that he laughed, the delicious deep sound reverberating about the room till it pelted against her skin like blissfully warm rain.

"You, Miss Nadia, don't have a polite bone in your body."

"I say please. I say thank you. If it's warranted."

"If you think it's not?"

"Then tough!"

His laughter this time was softer, deeper, more intimate. More knowing. It tripped and trickled all through her leaving a warm glow in its wake.

"Anyway," she said, shaking it off, "it doesn't matter why. All that matters is that we both agree, here and now, it won't happen again."

After the neat little speech he'd given her before the kiss, she fully expected him to agree. To make some excuse about how busy he was—eighty-hour weeks, solo winters in exotic Belize, the mysterious bachelor pad... About she and Sam being friends. How he was attracted to her, but...

"Why?" He took a step her way and, while her subconscious told her to bolt for high ground, she didn't move. "Why shouldn't it happen again?"

Simple enough question, with several fine answers. Yet as he prowled closer, all body heat and sex appeal, she could feel his wall of warmth before it should have been physically possible to do so, and there didn't seem to be a single reason why she shouldn't whip his top over his head and run her hands all over him, drag him to the floor and gain the release her body had been dying for all week.

At the very least she wouldn't send any more toddlers home in tears.

His hands gripped her waist, tugging her closer. She felt her breath leave her in a whoosh. He smelled like man, and sex, and it had been so long it was all she could do not to whimper.

Instead, she found her strength in the only place it still resided—she lifted their arms into a dance hold. And breathed through her mouth so as not to be bombarded by his masculine scent.

When the song began, she pressed and he pulled. Then he stepped towards her a fraction before she'd been about to encourage him to do so, kicking her out of step. And again when the time came to turn, he moved ahead of the beat instead of waiting for her cue. The frustration gnawing at her from the inside out finally gave.

She ducked out from his hold and glared at him. "Maybe you're used to being in charge out there in those suits of yours, but in this room I'm the boss. Can you handle that?"

"I thought the man was supposed to lead."

"Only if he knows what the hell he's doing. Until then, it's my job to make sure you don't injure yourself."

"Somehow I get the feeling you'd like that very much."

"And there I was thinking how good I'd been at keeping my feelings to myself."

The words dried up as the two of them stared one another down, breaths coming hard and heavy, awareness licking between them.

A dark eyebrow kicked up Ryder's forehead. "Fastest way to a stomach ulcer."

His retort was so unexpected; Nadia coughed out a laugh. Then laughed some more. Laughed, a little hysterically actually, till she had to bend over and clutch her side. But, thankfully, a measure of the tension that had been coiling her in knots all week scattered along with it.

When she caught her breath she looked the guy dead in the eye. "Then this is how I see myself avoiding one." She counted off her fingers. "No more Hollywood dips. No more flirting. No more pressing one another's buttons. And definitely no more kissing."

"I liked the kissing," he said, false contrition glinting in his gorgeous hazel eyes.

Yeah, she thought. *I hear that.*

Hands on hips, Nadia blew a wave of hair from her forehead. "Ever wish Sam hadn't decided on dance lessons?"

"Every damn day."

"Well, at least we're in step there." She checked the clock. Fifty minutes still to fill. "Speaking of Sam, she picked the song she wants the two of you to dance to. I think now's as good a time as any to hear it."

"Can't think of anything else I'd rather do."

A smile kicked at the corner of her mouth as she found the whimsical Norah Jones song Sam had chosen and pressed play.

Ryder's brow furrowed, before he nodded once. "I can handle that."

"Can you handle some choreography to go with it?"

Beneath his deep tan, the man paled.

"No pirouettes, I promise. Only one overhead lift, right at the end. It's tricky, but if you think you're not man enough to pull it off…"

His colour was back, and with it came a dangerous gleam in his eyes.

"You think I'm joking?" she asked.

"I think you have a sadistic streak. Makes me wonder why."

He said it as if it was a good thing, which sent utterly masochistic curls of pleasure straight to Nadia's belly. "I'm not a nice person."

"Nah, it's something else," he said, his gaze dropping to her mouth and staying there. "You're plenty nice."

"While you don't play fair."

"Where's the fun in that?" When his eyes lifted back to hers they were lit with laughter. And heat. And promise. And absolute resolution. Despite her pleas he had no intention of backing down.

She looked at the impossible man before her in consternation. "You're really ready for this?"

"Raring."

You better be, she thought.

For the next half-hour she clapped out the counts as her old ballet teacher used to, till the shouts of her commands—*knees straight! shoulders back!*—echoed off the walls.

And soon they were both sweating. Not glowing, not perspiring, but dripping wet. While Sam's song trickled through the room like water over stones in a brook, looming rolls of thunder in the distance brought with them an oppressive heat the industrial fans above merely seemed to push about the room.

But Nadia didn't let up. Especially when Ryder actually seemed to respond. The man was tall and broad, which could make for a Frankenstein approach to dancing, but he had natural grace when he stopped trying to cage his instincts and just let go.

Nadia eased herself into Ryder's frame, adjusting only slightly, using her body to urge him where he needed to go. And this time, as one, their feet began to move. Slowly, gently, no push or pull, just the music pulsing through the floorboards and rocking them to and fro.

Nadia nodded. *Good boy.*

The music swelled around them, all harp chords and piano keys, and the singer's husky voice crooning about spinning round and round, moving so fast. Nadia moved Ryder forward, and then he moved her backward, the rhythm so natural she let him. He slid his hand an inch further around her back until her belly met his, and she let him do that too. He tucked their arms nearer their sides, which wasn't classic dance hold, but even while it made Nadia's breath swell she didn't put a stop to it. The rhythm had other ideas as the dance swirled around and through them, binding them together and shutting out the world.

It was bound to happen, considering the way their bodies had fitted together in that kiss. That mind-blowing kiss—

Lightning lit up the room, followed by a crack of thunder, and then out went the lights. Then the fans. Music too. Not for the first time that week, but it was the first time they didn't flicker straight back on.

The heavy silence, the oppressive stillness in the air, the shards of moonlight the only thing between them, it should have been the perfect chance for Nadia to cut her losses and call the lesson over. Except neither of them stopped swaying.

In fact, Nadia might even have leant her head against Ryder's chest. Curled her fingers into the loops of his top. Melted a little when his chin landed gently atop her head. Melted a whole lot when his hands slid around her waist, across her tailbone, his thumbs dipping into the elastic of her skirt.

It was madness. Completely the opposite of what she'd set out to do with her hour. And not an altogether appropriate way to earn a fee.

But boy did she miss this. Not just the dancing, but the human connection. Skin on skin. Heat on heat. Feeling a part of something. Feeling discovered. Feeling *wanted*. And with every sway the sweetest sensation poured through her; a fragile serenity, not only filling nooks and crannies but opening them wide, till all that feeling pressed to the outer edges of her everything. And her heart became a bruising beat against her ribs.

Then, before she could talk herself out of it, she lifted onto her toes, wrapped her arms about Ryder's neck. And then easy as you please her mouth met his. Hot, wet, open, lush.

His tongue met hers, and she turned to liquid, melting against him as if she wanted to vanish right on inside. And with a groan he lifted a hand to the back of her head, the other gripping her backside, leaving her in no doubt just how much he wanted this. And the warmth inside soon spun into a crazy heat.

She tugged his top over his head, all but growling at the sight of him. Rippling, hot, golden, even in shadow. No wonder she'd been so bent out of shape all week. How could she function on a normal level, when there was *this* to be had?

Her nails scraped through those tight curls of hair covering his chest and he sucked in a breath between his teeth, and grabbed her by the wrists.

She shot him a look through the darkness. *Really?*

And with a flicker of the muscle in his cheek, he eased his grip. Shuddering deliciously as she continued her exploration. All that heat. All that strength. She kissed her way across his chest, the salty taste of him turning her thoughts into a faint grey haze.

She felt him bunch beneath her touch before the groan tore from his mouth. And then his hands were on her shoulders, clever thumbs pulling her shirt away giving his mouth better access to her neck, his tongue tracing her collarbone, his teeth nipping the swell of her breasts. And when her collar slipped another inch and his mouth found her nipple, at the curl of his hot tongue she began to tremble.

Nadia dragged her fingers through his hair and held on tight as Ryder proved himself greedy, taking her mouth, taking everything he wanted, leaving her weak, loose, nothing but impulse, and sensation. With no thoughts to cling to except a dull buzz inside her head.

It buzzed again, and through the haze Nadia realised it was the trill of a phone chirruping through the heavy air.

When Ryder pulled away Nadia went with him, following his lips with hers. Not done yet. Not even close.

When she came up with nothing but air, her eyes flickered open to find his: dark, tortured. The want she saw there, the reckless desire, teetering on the very edge of control and chaos, scared her. Scared and *thrilled* her. Because it exactly mirrored her own.

But instead of throwing her to the floor and having his way with her, he said, "I have to get that."

That? Oh, the phone.

"It's nearly eleven at night," she said, her voice ragged, her fingers tugging at the beltline of his track pants. "You really don't."

"It's nearly eleven at night. I really do."

He unhooked her hands, gave them back to her, then turned his back and answered his phone. Leaving Nadia to wrap her arms about herself to control the suddenly very cold shivers wracking her.

Ryder murmured into the phone so that Nadia couldn't hear what he was saying. Then he hung up, and grabbed his things, turning to her only when he had everything in hand. "I have to go."

Nadia breathed out long and slow, slowing her heart,

tempering the mortifying disbelief that this was happening *again* from ratcheting up to cyclonic levels inside her.

Then he dumped his things and swore effectively as he came to her, taking her by the arms and bending his head so that he was eye level, which was really the only reason she didn't boot him out of the flippin' door and demand he stay the hell away from her.

"Meet me," he said, command kindling at the edges of his voice. "Continue this. Tomorrow."

Not sticking a high heel in his ass was one thing, but asking for more? *Not on your sweet life, chump.* "I'm busy."

"All day?"

"Yep. Right this second, though? Not so much."

And there it was. If he wanted her, he could have her. Right there, right now. But not at his beck and call.

She'd been there, dancing to someone else's tune. And the fact that it wasn't a man who'd used her affections against her, who'd let her dangle, kept her at a distance even when they'd lived in the same city, danced in the same company, didn't mean it hadn't left a mean scar.

Ryder's jaw clenched, and he looked as if he wanted to shake her, or kiss her, or toss her over his shoulder and spank her. In the end he did none of the above; he rolled his eyes to the exposed beams he was so in love with, and left, muttering under his breath something about women being the death of him.

"Dammit!" Nadia cried out once he'd gone, shaking out her hands and pacing and kicking things.

If it wasn't so late she'd be on the phone to her boss telling her to find someone else to look after Ryder

Bloody Fitzgerald. She'd absolutely do it in the morning. First thing. Before her feet even hit her cruddy apartment floor.

Till then…

Till then she stretched her arms high over her head, lifted till the arches of her feet screamed at her to stop, shook out her hair and danced to the sound of the rain drumming on the windows. Danced till sweat dripped into her eyes. Danced until her breaths grew ragged, her heart hammered, and her legs could barely hold her.

Power still out, muscles shaking and spent, she rugged up, turned things off as best she could, and left.

By the time she got downstairs, the storm had passed. And Ryder's luxe car was long gone. Not even a dry patch on the edge of the otherwise drenched and shiny street evidence he'd ever been there.

For that she had the burn of self-disgust riding deep in her belly and the crescents of still-tender love bites on her chest.

Nadia twisted her summer scarf into a ball at her neck, and walked the other way.

It was closer to dawn than midnight by the time Ryder turned onto the beach road leading to his Brighton home to find a pancake-flat, electric-blue sports car facing the wrong way and blocking his driveway.

Angry and frustrated, and wishing that he were back in his suit and not the ridiculous workout gear he'd worn to score points with Nadia, he pulled to a stop beside the outrageous car. The window of the mid-life-crisis-on-wheels slid down at a sulky pace.

Ryder said, "What do you want, Fitz?"

Ryder's father glanced up at Ryder's home, three

stories of luxury living the younger Fitzgerald had designed himself, the daunting wall of dark windows looking out over Port Phillip Bay and the white stucco walls gleaming, even in the cloud-shadowed moonlight.

"Nothing more than I deserve," Fitz finally drawled.

Knowing he could spend a week giving his father the earful he truly deserved, considering the hour, and the fact that he wanted to spend as little time in the same vicinity as the man as humanly possible, Ryder decided on brevity. "I know what you tried to pull tonight. Just leave her the hell alone."

The man actually laughed, his light hazel eyes crinkling as he let loose a deep booming sound that made Ryder's teeth hurt. "Don't be ridiculous, kid. She's my daughter."

"And any *good* father would respect his daughter's decision."

"Respect? That's rich. Not only did she choose you to walk her down the aisle over me, she didn't even invite me to the damn wedding. I'm the only one should be harping on about a lack of respect right about now."

Yeah, Ryder thought, should have occurred to him "respecting others" wasn't a concept in his father's emotional vocabulary.

The man leant towards the window leaving only his eyes still in shadow. His infamous crooked smile, the one all those women had seemed hell bent on falling for, crinkled his age-defying face. "Come on, kid. Put in a good word. You know it's the right thing to do."

Ryder rolled his fingers into a fist before shoving it into the deep pocket of his track pants. Then he curled the fingers of the other hand over the window sill of the sports car, and felt a kick of satisfaction as his father reared back. "The right thing? Sam is your daughter, Fitz. One who has given you more chances to be an actual father than you could ever deserve. And your sweet, kind, only daughter is about to get married, and unlike you she plans for it to be the only time she does. So after a good deal of soul-searching she decided to spend that special day with Ben's family, a few close friends, her mother, and me. That's it. Because even while she loves you—heaven only knows why—she recognises that if you are there the whole day, her wedding day, will be about you."

Fitz scoffed, but Ryder went on, lifting fingers stiff from gripping the metal and pointing one at his father's nose. "And if you have even the slightest twinge of affection for Sam you'll do the right thing and suck it up. Because if you dare to turn up, if you send her a message, if you so much as *think* about her on that day…"

Before he did anything stupid, anything he'd truly regret, Ryder sucked in a deep breath and leant back, then he banged a fist on the roof of the car, only just stopping himself from denting it.

Either way, Fitz took the hint and with a kind of roar only a top of the range substitute for actual manhood could achieve he took off down the road in a screech of tyres and guttural noise.

Only after the sound of the car faded did Ryder close his eyes and suppress his anger. Or at least he tried. The man's influence echoed in the back of his mind, motivating him to do better, to achieve more, to prove the man wrong. But it had been a while, years in fact, since the effect had been so acute.

He couldn't remember feeling so incensed since that

moment on the worksite during that long-ago internship, when his father had dismissed him so inexorably.
A switch had flipped inside him that day. Emotions
cooled. Ambitions honed. He'd lived that way ever since.

But in that moment he felt anything but cool. Standing on the quiet footpath, the first rays of morning
blinking on the horizon, he struggled to get any hold
of his emotions at all. His muscles screamed for relief.
His heart pounded inside his chest.

And he knew that this time he didn't only have his
father to blame.

He'd been playing with fire of late, in the hope he
was cool enough not to get burned. Fire by the name
of Nadia Kent.

The quixotic, bewitching, tempting creature had
hooked herself into places deep inside him he'd long
since kept locked away. She called to his darker emotions, luring them out of hiding. Feelings that could
only do more harm than good.

And the whole time he was staring down his father,
when his ire ought to have been *all* about standing up
for Sam, there was no getting away from the fact that the
deepest root of his fury was that he'd been dragged away
from *her*. From that hellfire kiss that had been swarming them both headlong into something much more.

Not that he'd give his father an inch, ever, but the
episode was just the wake-up call he needed.

With every effort he slowed his heart, reclaimed his
breath, corralled the mixed emotions roiling inside him
and pressed them back down. Deep. Deeper even than

he ever had before, along with the big dark vault he kept
especially for anything to do with his father.

Until the heat relented. His enmity abated. And every
part of him felt blissfully, mercifully, icily cool.

Chapter Five

Times like this Nadia wished she could drive.

Living out of hotels, or in share houses, there'd never been much point. But as her arms ached and her fingers turned numb under the strain of grocery bags she'd filled on her weekend trek to the Queen Vic Market it felt like a really long walk to the train.

And she wasn't even done yet.

The boom of boutique butchers competing for business thundered across the white noise of happy crowds while mounds of mouth-watering cheeses, curtains of speckled sausages, and trays of speckled brown, free-range eggs fought for greedy eyes. But the final stall on Nadia's list sold wine. Great, gleaming bottles of the stuff.

Nadia tipped up onto her toes and over the seething swarm of locals and tourists alike spied her target. Then, eye on the prize, she nudged her way through the crowd. When she stepped back to make way for a group of little old ladies sucking down fresh-made caramels she glanced away to discover that smack bang between her and the Promised Land stood Ryder Fitzgerald.

But before she had the chance to do anything about it Ryder looked up and straight into her eyes.

Surprise washed across his beautiful face. Surprise

and heat. The kind that landed in the backs of her knees with a fiery *whumph*. But the moment passed as his brow furrowed into a scowl and wiped out everything in its path. *Seriously,* she thought, locking her wayward knees, like *he* had anything to damn well scowl about.

Resisting the desire to cut and run, Nadia stood stock still as Ryder began to stride her way.

She straightened her shoulders and lifted her chin. Not that it mattered any. She was dressed in her weekend gear of skinny jeans, pink ballet flats, a sleeveless top and thin summer scarf, her hair was a day late in the washing and twirled up into a messy bun, and she wore no make-up bar lip balm and wind burn. She was hardly at her best.

While he looked…breathtaking. His sharp jaw unshaven, his face all dark and glowering, his hair spiking up a little from the effects of the light drizzle outside, and in jeans and a dark grey T-shirt he was all broad shoulders and lean hips and the kind of swagger that came naturally or didn't come at all.

"Nadia," he said, her name in that deep voice doing things to her blood she had no hope of containing.

"Hiya!" said she in a high sing-song voice she'd never used in her life.

"Shopping?"

"Lunch. A bottle of wine to go with it, then home."

He eyed the two heavily laden bags then his eyebrows raised a smidge. "Expecting company?"

"Just me."

His eyes moved from her bags to her flat tummy, and she wondered if he could see the flutters she felt. Hoped not. Hoped so. Lost all hope in herself.

"Anyway, I need to get in line before it all sells out.

So…" With a quick smile, she saw a gap in the crowd and slipped through.

She felt rather than saw him follow, the heat of the man burning against her back till she couldn't help but arch away from it. And then he was at her side, walking with her as if it was all planned. As if the last time she'd seen him he hadn't had his mouth on her, and his hands, and so very nearly more.

Knowing she couldn't outrun him, and needing that promised bottle of red more than ever, she said, "Doing a little shopping yourself this fine Saturday?"

He held up a bag of sugared almonds, before tossing one in his mouth. "Best in town."

Nadia tried not to stare as his tongue darted out to swipe the sugar dusting his lips, tried not to remember the other skills that mouth could boast without boasting at all. "They'd need to be if you braved this multitude for them."

A smile darted across his eyes, her tummy rolled over on itself, and she looked determinedly dead ahead. "So how's life been since you bolted Tuesday night?"

There, take that.

"Busy." The look he shot her was cryptic to say the least. Unfortunately it wasn't accompanied with anything like an explanation.

And that was as far as Nadia intended to go. "Ryder, I want you to know I asked my boss to assign your classes to someone else."

The guy actually looked surprised. His next step faltered, leaving him a beat behind. He covered it well though, as she expected he would. Blinded by all that simmering heat, it had taken her a while to see it; Ryder Fitzgerald was one cool customer. With a staggering ability to disengage himself, and his emotions, from one second to the next.

She'd known people in her life with that level of detachment. Had spent so long trying to get through that wall it had near crippled her. She could only be thankful she'd come out the other end. At least with the sense to know when to stick up for herself. And when to walk away.

Having reached the wine stall, Nadia lined up and kept her eyes dead ahead, but from the corner of her eye saw Ryder lean against the divider between the elevated stalls.

He said, "Am I to expect someone new to grumble over my feet on Tuesday night?"

"Turns out none of her other staff are stupid enough to agree to see a strange man at ten o'clock at night."

She shuffled forward a step.

"So it's still you and me?"

Nadia breathed out long and slow. Truth was she'd floated the idea with Amelia about shuffling Ryder's class to another teacher, but when Amelia had struggled to find a replacement she'd told her not to worry, despite the saga so far.

Kiss and run once, shame on him. Kiss and run twice, shame on her. There would *not* be a third time.

In a nice moment of helpful timing, she hit the front of the line before she could give Ryder his answer. Ignoring the man leaning moodily against the wall beside her, she chatted to her favourite stand owner—a dashing sommelier with the most charming French accent. The man was a total darling—in his eighties he could flirt with the best of them. Charming, innocent, simple. Oh that all men could be so.

Nadia bought her wine, and, still smiling, she turned
to find Ryder watching her. There was nothing innocent, nothing simple about the way he looked over her
with those dark eyes. From the muscle ticing at his jaw
to the bunched muscles of his crossed arms, he was a
mass of coiled energy. And heaven help her if she didn't
want to be right there with him when he uncoiled.

Wondering just how much she was going to regret it,
she waited till his wandering eyes met hers, then said,
"This isn't fun and games for me. It's my work. My life.
I'll teach you on one condition. When we're in class I
need you to behave and do as I say."

"Okay." Ryder didn't even hesitate. As if he really
meant it.

Her success was short-lived as Ryder's eyes slid to
her lips and stayed there, staring, glaring, as if he remembered exactly how she tasted and wished he could
buy it by the ounce.

With a groan, she eased around the back of the queue
and walked away.

"Where's your car?" he asked, on her heels again.

"I'm taking the train."

"Fair walk with those bags."

"Don't have a choice," she said, picking up her pace
and shifting the weight of her bags. "I don't drive."

"Why on earth not?"

"I've lived in cities my whole life. Never needed to."
Grimacing, Nadia went to shuffle the bags again, only
to find herself relieved as Ryder reached out and slid
them from her fingers.

"Thanks, but I can carry them."

Ryder glanced pointedly at her red hands, which
curled into themselves in relief. He moved the bags

easily to one hand, using the other to herd her, protect her from the crowd. "My turn to put in a proviso."

Of course. "What would that be?"

"That was rough, last week. I could barely bend over at work the next day."

Nadia let out a laugh, and when their eyes connected a gleam lit Ryder's eyes.

Nadia looked straight ahead. "And what kind of work would that be, needing for you to do so much bending over?"

"On a construction site."

"You're a builder?" Huh. "So what's with the slick suits, Ace?"

"Architect, actually," he said, the gleam morphing into a sexy smile, which, when surrounded by all that rough stubble, was as good as a loaded weapon.

"Is that why you're interested in my building, then?"

When he was silent a while she risked a glance to find his sexy smile had faltered. *Right, back to being Mr Tall Dark and Taciturn.* She gave herself a mental slap, and a reminder not to forget it. Not if she wanted to make it through the next month and a half without becoming unhinged.

"That's not the kind of architecture I do."

"What is?"

"High rises. Skyscrapers. Big, tall shiny ones."

"Ah, compensating."

His laughter came from nowhere, his eyes crinkling as deep waves of joy rolled from his lungs. People stopped. People turned. People sighed. People closed in as if magnetised. All of them women.

Rolling her eyes, Nadia shouldered past them out of the food hall and into the weak wet sunshine. "Your car's not that flash, though," she threw over her shoulder, in case he'd made it out of there alive, "which always gives a girl hope."

"My car is plenty flash," he said, having caught back up. "You've just never been inside her."

"Your car's a girl? My hopes for you are falling."

He shot her a look that was half lit with laughter, but mostly lit with something else. Something that made her feel as if baby ants were tap dancing all over her skin.

"So, Miss Nadia," he said, leaning in close enough his voice rumbled through her, "care to tell me about these hopes of yours?"

Her tummy rolled in honeyed pleasure. She bit her lip in atonement. "Not on your life, Ace. Now, why *not* bring back the glory of beautiful old buildings with beams strong enough to swing from if it's not about—" she glanced at his crotch and whistled "—you know?"

He blinked, then grinned. And the honeyed pleasure hardened so fast it fractured into a thousand pieces that pierced her insides with hot little spikes of desire.

"I interned with a few mobs after I graduated. The first commercial firm offered me a good package and I took it. Learnt a lot, learnt fast. Went out on my own a few years later."

"Hence the eighty-hour weeks."

"Hence. Helps that it's immensely satisfying work. For the most part…" The frown was back a moment before it slid away.

"Well, good for you. And I'm sure your…*towers* are awe-inspiring."

He shot her another of those glances, those new ones, filled with humour and that flicker of heat that he could never quite quell even when he was being all distant and haughty. This one came with a new angle, as if he was trying to figure her out.

"How about you—you like teaching?" he asked.

"It pays the bills."

"Damned by faint praise."

"Said the man who finds his own work satisfying *for the most part*?"

She expected a frown, and instead got a smile. The kind that slipped under her defences like a hot knife through butter.

Mmm. She'd need a flashlight, a map, and a millennium to figure *this* one out. She only had a few short weeks. Not enough time. Yet way too much.

She stopped and held out her hands for her bags. "Thanks for the help, Ryder, but I've got feeling back in my fingers. I can take it from here."

He just stood there, the muscles in his arms bunching as he slowly rearranged the bags, his dark eyes unreadable.

She clicked her fingers at him but he still didn't move. "Ryder—"

"It was Sam on the phone the other night," he said, the words seeming to tear from inside him. Then, "She was the reason I had to leave."

As if he'd thrown a bucket of warm water over her, Nadia felt herself pink all over. The heat grew when she remembered the one part she'd made herself forget—the torture in his eyes that he'd had to leave *her*.

Sam. Of course. But what didn't make sense was that he hadn't just said so. Unless…

Nadia swallowed, her voice barely above a whisper as she asked, "Oh, Ryder. Is she okay?"

He lifted an arm, as if to reassure her, then realised

both hands were full. "Nothing like that. She's fine. But that night she was upset. Very upset."

Nadia kicked herself for not noticing anything at Sam and Ben's rehearsal Thursday night. It seemed the Fitzgerald family as a whole were good at keeping things close to the chest. "So what happened?"

"Our father happened," he said, and since he had her lunch and next day's leftovers in his hands, when he started to walk she had no choice but to follow.

"Your father's alive? I'd assumed… Since you're walking Sam down the aisle…"

Ryder's eyes became stormy. "He's well and truly alive, just not a part of our lives. He turned up at Sam's last Tuesday night. Tore strips off her for not asking him to walk her down the aisle. Father of the bride carries some social weight, don't you know. She was hiding out in the bathroom when she called; he refused to leave until she changed her mind."

While Ryder's voice grew hard as ice, Nadia's scalp felt all hot and prickly as she tried to picture Sam huddled in her bathroom, scared of her own father. "Ryder, I'm so sorry. I had no idea. What a creep."

Ryder's mouth twisted into a wry smile. "No apology necessary. Though I'd go more for bully. Or asshole. Selfish bastard pretty much covers it as that comes with the knack for abusing the trust of anyone who dares care about him."

Ouch. Literally. Nadia's heart gave her such an unexpected little pinch she rubbed the heel of her palm over the spot.

"When she rang he was… I could hear him… While Sam was…"

He stopped. Breathed deep. While Nadia couldn't breathe at all.

"Sam's had panic attacks before, but not for a long time. Not this bad. She was so distraught by the time I got to her I ended up calling an ambulance. It was nearly three before she was calmed and back home asleep in bed."

Nadia's fist curled against her ribs. Poor Sam. Poor Ryder. While Nadia had been pouting and kicking things and generally thinking the guy was a big jerk, he was going through all that. She felt like a fool. Then, "Where was Ben?"

At that Ryder's granite gaze skewed back to hers. Behind the surface she saw such a deep river of concern it made her thumping heart twist.

"She didn't call him," said Ryder. "She only called me."

"Oh, no."

"Yeah. Pretty much my first thought too."

After a few loaded beats, they both began walking again, close enough they were as good as bumping shoulders. The ground was hot and steaming beneath their feet, the rest of the world a blur as they remained lost in their thoughts.

After a good minute, Nadia asked the one question that had been left unanswered. "Where does your mother fit into the picture?"

A flare of something warmer pierced the granite. "My mother was…something else. A sculptor of found objects. A champion for the beauty redolent in bits and pieces others had cast aside. She could make something inspired out of detritus the rest of us wouldn't even notice." Then, as if he'd been working up to it, "She was sick for some time. I was eleven when she died. It took my father mere months to marry Sam's mother. And Sam was born weeks after that."

Nadia didn't ask how long after. She didn't need to. It was there in the set of his big shoulders, the tension of his beautiful mouth. His father hadn't waited for his ill wife to pass before knocking up wife number two.

Nadia couldn't imagine what it must have been like for a kid to go through that. Her relationship with her own mother was complicated, to say the least, but, even when she hadn't been around, she'd always been *there*. Even if "there" was the other side of the world.

In the end it hadn't taken a flashlight, a map, or a millennium. This big strong man had just given her a most unexpected glimpse behind the iron curtain. A glimpse at hidden depths, at the moral struggles that had been waged beneath that slick exterior. And even while she tried telling herself it didn't mean anything, that it didn't change anything, it felt like a precious gift.

Feeling a sudden urge to even out the score, Nadia picked the path of least resistance. "I never knew my dad."

Ryder's dark eyes flicked to hers.

"He was someone in the dance world, I gather. My mother was a dancer too. From bits and piece I gleaned over the years I think he was one of the owners of the ballet, or on the board." From the incessant mutterings of her sober grandmother, Nadia had also gleaned her mother had slept with the man in order to get ahead, and it had backfired spectacularly. No solos for a prima ballerina up the duff.

"Are you close to your mother?" Ryder asked.

"She lives in Toorak."

It wasn't what he'd meant, of course, and the clever glint in his eye, and hook to the side of his mouth, told her he was well aware of her prevarication. But he didn't push. Didn't ask for more than she was willing to give. This man holding her groceries. The same man who'd given her his jacket to keep her warm. The man who after every lesson—bar the one he'd fled to take care of his sister—had walked her out to make sure she stayed safe.

Emotions a little tender, a little raw, Nadia moved to the crossing lights, pressing the button to alert the machine she was there. When Ryder moved beside her, close enough now she could feel the shift of his body as he breathed, and goose bumps followed every time he breathed out.

"Hungry?" she said, before she'd even felt the words coming.

His gaze shot to hers, hot, dark, way too smart for his own good. Or hers.

But it was done now. Out there. The invitation for more. "Nothing fancy on the menu. Spare ribs and salad. Home-made cheesecake made in someone else's home. A bottle of really fine red."

He didn't answer straight away, and Nadia felt herself squirming in some deep, hot, hopeful place inside.

"I'm game," he said, his face creasing into the kind of smile that could down an army of women in one fell swoop. Then he started walking backwards, back towards the car park. "You cook, I'll drive. If you can bear to be taken about in my not so flash car."

She took a moment, as if mulling it over, all the while her still raw and tender emotions indulged in the provocative smile that spread across his face.

Then she fell all too easily into step beside him.

* * *

Ryder sat on the opposite side of the wobbly kitchen table watching Nadia slide the last pork rib between her lips, her eyes shut as she sucked the last of the meat from the bone.

Either the woman had no idea he was pressing his feet hard enough into the cracked vinyl floor to leave dual dents so as not to make good on the urge to tip the table over and kiss that sweetness right from her lush mouth, or she knew exactly what she was doing to him and loved every second of it.

He figured it about a ninety-five per cent chance it was the latter.

In an effort to save himself from doing damage, Ryder took in his surroundings instead. Turned out her place was as much of a mystery as she was. He would have imagined lots of rich earthy colours and unusual bolts of light, perhaps even a secret passageway or two. Instead her apartment was small, neutral, and undecorated apart from the basics. In fact, apart from a few photos of dancers on the mantel over an incongruously blank wall, it was devoid of any personal touches at all.

And yet sitting in the shabby kitchenette of the tiny apartment above the abandoned Laundromat below, sunlight pouring through the grubby old windows, he felt himself relaxing for the first time in days.

And from nowhere it occurred to him that his colourful mother would have liked her. Would have been drawn to her spirit, her pluck, the way she seemed to fit in anywhere, yet not much care what anyone thought.

As for what he thought? From the first moment she'd walked towards him in the dance studio, all dark and

mysterious and brazen, he'd thought her a creature of
the night.

But in the bright, warm, quiet room he felt himself take that assumption apart and put it back together
again.

In daylight her skin was beautiful, pale, and smooth.
Threads of chestnut and auburn strung through her dark
hair, which she'd twisted off her face showing off the
most graceful neck he'd ever seen. With one bare foot
tucked up onto her chair, her supple body curved over
her food, she looked casual, content. And smaller somehow, softer without the va va voom and invisible whip
that was such a part of her in teacher mode.

Which made it all the harder to remember why he'd
spent the past few days carefully, determinedly distanc-
ing himself from thoughts of her. Disentangling himself from the desire that had wound itself around him
like a straightjacket.

She licked her lips, and her eyes fluttered open.
When she caught him watching her, she gave a husky
laugh. The desire returned with all the force and ferocity of a rogue wave.

"Enjoying yourself?" he asked, his voice rough as
rocks.

"Yes," she said on a long slow sigh. She flicked a
glance towards the battered fridge-freezer in the corner of the room. "Dessert?"

He shook his head. Dessert wasn't close to what he
wanted. "I'm not sure where you could fit dessert."

Her leg splayed to one side as she patted her flat
belly and he had to hold back the groan that started
right in his crotch.

Blinking innocently, she said, "Dancing is a damn

fine workout, Ace. Which you'd know if you worked half as hard as I tell you to. I need all the energy I can get."

Ryder shifted on his seat, and struggled to find an innocuous change of subject so that he might get himself back under some semblance of control.

"Were you always a dancer?"

"Since the moment I came out of my mamma's womb," she said. "Family business."

Ryder stretched out the hand he'd bruised on the roof of his father's car and wondered at the kind of relationship where a child *wanted* to follow in a parent's footsteps. He nudged his chin towards the oldest photograph on the mantel—the image of a rake-thin dancer in full ballet regalia, her delicate face twisted in some tragic countenance. "That's her?"

"That was her. Before I was born. I've seen old videos," she qualified with a wry smile. "She danced like a whisper, soft, smooth, so quiet you'd never hear her land."

Nadia looked at the picture a little longer, blinked and sank her chin into her palm.

"Were you ever a ballerina too?"

She bolted upright at that, hand on her belly, mouth agape. "Good Lord, no! Do I look like a ballerina?"

What she looked was downright fit and lush and good enough to eat.

She let her stomach go, not that it went anywhere. "It takes a very particular kind of tenacity to make it in ballet, to have that level of control over your body. Over your whole life. Which is why Mum's ballet career was over the moment she fell pregnant with me. As for me, I like food too much."

Nadia waggled her eyebrows as she took a gulp of her wine.

Ryder quietly pieced together a relationship that might not have been so close after all. A mother and daughter living in the same city, yet not seemingly in touch. A mother who'd never revealed paternity. A mother who tangled the ending of her career and the birth of her daughter. And he shifted the conversation sideways.

"So if not ballet, what's your…speciality? Is that the right term?"

Nadia's mouth quirked and this time when she sank her chin onto her upturned palm the move was silken, slippery, sexy as hell. "I'm…well rounded."

"Learnt from Mum's mistake, then."

Nadia's laughter was scandalised. But she sank back into her chair with wicked wonder in her eyes. "I guess so. I've never been typecast, never been tied down to one style. I worked clubs in LA. A few stage shows in Dallas. My first solos were in a burlesque company off Broadway that was sold out for months."

Her gaze went to the mantel. Ryder's followed. "Seems a long way from ballet."

"You don't have to tell me. Especially considering Mum was working there at the time."

Ryder's eyebrows nudged up his forehead. "Well, I'll be."

While Nadia's eyes remained glued to the photo. "She'd always worked in America, but she had to leave her ballet company when she was pregnant with me and she came back to Melbourne. To my grandmother—picture Mum but humourless and grim."

Glancing at the photograph of Nadia's mother, Ryder thought it didn't take much picturing at all.

"Mum tried to stick it out once I was born. But when the dance calls…" Her fingers fluttered upwards in a move that seemed more of an impression than a natural movement of her own. "Then the life of a showgirl became too good to turn her back on. The hotel living. The rich men. The partying that reminded her she was still young, and helped her forget what she'd left behind…" Her eyes glazed for a second before she hauled herself back. "So I danced, and trained, worked my ass off and made it overseas. And then I got the call to work the burlesque club Mum had made her home. It was the first time we'd ever worked together, and I couldn't have cared if I was dancing Bollywood if it meant I was spending time with her. As for actually dancing with her?" She let go a long slow whistle. "It was amazing. For a little while. I was my own mother's protégé. We even had one act together, The Kent Sisters."

Ryder raised an eyebrow. But Nadia just grinned.

"I know. Hilarious, right? But despite *that* it was everything I'd ever dreamed of being since I first stuck my hands in the air and did a twirl."

"Since you're here, as is she, I take it things didn't last."

Nadia's gaze swung back to him as if coming from a long way away. She leant forward and cradled the glass of wine with both hands. "I got my first solo."

"Ah."

The wine was gone in a gulp. "And that was when she made it clear every job I'd ever been offered had only been after a phone call from her. That my name, *her* name, was the only reason I was anything at all."

Her mouth kicked into a wry smile, but Ryder caught the flash of hurt behind it. The disappointment. The disenchantment. He recognised the moment when you realised the parent you looked up to your whole life turned out to be, oh, so flawed.

"Anyway," she said, shaking out the funk that had settled over her, "after a particularly punishing day, I secretly auditioned for Sky High—at the last second using my grandmother's maiden name—and lo and behold got a place. Within the week I'd moved to Vegas, to the first real job that I'd ever been sure I'd got on my own. Not only that, it changed my life. Like I'd been dancing in shoes a size too small all my life and never known it. I'd found my bliss."

She finished with a soft sigh, a wistful and faraway gaze in her eyes. Then she looked around, seemed to realise where she was—or more precisely where she wasn't.

Her laughter was glib as she said, "I'm sorry. What was the question again?"

"I think you answered it." And then some. "I have just one more question. About your mother actually."

A flash of warning licked behind her eyes.

"She still pole dancing today?"

Nadia's laugh burst from her with such suddenness, such vivacious luxury, she near fell off her chair. "Ryder, if you knew her, you'd know how funny—I mean how *far off the mark* that was. A big Aussie mining magnate saw her on stage not long after I left New York, swept her off her pointy-toed feet and took her back home with him. She's retired. This time I'm the one who came home in disgrace."

"Back up a step now, Miss Nadia. Now we're getting

to the good stuff. What did you do to disgrace yourself? Rob a bank? Sell state secrets? Arabesque when you were meant to…anti-arabesque?"

Her lush mouth quirked into a sensuous smile, before her face scrunched up in what looked like embarrassment. This was turning out to be a day of revelations. "It's nothing nearly so dramatic or exciting."

He waved a hand for her to go on.

"I broke up with my boyfriend, quit my job, and fled."

And somehow the idea of a boyfriend, a man, being this close, closer, to her, ever, made Ryder's hackles rise more than the thought of her making off with an armoured car. "Poor boyfriend."

Her cheeks pinked even as she smiled that sexy, exuberant smile of hers. "Missing out on all this? You bet poor boyfriend. But you know what? In all honesty?"

His eyes roved over her, the beautiful bone structure, the sultry dark eyes, the sensual way she moved. "Hit me."

"I've spent the past year convinced I left because of a relationship that went embarrassingly south. But I've been dancing professionally without a break since I was sixteen. I wonder if it wasn't really a blessing in disguise, if my body told me this was my chance to get away from it all for a while so that it could recuperate. If my ego saw the chance to eke out some time to just grow up."

She shrugged and sat back in her chair, her nose buried in the empty wineglass in her hand.

While Ryder couldn't quite feel his centre on the chair any more.

Because somehow things had…shifted. As if in the

daylight, in her unassuming little flat, the normality of it all, having an actual honest conversation, caught at him, raw and arresting. Here sat a beautiful woman, slightly broken, but rich with substance and grit. And with his feet no longer pressing into the cracked old floor, there was nothing stopping him from perusing what his instincts had long since been screaming for him to do.

"Nadia."

"Yes, Ryder."

"You look plenty grown up to me."

The faraway gaze came back into sharp focus and her mouth curled into a smile. "I can assure you I am. All the way grown up."

And in the way that mattered most to Ryder, she was. What you saw was what you got with Nadia Kent. And there'd never been any question that what he saw he wanted.

"You missed some sauce," he said, eyes honed in on her lush mouth.

Her tongue flicked out to swipe the corner of her mouth. "Better?"

Better than what? "Still there," he lied, then lifted himself from his chair and leant over the table.

Her eyes darkened. "Ryder Fitzgerald. Not two hours ago you promised to be a good boy."

"And inside the dance studio, I'm yours to do with as you please. But I never made any promises about my behaviour elsewhere. And you never asked me to."

With a flare in her eyes that told him all he needed to know, Nadia hopped onto her knees on her chair, and bent forward, met him halfway. "Care to help?"

"Hell yeah," he said, leaning the last inch to cover her mouth with his.

He knew she'd be warm, knew she knew what she was doing; what he didn't expect was the complete shock of pleasure that knocked against his insides like a pinball gone rogue.

Her hand lifted to his cheek, her fingernails scraping his unshaven chin, and he had to grip the table edges to keep himself from taking them both down in a heap.

She pulled away, leant her forehead against his a moment, then lifted her head to look into his eyes, her irises swallowed by the pupils. "All fixed?"

He breathed in deep, out hard and said, "Not even close."

With that, she was on the table, crawling across the thing as it shook beneath her, the plates and cutlery bouncing to the floor with a crash. If she didn't care, neither did he.

He hauled her against him, light as a feather, sinewy and soft, every movement pure grace, pure sex. No sweet kisses, all voracious hunger.

She tasted of lemon and honey and contradiction and heat. And her hands were all over him. Tearing at his clothes till he was naked from the waist up. Running through his hair. Scraping down his back till he growled from the pure deep pleasure of her touch.

Fearless, she was, and with a mouth that drove him wild.

Pulsing with a craving he could barely contain, he whipped her top over her head, her tight belly twitching beneath his palms, then her small breasts perfect in his mouth. So sweet, so firm, so sensual. The power in her warm, supple body was killing him.

Mouths open, hungry, a hand at his neck, she dragged him down. As she arched into him her hands found his zip, freed him. She enclosed her palm around him and slid down the length till he had to brace his feet so hard into the floor he saw stars.

She freed him only to wriggle out of her jeans, her body shuffling against him. His blood rushed so hard through his veins he felt as if his very cells were reconstructing, like some damn werewolf at the full moon. Man, he wanted her, with a ferocity he couldn't remember ever feeling.

"Got something for the big guy?" she asked.

"Wallet," he managed, "back pocket."

With a sure hand she found his wallet, taking a moment to caress his backside while she was there. The woman was wholly corrupting, whisking him to the very brink of desperation.

Once she'd freed the square foil from within she tossed his wallet over her shoulder, flicked the condom packet between them, grinning, then tore the thing open with her teeth. Then, dark bottomless eyes on his, she sheathed him. Slowly. Torturously slowly. And thoroughly. *Wow*. Her fingers traced every inch, and then some.

Her hands moved around his thighs, tugged at a few hairs, sending shards of pleasure and pain through every nerve, then her legs wrapped around him, tight and strong.

He nudged her centre, her slick heat near sending him over the edge. Her eyes fluttered closed, her mouth sliding open on a sigh, her brow furrowing as if he wasn't the only one teetering all too close to the edge of eruption. And then with a gifted flick of her hips she enveloped him, deep and tight and gorgeous.

From there Ryder's vision collapsed till it was the

size of the table, everything else a red blur. His ears rang with nothing but the thud of his blood, with her gasping breaths. The scent of her, the feel of her, the sensual glory of her filling him from the inside and spilling out of him with a release so intense it near bled him dry.

He came to from wherever he'd gone, and realised his arm actually shook as it kept him from collapsing on top of her. He opened his eyes and his heart shook right along with it. The woman was an exotic mess. Her pale skin pink and shimmering with sweat, strands of her dark hair having fallen from her bun and spilling over the tabletop, her mouth open dragging in breath, her eyes dark pools of desire.

And he realised with mortification he'd been so far over the edge of need he had no idea if she'd been right there with him. "Did you...?"

"Not yet." And she clenched herself around him with a strength that made his head spin.

She kicked a leg over his shoulder and rocked, her eyes clenching shut, her mouth open wide as she took in short sharp gasps of air. He had the feeling she knew exactly what she was doing, that she could have got there without any help from him at all.

But that wasn't going to happen. Not on his watch.

Ryder swore and braced himself on two arms. He felt himself harden inside her, pressed deeper and smiled as her eyes flew open. Then, holding her leg in place, finding it flexible enough to handle the stretch, he slowly lowered himself to bury his face in her neck, drinking in the scent of her. Kissing his way down her neck, her fine collarbone. He traced her knee, ran his thumb down her inner thigh, found her centre right as his mouth found her breast.

He plunged deeper and she cried out, gripping the table with one white-knuckled hand. The other scraping down his back hard enough to hurt.

His tongue traced her nipple, desire knotting his insides. He swirled his tongue as he swirled his thumb, and felt her tremble, and fracture, and melt. Heat slid through him at her acquiescence, at her trust, wiping out all but instinct, pleasure, her.

And when she stilled, when her body contracted around him, as her body trembled and rose and lifted and hovered once more on the verge of collapse he plunged as deep as he dared, his own second release coming from so deep inside he roared till the building shook.

Spent, he collapsed on top of her, her hand sank into his hair, the other flopped over her eyes, and together they lay there until their breaths eased back to near normal.

She moved first, and insanely he felt himself twitch inside her. *Enough,* he urged himself. Any more and the rubber would be irrelevant.

He pulled himself free of her, and his body felt instantly bereft. How soon it was used to her shape, her scent, the feel of her wrapped tight around him. How soon it wanted all that and more. Not sure that his legs would carry him just yet, he perched on the edge of the table.

Distractedly, he noted that the floor was a mess: broken plates, a fork end up into a crack in the wood, sauce oozing under the cupboard. But he didn't have the energy to care.

It hadn't been sex as he'd known it—it had been survival of the fittest. And he wondered what it meant that they'd both lived to tell the tale.

Nadia pulled herself to sitting and leant against his back, laying a string of warm kisses along his shoulder blade. "Wow."

"You're welcome."

Her laughter tripped over his skin, then she slid from her table, stepped over the mess, till she was standing, naked, in front of him. Lean hips, beautiful thighs, small breasts with the most perfect pink nipples, a belly he wanted to rub his cheek against.

"Shower?" she asked. "Not much hot water I'm afraid, so we'd have to share."

A hair band between her teeth, she lifted her lean arms to retie her hair back into a chaotic bun and simply awaited his answer. Not an ounce of self-consciousness in the move. Just a woman who knew herself, liked herself, enjoyed the pleasure her body brought her.

For a man who'd spent a lifetime striving, soaring, hitting every pinnacle he'd ever aimed towards yet never reaching that illusive plateau of fulfilment, her effortless self-satisfaction was soporific, sinking into his bones like a drug.

"Coming?" she asked, a kick to her lush mouth.

Ryder didn't answer; his voice would have been little more than a hoarse croak as it was. Instead he lifted her up, threw her over his shoulder, her raucous laughter bouncing off the walls.

Then with a kiss to her gorgeous backside Ryder said, "Point the way, woman."

She did, with a neatly pointed toe.

Chapter Six

The Sunday sun shone upon the breezy St Kilda bistro. The chips were salty and hot, the drinks icy cold, and as Sam chatted away about how her wedding plans were coming along Nadia tried not to flinch every time Sam mentioned her brother's name.

It was less than twelve hours since the tryst in her apartment, and she could still feel Ryder in the ache of her muscles, smell him on her skin, see him every time she blinked her damn eyes.

"I tried to keep it small, you know," Sam continued. "But everything seems to be spinning further and further out of our control."

"It's your wedding day, Sam," said Nadia, shaking herself into the present. Though she wasn't sure how she could help; as a kid the only time she'd imagined herself in a white dress was if it was a tutu. "Let that bossy streak of yours run wild!"

"Yeah," said Sam, rolling her fey grey eyes before they faded flat, and Nadia had a feeling she knew why.

Nadia nudged Sam's foot with a toe. "Ryder filled me in some on what happened the other night. With your father."

"He did?" Sam managed to look both relieved and like a puppy remembering it had been kicked.

"Are you okay?"

"Most of the time. Nothing the right pills and some darned expensive therapy don't keep in check." When Nadia merely stared back, Sam put both hands over hers. "Honestly, I'm fine. The other night was horrible. Just really mean and ugly. But it only made me sure that I've done the right thing in cutting him off. Which, of course, my more astute brother did millennia ago. And speaking of Ryder. *He* talked about Dad? Using actual words? That's... I'm... Wow."

Nadia shifted on her seat. "Ryder didn't tell you we'd talked?"

Another eye roll. "Of course not. The man treats me like I'm made of glass. Though I get why. I do. What with his mum dying when he was so young, and our dad being...well, our dad, Ryder holds on crazy tight to the things that matter to him."

Sam curled her hands back into her lap and sighed.

"Don't tell Ryder this, but the only reason I'm going with a big white wedding is to give him the chance to give me away. I'd be happy to marry my guy right here, right now. But Ryder's so unwavering in his effort to do right by me I thought nothing less than an official ceremony would give him permission to really let me go."

Nadia nodded, even while she was only listening with half an ear. A warning bell had begun to buzz pretty insistently about a minute back when Sam had said *Ryder holds on crazy tight to the things that matter to him.*

It wasn't as if *she* mattered to him, not in the way Sam meant. Even if it was natural for a proprietary feeling to come into play when you'd been naked with someone, when that someone had taken you to heaven and back on your kitchen table, in your shower, and slow, tender, deep, trembling, and weak up against the front door, they'd never talked about the chance of an extended run. Or even going for a second act. In fact once their clothes had come off they'd barely talked at all.

"So you and my brother…"

Nadia found Sam watching her, chin on her upturned palm, grin spread across her face. "Excuse me?"

"You were looking all dreamy and far away just now. I know that look. I see that look on Ben's face each and every day."

Nadia brought her now lukewarm beer to her mouth while she tried desperately to fashion a response.

"At least I hope it's my brother you're looking so moony about, considering the last time I saw the two of you, you had your tongues entwined."

When Nadia near *choked* on her drink, she put it down carefully then sank her head into her hands, before sliding said hands through her shaggy hair. "What makes you think that was anything but a momentary lapse of reason?"

"I know my brother, Nadia. He's the human version of the skyscrapers he builds—big, strong, invulnerable. This is the first time I've ever seen him so struck he can't hide it and you, my sweet, did the striking."

At that her palms began to sweat, her blood rang in her ears, and she wondered if this was what one of Sam's panic attacks felt like. "Sammy Sam, I don't meant to burst your bubble, but there is *no* your brother and me. Not in the way you mean." She paused, knowing what she was about to say would complicate the simplest friendship of her life. "Melbourne was always a time-out for me, Sam. But that time's run out. In the next few weeks the reps from the new Sky High show are flying out to Australia to see a small contingent of Australian dancers who've been asked to audition by invitation only. I'm one of those dancers."

Sam's face fell, for a second seeming to literally slip down over her bones. "Does Ryder know?"

Nadia swallowed. "I never would have agreed to take on your wedding party account if I wasn't sure I'd be here until all your lessons are done."

Sam's next look was older than her twenty-four years. "That's what's my brother would call being deliberately obtuse."

Nadia breathed out hard and fast. Then threw out her hands in surrender. "No, I don't believe I've mentioned it to him. Or to any of my other students, for that matter."

She sent Sam a pointed glance, which Sam returned in good measure. And rightly so. Nadia hadn't spent a good many hours the evening before naked with any of her *other students*.

So why *had* she with Ryder? What made him so different from the dozen or so clients who'd made advances? Because there had been more. Plenty.

Ryder was beautiful to look at, sure, and unbelievably sexy in a prowling panther kind of way. But she was also fast gathering that he was ambitious and wry, complicated and intense, and while she'd gambled with more than her share of luck over the years he wasn't big on second chances. Maybe that was it—he had the right amount of emotional baggage to draw her to him, like moths to the same flame.

Sam held up a hand at Nadia, halting her mid-thought, before hailing a waiter, ordering more beer, then saying, "I'm going to say one more thing and then that's it, lips zipped shut. And that is Ryder would rather pull out his toenails with tweezers than talk about our father, though he will any time he knows I need to, which is only part of why he's a great guy. Any woman would be lucky to have him in their life. And no matter what's at the end of the road, for this moment in time, Nadia, that woman could be you."

Nadia slid the red paper serviette from around her unused knife and breathed in deep, hoping Sam couldn't see how shaky her breath was. Because in the quiet dark hours of night, she'd gone in circles thinking pretty much the same thing: that here and now didn't have to have anything to do with the near future.

But it did. It always did. She knew better than anyone that past and future were so tightly knotted and profoundly intertwined, if one didn't tread lightly they could strangle you.

"For as long as I can remember all I wanted to do was dance. Then a year ago I had it all—a job I loved, in a city filled with life and excitement and opportunity. And I threw it all away because—" *Because of a guy*, she'd been about to say. But no. She'd come to admit that had only been an excuse. Then why? Because she'd needed to take a breath? Because it had given her the perfect excuse to go running home to Mum? A little bit of all that. But also, "Because I didn't know what I had till it was gone. I've realised since then that life doesn't just happen, you choose it. And I choose dance. I'll always choose dance."

"Dancing means that much?"

"I wouldn't know who I was without it."

The waiter returned, condensation dripping down the brown glass of their beer bottles. When Nadia took the drink from his hand she realised she'd torn the red serviette to pieces.

"Man, I envy your passion." Sam stared at the red mess, before bringing the drink to her mouth. "And enough said. As for the other, apart from the fact that you've just broken my heart a little bit, now we'll have a couch to crash on if we ever get to Vegas, right?"

"For as long as you want."

With that, Sam let out a big sigh then closed her eyes to the rare bout of dry sunshine. Relieved at having told Sam her plans, Nadia tried to do the same. But now that she'd told Sam, now she'd brought that world into this, it somehow made it real. Like in the stars real. And anticipation flowed through her veins like liquid ice till the tips of her fingers tingled as they did when she worked the ropes too long.

As this time she understood the gravity of the opportunity.

Her year away from professional dance had helped her grow up, and it had started the moment she'd knocked on her mother's Toorak door, scoring nothing but a raised eyebrow.

It shouldn't have been a surprise; it was exactly her family's particular brand of solace. Twist an ankle? *Suck it up.* Bomb an audition? *Get over it.* And it certainly shouldn't have hurt so much. Rejection was as much a part of being a dancer as warming up. Still, it had felt like a punch right to her centre, and things had started becoming very clear.

What she wanted more than anything was to dance.

What she *needed* was to do so as far from her mother as humanly possible.

Necessity and desire burned within her and the reality check had just added fuel to the fire. Within the next six weeks she'd have the chance to have it all.

One wrong step and it could all go up in smoke.

Ryder pushed open the door to the dance studio, letting himself in.

After the day he'd had he was glad to be anywhere but on site. Accustomed to the politics of such a substantial and significant project, that day the trivialities had grated to the point he'd felt one problem away from abandoning the whole damn thing.

By contrast the studio was blissfully quiet. The lights dim. Slivers of cool moonlight shone through the bare windows painting patches of white on the scuffed wooden floor. He cast only a perfunctory glance at the beautiful beams above, as he was in pursuit of a different kind of therapy altogether.

It had been three days since that afternoon of delight in Nadia's battered little apartment. Three long days since he'd left her at her door with a long kiss, her face soft with release. Then he'd gone home. Gone to work. And pretended it had been a perfectly normal encounter.

Unfortunately, pretending hadn't made it so.

Normal for him meant no promises, no surprises, taking extreme care to leave no wreckage in his wake. Nadia turned him upside down and inside out until, even while he had no idea what he'd be walking into, or which version of the woman he'd encounter, he'd looked forward to Tuesday night more than anything else that week.

He dumped his gear on the moth-eaten old chair, and looked around. So where the hell was she? The eerie silence built inside him as he walked the wall of windows, anticipation and unrest mixing until his senses keened with every creak of an old floorboard, every shift of dust motes on the sultry air.

"Howdy," Nadia's voice twanged behind him.

Ryder spun on his heels to find her standing by the big old curtains; tiny curls that had escaped from her hair band framing her face, dark eyes a smudge, lush lips hooked into a smile. Her face and neck were dewy from exercise, the rest of her encased in a long-sleeved, cross-over-type top, a short black skirt, fishnet tights, and spiked high heels.

"Nadia," he managed.

Her eyes flickered reproachfully over his suit. "How was work, Ace?"

"Incessant." He'd spent the day battling unions and clients and staff and contractors and suppliers rather than doing any of the hands-on designing that his job was meant to be about. At least he'd thought so once upon a time. "Yours?"

"Hard, actually." She rolled her shoulders and stretched out a hamstring to bring that home. "Care to see what I've been up to?"

The unsettling inside out and upside down feeling came swarming back, yet he found himself saying, "You bet."

Without another word she whipped back the curtains at the corner of the room revealing...

"Holy mother of..." Ryder said, his feet propelling him forward as his eyes darted from runs of black ropes dripping from the beams above, over wafting swathes of red silk doing the same, to a sparkling silver hula hoop dangling six feet off the floor.

His eyes ran all the way up the heavy-duty wire wrapped about and bolted to the beams above. Architecturally inventive as he was, he was pretty sure he'd never look at a beam the same way again.

"You look a little freaked, my friend."

Ryder flicked a glance to Nadia to find her watching him, her arms folded over her chest. Defensive. And comprehension began to trickle down his spine. So this was how she was going to play it after their afternoon together. His little dance teacher was throwing down the gauntlet.

Schooling his features into the very definition of impassive, Ryder offered up a half-smile. "Dare I ask what it's all for?"

Nadia cocked a hip, all insouciance and grace. It was a heady combination. Especially since he now knew the curve of that hip, knew the taste of that dewy skin, the skill of that lush mouth, the light that shone from those guarded eyes when she was laid bare.

"How about I show you instead?" With that she unhooked her skirt, and nudged off her shoes, leaving her in the long-sleeved top, black bikini bottoms and fishnets. Holy hell.

With practised ease she slid fingerless leather gloves over her palms, snapping studs behind her wrists with an audible click that he felt right in his groin. A small voice inside his head told him to *Run!* A louder voice told him to stay the hell where he was, as he might just have found paradise.

With a few quick stretches, she breathed in, then out, ran the soles of her feet over a towel on the floor, stretched out her fingers, steadied her breath. Then she positioned herself beneath the ropes, taking care as she curled them about her wrists, tugging to—he hoped—check the tension. Then, with a quick glance over her shoulder, she said, "Ready?"

"As I'll ever be."

Her first smile, a glimmer of light in her eyes, she then lifted her feet off the ground and with deft rolls of her arms and flicks of rope behind her knees seemed to float up into the sky.

He'd been fully aware of the grace of her every movement before that moment. He'd danced at her side and in her arms. He'd been inside her and around her and beneath her and above, and been bewitched by the knowledge and control she had over her beautiful body.

But as she turned herself into and out of the grip of the shiny black rope, stopping only for her strong, lithe body to make the most insanely beautiful shapes, all he could think was: *upside down and inside out.*

No music rent the air as she continued her hypnotic routine; the only sounds the hot summer wind whipping against the window, the swish of the ropes as Nadia tumbled through the air, and the thunder of his heart as he stopped himself time and again from reaching out when he thought she might fall.

But she never even came close.

She knew exactly what she was doing.

She was a wonder.

And then she was falling, plummeting, the rope unwinding from around her.

Fear hurled into Ryder's throat, until she planted a foot on the floor; her ponytail swishing across her neck as her body came to a halt. Her chest rising and falling.

Tousled hair matted to her neck with perspiration. Eyes burning into his as if daring him to even try to think himself worthy of such a creature.

But for the first time in his life Ryder didn't give a flying hoot if he was worthy. He was a mass of pure instinct. Of need and fear and hunger; all of it primal, uncoiling from deep down inside, reaching out with perfect aim.

Nadia twirled her hands back into the rope till her arms were stretched up straight. "What did you think?"

As if she weren't fully aware blood was pumping so hard and fast through Ryder's body he could barely think at all. "If that's part two of the routine I've been sent here to learn," he said, his rough voice echoing across the huge space, "then Sam can think again."

Surprise flared in her dark eyes before Nadia laughed, the sound soft, husky.

Her fingers flexed, as if she was about to let go. But Ryder shook his head, infinitesimally, little more than a private wish. Then, after a long hot thick moment in which Ryder's blood rushed like a river between his ears, she instead rolled the rope higher, trapping her hands further, the stretch revealing a sliver of skin between her top and pants.

When she tilted her chin, she might as well have said, *Come and get it.* He didn't need to be asked twice.

Three long strides ate up the distance between them and then his hands were on her cheeks, his mouth on hers. The ropes swung her away from him, but he followed, ravenous, already pushed beyond the edge of reason.

His kisses moved to her neck, her throat, and then he was on his knees, not caring what the dust and old floorboards would do to his suit trousers. He had a million suits. There was only one Nadia, strapped up for his pleasure. And hers.

When he gripped her hips, she arched into him, again revealing a sliver of that delicious hard belly. He ran a thumb across the pale crescent, marvelling in the way her skin tightened, her muscles twitched. He followed with his mouth, running a trail of kisses in the wake of his touch, the scent of her filling his nostrils.

He looked up to find her watching him. Waiting. Anticipation kicking at the corner of her mouth. Desire flaring thick and fast behind her eyes. And something else. Defiance. As if they were playing on her terms.

And something came over him, a deep-rooted need to tame, to possess, to show her who was boss.

To negate his father's cavalier blood, Ryder had spent his entire life trying to be the most civilised man he knew. But this woman— One look, one cock of her hip, one tilt of her mouth, she simply stripped him bare.

Like a devil's whisper, it filtered through the haze of desire that if he gave her an inch this woman could well tear him apart. But it was too late.

He nudged her feet apart with his knees. She resisted, instinct kicking in. Too bad.

It was his turn to lead.

Eyes on hers, he slowly, achingly slowly, rolled the waistline of her pants and stockings down. Her mouth slid open to drag in breaths that were harder to come by. She tried biting her bottom lip, to retain control, but when he felt the trembling, heard it in the escape of a moan, he knew it was a lost cause.

When her tights hit her knees, he slid his hands up the backs of her thighs, desire knotting his gut as her head dropped back, her knees gave way, and the only thing holding her up was the rope biting into her wrists.

When his hands reached her backside, he breathed her in, desire pressing him near to the brink of control. Then he took her in his mouth, licking, nibbling, nudging, sucking, as she rocked and pitched and writhed above him.

When her trembling reached fever pitch, with one final deep lick he sent her over the edge. Feeling the strength in her sweet body, the tension in her arms, the utter freedom in her release, knowing he'd done that to her, this superwoman, was the single sexiest moment of his life.

He didn't wait for her to come down before he was on his feet, his hands making short work of her tantalising top, yanking it from her shoulder, needing more, needing to taste all of her, to imprint her flavour on his psyche and himself all over every damn inch of her.

No finessing, he took her breast into his mouth, hard, gripping her waist as she cried out from the new pleasures rolling through her. She hooked her legs around him, pulling him close.

Ryder glanced at the beams. His voice subterranean, he asked, "Can they hold the both of us?"

"We'll soon find out," she said, before taking his mouth with hers.

So hard he hurt, he freed himself, somehow found the cognitive wherewithal to protect himself. Silently berating her for not insisting, hating himself for liking that she hadn't, he pressed into her, hard, relishing every sensational second.

Her eyes snapped shut and she cried out. The muscles in her arms and neck strained, beads of sweat beaded all

over her chest, curls tight around her face. Her beautiful
face. And the sweet bliss of being inside her, pleasure
riding him as he stroked into her; hoping they weren't
about to bring the building down around their ears.

All too soon her climax came hard. Curling her into
him as she cried out. While his built from a tight knot
of need that unfurled until he felt it to the ends of his
everything. And he came with a roar that shook the
foundations of the old building till the thing near rained
down dust.

Her head dropped to his shoulder, her breaths fan-
ning against his ear, and he held her there, still inside
her, their heartbeats slamming against one another as
they drifted back to earth.

Ryder lowered her feet to the floor and since her
hands were out of action he gently rolled her tights back
into place. He uncurled one rope then the other, the red
raw ligature marks making him wince. Then when her
legs seemed about to give way, he scooped her into his
arms. Ryder carried her to the lounge, where he sat.
She sank into him, soft and warm, her head beneath
his chin, her hand on his heart. The quiet afterglow
washed over him, as a warmth in his muscles and a
sweet ache in his groin.

Then, just when her breaths grew so slow and heavy
he wondered if she'd fallen asleep, she spoke up, her
voice, soft and shattered, said, "Ryder?"

He wiped damp hair from her forehead. "Yes,
Nadia?"

"I'm leaving."

"I'd like to see you try."

Her fingers curled into his chest a moment before
she lifted her heavy head and looked up into his eyes.

And the distress that flittered therein made his gut con-strict—more than ropes, or studded gloves, or high heels that could castrate a man with one well-positioned step.

Then she said, "That routine was part of an audition piece I've been working on. Sky High, the company I used to work for, are casting a new show. And I'm on the shortlist." She paused to swallow. "If I get the job—*when* I get the job—as soon as humanly possible I'll be moving there."

"Where's *there* exactly?"

"Vegas."

"As in *Las* Vegas?" *The other side of the world.*

Her mouth twitched. "Is there any other?"

"Good point."

Truth was, he had no idea what he was saying; he was marking time. Dammit, his skin still thrummed from some of the hottest sex of his life. He couldn't think forward an hour much less weeks.

"Vegas," he echoed again. And as the ripples fanned to the corner of his mind, so many things began to make sense. Her reticence to make good on their attraction. Her drab apartment. She'd not put down roots because she'd never intended to stay.

"When?" he asked.

The flicker in her eyes making it clear she knew he'd been sideswiped. Damn. "They're en route now, but it depends how many dancers they decide to see in each place before they get here. I'm just waiting for the word."

She said it with a smile. Yet it was Nadia's complete stillness that got to him. Any other time even her very breaths moved through her as if she were dancing, yet she sat in his arms so still, so inert, she might as well have been made of air. Because this conversation was that important to her. Or that uncomfortable. Whatever it was to her, it clearly carried weight. *He* carried weight.

"Okay, then," he said.

It must have been the right answer, as her sinuous body settled deeper into his lap. He dragged his thumb gently over her lower lip and when she lifted her face to his followed with a kiss.

A kiss filled with sweetness, and tenderness, yet humming with heat.

And as his desire ratcheted up faster than ought to have been physiologically possible, he knew her imminent departure from his life was a blessing in disguise. He clearly couldn't keep away from her even if he wanted to. This woman who so effortlessly lured him into temptation. Who made him clamour to tap into the darkness, the consuming desires, the inner storm he'd all but eliminated from his life.

As for Nadia? There was no getting away from the look in her eyes as she'd told him she was going away. He'd glimpsed that look before in the rare moments when she let her guard down, when she'd unexpectedly opened up to him, when she'd forgotten to be on show and simply was.

A woman like *that* needed a different kind of man in her life. Not a man who worked more hours than not. Not a man with the complicated responsibilities he had. Not a man who'd never confuse lust for forever. And damn sure not a Fitzgerald.

Chapter Seven

Nadia stretched out her limbs and groaned; the slide of soft sheets over her body as lovely as her all-over ache was wicked. Her body was used to being pushed to the edge of endurance and then some, but the past couple of weeks with Ryder had educated her as to muscles even *she* never knew existed.

She tilted her head to find the man himself sleeping on his back, the crumpled sheet covering one thigh and half his torso, moonlight pouring through his bedroom window over the hard dips and planes of his body, glinting off the dark hair covering the gentle rise and fall of his chest, the heat of him warming even her side of his bed.

Watching him, this man who took her places she'd never before been, her hands circled her wrists, rubbing at marks that had faded days before. She'd underestimated Ryder in giving him a private dance. Expected him to be dissuaded by her stunts. She'd also overestimated her own willpower, as every day since, every time she was with him she told herself it would be the last, her resolve caved.

Her fault probably, for unlocking the danger junkie in him. How could she have known that beneath the slick suits he was so audacious, a sensualist, fearless? That she'd be the one left gasping, breathless, and shaken again and again and again.

The twin threads keeping her sane as they embarked on this impossible affair were the countdown to Sam's wedding and her impending audition. Not that they talked about the fact that their association had a big brick wall looming at its end, but they hadn't needed to; the ticking clock was simply there.

With a sigh she lifted her gaze to the two-storey wall of glass that filled the far side of Ryder's floating bedroom as well as the entire beach-side wall of the floor beneath. She guessed it was past midnight. Time to leave if she wanted some sleep.

Slipping from the bed, her toes curling against the plush rug, Nadia quietly gathered her clothes and got dressed. She nearly gave up on finding her strappy high heels before she saw them peeking out from under Ryder's side of the bed; by request they'd been the last item left on.

With the straps hooked over one finger, she took one last look at the big man sleeping in the big bed; his lips softly parted, dark hair falling over his forehead, the shadow of stubble already covering his cheeks and chin. When all that masculine warmth made her start to ache, she resolutely turned her back and walked away.

She texted for a cab as she padded down the circular staircase to the main floor of Ryder's amazing home. He'd designed the space himself—and for himself *alone*; that much was clear. All hardwood floors, and raw slate tiles, dark grey walls and sleek modern furniture. Downstairs was entirely open-plan with a sophisticated kitchen and a gigantic lounge that made the most of the beach views, with a cool art-deco bar and a TV you could see from space. Ryder had alluded to a garage, gym, and laundry in the subterranean floor below.

The only thing in the place that wasn't uber-masculine was a truly lovely antique-looking drafting table in the far corner. A more modern chair was skewed beneath and the wall beside it housed a wall of built-in blond bookshelves filled with rolled-up plans and books galore—all the accoutrements she assumed an architect must need.

And yet for all the modern, manly minimalism—the reclaimed wood, re-imagined steel, the huge artworks on the mood-lit walls that all seemed to be made from industrial cast-offs—the place was truly stunning.

He'd mentioned that his mother had been creative, a sculptor of some renown. No wonder Ryder Fitzgerald had talent; he had the heart of an artist.

Nadia snorted softly at her wayward thoughts, figuring she must be more tired than she thought. She dragged her hair into a ponytail, tugging her hair a little harder than necessary in order to wake herself up. Last stop, she ducked to the fridge, found an apple to appease her empty stomach—since they'd somehow forgotten to eat.

Padding towards the door, she sank her teeth into the skin, and a resounding snap of apple flesh split the air.

She stilled and heard the distinct rustle of sheets over man.

Swearing beneath her breath, she gathered her satchel from its place hooked over the back of a bar stool, then clamped the apple between her teeth and made a barefoot run for the door.

She'd almost made it when the floorboards creaked

ominously. Heart thundering in her chest, she took the apple from her mouth and glanced back to find Ryder ambling down the stairs; his hair dishevelled, his face soft with sleep. Previously discarded suit trousers covered his long legs, the clasp undone revealing the tantalising arrow of dark hair.

He stopped when he spotted her hand on the doorknob. "I thought I heard you decamping," he said, his voice deep and soft on the night air.

"You heard right. I also stole an apple."

He crossed his arms and leant a hip against the railing. "Consider it yours."

Nadia's pulse thudded at her wrists, behind her ears. All over. As even while he looked perfectly relaxed, she could feel the slumberous desire rolling from him in waves. And even while the muscle memory in her body begged her to make good on all that promise, she needed to be sure that when the time came, she *could* say no.

"See you Tuesday night?" she asked.

A beat throbbed between them before he said, "I'll be there."

He shifted, and her skin thrummed with the thought there might be one last kiss; a deep, sweet, lasting parting meeting of mouths that took her breath away. But one dark look later, he gave her a short nod and headed back up the stairs.

The tension drained from her until she drooped like a wilting flower. She let herself out, the cool darkness and soft salty tang of the sea air enveloping her. And then she began to laugh. It was either that or sob with relief. Or would that be disappointment? Argh!

And when her cab swished to a halt at the kerb, she

hopped inside, settled against the seat and closed her eyes, smiling until her cheeks began to ache.

As Ryder hit the stairs leading up to the studio the next Tuesday night, he heard Nadia's laughter echoing down the stairwell.

He was smiling by the time he pushed open the door, but at the creak of the hinges she spun on her heel, her hand flying to her chest, her cheeks glowing pink, her phone pressed to her ear. A couple of beats later she held up a finger, mouthing she'd only be a minute, then turned her back, talked in a low hum he couldn't make out.

Ryder dumped his bags on the couch and headed her way. He slid his arms around her waist, and ducked his face into her neck.

Frowning furiously, she tried to peel him away, to motion that she was on the phone.

He merely grabbed the offending hand and held it behind her, trapping it between them. He slid his other hand down the neck of her top until he found her breast, the hot sweet weight of it filling his palm and making him groan.

When he caught their reflection in the window, his hand down her top, her mouth open, her eyes hot and hard, he dipped his head to take her ear lobe in his mouth, not taking his eyes from her mirror image.

Then, husky as all get out, she said, "Thanks for the heads-up. Talk soon," and hung up the phone.

She pressed her sweet backside into him and curled the hand holding the phone around his neck to pull his mouth to hers for a long lush kiss. Heat thundered through him, making his whole world a tight sweet ache.

Eyes locked onto her shadowy likeness in the window, he peeled her top away to reveal her breast to the air, her skin so pale and sweet against the tan of his big hand. She shivered, her eyes fluttering closed, her head rocking back against his shoulder.

He grazed her nipple with his thumb, and again as it pebbled beneath his touch. Her tongue snuck out to wet her lips. She might as well have licked him lower for the kick of heat that knocked the breath right out of him—

Ryder leapt away from her as music blasted right next to his ear. Rubbing at his ear, he glared towards the offending noise to see the phone still gripped in Nadia's hand.

Already hooking her top back in place first, Nadia switched it to silent. "Sorry."

He tilted his chin to the phone gripped in her hand. "Miss Popular tonight."

"Hmm?" She blinked as if the lit-up phone weren't still vibrating in her palm.

Which was when Ryder felt a frisson of disquiet scoot down his spine. "You going to answer it?"

She shook her head. "No need."

"Why's that?"

"I know what it's about."

"Seriously, Nadia, you want to play twenty questions? Or tell me what's going on?"

A frown flickered across her brow and was gone just as fast. Then she lifted stubborn eyes to his. "The producers will be here in a little over a week. And I don't even have to go to Sydney, as they're coming to Melbourne. They're coming to me."

She didn't have to say which producers. Her return to her old life had been hovering between them since the night she'd told him it was on the cards. And after the initial bombshell it had morphed into something far more constructive: a neat little end point to the affair. And yet as it coalesced from an insubstantial notion into a concrete event everything inside Ryder distilled down to two thoughts: *one week* and *too soon*.

So immersed in his own reaction, he hadn't noticed that Nadia wasn't looking at him. Her cheeks were un-usually pale, and her knuckles had gone white around the phone. He'd seen her fierce. He'd seen her near bel-ligerent. He'd seen her sweet and soft and he'd seen her surrender. But he'd never seen Nadia Kent worry about a single damn thing.

He closed in and slid his fingers through her hair, lifting her head till she was looking him in the eye; the tumble of emotions ricocheting through her slid right into him. All he could do was hold on tight and barri-cade himself against the tide. "You okay?"

Her jaw clenched beneath his fingers as she lifted her chin, denial in her every movement. But he knew her, intimately. And from one blink to the next he saw her—the real Nadia, the raw Nadia, the one who'd yanked him from the safe side of the ravine to the other. The side where he wasn't in control of his actions. His thoughts. His desires. The Nadia that could only lead him into disaster. And yet he couldn't look away.

"You're nervous," he said as realisation dawned.

"Of course I'm bloody nervous! I hardly proved my-self reliable the last time I worked for them, so I'm com-ing at this with my chances hobbled from the outset. And what if I screw it up? What if I'm not in as good condition as I think I am? I haven't had to choreograph on my own for years—what if the routine sucks?"

He ran both thumbs over her temples. "I've witnessed your work, remember. Hottest damn thing I've ever seen. If they won't pay you to perform it, I will. Hang on a sec, I already did."

She laughed, and then slapped him on the arm. He grabbed her hand and held it behind her.

Her eyes turned wild. Rebellious.

So he slid his other hand through her hair, cradling the back of her head, holding her in thrall. Then he dipped his mouth to brush hers. When she didn't react, he kissed her again, barely a touch, then a luxurious swipe of his tongue across the seam. He felt her acquiescence in her melting body a fraction before she finally opened her mouth to him, sliding her tongue against his in a dance they both knew so well.

The kiss grew intense, heated, sumptuous, long. So long, when they finally pulled apart Ryder couldn't quite catch his breath. And—by the way Nadia's eyes flickered back and forth between his—he was pretty certain she felt the same way.

And yet she was leaving. Extremely soon. And while every impulse was to squeeze every last drop of passion from their affair that he could, he knew the level-headed move was to begin the gentle withdraw gracefully. Before anybody got hurt.

Ryder spun her about and gave her a little shove in the opposite direction. "Come on, Teach. You're not the only one with a countdown till the day you have to set the dance world on fire. The guests at the Fitzgerald-Johnson nuptials will not be disappointed."

She shot him a dark glance over her shoulder, but

when he didn't give her what she was looking for she rolled her shoulder, morphed into teacher mode. And gave Ryder one of the hardest workouts he'd ever had.

On their way out Ryder saw the extra bag he'd brought that he'd completely forgotten about in all the excitement. He thought about leaving it forgotten, but in the end he silently handed it over.

"For me?" Nadia took the bag and poked her head inside. She blinked. "Apples."

"I saw them and thought of you."

When she looked up her eyes were wide, and there was no hiding the flush that had risen to her cheeks. "But I only owed you one—now I owe you a tree."

"And don't think I don't have every intention of collecting on the debt. Before you leave," he added as he held open the door leading outside the building.

"The man's all charm. How will I ever survive the parting?" she said, voice dripping with sarcasm.

Yet the glance she shot him as she slid past him was not. It was quick; it was fleeting. It was *yearning*. And it had had nothing to do with what was ahead of her, and everything to do with him.

Ryder swung his keys around a finger as he opened up the passenger side of his car, trying to ignore it. The look, the way it had landed right in his centre with a thud, the way this woman managed to make his well-shackled ego roar to life.

Till she was about to slide inside. Then he whipped an arm across the door, blocking her way. His voice was subterranean as he asked, "Think you'll miss me when you head off to the bright lights of Sin City?"

Her eyes widened a fraction, her pupils swamping

her dark irises in a red-hot instant. Then she shrugged and said, *"Meh."*

His ego growled at the challenge. "You scoff now, Miss Kent, but just hope I don't really turn on the charm. You might never bring yourself to leave."

She breathed in hard, seeming to suck away all the air around them, and all the dangerous teasing of the past few minutes compressed until they were suddenly locked in their own personal pressure cell.

"Ryder." Her voice was deep, vibrating, but tinged with warning. "I will leave. I *have* to."

"I know that," said Ryder.

Her brow creased into a series of little frowns. Then, just before she slipped into her car, she said, "I will miss you though."

Hell. "Right back at ya, kid."

The ride back to his place was quiet.

"Crap!"

"Problem?" Ryder asked, glancing up from reading the "paper" on his tablet.

Nadia was settled on his couch wearing one of his T-shirts, glaring at his laptop perched on her bare legs. He'd woken that morning to find her still curled into his arms. The first time she hadn't snuck out during the night. It seemed he wasn't the only one debating the benefit of getting as much out of their last days together as they could.

She dug her fingers into her hair. "No. Yes. I don't know."

"Anything I can do?"

She pinned him with a dark look that didn't bode well. "Not unless you have any Mafia links."

"For what purpose?"

"I might be in need of a hit man."

Right. "I work in construction. What do you think?"

Her eyes widened and lost the dark clouds for a few seconds as she took that in, but they slowly slid back in. Then she lay back on the couch, an arm flung elegantly over her eyes, her feet hooked over the back rest.

"Nadia, you're currently more intriguing than today's news but I *am* about to hit the entertainment section…"

One eye poked out. "Nope. Don't want to demystify your elevated opinion of me."

When her feet began to point and flex coquettishly over the back of his couch, Ryder pressed himself away from his chair and went to join her. It didn't take much. "And what, pray tell, does this elevated opinion entail exactly?"

"That I'm formidable and focused and fabulous."

That pretty much covered it.

"Don't get me wrong," she said, hidey arm forgotten as she tilted her gorgeous face to him. "I am *all* of that."

"And more."

"Thank you."

"But…"

"I'm freaking out right now."

When her feet began to shake up and down, as if trying to lose excess energy through her toes, he knew she wasn't exaggerating. "Why?"

"Because I'd naturally assumed he'd be travelling to Europe with the old show, so never gave him a second thought. But I just got an email about the audition tour, and he's been listed as coming. Here. To watch me dance. I'm screwed. I'm royally screwed."

"*He* being?"

"My ex." She pulled herself upright and gave the laptop a little shove, tilting it his way. Ryder got a glimpse of a man with brown hair, pale skin, smouldering blue eyes. The fact that Nadia's lip curled as she said his name somewhat mollified Ryder's urge to rearrange those pretty-boy features but good.

"Associate producer, I see. You lost your job while he got promoted."

"So it seems. He always knew how to play the game. The woman—and she was barely that—he left me for was the niece of one of the producers. I, on the other hand, was dancing under another name so as *not* to cash in on my connections. And now look at us." Her tone was snappy but her body was so expressive he knew she was more upset than she was letting on. "There's also the fact that he is a brilliant dancer. One of those born with that elusive "X" factor. Stage presence like—"

"How could you bear to leave such a creature behind?"

Nadia didn't even have the good grace to blush. When her eyes skewed to his her mouth stretched into a knowing smile. "If I didn't know better I'd say you sounded jealous."

"Lucky you know better."

"Mmm."

When her gaze swept back to the laptop, caught on the image smouldering back at her, all humour faded and she shut it closed with a snap. Then she ran her hands over her face, before hunching and staring through the wall of windows to the sparkling water views beyond.

"If he has hiring rights, which is how it reads, then this ups the ante big time. I'm going to have to pull out all the stops." She swallowed, hard, then, "The entire time I worked for them they had no idea who my mother was. But what if letting it be known made the difference this time—" She nibbled at her bottom lip. "Because the thought of not getting this job…"

Her hand fisted into her T-shirt—which was actually his—lifting it from the long legs draped over the couch. How could she not know she had so much charisma, so much instant sex appeal she'd only have to saunter into that room and any producer worth his salt would hire her on the spot?

That bloody mother of hers had a lot to answer for.

"Nadia," he near growled.

"Mmm?"

"Nadia, look at me."

For once she did as she was told.

"Don't do it," he said.

An initial burst of shock lit her eyes before they narrowed. Like where did he get the right to have an opinion at all? He didn't care much if he had the right or not, she was going to have to hear what he had to say.

"You got where you were despite her once before. You can do it again."

"Sweet sentiment, Ryder. But you don't know that."

The number of people Ryder was certain he could count on in his life could be tallied on one hand. Less. Which was why he ran his behemoth business—from the plans to the paper clips—like a mini-monocracy. But in that moment he knew he could count on Nadia. To be true. To do her best. To aim as high as the sky. Because not only was she stunning, provocative, and slippery, she was brave, and gutsy, and honourable.

"When it comes to you, Nadia Kent, I most certainly do."

She swallowed. Then hooked her thumbnail against a tooth, a soft pink flush rising in her cheeks. "While you, Ryder Fitzgerald, might just be the most surprising man I've ever met."

When the intensity in her arresting eyes began to bring on that upside down inside out feeling, he ducked his chin to the simpering sap on the laptop. "All evidence to the contrary."

Yet her eyes remained on his. It was a long moment, a heady moment, before she glanced away and said, "Yeah. And you're right about the other thing too. A moment of weakness averted. Bugger it. It just means my routine will have to be so amazing, so beyond the edge of anything they've ever seen, they'll have to hire me."

She uncurled herself from the chair and shook out her whole body. Ryder's eyes roved over her mane of unkempt hair, her sexy bare feet with the faint crisscross of old rope burns and the sparkly hipster G-string under that T-shirt of his. She far from harmonised with the minimalist décor of his home. So why did she look so damn good inside it?

It hit him that it wouldn't be much longer before he'd no longer have this view to look forward to. No more of that soft, sweet warmth to smooth the edges off his busy days. No more of that spitting, sparking heat to set fire to his spacious bed. No more fogged-up bathroom after her decadently long hot showers. No more missing fruit. No more Nadia.

Glad she'd stayed, he reached out and snagged her hips, catching her off balance so she fell into him.

Laughing, she settled her thighs over his, shuffling till she was more comfortable, till he was anything but.

He slid a hand into her hair. Laughter lit her eyes, laughter and enquiry. When he ran a thumb down her cheek, tangling his fingers in that wild voluptuous hair, the laughter dried up. And he once again caught that touch of yearning.

And he knew he wasn't the only one now counting the days, the hours, wondering which kiss would be their last.

Nadia pressed her lips to his neck; it was so welcome he groaned. She kissed him again, more, until kisses rained all over his cheeks, his ear lobe, his collarbone. Her tongue following in their wake, warm and terrible in the reactions it invoked. The need, the tension, building and burning inside him, impossible and everything all at once.

Then gentle hands found his buttons and opened them one by one. Slow enough he felt each pop like something unhooking inside him.

Her touch was reverent, her mouth searching. The yearning not locked away this time, but right there. Every kiss honest and real, peeling away the layers of reluctance he'd spent years building. And by the time she laid his shirt open, she'd laid him bare.

He could feel his heart beating, not only in his chest, but in his wrists, in his feet, at the back of his head, as if a tornado were trapped behind his skin.

Then her mouth was on his chest, her lips following the rises, her tongue dipping sweetly into the falls, before her teeth closed over his nipple, biting down. It lasted a second, probably less, but the shock of it was like a dagger in his thorax.

He swallowed down the pain, owning it. He had to if he had any intention of enduring this as she slid his shirt from his shoulders and kissed him there. Her hands running down the flats of his blades, her fingers tracing his spine, spanning his waist till every muscle clenched with the sweet agony of her touch.

It was unbearable. Ryder clenched his teeth till his head rang from it.

And when her hands moved to slide under his backside, her mouth slanting over his, he gave up and took it. Took it all. He'd suffer the guilt another day. Right then he was too far gone to care.

In one swift move, he flipped her onto her back, her hair falling in waves across the cushions, her eyes bright, her luscious lips slick. And he made love to her right there. Slowly, gently, eyes on hers the entire time. Feelings sweeping through so strong him he could barely breathe.

Nadia came with a swift rise of heat, her neck arching, her hands gripping his arms, her mouth sliding open with sweet pleasure. And as she hit her peak his followed, pleasure riveting him inside and out, for the longest time, until he thought it might clear knock him out.

And then in a shudder of limbs and sighs they tumbled into afterglow. Together.

Her hand dove into the hair at the back of his neck, and she pressed herself closer, as if searching for an anchor. He felt it too; the wreckage, the insanity, the irrationality of how good they were together. How frustratingly perfect. It reverberated through him. Like a warning. Like a huge calamitous siren that any rational person would know meant go back, do not enter.

Danger lurked behind that door. The kind he'd long since vowed he'd never risk. And yet there'd been a moment back there when he'd shoved aside reason, knowing he was about to knock on that door hard enough to split the thing right down the middle.

Gripping onto his last tattered vestiges of sense, Ryder pulled himself away from her.

"Come on," said Ryder, taking her hand in his to haul her limp, soft, stunning body from his couch.

"Come on what?"

"Just come on."

"Don't you have to go to work?"

"Not today." He did, of course. But he wouldn't. For the first time in his life he was blowing off work. Today, it seemed, was a day of breaking rules.

"So where are we going?"

Anywhere but here. Anything but this.

"You'll see."

Chapter Eight

Which was how Nadia ended up on the side of a long straight road leading to the Yarra Valley, sitting in the driver's seat of Ryder's charming vintage coupe. Though from her vantage point, with all the old-fashioned dials and lights and pedals clogging her vision, the thing looked anything but charming. It looked positively petrifying.

Hands levitating an inch off the steering wheel she turned to glare at him. "You're kidding, right?"

"Not, in fact."

"But I told you I can't do this."

"I never thought I'd hear the word can't come out of that mouth."

"Well, you heard it here. Can't. Cannot. Unable. Now let's go. To the beach. I have a bikini that'll make your jaw drop—"

"If seventeen-year-old boys who don't even know how to pull their own pants high enough to cover their asses can drive a car, then so can you."

Nadia muttered a few things about seventeen-year-old boys and the men they turned into, before facing front. He'd pulled her out of the most intense bliss of her life for *this*?

She looked obstinately into the rear-view mirror as

the gently winding country road stretched behind her. The lanes were wide, with plenty of space to pull over. They'd been sitting there for five minutes and not a single car had gone by. And yet at the mere thought of driving, she came out in a cold sweat.

Which was ridiculous, really, considering what she did for a living. She'd long since proven she wasn't afraid of anything: heights, rebuff, pain.

All she could put it down to was that she was in some kind of delayed shock about her ex. Because while she'd thought she'd handled the news with about as much aplomb as any person could be expected to, seeing his face, knowing she'd soon see him, had rattled her.

But *this* was more than rattled. At the thought of attempting this thing with Ryder sitting there watching her like a hawk, her throat went crazy dry.

She looked over the bucket seats into the tiny back bench seat of the two-door beast, then back at Ryder. "Ever had sex back there?"

"Don't change the subject."

Nadia bit her lip and faced front. "Shouldn't I read the manual first? Or practise in a simulator of some sort?"

Ignoring her, Ryder went on, "Like most things in life the best way to learn how to drive is by simply doing it."

"What if we crash? What if I roll the car and we die in a burning inferno?"

"Then you can tell me you told me so."

"Don't you have a smaller car? Something a little less magnificent?"

That hooked his attention. Finally! "I thought you didn't think my car all that fancy."

"It's grown on me. And at some point I might have looked it up on Google, you know, in case I one day did want a car. Turns out I'd have to sell a kidney, and a lung, for the privilege of owning one of these babies. I took it as a sign."

He laughed, the sound filling the car with its husky gorgeousness. Nadia looked to him in appeal.

"Stop being such a wimp, Nadia, and do it already. Turn the damn key."

"I'm not a wimp! I'm stronger than I look. I'll prove it. Get out of the car. I'll lift you off your feet right now."

Her hand went to the door handle, but he reached over and locked the door. There his arm remained, pressing her to the back of the seat, the heat of him burning across her chest. But it was his eyes, his stunning hazel eyes, and his voice, smooth and sexy, that had her pinned as he asked, "What are you so afraid of?"

"Not a damn thing!" she said, but even as the words came out of her mouth she knew he was right. She *was* afraid; heart beating in her throat, prickly-skinned, blurry-visioned scared out of her mind. So it was a blessed relief when, like a familiar security blanket, her mother's voice slipped all too easily inside her head: *Grow a spine, kid.*

"Ryder, no, I've had enough—"

"You can do it," Ryder said, his voice deep, demanding, but most of all indulgent, and the anaesthetic dogma that had protected Nadia for so many years simply failed to work.

And through the chink in her armour, she saw, with a flash of insight, what she'd been trying to disregard. She'd never feared being rebuffed by a panel of experts looking for a very specific person to fill a dance role. That was their prerogative. But rejection by someone she respected, someone she trusted, someone she admired...

Ryder. This current craziness was about Ryder.

She pressed her eyes shut tight and swallowed hard. But there was no stopping the feelings, the knowledge, now they'd been set free. She cared what he thought, he mattered to *her*, and she didn't want him to see her fail.

Because at some point in the past few weeks, she'd dropped her guard. Maybe because the auditions were so close. Maybe it was the fact that it was hard to be impervious when completely blissed out by afterglow and you felt as if you'd been melted from the inside out. Whatever the reason, even with her eyes closed, when she breathed in and caught Ryder's masculine scent her heart skittered against her ribs, heat slithered below her skin, and she felt jittery and feverish, and yet somehow at ease. Things she'd never felt before. Not with the same purity, the same effortlessness. Because she'd been taught very early on in life to press all her feelings deep down inside. The bad *and* the good.

Give a damn and they'll eat you alive.

And the second she stopped pushing it all back down, it bubbled up until she felt it all—the breakdown of the first, real, long-term relationship of her adult life, her mother's cruel reaction, the senseless flight from the career she adored. She'd honestly thought she'd taken it all on the chin, but she'd only pressed it down, the whole big hot mess that had led her to that point, spilling into her nerves, her heart, until she couldn't breathe.

"Nadia."

Ryder's voice hummed through her like a tuning

fork. She shook her head, no. No. No! Formidable and focused and fabulous, she was invulnerable. But she felt so raw her skin might as well have been flayed from her chest.

Unfortunately he was made of as stern a stuff as she. He grabbed her by the chin, turning her head to face him. She looked at the neckline of his T-shirt instead.

At her obstinacy he laughed—laughed!—before saying, "You asked me to let you lead on the dance floor, and I deferred to you once I grudgingly admitted you had the wisdom of experience over me. I've been driving for well over a decade. Not a single traffic violation to my name. Defer to me, Nadia. Trust me."

She let out a roar of frustration and shook the steering wheel some, but this time didn't let it go. Trapped, panic-stricken, she lifted her eyes to his, all set to tell him to bite her. But the moment her eyes found his, she jammed up. Those eyes. So deep, so beautiful, so patient. And so damn smart.

As if he knew. As if he'd known for some time that she'd been in denial about how quickly she'd gotten over the multiple layers of embarrassment and pain of the events of months past. All she could hang onto was the hope that that was *all* he'd deduced she was in denial about.

At least she'd learnt one thing from events past—the only way out of any mess was through. Nadia breathed in deep and breathed out shaky, happy right then to be breathing at all. "Okay," she said. "Tell me what I have to do?"

"Foot on the clutch," he said. "Gear into First. Key's in the ignition. Turn it right, wait till the engine hums and let go."

Sweat prickling down her back, Nadia followed Ryder's instructions as best she could. And the car bunny-hopped a few feet before wobbling to an ignominious stop. Heat landed in her cheeks with a humiliating thud. "I totally suck."

"Nobody gets the waltz right first go."

"I did."

"And I've never stalled. Duck to water."

At that she laughed; shocked blissful laughter that shaved the sharpest edges off her agitation. With a slow breath out, she resettled herself, went to that quiet place she went before a routine: darkness, silence. Not discounting the natural fear, harnessing it.

In the quiet she heard Ryder's litany of instructions, and, after a few more false starts, the directions began to blend from one move to the next, until it all seemed to click and she was easing out onto the road proper, rural scenery sliding past the window.

"I'm driving!"

"Yes, you are."

"It's easy!"

"Look at the road. Not me."

She swung back to face the road to find herself veering. She nudged the car straight, her eyes on the horizon as he'd taught her. She pressed a little harder on the accelerator, adrenalin spiking as she was pressed back in the seat. "How far can I go?"

"Do you have a learner's permit?"

"What?" Nadia said, her hands flinging off the wheel and feet off the pedals in panic. "Of course not."

The engine stalled and with an oath, Ryder grabbed the wheel and shifted it a fraction so they could ease off the side of the road, where he yanked the parking brake. "Then we'd better stay away from town. And schools, and police, and people in general."

His voice was rough, but when she looked at him he was smiling.

While Nadia let out a "Woop!" of pure delight and laughed till her sides hurt. Relief and joy spilling through her unstoppered. And like a street after a rainstorm, all the muck that had flooded to the surface before had been washed away leaving her feeling shiny and new. "That was awesome. And even better for being illicit, right? What next?"

"Next we lunch. I'm driving." Ryder got out of the car and motioned she do the same.

Lunch? He wanted to *eat*? She was so wired she could fly! Nadia gripped the wheel a moment longer and wondered how far she might get if she just took off. When he opened her door she squinted up at him. "Bonnie and Clyde had to start somewhere."

He merely held out a hand. She let him help her out of the car when she realised she was trembling all over, adrenalin knocking about her insides till her nerves sang. He must have felt it as he cupped her elbows in an effort to steady her, which was kind of sweet. Then his eyes turned dark and he pressed her back against the sloping side of the car which was anything but sweet. "Tell me how that felt?"

Shaking hands running over his chest, she said, "You were the one putting your life in my hands. How did *that* feel?"

His eyes narrowed. "Not in the least bit unusual."

"Oh," Nadia said in barely a whisper. While in the cocoon of the car she'd managed to just hold herself together while being cracked apart. Now, out in the open air, the country breeze tickling at her hair, sunshine pouring down over her bare shoulders, Ryder's challenging hazel eyes looking deep into her own, she felt…too much.

Heat rising, everywhere, she looked up at him. "I know I was a bit of a beast to start with, but thank you for today."

"It just seemed like a nice day for a drive."

Said the man who worked so hard that he never had time to change out of his suit for a ten p.m. appointment, who'd taken a day off because he'd seen she was about to crack and chose to be there to hold her together when she did. "Come on, Ryder," she said with an unsteady laugh. "I doubt you've done a thing in your life that wasn't entirely deliberate."

Something slid behind his eyes like quicksilver, something deep and onerous. "So I might have had an ulterior motive."

His gaze slipped to her neck, the hot spot below her ear, before landing on her lips, and any breath she'd managed to gather in her lungs poured out of her in a shaky sigh. Then his eyes slid back to hers. "You, Nadia Kent, have reserves of strength inside of you you've not yet tapped. Add drive, talent, panache, and you can do anything you set your mind on. You don't need your mother's permission to soar."

Mention of her mother was quite enough for the adrenalin still sliding hot and molten through her veins to solidify like cooling candle wax. "Ryder—"

"Tell me you know it."

His eyes were no longer smiling. They were intense. Serious. Unrelenting. As if he believed in her. Not just her ability to dance. To do well despite her ex watching on. But *her*. And he wouldn't give up until she believed the same.

"I know it." And like a flash of white-hot light bursting inside her, illuminating the shiny new places inside her she'd only just begun to feel, she did. In fact in that moment she felt pretty much invincible.

Pure and unadulterated instinct taking her over, Nadia lifted up onto her toes, slid her hands over his big shoulders and kissed him. Soft at the start. Appreciating every lick of heat building in its wake. And when his hand moved to her breast, kneading, running a thumb over the centre, it ached. She ached. Every last bit of her inside and out, filled with such sweet pain she could barely stand it—

A car zoomed past, flushing them with a burst of hot air, and a beeping horn that echoed off into the distance. Still, they were slow to pull apart, and when Nadia leant her forehead against Ryder's shoulder the erratic beat of his heart more than matched her own.

"Lunch?" Ryder asked, his voice coarse.

"Sounds like a plan."

When Ryder dropped Nadia home late that evening, he helped her from the car once more. And once again made a meal of her self-control, the cold metal of the car at her back doing nothing to dampen the heat of the man kissing her senseless.

But after the events of the day—the news, revelations, and realisations—she was exhausted, emotionally and mentally wrung out. The thought of putting one foot in front of the other to get to her door was enough to make her whimper. So she pressed a hand to his chest. "Ryder, wait."

When he growled in frustration, she bit her lip so hard it bruised. She swiped her tongue over the spot, then said, "I've been thinking, and I need to cool things between now and the audition."

Hard, and hot, and breathing heavy, Ryder didn't move for a long while. When he did it was to curl away from her and lean back against the car, where he crossed his arms and looked out into the night.

"Like a football player," she explained, turning to face him, the cold of the car now seeping into her skin. "No sex before a big match. I'm going to need all the reserves of stamina I can muster. You understand, right?"

It shouldn't have been so hard. They both knew that with the audition looming, and Sam's wedding right on its heels, their places in one another's lives would lose traction and wind up. That time apart would all too soon be a final goodbye. And yet Nadia held her breath as she waited for his response.

"Yeah," he said, running his hand through his hair, before piercing her with a dark glance. "I understand."

Then casual as you please he ambled back to his side of the car, leaving Nadia to feel horribly bereft. Even though he'd given her exactly what she wanted. What she *needed*. Heck, he was the one who'd relit the fire under her with all that "you don't need your mother's permission" nonsense!

Desire, and exhaustion, and a goodly head of inner steam giving her a second wind, Nadia jogged across the cracked pavement leading to the heavily barred door below her apartment, and jabbed the key in the rusty lock.

"Nadia."

She turned to find him watching her over the car. His face in near darkness.

"Break a leg," he said, his words carrying a level of intensity that made her skin tighten all over at the thought he might not be wishing it in the spirit in which it ought to have been meant.

Nevertheless she said, "Thanks, Ryder."

Then without looking back she jogged up the skinny steps leading to her first-floor apartment, and went straight into her bedroom, and to the drawer where she kept her choreography notes.

She spent the next few hours staring at them, poring over them, tweaking them. Imagining herself going through the motions until she was sure the routine was the best thing she'd ever created. Because despite her exhaustion, her head was clear. Clear of the muddy conflicts and doubts and strangled hopes that had suffocated her efforts for as long as she could remember. And in the clarity she knew. She was ready. More ready than she'd ever been. To dance. For her. Just her.

Nadia ducked out of the train at Richmond Station.

Turning the collar of her light jacket against the shimmer of summer rain, she made her way along the platform, down the ramp and out onto the street leading to her apartment, where the malodorous scents of Laundromats, and student accommodation, and a million different kinds of international cuisine fought one another on the hot hazy air.

Adrenalin sent wings to her feet and she found herself doing her best *Singing in the Rain* all along the edge of the footpath, her feet feeling as if they barely touched the ground as the audition she'd just left played over and over in her head.

Not so much the moves; truth was she could barely remember a moment of the actual routine. It was the conversation afterwards that was still blowing her mind. Not only that the producers had been so lovely, so welcoming, so honestly thrilled to see her, but how they'd raved at her transformation.

Her technical perfection, they'd gushed, had been supercharged by some new raw emotion. A new-found vulnerability had added layers to her performance. A breakthrough, they'd said. Goose bumps had been mentioned. One woman claimed that with that final tool in her arsenal she was unstoppable. With that ringing in her head, who the hell cared that her stupid ex had barely looked her in the eye?

Seeing him had been *less* than she'd expected. Less hurtful. Less embarrassing. Maybe because she understood his part in the debacle, maybe because she'd recently begun to understand her own. Could she work with him if she got the gig? Hell, yeah. Could he work with her? That was his problem.

Needing to share this feeling before she burst, she pulled out her phone, opened her contacts list and there her thumb hovered. She wanted her friends in Vegas to know—they'd be cheering for her. Her reasons for wanting her mother to know were thorny and complicated. And yet there was only one person she truly wanted to tell, one person who would understand the layers of pride and relief and fear and excitement it had taken to dance on her own terms…

"Hey, Ginger Rogers," a deep voice called out.

Stopping short with one foot wavering in the air, she

grabbed a lamppost to steady herself and held on tight. For there was Ryder, outside her apartment, leaning against his beautiful car in a pose that was as familiar to her as the man himself.

"Gene Kelly, actually," she said, her voice breathless, pocketing the phone with his number still on the screen.

It had been days since she'd seen him—since the driving lesson with the life lesson thrown in. It felt like weeks.

Pushing away from the shiny black hull of his car, he came to her. A tall, dark presence who somehow still made her feel so light. "What's up?"

"You tell me. How did the audition go?"

"Seriously?" she blurted, fatally rapt that he'd remembered the time, the date, everything. She couldn't remember another time in her life when anyone cared enough to ask, at least not someone not competing against her for a part.

Then Ryder was there, his hands sliding around her waist, and she let go of the slippery post to hold his elbows. Tight. The familiar scent of him mingled with the rain in the air and she breathed it in deep. The heat of him coursed through her and her pulse thrummed right down deep.

"So?" he asked.

"Hmm?"

"The audition?"

"Right. Of course. It was…fabulous. I didn't want it to end. And they liked it. And me. And…well, that about covers it!"

His eyes roved over her face as she spoke, such intensity, such desire she near lost her train of thought. Then, eyes on hers, he slid a hand over her hair, coming up with a damp tendril. He wrapped it around a finger and tugged. "And the ex?"

Her skin, already feeling a size too small, zinged from his touch. "Still a douche."

He laughed, the deep sound rumbling through her, coiling the tension inside her tighter still. "And to think I'd been worried the guy'd take one look at you and fall to his knees and beg to have you back."

He'd been worried? Nadia felt so light-headed at the thought she figured she was way too low on electrolytes. But first she slid her hands up Ryder's big arms, over his strong shoulders, and she said, "He could beg all he likes. He's never getting me back."

He lifted his chin in acquiescence. "Good… For you," he added as an afterthought. "So how's your stamina, now the big match is over?"

That brought a grin to Nadia's face as she lifted onto her toes and pressed her mouth to his. The touch of their lips was gentle, tender even, as if they were relearning one another after their time apart. So tender her heart felt as if it was beating in her belly, emotion tightened the back of her throat, and she was pretty sure she'd begun to tremble.

Feelings tumbling through her like a waterfall over a craggy rock wall, Nadia tipped so high onto her toes she was practically *en pointe*. Then, though she wouldn't have thought it possible, when he held a soft hand at the back of her head the kiss grew deeper, more connected, and infinitely more precious.

Was it raining harder? Who knew? Who cared?

Wanting more, craving all, needing relief from the knots of pleasure twisting in her belly, she opened her mouth and Ryder took complete advantage. His tongue slid against hers, slowly, gently, but with absolute intent. When his tongue slid cruelly away, her teeth sank into his bottom lip in retribution, hard enough he hissed in a sharp breath.

Nadia stilled, while the heat continued to pour through her. Then with a groan Ryder swept his mouth over hers, enveloped her in his strong arms and kissed her till she saw stars.

Relearning done. This they knew how to do.

Her hands were beneath his jacket, sliding up the long flat muscles of his back, which twitched beautifully at her touch. Then with something akin to a roar he lifted her into his arms. She let out a loud *whoop* of surprise and held on tight—her arms around his neck, her legs around his waist.

"Keys?" he demanded.

"Back pocket."

His hand slid over her butt cheek until he found the necessary. Then, while she held on tight, laughing raggedly, breathlessly, by that stage, Ryder made his way to the door that led to her apartment and struggled manfully to unlock the thing, practically tearing the bars from their hinges as he let them inside.

And then Nadia's laughter disappeared as—compared to the bright shimmery light outside—they hit relative darkness. The naked globe at the top of the skinny stairs swept shadows across their faces, and the sounds of their intermingled breaths echoed off the old wallpapered walls.

Yet, even then there was no denying the hunger in Ryder's gaze.

Or the sudden dazzling wish in her heart that somehow it didn't have to end.

Nadia closed her eyes tight against the daze and kissed him. Out of sight of the rain and sky, away from prying eyes, just the two of them in the private contained space, the intensity of the kiss heightened. Deepened. Bringing with it an ache from where the wish had been born.

Nadia wriggled from Ryder's arms, and proceeded to tear her clothes from her body. Her frustration only built when it turned out the rain had stuck the cotton to her like glue.

"Oh, come on!" she cried out when her bra strap got caught on the strap of her top and held her like a straightjacket.

Ryder lifted her bodily till she was a stair above. Then, face level with hers, he placed his big hands on her bare waist. Her muscles leapt at the skin-on-skin contact. His thumbs circled the edge of her ribs, his dark eyes following. She couldn't have been more glad that his eyes were anywhere but on hers, as there was no way she could hide the foolish feelings rushing about inside her, and no way she wanted him to see.

Fingers spanning her ribs, he rolled the layers of wet cotton up her body, over her breasts, and away. Her relieved sigh swept up the stairs, but was soon cut short as Ryder found her bare breast and took it in his mouth. His hot tongue swirled about the cool peak and her vision turned black.

With a groan that rocked the walls he arched her back as he took her other breast in his mouth. She trembled so much with the pleasure of it all she was very much afraid she might cry. She emptied her lungs on a long juddering breath and gave herself over to it. To him. To the absorption of his touch. The sexy shadowy darkness of the stairwell intensifying every shift, every sound, every slide of skin on skin.

When he lowered her to the stairs, she braced herself on her elbows. He tore her jeans down her thighs, taking her ballet flats with them, leaving her butt naked, while he was still fully clothed.

Before she even had a chance to rectify that, Ryder fell to his knees, pressed hers apart and took her in his mouth, his tongue, his hot lips, his not so steady breath driving her to an absolute craze until everything inside her spun out of control, and all she was, all she felt, was wave after wave of hot pleasure as it swept into a great aching that scooped her hollow. And just when she was sure she couldn't take it any more, the world stilled, lifted, swelled and splintered into a million points of light.

Body like rubber, mind complete pulp, her name came to her, the sound rolling over her skin like a caress, drawing her back to the present to find Ryder poised over her, his dark eyes burning into hers.

"Nadia," he said. That one word making her feel so much. Too much.

Closing her eyes against all it meant, she slid a hand behind his neck and pulled him to her. Vanishing into his kiss, his touch, his latent heat. This man who'd thought of her, waited for her, worried about her, and hadn't been able to keep his hands off her long enough to make it up one tiny flight of stairs...

She slid a leg along his to find his pants were gone. And with a smile she arched away from the stairs, wrapped her legs about the man and took him. Deep, hard. Her turn to cry out his name as he once again swept away every effort to keep him at emotional arm's length and once again sent her world crashing about her.

As they came back to earth Nadia held Ryder's head in the crook of her arm, breathing in when he breathed in, and staring at the paint peeling off the ceiling a half a floor above. As only now lying in the quiet with the big man's breaths easing over her skin, making her feel as if she were pure energy, barely bound, she knew where the "new raw emotion" the producers had raved about had come from. How she'd been able to "leave herself vulnerable" for the first time in her professional career.

But bar a malevolent miracle, or her ex having more influence than he deserved, she was going to Vegas. And soon. Her initial contract would be for six months, with an option to extend it out to two years if the show was a success. And it would be a success. Sky High was a phenomenon that showed no signs of waning.

And yet for a second, she let herself wonder…what if? What if she didn't get the job? What if they actually had a chance to take this thing for a spin and see where it might lead?

But a second was all it lasted. After Sam's wedding there would be no more dance lessons to keep them together. And the decision to remain so after that had been made before they'd even met. Because Ryder had been nothing but honest about his limitations as he saw them. About how his father's indiscriminate behaviour had burned him to the thought of for ever. And even while Sam claimed he held on tight to the things that mattered to him, despite the spark, despite the reverence in his touch and unquenched hunger in his eyes, despite the way he saw into the deep dark heart of her like nobody else she'd ever met, he'd never asked anything of her.

Not because she didn't matter; she just didn't matter *enough*.

And she'd been there, taken whatever scraps she was fed in the hopes of being loved. But something had shifted inside her these past few weeks. And she'd never *choose* to let herself not matter again.

Ryder lifted himself with a groan, his voice drugged, slow, deep. "Can you walk?"

"I've been known to."

They peeled themselves off the stairs, straightening as much clothing as possible.

She held out her hand, and after a moment Ryder took it, curling his big warm hand around hers before taking the stairs two at a time to lead the way. And when her heart thumped against her ribs at the feel of him, the sight of him, the knowledge that one day she'd wake up and know she'd never see him again, a little piece of her heart broke away from the whole.

And never, not once, for any other reason, did she wish harder that the Sky High gig would be through, and soon.

Chapter Nine

Ryder didn't realise that he and Nadia had cruised into a kind of routine until the night it came to a halt.

The unions were threatening a city-wide walkout right when his latest project was at a crucial stage, and it had taken his team every ounce of charm to keep the worksite actually working when tension ran high enough to bring the whole thing crashing down on all their heads. But even as he'd headed back to his quiet apartment for a shower before he had to head to class, all he'd wanted to do was go to her.

Even considering the seismic scene on the stairs leading to her apartment, the thing he hadn't been able to get out of his mind was the volatile feeling that had erupted inside him when after few impossible days apart he'd seen her appear out of the mist, dancing in the rain.

He pressed the door open; the thought of catching her swinging from some dangerous contraption had him already harder than a beam.

He slowed when he saw she was already with someone—a skinny brunette he knew all too well. "Sam?"

"Hey, bro!" said Sam, a foot up on the barre, pretending to stretch like a knobbly-kneed ballerina.

"Hey, Ryder," Nadia called out, her back to him as she fiddled with the stereo.

Brow tightening, Ryder dumped his bag on the pink lounge. "What is she doing here?"

"Rehearsing," Nadia said, flicking him a glance that was far too perfunctory for his liking. "On the big day you'll be dancing with her, not me. So we thought the time had come for you to practise together."

Ryder would have bet his right elbow there was far more Nadia in that decision than *"we"*.

Sam ambled over to him, bumping him with a hip as she passed to grab a drink. "What she's too kind to say is I want to make sure you're not going to make a complete fool of yourself before I sign off on this thing."

Momentarily distracted by Sam's outfit—hot-pink leg warmers and an obscene green G-string leotard over shiny silver tights; she looked as if she'd stepped straight out of an eighties aerobics video—when he looked to Nadia there was gloom in her gaze. Though compared to his sister a disco ball would have seemed sinister.

Nadia clapped loudly, snapping him into reality. "Warm up!"

And Ryder gave himself a mental shake. Having a joint rehearsal was completely fair. And after an hour of the closest thing to living hell—dancing with his G-string-clad little sister—he'd have earned himself a trip to heaven.

Nadia took them through a few twists and bends and loosening exercises, then asked them to drop into a standing forward bend. He and Sam groaned and barely got their fingertips to their knees, while Nadia folded gracefully in half, the tips of her dark waves brushing the dusty floor.

"I've never been able to do that," Sam groaned.

Ryder squeezed his eyes shut when the thought that slipped into his mind was, *Poor Ben*.

"Practice, my sweet," said Nadia, not an ounce of strain in her voice as she lifted herself up straight. "After about the age of three being bendy only comes with practice."

Bendy, twisty, tricky, intoxicating, Ryder thought, catching Nadia's gaze before it slid past him and away. Okay, that time he knew he wasn't projecting. Definite shadows therein. And while that darkness did wicked things to his composure as it always did, he had to fight the urge to grab her by her bendy elbow and drag her to a quiet corner and ask her what the hell was going on.

Oblivious to the undercurrents, Sam groaned again as she pulled herself upright. "You've really been dancing since you were three?"

"Yep," said Nadia.

"So I'm a tad past it, then," said Sam. "Becoming a pro-dancer, that is."

Nadia laughed. "You've got a sudden hankering to go from standing ovations one day to in-your-face rejections the next?"

"I'd never looked at it that way. Harsh. How do you do it?"

"It's not so bad. I'm lucky I went in with my eyes wide open."

"Why's that?" Sam was bouncing from foot to foot by that stage, rolling her shoulders as if she were about to enter a prize fight, not practise a modified sway.

But Ryder only saw it from the corner of his eye as his focus was absorbed by Nadia, who looked as if she'd been jabbed with a cattle prod. And Ryder realised with a slow dawning that she must never have talked about this side of her life with Sam. Yet she had with him. The alpha wolf in him roared to life.

"Mum was a dancer," Nadia finally answered, staring at the remote as if it held the answer to life, the universe and everything. "And should therefore probably have been my cautionary tale. Alas, I caught the bug and that was the end for me."

With the alpha roar hampering his thought processes, Ryder slowly caught up. Something had definitely happened. In the hours since he'd seen her last, something had knocked her back into the darkness. Something that had made her bring Sam along as a shield. Ryder took a step her way, but whether by accident or design Sam bounced smack bang in front of him.

"Well, you're in the right city for it now," said Sam. "Melbourne is one of the most culturally rich cities in the world. There must be more work for a talent like you than you can bat away with a stick!"

Which was the moment Ryder realised *he'd* been the only oblivious one in the room.

His urge was now to drag *Sam* into a corner to ask her to explain herself. But Nadia's gaze had already zeroed in on his sister; his sensitive sister who didn't cope well with change, but who was also struggling with self-determination. Was *that* why she was doing her all to get him and Nadia together? Nadia who was in turn using Sam as a blockade.

And as the two women in his life stared one another down, hearts on their sleeves, his feet turned to lead. As for the first time in memory he didn't know what to do.

Nadia didn't have the same problem. She walked over to Sam, took her by the hips and spun her to face the windows; using one as a mirror, she pressed Sam's shoulders back and lifted her arms into a dance hold. "I'm going to miss you like crazy too, Sammy Sam. But I can't stay here. Even if I don't get the Sky High job, there'll be another. And it will be somewhere else other than here."

"Why?" Sam asked, tears springing into her eyes.

Nadia leant her chin on Sam's shoulder. "Because while this has been lovely, and wonderful, and curative, it's time for me to get back to my real life."

Sam's mouth twisted as she looked at Nadia's eyes in the reflection. Then Nadia gave her a squeezing hug from behind and said, "Okay?"

Which unbelievably made Sam laugh and say, "Okay."

While all Ryder could think was, *She's leaving. She's really leaving. And she's started saying goodbye.*

Nadia sat perched on the edge of the pink velvet chaise and simply breathed.

It had taken a good half-hour before things finally settled into the groove she'd been desperate for when she'd called Sam that afternoon and all but begged her to come. A conversation she'd had about fifteen minutes after getting off the phone with her mum.

Determination giving her wings, she'd called to tell her mother about the awesome audition. She'd couched it in wanting Claudia to know she might be leaving the country soon, in case she, you know, actually cared. When that had made little discernible impression on the woman Nadia had turned into a babbling idiot—*they loved me, they really loved me!* And it had only gone downhill from there.

Nadia dropped her head into her hands and groaned under her breath. She was a lost-effing-cause. She could dance without her mother's acceptance; Ryder had been right about that. But it seemed she still couldn't *live* without it.

Sky High or no Sky High, the only way she could see to cut herself off from the passive-aggressive abuse for good was to go away, far away, and this time to stay.

And no matter how appealing, how enticing the possibilities that had barreled through her after Ryder had come to her after the audition, all the glowing what-ifs in the world couldn't stand up to that one great truth.

Laughter spilled from the centre of the room, cutting through the dulcet sound of Norah Jones. Nadia followed the sound to where Sam was in Ryder's arms, their dark heads tilted towards one another. They laughed softly as they danced, Sam instructing, Ryder telling her to shut the hell up and let him lead, eyes mostly on one another's feet.

Not a subtle bone in that girl's body, Nadia thought, her heart giving a little squeeze. Sweet though, what she'd been trying to do. Bittersweet. As for her brother...

Nadia's breath lodged in her throat as Ryder's eyes found hers, and not for the first time. As he moved confidently through the steps, he couldn't seem to keep from looking her way. Every glance forcing her to add a new brick to the wall she was rebuilding around her heart. Because he'd taken a piece of it the other day, turning up after her audition as he had.

But she couldn't hope to really make the very most of this next phase of her life clinging to the previous. She knew better than anyone.

The song ended and Ryder twirled Sam out to the

end of one hand before twirling her back again, Sam's adorable laughter filling the studio till it tinkled off the windows. One of the bricks around her heart crumbled and fell.

When Ryder wrapped his arms around his little sister and dropped a kiss atop her head, it took everything Nadia had not to crumble completely at the tenderness of it all. The adoration. Intimate, private, true. It was like a foreign language to Nadia, and yet in that moment she felt a funny flicker of comprehension. As if she just needed to tilt herself on the right angle and she'd understand it all.

And then, when Ryder's gaze once more landed on hers, and he smiled just for her, like a flash bomb blooming from the centre of her heart and all the way out to her extremities, she understood all too well. She did everything in her power to contain the ominous surge, employing every formidable muscle, every bullet-proof nerve, every form of self-protection she had in her potent arsenal.

They didn't make a dent. The light of her tender feelings for Ryder filled her till it all but lifted her from the chair.

Her heart continued to beat. Her lungs continued to breathe. Yet she knew everything had changed. Only with the familiar dull ache of her messy conversation with her mother still riding her, and with no example of what the hell to do about these wholly new feelings flinging about inside her, all she could do was rewrap herself in the scattered remains of her fortitude, and hold on tight.

Her throat felt raw when she called out, "That's a wrap, kids."

"But we have ten more minutes!" said Sam, the adrenalin of the dance still pouring through her.

"I do believe Miss Nadia intends for us to quit while we're all ahead."

Nadia flinched as Ryder's deep sonorous voice slid inside her as if he had some kind of inside track. Some door only he knew how to open. She wished she could just shut it down, but she hadn't a clue where the opening was.

"That's right, kid!" she said, standing and wrapping an arm about Sam's shoulders. "You done good. So scat."

With a sigh, and a twirl, Sam gathered her things, gave Nadia a kiss on the cheek, informed them Ben had been waiting in the car below the whole time, then disappeared out the door, leaving Nadia alone with Ryder after all.

"Are you going to tell me what happened?" Ryder said, cutting to the point.

"You're ready, that's what," she said, avoiding eye contact as she pretended to tidy sheets of piano music that hadn't been looked at in decades. "Now I can safely send you two out onto that dance floor and not be mortified to put my name to it."

"That's not what I mean and you know it. You've had news?"

News? The auditions. Right.

She tensed when she felt him move in behind her. And when Ryder's hand landed on her waist the light inside her shone so bright it was blinding. It took everything she had not to lean into all that strength and warmth. Instead she turned out of his grasp, and held onto the bookshelf behind her for support. "No news. Not for a few days, I'd say. Maybe longer."

Ryder's hot eyes landed on her mouth, and her brain waves skittered out of control. Only now she'd somehow lost the ability to bring them back to earth.

"I'd wondered," he said, frowning even as his eyes darkened. "Considering you've been acting like a cat on a hot tin roof since I arrived."

She had? Oh, right. Her mum. The light inside her dimmed a fraction, which should have been welcome, but instead she fisted her hands at her side and tried to press her mother out of her head. Out of her damn heart. The reason Nadia wasn't coping with the feelings skittering about inside her like a normal person was because of *her* in the first place.

"Everything else okay?"

She shook her head. Nodded. Opened her mouth to tell him about the call, knowing this man of all men would understand better than anyone.

But it wasn't his concern. Could never be.

She took a deep breath and looked him in the eye. "Everything's hunky-dory."

Smart guy, he clearly didn't believe her. But for whatever reason he didn't press. Instead he said, "Prove it. Let go of the damn shelf, woman, and come here."

Despite the emotional roller coaster going off the rails inside her, Nadia's mouth twitched into a smile. And following her wicked feet and anaemic heart, she went to him, but at the last she pressed her hand against his chest, as if keeping their hearts apart was her last stand.

"You may have led Sam with some aplomb back

there, Ryder, but I'll have you know I'm still the boss in this room."

One dark eyebrow slid up his forehead. "You just go on thinking that, Miss Nadia," he said, his voice gruff as he pressed her back against the shelves, dust and papers raining down upon their heads. "If it helps you sleep at night."

Her heart kicked like a wild thing as his eyes dropped back to her mouth, eyes filled with desire and defiance, and she knew that she wouldn't be sleeping much that night, if at all.

It's sex. Just sex. Delicious, exquisite, earth-moving sex. He's been your port in a storm. A little night comfort in a far-off land. Nothing new there; that's totally your MO.

Yeah, she thought, *you just keep telling yourself that*, as his mouth descended on hers, sensation took over and all thought fled.

Ryder ran a hand over his neck. It ached from too many hours at the computer in his office atop a giant Collins Street edifice.

And yet it hadn't been a skyscraper keeping him locked to his chair. It had been sketch after sketch of a large space filled with arched windows and high beams and old wooden floors. A building with a broken lift, lights that appeared on the verge of burning the whole place down. With strips of red silk floating from one discreet corner.

He'd been thinking about the place so much of late, to the detriment of his real work. His only option as he saw it was to get the thing out of his head. The sheaths of paper curled up on the carpet beside his shoes proved it hadn't worked.

Ryder stood, stretched his arms over his head, and felt his spine crick and crack. Then, remembering the posture Nadia had shown him, pressed his feet into the floor from his hips down, and pulled himself as tall as possible from his hips up, as if his body were squashed between two panes of glass… His muscles sang with the relief and release of it, until he caught sight of how ridiculous he looked in the window.

He could have kissed his mobile when it rang.

"Hey, kiddo," he said, after seeing Sam's number on the display, "just the distraction I needed."

"We got married!" her crackly voice exclaimed.

"Say again?" Ryder stuck his finger in his other ear and headed to the window to make sure he had the best reception possible. Because she could not possibly have just said—

"We eloped! I am now officially Mrs Ben Johnson!"

"It sure as hell sounded like you just said that you eloped."

A pause, then, "That's because I did. I told Ben everything. About Dad, and the other wives, and the panic attacks. And he was a rock, Ryder. He was beautiful, and perfect, and strong, and wonderful. And we're in Las Vegas right now. And it's gorgeous. We flew in at night and the lights—"

But Ryder hadn't heard much past *Vegas*. The bloody place was fast turning out to be his arch enemy. "Did Nadia put you up to it?"

After a long pause, Sam shot back, "In what possible way?" her voice tight. When he was the only one with any right to be pissed.

"She's from Vegas. And don't try to say you didn't know."

"She's not from here. She's *from* there."

"Well, she's moving back there any day now." He knew he was pulling at straws, but he was struggling to get his head around it all.

"Oh." Sam's suddenly soft voice broke through. "Has she heard when?"

She hadn't. Not when he'd left her soft and warm and naked in her bed at five that morning. When he'd actually toyed with the thought of doing the walk of shame into work in the same suit and tie he'd worn the day before, just to get another hour in her arms.

"That's not the point," he growled. "What the hell possessed you guys?"

"It had all just spun so far out of control, Ryder. It was meant to have been small, just us and Ben's family, and you giving me away. And then all that stuff happened with Dad, and on Ben's side a fight had erupted over what flavour cake might offend Great-Auntie Wallace. In the end we realised we just wanted to look one another in the eye and say, *It's you. You're it. You're the one who makes my heart race and my bed warm and I'll take that for ever, thank you very much*."

Ryder closed his eyes and rubbed his thumb and forefinger over the bridge of his nose. What the hell could he possibly say to that? "And Vegas was your only option?"

"It was quickest," she said, and he could all but hear her grin. "A sixty-dollar licence and a five-minute ceremony and you're done. You should have seen the line-up at the courthouse. Picture women in full bridal regalia, their limos waiting at the kerb. Men in Elvis wigs, their luggage at their feet as they'd come straight from the airport."

Picturing it wasn't helping. "I just wish…" He wished what? That he could go back to the way things were when he was her everything, and she was his, and his life was laid out ahead of him like a long dark tunnel of more of the same? "I just wish I'd been there to see it."

"I know." He heard the wobble in her voice, before she took a great big sniff. "But then we had that dance, you and I. That perfect, lovely dance at Nadia's. *That* was our dance, Ryder. Not in front of a million people I barely know. Not looking over our shoulders waiting for Dad to ruin everything. That night at Nadia's studio—you gave me away."

His thoughts slipped back to that conversation in his car a few weeks back when she'd "set him free". And he knew then why it had felt like a false victory—it had never been about Sam setting him free; he was the one who needed to let *her* go. And that night in the dance studio, watching Sam and Nadia go head to head, he'd not only given her her first real taste of independence, he'd taken his first step into his own.

"Yeah," he said. "I did."

"Lucky for you," said Sam, "the cabana boy wants to be a cinematographer so he took the video for us."

"Lucky me."

And then his sister was babbling about the lights and the casinos and that you could sit in the Keno bar all night, play a game an hour and get as many free Long Island iced teas as you wanted.

"You sound happy, Sam."

Her breath shook. "So, so happy."

"Love you, kiddo," Ryder said before he bloody well joined her.

"Love you more."

And then she was gone. Leaving Ryder alone in his big office, with the moonlight and etchings his only companions.

He looked out at the view over the city, glancing over the number of significant new buildings he'd had a hand in creating. His legacy. And he waited for…something. A feeling of satisfaction. Or pride. Even relief that for the first time in more than half his life he had only himself to consider.

But no matter how long he stood there, he didn't feel a damn thing.

Because the honest truth was, the only decision hanging in the balance in his life wasn't up to him. It was in the hands of a bunch of tights-wearing strangers on the other side of the planet. And there was not a damn thing he could do about it.

Chapter Ten

Long shadows sliced through the golden glow of the street below as Nadia left the studio in daylight for the first time on a Tuesday in over two months.

She knew Ryder wouldn't be there leaning against his big black car. Dance lessons were over; Sam's crazy, wonderful elopement a couple of days earlier had put paid to that. Yet the empty street tugged painfully at her stomach.

She jogged down the steps and headed towards her spartan rooms where everything was so temporary. So quiet. All those hours ahead of her in which to think.

She could have stayed and rehearsed, but she just didn't have the urge. And with Sam and Ben away she couldn't call on them to go out dancing to shake off the odd sense that she was in limbo. Waiting. As if the other shoe were out there, dangling above her and about to drop right on her head.

She turned up the collar of her light jacket, shoved her hands into the pockets and turned the corner, picking up the pace as a light drizzle filled the air, taking the edge off the heat as the longest, hottest summer of her life drew to a close.

But in spite of how far she walked, the tension still rode her, made her muscles tight, her stomach hard, her head jittery. Another day of not knowing what was around the corner for her—much less another ten—and she'd be off her nut.

And there was only one way she could think to ease the pressure that had been building inside her for days. *Ryder*. She walked faster instead. Because she couldn't go there. Especially not after she'd taken that swan dive into fairyland the other night.

In retrospect she put the whole thing down to a mini emotional breakdown. Still roiling from the aloofness of her mum's phone call, and then mixing in Sam's supreme happiness and the big man's total tenderness, as well as the realisation her time in Melbourne was coming to an end—it had all whirled into some great vortex of syrupy sentiment.

Which meant that Sam's elopement could *not* have come at a better time. If they wanted a neat and tidy end to what had been morphing into a more complicated affair than either of them had signed up for, they'd been handed it on a platter.

Unfortunately her body didn't agree. Turned out she couldn't walk fast enough to get away from thoughts of his hot touch, his strong hands, his devastating mouth.

A cab pulled up at the kerb ahead, letting out a passenger. Her feet stalled to a halt, her knees twitching, her teeth clamping down on her lip.

Then before she knew it she was running up to the driver, asking if he was free to do a drop-off in Brighton, and was in the back seat and away. It felt like less than a minute before she was out of the cab and walking up to Ryder's stunning split-level near the beach.

Her hair was damp from the rain. Goose bumps tightened her skin to the point of pain. Her heart knocked hard and heavy against her ribs, opening them up with each beat until she felt as if she were completely exposed. Then, as if she were a magnet and Ryder the centre of the earth, she lifted a hand and knocked.

Blood pumping so hard she could barely hear the traffic and waves and thrash of the wind as the drizzle whipped up into a late summer storm, Nadia waited. The ground tilting out from under her as she realised he might not even be home. And worse, if he was, the second he opened the door and saw her there, he'd know—

"Nadia?" Ryder said, surprise lighting his voice as he did just that.

He was decked out in old jeans that had clearly seen a worksite or two and a black shirt untucked with the sleeves rolled up. His hair was mussed and his jaw unshaven. And he looked so beautiful, so strong, so vital Nadia's thumping heart leapt right into her throat and stayed there.

Her mouth opened but nothing came out. What could she possibly say? The truth? That her last few days were a fog? That her feet had just brought her there? That her mini emotional breakdown was still very much in force? Either that or she was falling in love for the first time in her life and that she was terrified she'd spend the rest of her life aching without him.

But she'd never had a relationship that didn't end. Had never had anyone in her life who'd stuck around. Not when she'd asked, not when she'd enticed. Not when she'd out and out begged.

Give a damn and they'll eat you alive.

Which was how she summoned the remaining echoes of a lifetime of feigned ambivalence, ducked a hip against the doorjamb and looked up at him beneath her lashes. "It's Tuesday night. And for the first time in for ever I have no plans. You?"

He stood there, a wall of strength and quiet, saying nothing. And a flood of mortification flowed thick and fast through her. Oh, God, she was really alone in this, wasn't she? The only one feeling at a loss. Like every other time she'd dared to reach out to someone in her life. She took a step backward—

Ryder's hand clamped over her wrist, and he pulled her to him, and his lips were on hers, her hands in his hair, not an ounce of dying daylight between them as he walked her inside.

He slammed the door shut with his foot before he was all over her again. Ridding her of her bag, her scarf, her jacket. Flicking her hair out of the way to get to her neck.

She leant into him with a sigh, sensation pummelling her; her hair was everywhere, her skin already slicked with sweat. Too much feeling shooting through her to slow it down before it consumed her.

Not that Ryder gave her a chance. With a growl he found a wall and pressed her up against it. And their clothes were gone, skin on skin, his heat filling her up, the light inside her so bright it spilled over in her sighs, her moans, the damp gathering at the corners of her eyes.

And then he was inside her and Nadia spiralled so far down the rabbit hole there was nothing but the deepest delectation and absolute relief.

Ryder held the mobile phone tight in his hand, not sure how long he'd been sitting up in his bed staring at the screen. Seconds probably, considering it had yet to hibernate to black, and yet it felt like for ever.

"Ryder?" Nadia's sleepy voice murmured from beside him, just before she snuggled her face into his hip, her arm curling possessively about his thigh. "Was that my phone?"

Ryder gripped the thing a moment longer, stalling, stretching time, before he accepted time had run out. "It rang. I didn't get to it in time."

Nadia dragged herself to sitting, bringing his sheet with her. Knees to her chest, she swept the messy mass of her hair from a face soft with sleep and swiped a thumb over the screen. She got halfway through a yawn before she saw the name that had stopped his heart.

Wide awake now, her eyes shot to his. Even in the soft wash of moonlight he saw how big they were. And how damned excited. "I was expecting an email. They said they'd email." She swept her hair from her eyes again; this time her movements were quick, breathless. "I'm sorry. I have to—"

"Go ahead," he said, leaning back against his pillow with his arms propped behind his head, like a man with not a care in the world. When truthfully, his insides were coiled so tight that his lungs struggled to fill.

She spun away from him, her toes dropped to the floor, and she curled over her phone with both hands as if it were something precious. Within seconds her voice hummed into the thing. "Sorry, Bob, I was asleep." Laughter, then, "No, that's fine. But only because it's you." Then came a series of quiet *mmm-hmms*.

Ryder closed his eyes and, for the first time since he found a thirteen-year-old Sam in the midst of her first panic attack frozen to the point of near catatonia, he prayed.

When he realised what he was praying for, his eyes snapped open. And his blood ran cold.

Nadia slowly hung up the phone and held it in her lap, her naked back curved towards him, her dark waves spilling over the unearthly pale skin, her scent of her all over his sheets, all over his skin.

And he knew.

Strike that. He'd known from the moment she'd walked towards him so dark and lush and tempting that any part she played in his life would be transitory, titanic, fatal.

"When?" he asked.

She turned so one leg was hooked onto the bed, and glanced quickly over her shoulder before turning back to the phone, and in that glance he saw that any excitement that might have been there was now lost beneath the quicksilver mess of emotion shimmering across her face. "Next weekend. No, *this* one. Bob's emailing flight details right now."

Ryder somehow nodded, even while he was blistering on the inside from the effort not to hold her, touch her, lose himself in her every last moment they had together. But mostly from the effort not to make good on his prayer and do whatever it took to make her stay.

Because it was going to be brutal. Hell, if she hadn't come to him that night, by five minutes to ten he'd have been ripping her door off its hinges. Like some seductive vapour she'd invaded his thoughts, his needs, his life. At times when they were apart he could have sworn he could feel her energy flowing through him as if she'd seeped into his very marrow.

And considering her history, he had no doubt he could chisel that fissure of hesitation into full-blown uncertainty. A kiss just below her ear, a thumb run softly along her jaw, a stroke of her inner thigh and he could make her his. But for how long? Until another opportunity like this came along? Until things naturally simmered down? Until disillusion leached in, restlessness took hold, and he realised he'd had enough?

He knew how badly she wanted the job, how much of her own self-worth was wrapped in whether or not she had it in her to succeed on her own, how much healthier it would be if she got as far away as possible from the insidious destructive influence of her mother, and yet he'd yearned for her to fail. Just so he could keep her close.

If he'd ever harboured any small hope that he might one day be able to love a woman in a more honest way than his own father ever had, that doubt had just been pulverised.

He was a selfish bastard. Which was his problem, not hers. His hit to take.

As he saw it he had one chance at redemption. He had to let her go. And he had to do so in a way that meant she'd never look back.

"You appear a little shell-shocked, Miss Nadia."

In profile her forehead scrunched into a frown. "Probably because I am."

"I thought you'd be bouncing off the walls. Literally." He said it with a smile that felt as if it had been cut into his face.

Then she turned to him, her eyes wide, her lips pursed, her expression…lost. "What if I'm not ready? What if I'm kidding myself? What if it's not what I really want? What if I've been too busy running towards what I think I should want to see that what I really want is something else—something right under my nose?"

Dammit. Nadia. Sweetheart.

Ryder lifted off the pillow and slid a hand up her spine before it curled around the back of her neck. Her soft skin and sleepy warmth carved a hollow in his chest. "You forget, I've seen you spinning circles in the sky. Of all the people I've met in my life, you are the one who's had the most manifest purpose. That show is what you were born to do."

"You think?"

"I know."

"Ryder," she said, pulling away. Her eyes glistened, swarming with emotion he understood more than he let himself dwell on. What had happened between them might be real, it might feel rich and thick and true, but he couldn't promise it would last. And he wouldn't risk hurting her simply for the chance to find out.

"I *know*," he said, holding her gaze until she breathed out, and belief poured back into her dark, soulful eyes.

And then she leant into him. Snuggling into his touch. Trusting and soft and small. *Adorable*, he thought. And between breathing out and breathing in again, Ryder felt something inside him split right in half, the pain of it cracking through him like a gunshot.

But she didn't need to know the arguments his conscience and his ego were battling out inside him. What she needed was sleep. And to feel damn proud of herself. So he laid her down, and rolled her into his arms, wrapping her up until her head fitted just under his chin and her breath shifted against his chest.

He lay there, all night, staring at the phone still clutched in her hand, telling himself he'd done the right thing.

When Nadia woke up the next morning, Ryder was gone.

She reached out for him to find his side of the bed empty and cold and on his pillow a note. A note and an apple.

For the road, the note read.

And the lump that had formed in her throat the moment she'd seen the Sky High producer's name on her phone dislodged itself and the tears that had gathered behind it poured from her eyes like a damn waterfall.

Because she loved the idiot.

Up and down, through and through. She'd known it with absolute certainty the moment Bob had told her she was in. She should have felt elated, over the moon, vindicated, relieved. Instead all she'd felt was a keening sadness whistling through a hole in her heart.

Even while she'd seen in his eyes that he felt…something, if not love then a definite desire to keep her close, he'd congratulated her, wished her luck, and held her with such tenderness she'd slept like a log. And woken not to the man who'd misappropriated her heart, but a damn apple, and a note that as good as warned her not to let the door hit her on the backside on the way out.

Was that it? Good luck and thanks for all the sex? Because he simply didn't care, or because he cared too much for some drawn-out farewell?

She couldn't think surrounded by his heat, his scent, the bachelor pad to end all bachelor pads. She had to get out of his bed. She swiped her palms over her damp cheeks, and then tried to untwist herself from the sheets, but they fought back. By the time she'd yanked herself free she tumbled out of bed and onto the floor with a thump.

And there she lay, breathing heavily, looking up at the ceiling as she had the first night she met him. Only this time it wasn't the ceiling of her lonely little flat. And this time she wasn't lost, wasn't filled with hope that she might one day get her act together. This time all her dreams had come true.

All the dreams she'd ever had until she met him.

With a groan she pulled herself upright, wincing at the bruises on her backside, which would be black and blue by the time she got to Vegas in a few days. *A few days*. That was all the time she had to tie up the loose threads of the life she'd built. And the more she thought about it, the more threads there were. So many unexpected goodbyes.

"Then you'd better get cracking," she said, the croak less convincing than she'd hoped.

She was dressed and out of the door within minutes. She only held onto the doorknob a moment. Okay, a few moments. But she had to be sure this time, certain of what she was walking away from.

"Love," she said out loud, the word picked up by the sea breeze and carried away on the wind. For the first time in her life, love.

But Sky High was what she wanted. It *was*. It had better be, because it would be her whole life now. Her days and her nights. Her blood and her sweat. Her bruised bones and her tweaked tendons. And as for her inflamed heart?

With a growl she pushed away from the door and jogged down the steps to the footpath.

She'd had her heart crushed a thousand times in her life and survived. So long as she had dance, she'd survive Ryder Fitzgerald too.

With that mantra on a loop inside her head as she walked down the beach road towards her tram stop, Nadia didn't look back.

Chapter Eleven

Melbourne put on a most beautiful day. After the weeks of rain and overcast skies the heavens were clear, only a few puffy white clouds marring their perfection. Down on the peninsular the air was more fresh, the salty breeze a reminder how close Ryder was to the sea.

With a plane taking Nadia away that day, Ryder hadn't trusted himself not to bite the head off some poor contractor on site, so he'd taken a road trip south until he found himself on a very different kind of site, the kind he hadn't set foot on in years.

Before him loomed a big old house. It listed away from a dangerously pitched cliff face as a result of years of buffeting winds and was now held in place by carefully built scaffolding. Around the property lay palettes of stained glass, piles of old wood, and mounds of new bricks peeking out from beneath paint-speckled tarps.

And just like that his palms itched with the memory of having an actual hammer in his grip, wood and nail meeting with a satisfying jar. It was a memory of his summer days learning the trade in places like this, and of watching his mother grin as she knocked together creations of her own. Either way it felt…good. And after the oblivion of the past few days he'd take all the therapy he could get.

"Ryder!" a familiar voice called out, and he turned to find Tom Campbell bearing down on him.

It had been over a decade since he'd last worked for the guy, acting as labourer's apprentice down in Portsea in his determination to pay his own way through college. Even with the salt-and-pepper hair and deeper crinkles around his eyes, he looked more robust than ever.

"You look ridiculously healthy," Ryder said, shaking his hand. "Sea air? Honest work? Botox?"

"Try the love of a good woman."

Right, shouldn't have asked. "Show me what you're up to."

With a grin of pure delight, Tom distracted Ryder beautifully by taking him through his latest house project, a renovation job he didn't need for the guy was loaded, but one he did for the thrill of bringing old glory back to life.

And as Ryder took in the beautiful mouldings, the original stone fireplace now peeking through a hole in the horrendously wallpapered plasterboard, of all the spots he could have gone in an effort to find his feet again, this was the place. He felt more grounded here than he had in a long time. More stimulated by the random house than any building he'd produced from scratch. Because this was what he'd gone into architecture *for*.

Uncovering the inherent beauty in lost things.

And the years began to tumble in on him, brick by brick, till he was breathing in the dust of his memories, the ache of that long ago day when, covered in sweat and grime and speckles of paint, he'd had the future of his dreams in sight only to have his father corrupt it with his cruel words and snatch it right away.

Only from the outside looking in he realised that it wasn't that simple. Fitz had been his usual ruinous self—but so full of spit and fire and hostility the decision to quit had been Ryder's own. His father had altered the course of his life because Ryder had let him.

The irony hit like a roundhouse kick to the solar plexus. Like that long ago day, he'd let the bastard do it again. And this time he hadn't even been in the same room.

Needing air, space, perspective, Ryder excused himself and steered himself back outside. And the moment he stepped into the sunshine he saw it—a plane soaring overhead. Who knew where it was headed? Probably Sydney, or Brisbane. Outer Mongolia for all he knew. The chances it was heading to Las Vegas were slim to none. And yet he didn't look away. He couldn't. He watched, lungs tight, skin tingling, feet pressing hard into the rocky ground until the plane was well out of sight and he could tell himself Nadia was gone. Really gone.

He'd lost her. Hell, he'd miss her. He tried telling himself he'd done the right thing. The benevolent thing. That nothing lasted for ever. Not relationships. Not old houses built on windy bluffs. Not even skyscrapers built of the strongest materials known to man.

Except for the fact that he hadn't lost Nadia, he'd *let her go.*

And she'd let him let her go because she'd been let down so many times in her life it was all she knew how to do.

Dammit, thought Ryder, closing his eyes tight, blocking out the light as he tried to capture any one of the fragile threads of thought shifting through his head. That somewhere there was an answer. A different answer. The real answer. *His* answer.

Something about Sam. His little sister finally putting her foot down and living her life on her terms. Because of Ben. Because the kid's love meant more to her than their father's betrayals.

And then—lungs filled with the heady scents of paint stripper and putty, of wood varnish and plaster dust, of imagination, dedication, and optimism—he caught it.

He loved Nadia.

He *loved* her with a depth he couldn't see to the bottom of. And, try as he might, he couldn't imagine a time when he wouldn't feel the same way. Because Nadia wasn't some girl he was trying to forget for her own good. She was *his* girl. His equal, his foil, his conscience, his advocate. His partner.

Ryder had believed it was in his genes that he'd never be able to love that way, and time had never proven him wrong. But the truth was, he just hadn't known how until he met her. She'd filled his life, connected him deeper to himself than he'd ever been. And in that darkness, deep down inside, she flickered. She'd always flicker. His truth. His light. His love.

Ryder ran a hand through his hair and took a few steps right, then left. But he had no idea where he was meant to go. Only that he hoped it wasn't too late. That he hadn't martyred himself out of the best thing that had ever happened to him.

When it finally hit him where he was meant to be he called out his goodbyes to Tom and took off towards his car at a run.

* * *

Nadia leant her head against the window of the cab and watched the Las Vegas scenery flicker by—wide plots of vacant land populated by dry brown scrub and tumbleweed, huge outlet malls, wedding chapels, drug stores and casinos so big that the time away had made far smaller in her mind.

The years she'd looked out over Vegas' shimmery horizon every day felt like a lifetime ago. Her year in Melbourne was still far too significant. The memories too raw. The people left behind like anchors around her neck.

But seeing old friends, visiting old haunts, making new memories would take care of that. As would setting up her silks, getting back into the swing of the hoop and enduring the punishment of the rehearsal schedule. She would immerse herself so deeply in the dance that by the time she came blinking back out into the real world the permanent ache in the centre of her chest would have faded. Some of it at least. Oh, she hoped so.

And then Norah Jones came on the cab's radio.

Her mind filled with the memories of other car rides. Of Melbourne rain sliding down other windows, and down her back. Of dancing with a deep voice in her ear, a hot chest against her own as she swayed with no purpose other than to be near. Of sharp suits and shiny shoes. Of bare feet curled over hers in bed, a strong arm wrapped possessively over her naked waist—

"We're here, missy."

The taxi driver's twang snapped Nadia out of her reverie. She stared blankly at the guy, who grinned as he leant his arm on the back rest of his seat, no doubt mistaking her silence for awe.

"What's the plan?" he asked. "Gonna win big? Get yourself hitched?"

"I'm a dancer," she said, the words settling her some. "In the new Sky High show."

His eyebrows disappeared beneath a thatch of dyed black hair; the guy probably moonlighted as an Elvis impersonator. "Never seen a show, but my girlfriend can't get enough of them. Know what? I'll be sure to see yours, since I can say I met you and all."

Nadia paid out the fare. "Do. It'll blow your mind."

The driver shrugged, as if being local to this part of the world it'd take a hell of a lot more than a fancy dance show to surprise him.

Check-in papers in one hand, handle of her small wheelie case packed with her meagre worldly possessions in the other, Nadia looked up at the multicoloured façade of the structure that would be her home until she found herself a place. She would be sharing accommodation with a bunch of the other dancers, no doubt. Rehearsing all day. Partying all night. And when the show began it would be two shows a day, six days a week, for months on end. Her ankles killing her, her knees protesting, her hands worn till they resembled those of a woodchopper...

Her dream come true.

The double doors slid open and she was instantly hit with the sound of slot machines a level above. The carpet was a Harlequin pattern in a riot of eye-watering colour, the walls just as chaotic.

She joined the line at Reception behind a group on a girls' weekend, and another at a buck's party. She could all but see tomorrow's hangovers in their eager faces.

Better get used to it. They were the minutiae of her

new life. Her people. Day trippers and weekenders.
Honeymooners and gamblers. And a dance company
of thick-skinned kids with hollow legs and a taste for
danger. Transient and impulsive. Drawn to the bright
lights and constant noise. Never wondering if they were
really living the dream or simply blinded by fluores-
cent lights, endless buffets and not a second's down
time to just think.

No shiny-faced Tiny Tots who thought her an honest
to goodness fairy princess here.

No senior pole dancers who found more simple joy
hooking a leg around a chair than most of her peers
did successfully completing a triple-twist death drop.

No boss who remembered her birthday and gave her
the day off, and gift certificates to get massages if she
looked worn out.

No local markets where the stall owners knew her
by name.

No Sam and Ben. Or the sweet crew of fun, crazy
friends who actually cared about one another and would
have laughed themselves silly at the very thought of
competing against one another for anything.

Nadia breathed deep, held the suitcase handle tighter
again, and did her all to stop the next name from slipping into her mind. But there was no stopping it. No
stopping him. There never had been. From the moment
he'd waltzed into her studio, so magnificent and fore-
boding, it was as if her soul had said, *So there you are*.

But he wasn't there now. Not any more.

As it always did at such moments, her mother's voice
seeped in knocking her to *get up, move on, stay tough*.
And most of all not make the same mistake she had, in
letting her future go up in smoke for some guy. Well, it

had sunk in all right, because here she was, with the job of a lifetime in the palm of her hot little hand, while the guy she loved was thirteen thousand kilometres away.

It might as well have been a million, she thought, looking over her shoulder where the automatic doors slid open and closed to accommodate the constant stream of strangers. The angle showcased a handful of hotels down the strip, the peculiar golden sun of Nevada making them appear like a mirage, a fantasy that would dissolve into sand at the first strong wind.

"Welcome to the King's Court Hotel and Casino!"

Nadia flinched and turned back to Reception to find a woman in a red and navy jester's outfit with big silver bells tinkling on the tips of her crazy hat.

"Pray tell, what can I do you for, today?" When Nadia didn't answer, the receptionist waggled her fingers at the passport and papers in Nadia's hand. "Checking in?"

Nadia nodded, and handed over her work papers, unable to take her eyes from the bells. *Tinkle tinkle.*

"Oh, wonderful!" said the receptionist. *Tinkle tinkle.* "You're with the new show! I wish I could dance— two left feet though. Though I guess there's dance and there's what you lot do. I poked my head in on rehearsal the other day and…wow! You are so lucky, to have the ability to back up what you want to do with your life."

The woman's hat tinkled some more as the automatic doors again opened behind Nadia, bringing with them a gust of dry desert air that lifted the hairs on the back of her neck. When, after a pause, the receptionist's smile began to waver, Nadia realised she was still gripping her papers with one hand.

Because as if the blast of air had dumped a flurry

of pixie dust from one of the magic shows down the strip onto Nadia's head, her mind emptied till it was left with the receptionist's perky voice saying, *You are so lucky, to have the ability to back up what you want to do with your life.*

She absolutely had the ability to back up what she wanted to do with her life, and she always had, because she *hadn't* made the same mistake her mother had.

Her mother had fallen pregnant to a man she didn't love. If she'd loved him she'd have stayed. She'd have fought. Kent women were fighters after all. No, Claudia must have had to make a choice, probably on her own, and she'd *chosen* to sacrifice her career at its pinnacle. To keep Nadia.

Nadia didn't even realise she was halfway back across the lobby until the woman on Reception called out her name. But she wasn't stopping for anything. Because Nadia wasn't in the same unimaginable position as her mother at all.

She didn't *have* to make a choice.

She *wanted* to.

And what she wanted was Ryder.

Sky High had been her saviour. The place she'd found her feet, found freedom. But that was then. Before she'd grown up. Before she'd gone home. And now she'd take her cramped little apartment, crazy-making Tiny Tots, the occasional ass-grab from salsa-dancing widowers, even occasional mind-bending conversations with her misfortunate mother if it meant she had *him*.

Eyes darting across the way, she spotted an empty cab and leapt right on in, only to find it was the same one she'd just left.

The taxi driver looked up, surprised to find himself actually surprised. "Forget something, missy?"

Nadia shook her head, adrenalin pouring through her at such pace she could barely sit still. "Remembered something, actually. The airport, please."

"Well, then," he said, revving the engine and turning the cab into the arc of the driveway that took them back to The Strip, "ten minutes in Vegas and you're all done with the place. That's an honest to goodness first for me."

And even while Nadia's heart fair thundered against her ribs, the space that had been pressing so hard since the moment she'd left Australian shores no longer hurt. It settled, warmed…

And waited.

Ryder squinted against the sharp sunlight filtering through the clouds above. The car at his back quiet, its engine cool, its doors unlocked, its presence forgotten.

The large brown building before him sunned itself in the morning's warmth like an old alley cat—worn, neglected, clearly in its twilight years. And yet Ryder's gaze was fixated higher—on the row of arched windows reflecting the sun like mirrors on the top floor.

And he silently cursed his sister.

A week earlier he'd handed over all the work on his desk to his shocked employees and left the office. Then, he had boarded the first plane to Vegas, intending to knock on each and every one of the million hotel-room doors in the big, vibrant, elusive city, until he found Nadia.

Sam, still honeymooning, had met him at the airport

and looked at him as if he'd gone off the rails. She'd turned out to be right.

Sam had looked up on Google the casino in which Sky High would be performing later in the year. He'd called. No Nadia Kent was booked in. And hell if he knew her grandmother's name, the name she'd once told him she'd danced under. Meaning she could be anywhere, no doubt becoming more and more ensconced within that dazzling, decadent place with every second that passed.

So he'd gone home, only to end up back to the building housing the Amelia Brandt Dance Academy so often it was practically a second home. All to no avail.

Now he'd reached the end of his patience. If it took for him to stage a sit-in in order for Amelia Brandt herself to tell him where Nadia was, then that was what he'd do.

Then a flutter of movement appeared at the window. A flicker of dark hair, a press of a pale hand. It was doubtless all in his head, some desperate manifestation of his desire, but he was through the cracked front doors and up the rickety stairs before he even knew he was moving.

It was too late before he remembered that at some point on Tuesdays the studio took seniors pole-dancing—and that he might be about to witness something no man in his prime ever should—because he'd already pushed through the studio doors.

Music filled his ears. Music and giggles and the sound of a hundred elephants thundering across the floor. But the daylight pouring through the windows had hit him right in the eyes. A hand as a shield, he blinked away the spots, and then promptly forgot how to breathe.

For there she was, chatting and laughing with a tall lean woman in black while a bunch of little girls in ridiculous pink tutus went mad in the background.

Nadia.

He was sure he hadn't said her name, that his thought had been enough to capture her attention. As her ever-dancing hands stilled, her pointing toes lay flat against the floor. And she turned.

Ryder might as well have been slammed across the head with a plank as in the next moment his life flashed before his eyes. Only it wasn't his past. Not his father, or Sam, or the business that had taken him so far off course from his original dream as to make it unrecognisable.

It's you, Ryder thought, his future hovering in front of him like a juicy red apple just waiting to be plucked. *You're it. You're the one who makes my heart race and my bed warm and I'll take that for ever thank you very much.*

And when she began to walk his way, he felt the same way he had the first time, stunned by the instant impact of her earthy beauty, the awareness that sprinted up and down his arms, the eyes that looked past the all the nonsense and consequential career and fancy wheels and right into his soul. A place he'd avoided for a very long time, a place he'd rediscovered because of her.

"Ryder," she said, licking her lips as if his name were as sweet as honey. "I was just about to come and find you. Bearing gifts."

At which point she glanced beside him. He followed her gaze to the pink velvet chaise longue, where beside her patchwork handbag sat a massive net bag filled with apples.

He coughed out a laugh, surprise and desire gathering within him like a perfect storm. When he turned back to her, his smile had a dangerous edge. There was only one gift he'd take from her, and it didn't come in a bag.

It started with a touch. Although worried about for ever damaging the psyches of a plethora of sparkly, pink three-year-olds, Ryder held out a hand. Nadia took it. When he ran his thumb down the centre of her palm and she sighed, desire morphed into need. Need to have, to know, to *keep*.

"You're back," he said, his voice barely a hum.

She nodded.

"For good this time?"

"Depends."

"On?"

"Well, I quit my job when I left, and then I quit my *next* job to come back here. And then the airline went and lost my luggage. So I am currently homeless and unemployed and without stuff. If there's a way I can get those things sorted, then I'm home free."

Feeling as if the pieces of his life were floating about his head, just waiting to settle into perfect place, Ryder said, "I may have the solution."

"Really?"

"I always keep a spare toothbrush on hand, and you already look better in my shirts than I do."

Nadia let out a breath and Ryder wondered how long she'd been holding it. Unable to hold back any more, he pulled her closer, close enough to see the sparks of hope and swirls of shifting desire in her dark eyes.

He spared a glance over her shoulder where a dance teacher—possibly even Amelia Brandt herself—was watching with one hand to her heart and another to her cheek.

"She's the best dancer you'll ever see, and you know it. Give her a job!" he barked.

The dance teacher jumped, nodded, and proceeded to herd the tutu brigade into some sort of line away from the big grumpy man.

But Ryder needed more privacy than that in order to do what he intended to do. He grabbed Nadia's gear and tugged her out the door. Noise spilled from the floor below for the first time since he'd ever set foot in the joint, as what seemed like a never-ending stream of uni-student types in too-skinny jeans and ironically labelled T-shirts bundled into the dubious writers' centre space on the second floor.

When it looked as if the procession would never end, Ryder took the only option. He pulled open the doors of the lift, which now swung happily at the top floor. And as he wrenched the old glass doors closed, then the rusty wrought iron bars behind them, the sounds of the stairwell lowered to a mere hum.

"Daring," Nadia said, looking up through the glass ceiling to the old cables hulking above, before jumping up and down till the thing began to swing. "My kind of place."

The moment her eyes dropped back to his, hot, hooded, and dark with desire, Ryder dropped her bag and his apples, dragged her into his arms and kissed her as if his life depended on it. Hell, it did depend on it. And by the way she kissed him back—clinging, desperate, pressing herself into every part of him—her life *had* to depend on it too.

When he pulled away the ground beneath his feet continued to shift, even as the lift settled to a halt. He tipped his forehead against hers, waiting until their laboured breaths found a matching rhythm, and then he looked inside himself for the words he'd spent days trying to shape into some kind of sense.

"I'd like to give it a shot."

"What's that?"

"Adoring you."

At that she shuddered, her body melting against him, her head lying against his heart. Then she melted some more.

Intending to keep her there as long as he could, for ever sounded about right, Ryder ran his hand down her back, sliding his fingertips under the belt-line at her waist, her warm skin sending his heart rate thundering and turning his vision red. He kept it together, just, because there was more he intended to say. More she deserved to hear.

"I've been thinking for some time now that it's a damn shame a woman like you hasn't felt adored. And I want to be given the chance to be the man who adores you on a regular basis. Daily. Multiple times a day. Every minute. Every second."

He pulled back to find Nadia's head still tipped down. Her eyes closed. And when he propped a finger beneath her chin and tilted her face to his, he saw tears flowing down her cheeks. He leant in and kissed them away.

"Ryder," she said on a gulp.

"Yes, Nadia."

"I love you."

Well, he thought, his face splitting into a smile, *I should have just started with that.* "I know, sweetheart. This I do know. What I need to know, for sure, is if you're sure about being back. I know how much getting that job meant to you—"

She shut him up with a finger to his lips, and it took everything not to suck it into his mouth and taste her. Every bit of her. By the darkness that spilled into her eyes he knew she was feeling it too.

Rather than tempt fate, she curled her finger away and lay her hand on his chest, right over the beating of his heart. "I got all the way there, right up to the reception desk, but I couldn't check in. I couldn't pretend, even for a second, it was where I was really meant to be. Easiest decision of my life was to come back. To find you, Ryder. To tell you—"

"I love you too, Nadia," Ryder said.

It was Nadia's turn to beam, her smile turning her dark eyes bright, the utter happiness lighting that beautiful face sapping his breath straight from his lungs.

And in that moment, Ryder Fitzgerald—long-time lost thing—found himself.

All because he'd found her.

And now he was never letting her go.

This time the kiss was slow, this time deep, this time he took his time to bring her to the edge of thought and feeling. Because for the first time since he'd met her all they had was time. Years. For ever.

And then the lift began to move.

Nadia squealed, or at least Ryder hoped it had been her squeak that echoed in the small box.

"It works!" she said, laughing and spinning by that

stage. "Near a year I've been teaching here and it's never worked."

"It's a sign."

"That while maintenance ignored Amelia's pleas they responded to her lawyers?"

"That this big slumberous lump of a building wants us here. Together. On one condition," said Ryder, waggling a finger at the lift as it drifted and screeched all the way to the ground floor. "No more dance lessons. Ever."

"Deal," said Nadia, sliding her hands around his waist as he pulled her deep into the circle of his arms, where she plastered herself against him, resting her cheek against his chest, her hip bumping his as the lift shook them side to side. "We can sway though. We're good at that."

"Yeah," he said, his voice a rumble, "we sway just fine."

They hit the ground with a thud and Ryder dragged the doors open, leaving them to spill into the sunshine.

Out on the street Nadia spread her arms, bags dangling from each hand, and closed her eyes and filled her lungs. With feet that seemed to float across the ground she twirled out into the middle of the deserted back street. "It feels like a brand-new day. Doesn't it?"

"A brand-new world," he agreed.

She looked over his car at him with a dark smile, a smile that spoke of cool sheets and hot limbs and getting all that as soon as possible, and said, "I do have a couple of hours before senior pole-dancing starts."

He laughed so loud it echoed off the buildings around them. "You little con-artist. You do have a job."

A shrug. Then, "For now. Until I find my real thing. Which I will do."

Ryder took her scarf and looped it around her neck, tugging her closer. "Of that I have no doubt. And... until then?" he asked, in a voice loud enough only she could hear it.

A finger running down the spine of his car, she sauntered around the thing, every step an exquisite sensuous thing he'd never become immune to. Neither did he want to. "I don't know—we could walk? Window-shop? Coffee?"

"I thought you hated coffee."

"Please, when did I say that?"

"First time I asked you out. *Stunts your growth* were your exact words. Miss Nadia, were you playing hard to get?"

"Ha! I've never played hard to get in my life. You just...overwhelmed me."

Ryder found it hard to imagine that this creature of his was overwhelmed by much in life, but he'd take it. "And now?"

"You still overwhelm me." At his side now, Nadia lifted onto her toes and pressed a soft, sweet kiss on his lips. Then, holding his cheeks between her palms, said, "Lucky for you I appreciate the thrill of being up high looking down, on stage looking out, eyes closed or blinded by stage lights, nothing but a ribbon and practice between me and certain death. But you, gorgeous man, are the greatest thrill of my life."

When she kissed him it was anything but sweet. It was deep, real, so far beyond a mere thrill.

"I'm thinking takeaway," said Ryder. "And they rent rooms above the pub around the corner, right?"

"Man after my own heart."

He held out an elbow, she slid her hand through the bend and rested her head on his big shoulder as together they walked down the thin Richmond street, sunlight filtering gently through the patchy clouds, the soft swish of their shoes on the crooked pavement in perfect time.

Epilogue

Nadia dodged the piles of plasterboard and plastic sails hanging from the scaffolding as she headed out of the soft double doors and down the stairs of the old Richmond building she now called home.

From the second-floor landing she caught Amelia's eye through the open doorway of the makeshift studio she was using while Ryder's company decked out the new slick arts studio near his old place in Brighton.

Wrangling a group of teenagers, no doubt forced to attend class to get ready for the senior formal, Amelia beckoned Nadia inside mouthing, *Help me!* But Nadia waved the appeal away. Been there, done that.

She wrapped her thick scarf around her neck and tugged her beanie tight about her ears, then pushed open the brand-new, shiny red doors at the front of the building and jogged down the tidy steps. Once she hit the far edge of the footpath, she walked backwards and as always marvelled at how warm her building looked even in the winter light with the scrubbed façade, windows all now free of bars and gleaming with the light of endeavour, the neat row of apple trees and box hedges planted along the entire front.

Hands in pockets and shoulders lifted high to her ears with pride, she glanced up at the arched windows of the third floor; the one with the window seat at which she sat and sketched ideas of a weekend. The other up against which their huge king-size bed had been shoved that first night the place was officially theirs and had never been moved. The next one that gave the most light for Ryder's vintage drafting table that he used in the morning while she slept in; the one that had been his mother's before him.

To think in a few short months it would all be done. The bottom floor for Ryder's new boutique firm—RF Renovations. The middle floor for her very own private studio—or her "swaying and swinging room" as Ryder called it. The top floor with its windows and beams, big industrial fans, crazy chandeliers and Ryder's imaginings for the layout of their first home, just gorgeous and perfect.

To think how much had changed since she'd made the choice to come home. After Vegas, she'd also made the choice to give her mother a break, because, no matter how tough the woman was, she mattered and always would. They were stuck with each other. Nadia had sat her mother down and told her exactly that and then had neatly put the onus on her mum to deal with it. Or not. Amazingly, she had. Slowly though. Kent women were stubborn after all.

"Hey, kiddo."

Nadia spun on her heels to find Ryder coming up the

street towards her with breakfast for the crew: a tray of coffee and a bag of bagels from the most *amazing* pub just around the corner. It had become their local. For coffee, and for occasional accommodations when they couldn't wait for the restoration crew and/or dance students to vamoose for the night.

"Hey, handsome!"

Ryder's beautiful face broke into a grin. She'd thought the man the most gorgeous male specimen on the planet in his slick suits and shiny shoes. Turned out in old jeans, long-sleeved T-shirt and plaster dust in his hair he was even better.

"Off to work?" he asked, leaning in for a kiss.

"And lucky I'm not late. You were meant to wake me," she chastised.

"You looked too rumpled to move. I like you rumpled."

Coming over all warm, she hooked a finger into the beltline of his jeans and tugged. "Rumpled will not endear me to my new boss."

Ryder scoffed. "Your new boss adores you. The crazy, high-flying, death-defying acrobats you are choreographing adore you. I adore you. Now shut up and give me a kiss and get out of here. Or you'll really be late."

Nadia did as she was told, wrapping herself around her man while he held coffee and bagels out of her way.

"Here." He gave her a coffee and she gave him one last kiss. "Go teach them a thing or two."

"Planning on it," Nadia threw over her shoulder.

"If they need to know how to sway—"

"I know who to ask!" she added with a laugh.

And even as the laughter faded, the smile stayed. Stuck. A permanent fixture. Like so much else in her life. Her extraordinary, adorable life.

* * * * *

AIMEE CARSON

The summer she turned eleven, Aimee Carson left the children's section of the library and entered an aisle full of Harlequin novels. She promptly pulled out a book, sat on the floor and read the entire story. It has been a love affair that has lasted over thirty years. Despite a fantastic job working part-time as a physician in the Alaskan Bush (think *Northern Exposure* and *ER*, minus the beautiful mountains and George Clooney), she also enjoys being at home in the gorgeous Black Hills of South Dakota, riding her dirt bike with her three wonderful kids and beyond-patient husband. But, whether at home or at work, every morning is spent creating the stories she loves so much. Her motto? Life is too short to do anything less than what you absolutely love. She counts herself lucky to have two jobs she adores, and incredibly blessed to be a part of Harlequin's family of talented authors. Visit her online at www.aimeecarson.com.

DON'T TELL THE
WEDDING PLANNER

Aimee Carson

Prologue

Dear *Ex Factor,*

I'm in desperate need of help. My best friend is marrying my former boyfriend and now she's asked me to be her maid of honor. My ex and I dated for over three years and everyone thought we'd eventually marry. The breakup was messy, but when he started dating my BF we all managed to reach an understanding. I'm really happy for my girlfriend and I want to be there for her on her big day, but I dread all the comments from friends and family. What should I do?

Callie: First off, congratulations to all three of you for working through your differences so that everyone remains friends. Secondly, I've been in your shoes, having recently arranged the Ex-Man's wedding—*my* ex-boyfriend—which he ruined with a zombie invasion. :) If *you* are happy for the bride and groom then most of the guests will see this. Unfortunately, there will be those with thoughtless comments and questions. I found it best to be prepared. So formulate a few vague, generic responses beforehand so you won't get caught unprepared.

Ex-Man: I think you only need one response: "I'm mainly here for the free food and beer." And if you're planning a zombie invasion to liven up the reception, don't tell the wedding planner.

Chapter One

Man, what a lot of work just to get hitched.

Matt weaved his way through the sightseers enjoying the ballroom of the historic Riverway mansion, a plantation that had once taken part in producing 75 percent of the world's cotton, but was now reduced to group tours and a venue for weekend events. He knew he was headed for the outdoor, private wedding reception when he spotted two Southern belles in authentic dress.

Choosing a Civil *War* theme to celebrate a marriage seemed wrong. But who knows, maybe the couple enjoyed the irony? Regardless, given the authentic mansion worthy of Scarlett O'Hara and the costumes of the guests, the wedding planner was either a genius...or insane. Matt was pulling for the latter, because he absolutely needed Callie LaBeau to be insane. If she were a reasonable, rational individual, she'd refuse Matt's request. Which meant his plans to fly in, fix his problem and fly back home would be over. And he'd be screwed.

Catching up with the two ladies in 1800s dresses, petticoats rustling beneath, wasn't hard. Their hoopskirts caught as they tried to open one of the French doors leading to the backyard, and their attempt to cross the threshold side by side didn't work out so well.

Matt bit back the grin and the fatigue of thirty-six hours on two hours of sleep, pulling open the other door.

The one in an ugly yellow-colored dress tossed him an inviting smile. "Thanks."

"Bathroom breaks must be a real bitch," Matt said.

The lady in lavender laughed. "You have no idea."

"Do either of you know where I can find Callie La-Beau?" he asked.

Lavender lady jerked her thumb toward one end of the outdoor reception. "Last time I saw her, she was over by the bar."

Matt took that as good news. Alcohol would definitely be a requirement in a crazy setting such as this, hopefully softening the wedding planner toward Matt's cause.

"I think she's the only one in royal-blue." Yellow dress sounded a little jealous.

Matt took the exit leading out to the twenty-acre grounds that smelled of freshly cut grass and held the crowd of wedding guests in Civil War costumes. Kerosene lamps sat on tables covered in white and dangled alongside Spanish moss in the giant oaks. The trees provided a canopy for the reception, the soft lamps casting a glow against the twilight sky.

He hoped the lamps were fake or the theme would soon be overrun by the yellow of firemen suits.

Fortunately, the lighting was low enough that Matt's dark pants and white, button-down shirt blended with the attire of the staff posing as servants. As for the male guests, half wore blue Union uniforms while the others sported gray Confederate uniforms—given the choice of a Southern theme, most likely the bride's side of the family. Matt scanned the brightly colored Southern belle dresses dotting the scene and spied one of royal-blue in front of an old-fashioned buggy being used as a bar.

Relief relaxed his shoulders. Today's four-hour flight to New Orleans had been turbulent and hot, hopeless for snagging a few minutes of shut-eye. A cold beer would go down good about now.

He approached the makeshift bar and leaned a hip against the wagon. "Callie LaBeau?"

The woman turned, and Matt was hit with a vision of hair the color of dark honey, wide, brown eyes and a slim but clearly female body filling out the bust of her gown. Appreciation thrummed through his veins, but he ignored the distracting sensation.

"Matt Paulson." He stuck out his hand.

"Colin called and said he was sending you my way."

A palm briefly pressed against his. The soft skin and the drawl, as honey-soaked as her hair, brought to mind hot, Southern nights filled with heated skin and sweat-soaked sheets.

Stick to the plan, Paulson. Get in, take care of the problem and get out.

She released his hand and her lips quirked. "Though Colin didn't mention he was sending you *now.*"

There was no irritation in her voice, only the calm tone of one who dealt with life's surprises and upsets with grace and dignity. He liked her already.

She'd need that skill set for what he had in mind.

"Colin told me I could find you here." He scanned the guests milling about. "I assumed you were scoping out a venue for an event. He didn't mention I was walking into the middle of an actual wedding reception."

"Colin's a good friend, and I owe him a lot. But he's

an obsessed gamer," she responded with a shrug that said it all.

Matt understood. Over the course of the past two years, he'd learned that the geekdom world was built on the backs of those whose lives revolved around the game. Outside social conventions often didn't compute. His brother's life currently consisted of work and spending hours immersed in the world of *Dungeons of Zhorg,* having traded one obsession for another. Matt just hoped Tommy's current fixation lasted.

Because dungeons and dragons and trolls beat the hell out of crystal meth.

As always, the years-old ache in his chest hurt as he remembered a time when his brother was gaunt, paranoid and delusional. Sick and wasting away right in front of Matt's eyes.

His stomach roiled, and he pushed the memories aside. "Should we meet up tomorrow or do you have a minute?"

"I'll be out of town all day on Saturday. How long are you in New Orleans?"

"Until Sunday morning."

She let out a huff of humor. "Now it is, then."

Callie reached into the bodice of her gown. The sight of those graceful fingers dipping into her cleavage hiked his brow and tightened his groin. Fortunately, he kept his expression one of amused sarcasm rather than the truth: a sleep-deprived guy who found the sight a total turn-on. A grin curled her mouth as she pulled out a tiny pocket watch.

"I try to keep things as authentic as possible. As the one in charge, that makes things difficult. Working without my tablet has been a real pain." She glanced at the time and blew an escaped strand of honey-colored hair from her cheek. "My assistant can keep an eye on things for a bit. But you only have twenty minutes until I need to prepare for the cutting of the cake."

Twenty minutes wasn't a lot of time to convince someone to do the impossible.

He ordered a beer and Callie requested a club soda. After she spoke with her assistant, who wore a similar gown in red, and looked a lot more harried than the wedding planner herself, they headed to a small bar along the back of the house that wasn't in use.

"What I wouldn't give to lean back in that seat right now." Callie looked longingly at a chair at one of the few empty tables, like a student eyeing an espresso after an all-nighter. "But this dress makes relaxing impossible. And I'm tired of sitting up straight."

"That getup doesn't look comfortable, either."

"The petticoat is stiff and the corset makes breathing impossible." She leaned against the counter, her brown eyes intrigued. "So tell me about your wedding-day fantasies, Mr. Paulson."

A bark of shocked laughter shot from his mouth. Hell, before he could think about tying the knot he'd have to be in one place long enough to successfully date someone. And that wouldn't happen anytime soon. If ever.

How many times had he tried, and miserably failed, to be the long-distance boyfriend? How many times had he tried, and failed, to keep a relationship going? An occasional round of great sex was one thing, but that held a woman for only so long. And there weren't many willing to play second chair to his responsibilities to Tommy. Eventually, they all left, the resentment toward his priorities too much to overcome.

Matt cleared his throat. "I'm not here to discuss my fantasies."

Fantasies.

Another stab of awareness hit, stronger than the one before. Damn, why were they even using the word? Currently *his* fantasies consisted of a brown-eyed beauty wearing an old-fashioned dress with a ridiculous hoop beneath. But the thought of unlacing a corset was surprisingly…hot.

He settled next to her at the counter. "I'm here about my brother's wedding."

Was that a hint of interest that flickered through her eyes?

Before he could decide, she glanced down at her drink and took a sip before carefully setting down her glass. "So why isn't he here?"

"Can't get the time off work."

More accurately, with Tommy's track record, he couldn't risk losing another job.

"And the bride to be?" she drawled.

A history as bad as the groom's. Perhaps worse.

"They had prior commitments," Matt said instead, sending her a smile that didn't encourage further questioning. "I had a few days off, so I volunteered to come down and get the ball rolling."

She eyed him steadily. "Dedicated of you."

Matt's lips quirked dryly. She had no idea.

"What can I say?" he said with an easy shrug. "I'm a hell of a brother."

Matt glanced down at the woman who stood a good six inches shorter than him. A height which was just high enough for a great view down the front of that ridiculous outfit that displayed her breasts as though they were a commodity. Perhaps during the time period of the dress, they had been.

Man. He rubbed his eyes. The fatigue was clearly getting to him. He'd worked four twelve-hour shifts in a row, the E.R. packed with patients every night—just how he liked it. The last night he'd encountered a trauma case that left him flying high on adrenaline, unable to sleep. He loved the challenge, and he was damned good at emergency medicine, too. He'd finished up a satisfying two weeks of work in one of the busiest E.R.s in Los Angeles and had been set to climb on a flight back to Michigan to check on Tommy. Until his brother had called and shared his and Penny's plans for the wedding. So, instead, Matt had headed to LAX and climbed onto a plane bound for New Orleans.

"Don't be too impressed, Mr. Paulson."

Matt blinked, forcing himself back to the present and the lovely set of boobs. "Come again?"

"The corset pushes everything up. They're not as big as the dress makes them look."

He quirked an eyebrow, amused by her admission. "Who said I was looking?"

Even the laugh that escaped held a hint of the South. "No one had to say anything, Mr. Paulson. I can see your eyes with my own."

Matt scrubbed a hand down his face. "Sorry. I haven't had much sleep in the past thirty-six hours and I got a little distracted. And I think you should call me Matt." A hint of a grin finally crept up his face. "I'm guessing the formalities aren't necessary once you get caught leering down a woman's dress. How much time do I have left?"

Her lips quirked as she reached in to her bodice "It's now seven forty-five. You have ten minutes left." She tipped her head curiously. "Don't you wear a watch?"

"I do," he said. "I just enjoy the sight of you pulling that watch out of your dress."

Her warm laugh encouraged him to settle more comfortably against the counter.

"So tell me about your *brother's* wedding fantasy," she said.

She turned and leaned her elbows back on the counter, and he wondered if she knew the position put her on even better display. From the focused look on her face, he'd say no. The woman had slipped fully into themed-wedding-planner mode. He forced his eyes away from the expanse of skin of her bared shoulders and the line between the curve of her breasts.

"Simple," Matt said. "His fantasy involves a video game."

Callie groaned. "That's why Colin sent you to me."

"Tommy and Penny want their wedding to be a *Dungeons of Zhorg* weekend set here in New Orleans," he said. "And since I volunteered to come and hire someone to organize the wedding, I wanted to check and make sure there wouldn't be any legal problems with the plan. So I hunted Colin down to clear up any copyright hassles."

"Which would only be a problem if you were selling tickets to the public. I assume this is a private party."

"More or less."

Her eyebrows drifted higher. "So which is it, more or less?"

Here was where things were about to get tricky.

Matt shifted on his feet, trying to get comfortable against the counter. "They want to combine their wedding with a LARP event for their fellow gaming friends. You know, a live-action—"

"Live-action role-playing. Yes, I know. I dated Colin long enough to be well versed in geek speak."

Matt felt his brow crinkle in surprise.

So Colin was her ex. When Matt had searched the creator of *Dungeons of Zhorg* out at Rainstorm Games and found him in his office late on a Friday afternoon, Matt's opinion of the geeked-out gamer had been complete. Fortunately, the man had no problem with Tommy and Penny's plans. In fact, Colin thought a newspaper article about the event would be good publicity for his game. Matt had told him he'd check with Tommy before agreeing, but figured his brother and the equally geeked-out fiancée would be thrilled. Matt could just see the headline now.

Ex-Drug Addicts Saved by Finding True Love Through the *Dungeons of Zhorg*.

Everyone would love the story. Hell, *Matt* loved the story.

He just wished he could believe the current state of affairs would last.

The familiar surge of unease filled his stomach like a concrete truck unloading its contents. Damn. If he'd learned anything over the years of Tommy's addiction, it was that taking care of today was the best Matt could do. Sometime it was *more* than Matt could do.

And often, his best just hadn't been good enough.

Matt pushed the thought aside and returned to the more interesting topic of Callie. "You and your ex must have remained pretty good friends if he's sending you my business."

Her eyes crinkled at the corners. "You'd have to pry the game controller from his cold, dead fingers before the man would admit the truth, but he owes me. I helped him track Jamie down after they first met. Now they're married." Callie let out a chuckle. "That and he wants to ensure the wedding gets done right. You know, with the proper attention to Zhorg detail." He heard, rather than saw, the roll of her eyes in her tone. "But a ceremony shouldn't be too hard to pull off."

"Actually, the entire weekend needs to be planned."

"Wait," she said, straightening up from the counter to face him. "I thought you just needed me for the wedding part. You want me to be in charge of the entire LARPing *event?*"

After several years of experience as the locums doctor in various E.R.s located in big cities across the country, Matt had learned how to handle addicts flying higher than a kite, as dangerous as a violent criminal.

Much like a cornered wild animal, the key was to never let 'em see you flinch.

He maintained her gaze and adopted his best soothing tone. "Yes. But the weekend doesn't need to be that elaborate. Throw up a few tents, offer a little food, and the guests bring their own costumes. And we can call it a day."

He knew he'd totally downplayed Tommy and Penny's vision for the weekend, but Matt thought they were dreaming too big anyway. He'd told them both pulling off exactly what they wanted would be impossible, short of crawling into the video game itself.

Her brow scrunched and several seconds ticked by.

"How much time do I have?" she asked.

"Two months."

"You're kidding, right?"

"I'm completely serious."

"Impossible. Sorry, Mr. Paulson, you'll have to find someone else." She reached out and took his wrist, pushing up his sleeve to peek at his watch. And then gave him a pretty smile. "Time's up."

Momentarily stunned, he watched her head toward the cake table.

Until he remembered his goal, and took off, following her through the crowd. "I love what you did with *The Wizard of Oz* wedding," he said, keeping stride with Callie. "And having the Mad Hatter as the wedding officiant in the *Alice in Wonderland* theme was inspired."

Did he sound as stupid as he felt?

"How did you learn about that?" she asked.

"Colin gave me one of your brochures. He said you're the best in the business."

Callie cast him an amused glance but kept on walking. "Are you trying to use flattery to change my mind?"

"You bet," he said. "Is it working?"

"Not yet, but feel free to keep trying."

"The Elizabethan venue was spectacular—" he dodged two Southern belle dresses and a Confederate soldier "—and *The Three Musketeers* theme was cool, as well."

She shot him a wry look. "Pirates," she said. "It was a pirates theme."

"Whatever," he said. "Who else is better qualified for a *Dungeons of Zhorg* themed wedding?"

Callie stared out across the crowd of guests milling about as they enjoyed appetizers. A furrow of concentration between her brows, she appeared to be running through the idea in her head. She chewed on her cheek before swiping her lower lip with her tongue. The sight of the now damp, full mouth was putting a whammy on his libido.

Huh, if he was this easily distracted, it was well past time he sought out some female companionship. To take the edge off, so to speak. Or maybe he simply needed sleep.

"Okay. It might be doable. Crazy, mind you. But doable," she drawled, and then looked around the current scene. "After all, crazy *is* my specialty."

Matt smiled his first real smile since Tommy had shared his engagement news and Matt couldn't decide if the marriage would make conditions better...or worse.

The potential for an epic screwup was great.

Callie sent him a wide smile back. The gesture wasn't sexual, but the genuine nature lit her eyes in a way that left them sparkling, sending another bolt of heat and awareness up his spine.

Too bad his flight out was Sunday. And there was no way he could delay the trip. He'd already gone two weeks without flying back home, to the childhood house Matt had moved back into, sharing the residence with Tommy since the very first round of rehab had failed, all those years ago.

He cleared his throat. "Fantastic," he said.

Mission accomplished. Problem addressed, solution found and past time to move on. Or, as the motto went in the E.R., treat 'em and street 'em. Everything was turning out better than he'd planned. He'd even get a full night's sleep tonight.

"Let me know how much to put down as a deposit.

I'll get you my email so you can send me the invoices as we go." He slipped his wallet from his pocket and pulled out his card, filling in the contacts. "And here are Tommy and my cell phone numbers too, just in case you have any questions—"

"Wait." Her brown eyes grew even wider as she took his card. "You're not leaving, are you?"

Concern edged up his back, making his shoulders feel stiff. "I have a hot date with the king-size bed in my hotel room—a rendezvous I'm really looking forward to. And Sunday I *have* to head back home."

Callie leaned closer, bringing that lovely view in a more direct line of vision. "Listen, Mr. Paulson."

How was he supposed to listen, much less concentrate, with a view like that? And clearly the stress of the upcoming event had knocked them back to a last-name basis instead of first.

"You're lucky I have a light enough schedule and an assistant to help me," Callie said. "But I can't do this alone. There are too many decisions that need to be made, and made quickly, too. I won't take responsibility for making the wrong ones. Someone needs to be around to help."

"Both me and my brother will be available by phone and internet."

"Not good enough. We can't afford to play phone tag. Not with so little time and so many big choices to be made."

"What choices?"

"Venue, for one. This won't be your average setting. We'll need a large outdoor park with adequate parking. Food, for another. A menu based on medieval times? Complicated. And from what I remember about LARP, there are games revolving around the video. And they'll need to be authentic."

"Tommy and Penny won't care about the details," he lied.

They would care. In fact, they'd care too much. That's what made a fan crazy enough to base their entire wedding around a video game. An obsession about even the minutest of details.

"I once had a client who said she didn't care. But she did," Callie said. "Despite the fact the bride and groom were thrilled with my work, the one paying the bills wasn't." She tipped her head. "Who's paying for all of this?"

"Me."

Something flashed in her eyes that he didn't recognize. Probably questions and comments and opinions about a wedding being paid for by the brother of the groom. Not your traditional arrangement. But then again, who else was there? No one.

And there hadn't been for a long time.

Callie, to her credit, didn't pry. "Then, officially, you'd be my boss. If you want me to agree to plan this event, you're going to have to at least stick around long enough to make a few of the major decisions."

"How long?"

"Depends on how our hunt for a venue goes. Can't say for sure. Maybe a week?"

Damn. That would mean he'd go almost a month without physically checking in on Tommy. The last time Matt had done that, he'd missed some early clues, and Tommy had wound up in rehab again.

But that was two years ago and he'd promised Tommy he'd take care of this.

Matt turned his options over in his head. As far as he could see, he didn't have any. He'd only just convinced the woman to take this project on. Refusing her now would be counterproductive. And finding someone else to participate in this harebrained idea would be absolutely impossible.

"All right," he said, raking a frustrated hand through his hair. "I'll give you until Tuesday and then we can reassess from there."

"Fine. But we need to get started right away, beginning with a meeting to list exactly what y'all want. I have to go out of town tomorrow, family stuff I have to take care of. But I'll put together a list of potential park sites and Sunday we can make the rounds to check them out. We can use the drive to put together our ideas for the wedding weekend."

Sticking around to help nail down the details for this crazy event? Not exactly what he'd had in mind when he'd climbed on the plane today. Matt could afford two more days in New Orleans before heading home. And Callie's brilliant smile helped ease the frustrating turn of events.

"Sunday morning it is," he said.

"Forecast calls for a heat wave the next few days or so." Callie's grin grew bigger. "Hope you like the weather hot, Mr. Paulson."

The playful grin brought about one of his own.

"Ms. LaBeau," Matt said, leaning close. "I like everything hot."

Matt entered his hotel room and toed off his shoes, unbuttoning his shirt as he headed toward the bathroom. Fatigue made his movement clumsy as he flicked open the front of his pants. After tossing his clothes aside, he flipped on the water and stepped inside the marble shower, groaning as hot water coursed over his hair and down his skin.

The ache in his muscles had started during the cramped four-hour flight, and now finally eased. Matt leaned his hand against the wall and bowed his head, letting the wet heat wash away the remainder of the stress of the past thirty-six hours.

It looked like his plans to get in and out of New Orleans quickly so he could check on Tommy had just bitten the dust. As a consolation, he now had a little more time to spend with Callie LaBeau. And the next time they saw each other, he will have had a full night's sleep.

As far as screwed-up plans went, this one could have been worse.

But the time had come to rethink his approach.

First up, place a call to Tommy. A phone check never gave as much information as a face-to-face interaction, but it beat no contact at all. Unfortunately, no one could assess weight loss and skin color over the phone. Of course, the first sign Tommy was slipping was the way he refused to look Matt in the eyes.

Second, the trip around town to locate an available park. Matt ignored the tightening in his groin as he considered a day in the car. With Callie. Alone. Awareness definitely hung in the air around them, though he sensed a hint of reluctance on her part. A reluctance that could have meant anything.

Because they were working together.

Because she had a boyfriend, though Matt doubted that to be the case.

Because she still carried a torch for Colin…

Matt soaped himself clean, picturing the golden skin and the honey-colored hair and big brown eyes. The little dip in her upper lip. The way she nibbled on the inside of her cheek while lost in thought. The pink tongue that licked the corner of her wide mouth.

He pictured that mouth on his skin. The teeth. The *tongue* traveling down his chest. Past his abdomen. The lips closing around his—

He slammed his eyes shut.

Fifteen minutes later, clean and refreshed and a whole lot more relaxed, Matt padded from the bathroom and into his bedroom. He dried his hair and wrapped the towel around his waist, heading to the window and pulling back the curtain. The lights of New Orleans spread out before him. As much as he dreaded the conversation, he picked up his cell phone and punched speed dial.

He hated the way his stomach tightened before every contact. After two years of a sober Tommy, Matt should have stopped bracing for the worst every time. Only problem was, Tommy had achieved sobriety before. Six times total. Every relapse had gotten harder than the one before. And had broken Matt's heart a little more.

"Hello?"

Despite everything, as always his brother's voice made Matt smile.

"Tommy. Fought any good dragons lately?"

The laugh on the other end sounded robust, easing a little of Matt's nerves.

"Dude, you should have seen the troll that Penny took down the other day," Tommy said.

"Big?"

"Massive."

"Hope her cooking isn't going to your waist. Your chain mail still fit?"

When Tommy's chuckle finally died down, he said, "That headhunter called again today."

The news formed a knot in Matt's chest and expanded, the pressure creating a wound that would never fully heal. The first time the recruiter from Jaris Hawking Healthcare had called about a job, Matt had been thrilled. At the time he'd been too busy cleaning up the last of his brother's latest mess to search for a job, but things with Tommy had seemed to be settled and Matt was ready to finally make the longed-for career move. Matt had spent hours researching the busy hospital in Miami, looking forward to the excitement he craved. But just when he'd been set to sign the papers, Tommy had relapsed again, requiring another round of rehab. And a family member to be there to ensure it happened. Matt had finally realized that he'd never be able to move.

Giving up that dream had hurt like hell, but there was no sense rehashing old disappointments.

Tommy went on, "They said they were desperate for someone with your talents."

"I hope you told him I'm still not interested." If he repeated the lie enough, he just might begin to believe it. Besides, he had more important things to ask. "How's work?" He aimed for a nonchalant tone, but he knew Tommy saw straight through the question.

"You don't need to check up on me, Matt." Tommy didn't sound annoyed, just resigned. "Work is fine. Penny is fine. *I'm* fine."

"You sure you two geeked-out lovebirds want to get

hitched during a lame-ass reenactment of a video game? Not too late to go for the Elvis wedding in Vegas. Or better yet, a pirate-themed adventure wedding in Hawaii. Think of it. A week's vacation in Maui with all expenses paid by yours truly. What better wedding gift could a brother ask for, huh? I could do with a base tan myself."

"The wedding absolutely has to be in New Orleans. We want trolls. And dragons. And Matt...?"

Matt dropped onto the bed, leaning back against the headboard and propping up his feet. "Yeah, sport?"

"I'll pay you back."

Matt's lips twisted wryly as affection kicked him the chest. Every goddamned time. The kid had spent the past twenty-five years worming his way into Matt's heart, until Tommy was so firmly entrenched, there was nothing Matt could do. He could picture his brother's wavy brown hair, earnest face and appreciative gaze. Beneath those ribs beat a heart of gold.

Amazing what havoc an addiction could inflict.

"You bet you'll pay me back," Matt said with a teasing tone. "With twenty percent interest. Wait, I forgot about inflation. Make that thirty percent. Didn't I tell you? You're my retirement fund."

"Which means you're screwed, bro."

Matt let out a scoff. "Better odds than on Wall Street."

Tommy laughed. When his brother finally grew silent, Matt went on.

"Seriously, though?" Matt said. "Don't worry about the money. That's what brothers are for. Just..."

Keep it together.
Stay clean.
Don't break my heart again.

"Just make sure that future wife of yours doesn't kick your ass on level ten like last month or I'll have to disown you," Matt said.

Matt could hear the smile in Tommy's voice. "You got it."

Chapter Two

Two days later Callie studied Matt as he drove her Toyota out of New Orleans. It had been a long time since Callie had been so curious about a guy. Matt was friendly, charming, and sexy enough to eat with her fingers. There'd been no sign of embarrassment at being caught staring at her cleavage.

Even now the memory left her body vibrating with energy.

But a lingering hint of hesitation clung to him, a reserve that was fascinating. Intriguing. He'd shown up at the reception two nights ago with *goal* written all over his face.

They'd been traveling for about an hour now, but hadn't had a chance to talk much about business. Callie had been too busy directing him around town to potential parks to use as the site for the *Dungeons of Zhorg* weekend. The first two were mostly a bust. But she had high hopes for the one they were heading to now.

She'd asked Matt to drive, explaining she needed to take notes while they discussed the plans for the event, listing out the pros and cons of the two sites they'd just checked out. But the excuse sounded lame, even to her. Especially considering she spent half her time giving Matt directions. But she didn't care. Because with his attention on the traffic, and her vantage point from the passenger seat, she was free to enjoy the view.

And she wasn't talking about the city she loved.

Matt's lean, muscular frame filled the driver's seat of her car. Given the heat wave that had settled in yesterday, he'd wisely chosen to wear shorts. Shorts that allowed a view of hard thighs. Muscular calves.

He'd had to push the seat all the way back to allow room for his long legs. His olive-colored T-shirt clung to a broad set of shoulders and biceps that flexed with every turn of the steering wheel. Not grossly big. More like well-defined and…just right. Enticing. Callie preferred the casual clothes to Friday night's slacks and button-down. Because today he looked more relaxed. He also looked as though he'd gotten some sleep.

A large truck ahead of them whipped into their lane, and Matt reacted instantly to avoid the hit. No cursing. No frazzled look. Not even an indrawn breath or a frown for the dangerous driver.

Just like Friday night, when he'd shown up so focused, he employed a plan-and-attack mantra while driving. *Goal* written all over his face. Focused. Decisive. He never hesitated. And he had lightning-fast reflexes, if the maneuver he just pulled was anything to go by. They turned into the parking lot of their next potential venue, a grassy park on the outskirts of town.

Matt turned off the car and glanced at Callie, and she realized he'd just caught her studying him. Very closely. And thoroughly.

"Is this the equivalent of me staring down your cleavage?" he asked.

She ignored the heat thrumming through her veins and exited the car, missing the air-conditioning already and waiting for him to follow suit to respond. "Just admiring your quick reflexes."

From across the roof of her Toyota, his lips quirked. "So you were checking out my…skills."

She bit back a smile. "We have a lot of planning to do, Mr. Paulson."

"Matt."

"Matt," she said without missing a beat. "I'm just trying to figure you out. And decide whether you're gonna be the guy who makes my job easier or harder."

Normally she meant the words in the sense of a client being difficult. Hard to please. And far too demanding in their wedding-day wishes. Or incapable of making up their mind.

With Matt she knew the decisions would come quickly and decisively. Yep, with Matt the easier or harder delineation was based on Callie's ability, or inability, to stay focused with such a fine specimen of male anatomy on display.

"What have you decided?" he asked.

"I'm not sure yet," she said with a tiny grin. "I'll let you know when I figure it out."

After a few beats filled with a scorching temperature courtesy of New Orleans's latest heat wave and Matt's assessing gaze, he gave a sharp nod and headed up the brick walkway.

Fortunately the path was lined with oaks providing shade from the relentless sun. The playground to their left hummed with the activity of a few families crazy enough to brave the temperatures. An ice-cream truck was parked along the curb. The beautifully maintained park was clearly well run, the amenities nice. Even the current weather had been addressed. Misting machines with large fans had been set up along the path in front, providing blessed relief from the heat.

A drop of sweat trickled between her breasts and she ignored the long, lean legs of Matt as he walked beside her. The view wasn't helping her struggles with heat stroke.

"So there's a large private area of the park that is available for rent on the dates we need," she said. "This place is a little farther out of town than I wanted, but there's ample parking." She could feel his eyes on her, but she kept her focus forward as she came to a stop at the field.

She pointed at the outdoor building sitting in the middle of the field. "The pavilion can be used as the main structure and where the food will be served. We're going to want the restrooms close by, even if it does ruin the medieval feel."

"Better to ruin the Middle Ages feel than contract cholera."

Callie smiled but continued on, "There's more than enough space to set up the tents and the sites for the various games." She studied the grassy field, a natural border provided by oak trees. "We can set up the gaming tent over here."

He shot her another appreciative glance, and this time she couldn't resist.

"What?" she said.

"You've already given this a lot of thought."

"We don't have much time."

Matt leaned back against the oak. "Why did you agree to arrange this event?"

"It's my job. This is what I do."

He hesitated and crossed his arms as if settling in to

wait for a better reason. Callie longed for a cool breeze, or heck, just a breeze would do. Anything to lower the temperature brought about by the Southern climate and Matt's disturbing eyes.

"Because I owe Colin," she said. "Our breakup was… complicated."

Translation: I screwed up big-time.

"But we've managed to remain friends," she went on. "And he's a regular contributor to my blog, *The Ex Factor*."

At his look of confusion, a grin slid up her face. "It's a he-said, she-said column where readers can pose questions and we offer opinions from our unique perspectives."

"Is that the only reason you agreed to take this on? Because your ex helps you out?"

"Isn't that enough?"

He squinted across the field. "I'm sure you have better ways to spend your time than arranging a weekend LARP event."

Was he speaking for her or for himself?

Callie nibbled on her lower lip and looked across the field. How to explain? Because if her business became successful enough, everyone would forget about her mistake in college? Because maybe, just maybe, if she landed a big enough event with the proper publicity, her parents would stop waiting for her to muck up again?

She liked her life, damn it. And while she hadn't left for college with the plan of losing her scholarship and getting kicked out, she was delighted with what she'd built. She was happy, *proud* of all she'd accomplished despite her initial flub.

Now if she could only convince her family to be proud, too....

She pushed the thought away and shrugged. "Every little bit of publicity is good for business."

Matt studied her with those observant brown eyes that always set her on edge, mostly in a good way. Making her aware of what she wore. Making her aware of what she said. Normally she focused on business or was totally relaxed. Then again, her clients usually consisted of happy couples or middle-aged parents. Dreamy *eligible* men didn't knock on her doors wanting her services. And it was a little disturbing to be second-guessing every little thing as she went.

And if he thought her answer to his question was bull, he didn't say.

When she couldn't take those eyes studying her anymore, she turned her attention back to the field before them. "It's more than we need, but I think this works perfectly. You agree?"

"You're the expert."

"I'm sure I'll have to remind you of that sometime in the future." She lifted her hair from her neck, longing for a cool breeze. "Let's head back before you're treating me for heat stroke."

The walk back toward the car was even more uncomfortable, the sun now higher in the sky. Matt's silence and his occasional glances left her thinking he planned to quiz her further. And with the hot temperature, and the hotter gaze—not to mention the zillion questions she saw in his eyes—didn't make for a comfortable walk. Perhaps she should do a little quizzing of her own.

"So, tell me why you got elected to travel to New Orleans to arrange a wedding," she said.

His lips twisted wryly, but he didn't answer right away, so she went on.

"Over the years, I've worked with mothers, fathers, sisters and friends of the bride," she said. "But I've never worked with the brother of the groom before."

An amused light appeared in his eyes. "It's an honor to be your first."

She kept her gaze on his profile as they headed up the walk, the sound of the misting fans droning ahead. "Which doesn't answer my question."

"I told you, Tommy and Penny are up in Michigan. They both have jobs they can't afford to lose. And I happen to have the time."

"Where are your parents?"

"Dead."

A pang of sympathy hit, and she studied his expression, looking for clues to his thoughts. There weren't any.

"I'm sorry," she said. "How old were you?"

"Twenty-one. The year Tommy turned sixteen."

Leaving you in charge, she didn't say. Raising a teenager when Matt was barely past the stage himself had to have been a massive struggle.

Turning the news over in her head, Callie headed for one of the few massive fans that didn't have kids hopping up and down in front of it. A large oak provided shade and when she stepped closer to the machine, the cool mist hit her skin, and Callie almost groaned in relief. A fine spray of water coated her face, her neck, and her T-shirt and shorts. But she didn't care.

With the way Matt looked at her, a hosing off wouldn't be out of order.

"Where are Penny's parents?" she asked.

"They disowned her four years ago."

Disowned? Her eyebrows shot higher, but Callie held her tongue, despite the curiosity. What kind of parent abandoned their kid?

When she didn't respond, the buzz of the huge fan filled the air, and Matt shot her a look. "She's a recovering drug addict."

No wonder. The news explained the edge she sensed churning just beneath the surface of one Mr. Matt Paulson.

"That must be hard on your brother," she said.

Matt turned and faced the fan, closing his eyes and letting the mist hit his face. "He's a recovering addict, too."

She lingered on his profile as the words and everything he *hadn't* said settled deep. So much tension. So much emotion. She couldn't read the thoughts in his expression but they were present in the taut shoulders, the flat line of his mouth. His short, sandy hair grew damp and curled at the edges, just above his ears. His bangs, thicker than the rest of his hair, developed a wave as water accumulated. The drops left a sheen to his skin, his throat and those lovely, lovely arms.

Matt definitely had the sexy shtick down pat. A wet Matt? Even more so.

"Sad that Penny's parents won't forgive her," she said.

"They have their reasons." Matt didn't open his eyes, just continued to enjoy the cooling mist. Or pretended, anyway. "She put them through a lot. Lying. Stealing. Disappearing for weeks on end until they weren't sure if she was alive or dead from an overdose. I'm sure they just couldn't take it anymore. They're just trying to protect themselves."

Had Matt tried to protect himself?

"But still…" she said. She knew what it was like to screw up. Not in as grand a fashion as a drug addiction. Her screwup was tiny in comparison. But she knew how it felt to work hard to overcome your mistakes, only to have nobody let you forget.

"Now she's clean," she said.

"She's been clean before."

Callie let out a scoff. "'My good opinion once lost is lost forever.'"

He opened his eyes, and that brown gaze landed on hers, sending a self-conscious flush up her face. She could read the question and surprise in his expression. She hadn't meant to wear her own struggles quite so clearly, or to sound quite so personally invested.

She shrugged, trying to ease her discomfort. "Just a quote from Mr. Darcy, from *Pride and Prejudice*." When he didn't comment, she went on, "My favorite book."

On her thirteenth birthday her mother had taken her to the library and she'd checked out the paperback. She'd spent the next two days glued to the book, her mother practically dragging her from her room to come eat dinner. Growing up poor meant Callie could relate to the Bennet sisters. She'd admired Lizzy's courage and her determination to marry for love only, despite the very real risk of poverty, causing Callie's transformation from a total tomboy into a romantic. The book had had such an impact, she'd spent the weeks after imaging Lizzy and Darcy's wedding, and she'd developed a passion for bridal magazines and picturing the perfect ceremony.

Starting Fantasy Weddings had been a natural extension of that passion.

"I've never read *Pride and Prejudice*," Matt said.

"I'm not surprised."

A lull in the conversation followed, and she wanted to ask about Matt's experiences with his brother, to learn the details about the current state of the relationship between the two. However, Callie sensed asking anything more would go over like a hot toddy during a heat wave.

"How did Tommy and Penny meet?" she asked.

"As total geekster gamers and pros at your ex's zombie apocalypse game, they were selected as beta testers for *Dungeons of Zhorg*. That was how they met online. And then they discovered they'd fought the same addiction, and eventually fell in love. I think—" He pursed his lips. "I think the game helped keep them from slipping. Gave them something to focus on."

Which would explain Matt's willingness to take on this crazy task.

"I have to admit," she said softly, "I'm a sucker for a romantic story." And this one really struck a chord. Two people who'd lost themselves in a dark world and managed to pull out with the help of each other and a video game. Slaying dragons online as they fought their personal demons.

Callie smiled at the ridiculously fanciful thought. But no wonder Colin agreed to the weekend wedding/festival named after his latest game.

When Matt didn't comment, Callie went on, "Who's going to give Penny away?"

"She asked me, but I told her to get one of her *Dungeon of Zhorg* buddies. I can't do it because I'm Tommy's best man."

She let out an amused huff. "It's not like this is a traditional wedding. No reason why you can't be both."

"I'm not her family."

"You will be."

Two seconds ticked by before he hiked a brow. Mist had accumulated on his neck and trickled down to gather in the hollow at his throat. She had the sudden urge to lick the spot, and heat shot up her limbs and settled between her legs.

Shoot. Admiring the man was one thing. Wanting to treat him like her favorite brand of ice-cream cone was another.

And while he looked slightly put out by her pushing, the light in his eyes held a hint of amusement. "Does the family counseling come with the cost of your services or will that be extra?"

Callie grinned. "Just the cost of a trip to the ice-cream truck."

If she couldn't lick the real thing, she could at least enjoy the substitute. The lopsided smile he sent her did nothing to quell her appreciation of his form.

"So I'm buying?" he asked.

"You're buying."

In the end Callie chose a lemon-lime Popsicle, while Matt went with his favorite, chocolate. Cooler now that they were damp from head to toe, they wandered beneath the oaks back to Callie's car, in no particular hurry. Not only because of the relief they'd accomplished the most pressing task, selecting a site for the

DoZ weekend. But also because Matt felt no sense of urgency to leave.

Especially when Callie looked as if she'd just entered a wet T-shirt contest. It had been a while since his college buddies had dragged him to such an event during his relatively carefree undergraduate days. At the time he'd thought the rigors of academics and obtaining the grades for medical school had been stressful.

But then his parents had died, leaving him solely responsible for Tommy.

And the sight of Callie's lovely chest beneath the wet garments did more than just bring back great memories of happier times, it also turned him the hell on.

Not exactly conducive to his get-in and get-out goals.

Her damp shirt clung to her skin, and he could make out the lace of the bra beneath. White, if he wasn't mistaken. And if he tried hard enough, he could imagine the darker circle of skin beneath the center of each breast. He could definitely make out the rounder buds.

"I told you they weren't as big as the slutty Scarlett O'Hara dress suggested."

Busted.

The relaxed look on her face eased the tension in his shoulders. Though she certainly had good reason, she didn't appear overly annoyed by his tendency to check out her form. In fact, she seemed more…amused. As though he was just a stupid kid who couldn't help himself.

Which wasn't too far from the truth, aside from the *kid* part. The *stupid* description fit just fine.

"I promise," he said. "I'm not a total pervert."

"Does that mean you're a partial one?"

He threw back his head and laughed. When the

amusement finally passed, he shot her a grin. "I guess it's up to you to let me know."

They reached her car and Matt opened the door for her before rounding and climbing into the driver's seat.

He closed the door and faced Callie, who was still licking the Popsicle.

Why hadn't he noticed how hot the image was until now? The tip of her tongue catching the drips. The way she nibbled at the side. How much the vision reminded him of his fantasies during the jerk-off session in the shower that first night. Probably because he'd been too distracted by the sight of her breasts beneath that wet shirt.

Maybe he really was a perv.

He gripped the steering wheel. "Where to now?"

"Home," she said.

A completely inappropriate surge of adrenaline shot through his body, only to be doused by her next statement.

"I have some things I need to do today for another event coming up in two weeks," she said. "And I really want to take a shower and wash off all of this sweat. Where do you want to meet tonight to discuss the rest of our plans?"

She twisted in the seat to face him, one long *bare* calf curling beneath her. The tanned leg looked smooth and he wondered if the skin was as silky as it looked. Heat gathered at the nape of his neck, and the relentless sun through the window lit Callie's form, making ignoring her impossible.

He cleared his throat. "Preferably somewhere cool."

Her eyes lit, and that wide grin returned to her pretty face. "I have just the place."

Chapter Three

Christ, this wasn't really what he'd had in mind.

The chill seemed to hang in the air of The Frozen South, an ice bar taking up the top floor of The River's Edge Resort and Casino overlooking downtown New Orleans. The crowd fairly thick, the noise seemed even thicker. Most likely everyone else had the same idea: escape the heat wave outside. And the establishment was the perfect choice.

Ice blocks holding tiny neon lights made up the bar. Ice sofas, ice chairs and ice sculptures were the mainstay of the furniture and the décor. Fortunately, fur rugs lined the seats. Good thing, too. Anyone bold enough to drink too much in this environment might forget to protect their skin and wind up stuck to their chair. Some of the patrons chose to have their drinks served in ice cups. And because the management clearly had a sense of humor, costumers could even keep their cups. Of course, with the hot weather still chugging along outside with a relative heat index nearing one hundred degrees, by the time the club goer arrived home all they'd have is a wet hand that smelled of vodka.

But Matt's beef with the choice wasn't the crowd. Nor was it the cool temperature, a relief after the blistering day outside. Callie's frozen margarita looked inviting and his beer was the perfect temperature.

No, Matt hated the need for Callie to be covered in so many clothes.

Matt had sprung for the best cover package, which included a parka best suited for exploring the Arctic and a hat that framed her face, limiting his view of the honey hair he enjoyed. The only thing he had going for him was that she hadn't zipped the jacket closed.

He leaned in to speak at her ear. "You sure you don't want to go somewhere quieter?"

She turned to look at him. A maneuver that brought them face-to-face, her lips close to his.

Huh. The impulse to lean in and kiss Callie smacked him across the face like a pheromone-soaked glove, but he squelched the urge. How the hell could he plan this crazy wedding and get home to check up on Tommy if he was constantly looking at Callie, wondering what she'd taste like? With that honey hair and that honey accent, would her mouth have the same flavor?

A stupid, fanciful thought that was getting him nowhere closer to his goals.

He cleared his throat. "We might accomplish more without the noise."

Two beats passed, but Matt couldn't read the look in Callie's eyes.

"It feels good in here," she said. "Besides, the view is awesome."

Matt mentally shook his head and forced his gaze out the large window.

True, the lights of downtown New Orleans at night were definitely awesome. Unfortunately, he hadn't traveled to New Orleans to enjoy the view. But Callie in a blouse, wearing a sweater zipped up to her throat, paled in comparison to her breasts on display in a slutty Scarlett O'Hara dress. Or a wet T-shirt.

Though the gently curved hips and the shapely butt in formfitting jeans almost made up for the lack of cleavage.

Almost.

"So…" Callie stared down at her notebook, obviously completely unaware of the distracting thoughts mucking up Matt's concentration. "The games we've got listed so far are an ax-throwing competition, an archery competition and sword fighting. Though having all three feels redundant. Today I made a few calls and found a magician available those two days."

Magicians. Great. But Matt was too caught up by the play of beautiful lips and teeth and tongue as Callie spoke to pay much attention.

"A local group can provide something resembling strolling minstrels," Callie went on. "Though they won't be quite as authentic as we'd like. I checked with the park this afternoon, and horses are allowed. Which is good because apparently Penny would love to have jousters, so I contacted a branch of the Society for Creative Anachronism and—"

"Wait. *What?*"

Matt's mind stuck, spinning on all the information. Though only one piece of news stuck out.

Callie set her list down and looked at him. "The society is a living history group that's devoted to re-creating the Middle Ages. There's a branch just outside of—"

"No." Matt shook his head. "You spoke to Penny?"

For some reason the news felt odd. Strange.

She tipped her head curiously. "You gave me the

contact numbers, remember? So I called and spoke to both Tommy and Penny today." She hiked an eyebrow. "After all, I *am* arranging their wedding."

Matt couldn't speak, and Callie went on.

"Anyway, Tommy is gathering volunteers among their DoZ friends attending to run the sign-up for the competitions and then the competitions themselves during the event. And Penny is going to coordinate any of the Society of Anachronism volunteers who can attend on such short notice."

"Damn." Matt plowed a hand through his hair. "This thing is growing out of control."

At this rate he'd never get back home to check on Tommy. Matt's stomach tensed. It had been *how* many days since he'd last laid eyes on Tommy?

Regardless, if the explosion of the wedding weekend kept up, Matt would be stuck in New Orleans figuring out how to clean up horse dung from a park and how to find swords and— *Jesus,* why did Callie have to smell so good?

"I suppose now wouldn't be the time to tell you about the dragon Colin is donating to the cause?"

Matt rubbed his forehead. "Dragon?"

Callie's lips twisted wryly. "Not a real one, of course. One they used at the launch party of *Dungeons of Zhorg.*" She eyed him closely, like he looked as if his head bordered on exploding.

Matt wasn't sure but it might have been true.

"At least all of Tommy and Penny's guests are DoZ friends who are bringing their own costumes. Looks like you and I are the only ones who need to rent something."

Matt blinked, biting back the urge to call the whole damn thing off. "I am not dressing up as a troll."

Callie laughed. "I pictured you dressed more as a crusader. You know, chain mail and the whole nine yards. Anyway, because of Mardi Gras, New Orleans has great costume shops. I have several we can visit tomorrow."

Chain mail?

A crusader?

Christ, he'd almost rather go as a troll. The only thing he had left to hope for was finding Callie a slutty medieval gown.

"How does the dress fit?" Matt called through the dressing-room door.

"Give me a minute. I have to find my way inside the stupid thing before I can tell you. If you don't hear from me in ten minutes, send help." Callie stared down at the mound of fabric big enough to hide a nest of baby gators and their mama in. "Make that fifteen."

In truth, she needed a few minutes alone to recover.

Last night's graphic dream involving Matt made looking him in the eye this morning pretty gosh darn difficult. Colin's plans for publicity were growing and, as the publicity plan grew, so did the importance of this event. Now there was the potential of the story getting picked up by a local channel, so she did *not* need to be getting sidetracked by the killer hot looks of the brother of the groom. Still, looking hardly hurt anything…

Until the looking did indecent things to her dreams.

Callie pushed the thought aside and searched for the bottom of the dress. Actually, the outfit consisted of two pieces, the first part white satinlike material with a beautiful gold brocade pattern on the skirt. The second part was an overdress of robin's-egg-blue with a solid gold band at the bodice and split in front, forming an inverted V to showcase the design of the skirt beneath.

She slipped the first part over her head, wondering how Matt was faring with the costume-shop owner, an eccentric elderly man Callie had instantly adored.

Callie hadn't had an occasion to use this establishment before, but the moment she entered she'd known she'd found a gem of a resource. Not only did the owner carry a wide variety of quality costumes, he had a serious collection of props. And the stuff wasn't cheap and flimsy, either, but high-quality.

The huge crucifix on the shelf would be perfect for the *Interview with the Vampire* wedding she was organizing. Callie longed to come back and comb through the assortment of odds and ends, though the process would take some time. The owner was sweet, eccentric and carried a wide assortment of interesting items. Unfortunately, his organizational skills sucked. Searching through the racks and racks of costumes would have been easier if the shop was organized better. But their high-quality costumes made up for the inconvenience.

Matt probably would argue no.

A sharp knock on the door pulled her out of her thoughts. "Need help?"

She bit her lip and stared in the mirror. Handling the complicated fastening system in the back would be impossible on her own. Then again, having Matt in here, alone with her. Her back so exposed…

Say no. Tell him to go away.

"Sure," she said instead, opening the door.

In a medieval costume that would do a knight proud,

Matt stepped inside. And there wasn't a woman alive that wouldn't have been satisfied by the way his gaze landed on her figure and his eyebrows shot higher.

He let out a low whistle. "That gown is something. You look gorgeous."

A flush of heat left her feeling stupid.

Come on, Callie. Get your act together.

"Thank you," she said. "You, uh, look good, too."

Matt's pants looked appropriately made of unrefined material. Over the crudely cut, long-sleeved shirt, he wore a chain-mail shirt. A huge sword hung on the scabbard at his waist.

Matt let out a scoff. "Maybe, but this stuff is heavy."

"Most authentic costumes in New Orleans."

"I think I'd rather go with the cheap stuff that doesn't weigh a thousand pounds." He rolled those broad shoulders. "Man, how did men fight in this getup anyway?"

"I have no idea. But at least you don't have to wear a dress that pinches your waist to nothing and flattens your boobs," she said dryly.

Matt was clearly biting back a grin. "I definitely prefer the slutty Scarlett O'Hara over the prim and proper medieval princess. Allow me?" He nodded down at the laces hanging open in the back.

She hesitated a second. Was that amusement flickering through his eyes? Gritting her teeth with determination, she then turned to face the mirror. Matt stepped closer, bringing a scent of spicy soap. When she briefly met his gaze in the reflection, a shock of awareness jolted her limbs and burned her belly.

The intimacy of the room, the muted lighting and the strange costumes made the whole situation surreal and, God save her from her overactive imagination, a little romantic.

Given this was Matt in chain mail with a sword at his side, a whole lot of sexy was on display, as well. Her heart did a crazy twist when Matt reached for the laces at her back.

Crap, don't picture him undoing the dress. Just… don't.

Dying to cover her nerves, she eyed him speculatively in the mirror. "Does this make you my lady-in-waiting?"

One side of his mouth curled up in amusement. "No," he said. "And before you get any other crazy ideas in your head, I'm nobody's knight in shining armor, either."

Matt's fingers whispered against her as he fixed the corset-inspired lace-up fastening in the back. Careful not to move, Callie concentrated on the warm brushes of skin on skin that sent currents of electric heat skittering up her spine. As touches went, this one bordered on being an incredible tease.

His gaze on the task at hand, lips set as if in concentration, Matt said, "You sure are going all out on this. I mean—" his eyes crashed into hers "—Tommy's *my* brother."

Callie blinked and mentally shoved her libido in a box. The most truthful explanation wouldn't go over so well, for sure.

Especially with Matt.

She held his gaze in the mirror. "They deserve the wedding of their dreams."

She'd never meant the words more, but she also knew reciting the slogan from her website didn't cover everything she'd poured into this event so far. And everything left yet to do. After talking with Tommy and Penny yesterday afternoon—they'd both sounded so sweet and sincere on the phone—Callie's heart had melted more.

In a way, her screwup had torn her and Colin apart. Years later, and she was *still* alone. Tommy's and Penny's screwups had led them to one another and now they were getting married. Their heartwarming story was one of the most inspiring Callie had ever heard. And she'd heard some doozies, stories of lost loves reunited and second chances and those who'd survived devastating illnesses to go and achieve their happily-ever-after.

But Tommy and Penny's tale of overcoming the effects of the bad choices they'd made struck a chord in Callie. After talking to the two, Callie's ideas for the weekend had exploded. So now there was more work than originally planned. Not that she feared hard work. In fact, she'd grown quite used to it.

But Matt clearly couldn't figure out why she'd brought more work on herself.

"I guess because I know what it's like to mess up your life," Callie said. "In college, I made some seriously stupid decisions."

The fingers on her back grew still, and Matt's eyes met hers in the mirror again. His gaze didn't budge as he remained silent, most likely waiting for her to go on. Callie's throat suddenly felt twice baked and lacking in all moisture.

"I let a lot of people down," she said. "Including my parents. And Colin."

"Tell me."

With those words, her immediate thought was *no* because the story was too personal, cut too close to the bone. But maybe if she shared the ugly truth about her past this would help Matt. She'd sensed there was tension between him and his brother. Maybe he'd find a way to move on, as well. The idea of her story helping others was kind of appealing.

Time to put your big-girl panties on, Callie.

Matt's focus dropped back to her dress and he resumed his task. Maybe he sensed that telling the story would be easier without his eyes studying her so closely. Despite his focus being elsewhere, she could tell by the tension in his shoulders and the set of his mouth that Matt's attention was solely on her.

She cleared her throat to loosen the muscles. "I grew up poor, in a little town north of here. My parents sacrificed a lot to move us to the city so I could go to a better high school. They wanted me to attend a university and be the first LaBeau to get a college degree."

"Did you have trouble in high school?"

"Nope. I did well," she said. "Straight-A student. I wound up with several acceptances to excellent schools. My parents wanted me to accept the scholarship at a smaller college closer to home, but I…"

Callie stared at her reflection in the mirror. She'd been so dumb, thinking her ability to adjust to a new high school translated into an easy adjustment to a new town and a large university.

"I wanted to get out and see the world," she said. "I mean, high school seemed fairly easy. How hard could an out-of-state larger university be? So I accepted the Wimbly Southern deal."

His gaze ticked back to hers in the mirror. "Scholarship?"

"A full ride," she said with a nod. "Tuition. Room and

board. Books. The works. Even some spending money so I didn't have to get a job. I only had to concentrate on my studies. For a girl with parents who could barely afford the rent, it was a big deal."

He cocked his head, the fingers at her back now motionless. "Let me guess. You flunked out and lost the scholarship."

Callie hesitated. She could say yes and let that be the end. His short sentence summed up the events accurately. But she knew leaving out the most important bits would be taking the coward's way out, and certainly wouldn't explain about her commitment to Matt's brother and his fiancée—a couple she'd only spoken to once on the phone.

"Yes, but there's a little more to the story," she said.

"How much more?"

"My grades slipped because I fell in with the wrong crowd. I was lonely, and the party kids were the only ones who would have anything to do with me."

In hindsight, she realized how lucky she'd been in high school. Moving just before the tenth grade should have meant she'd been the odd one out, friendless and alone. Instead, things had come together easily. She'd had plenty of friends and was well liked by her classmates. Some of that might have had to do with her dating Colin, his popularity rubbing off on her. Either way, things had fallen into place and she'd never missed a beat.

College, on the other hand, had been a disaster.

Callie cleared her throat. "But the party crowd comes with certain expectations, and I went out too much." She rolled her eyes. "That alone would have been enough for the Moron of the Year Award, but one night I went to a party at a house."

Matt's going to hate what comes next.

She gripped the skirt of her dress, wishing the silken folds could sooth her nerves, and she gathered her courage before she went on. "The police raided the place because the man was a drug dealer."

Matt sucked in a breath and his lips went white, and she knew the news had hit him viscerally. He looked as if he'd received a solid punch to the solar plexus. She whirled around to face him, laying a hand on his arm. Her heart pumped hard in her chest.

The rest tumbled out of her mouth. "I didn't know who he was or what he did to make money, Matt." She stared up at him, emphasizing every word and trying hard to convince him of the truth with her gaze. "He was a friend of a friend of a friend. It sounds like a stupid cliché, I know, but I honestly had no idea who the man was. But—"

She bit her cheek and held her tongue, staring at Matt. Callie shoved her hair back from her face, disturbed by the slight tremor in her fingers.

"We all got taken down to the station and…and they found marijuana in my purse."

"Jesus, Callie."

And then Matt just seemed to stop breathing, as if this final piece of the sordid story was just one insult too many. There was no way out but the truth. And the faster she got this over with, the sooner her heart would start beating again.

Callie drew in a shaky breath and pushed on. "I know. I *know.* I was stupid and depressed and I just wanted something to make it all go away. It was the only time, I swear."

The stupid move would follow her around the rest of her life. She briefly pressed her eyes closed. The shock of her arrest had been difficult enough for her, but it had been horrible for her parents. Years of being the perfect kid, the perfect student, had made her fall from grace all that much more painful. Especially given their car had been plastered with so many Student of the Week bumper stickers the chrome on the bumper had all but disappeared.

"I called my parents, who couldn't come to help me out, so they sent Colin." She winced at the memories of the complete and utter humiliation when Colin had strode into the police headquarters, clearly furious. "He drove up to Wimbly, even though I didn't ask him to," she said, realizing she was rambling again. "And then, of course, things between the two of us started to fall apart and I—"

The look on Matt's face gave no indication as to what he was thinking. The knot in her stomach tangled a little tighter, so she hurried on, beyond ready to push on to the next subject.

"I just think, after everything they've been through, Penny and Tommy deserve the wedding of the century," she said.

The tension in his body had eased a bit, and he leaned back against the wall, arms folded across the chain mail on his chest. For one bizarre moment, she realized she missed his hands on her skin. Callie smoothed her hand down the satiny skirt of the underdress.

"And if I can help Colin out with a fantastic publicity opportunity *and* prove to my parents my business is a success, all at the same time, so much the better."

Parked against the wall, Matt continued to study her.

She still couldn't tell what he was thinking. That she was an idiot? That she deserved to return to New Orleans, the stink of shame following on her heels? True.

But jeez, the whole mess had taken place ten years ago.

"Aren't you going to say anything?" she asked.

There was a two beat pause before he answered. "You're right." She held her breath as he went on. "The dress does flatten your breasts too much."

A bark of surprised laughter escaped Callie, one part humor and a hundred parts absolute relief. "Oh, my God, you really *are* a perv."

He smiled, crinkles appearing around his eyes, the tension of the moment finally broken. "Are we done with the confession now?"

Callie released her death grip on her skirt, muscles finally relaxing.

"Beyond done," she said.

"Good. Now could you please help me get this son of a bitch off?" He pulled at the chain-mail shirt a bit, letting it drop back to his chest with a *ching*. "I'm about to die of heat stroke here. And no way in hell do I want to pass out and be carted off to the nearest emergency room in this getup."

"Sure, turn around."

She spent a minute wrestling with the clasp at the nape of his neck, her fingers fumbling a bit as she tried to ignore the soft tickle of hair against her fingers. Against her will, awareness washed over her again, and her gaze slid past his broad shoulders down to his trim waist and lean hips. The body looked solid and rugged and was impossible to ignore, especially in the kind of getup that hinted at strong heroes, epic battles and undying devotion to a lady.

Ridiculous, Callie. You're absolutely ridiculous.

"Now face me and lean in," she said.

Matt turned and bent forward at the waist, and Callie pulled the hem up his trunk and over his head. The chain mail was heavier than it looked, pulling the shirt beneath along, as well. The whole ensemble dropped to the floor with a *clank* and Matt straightened up.

Holy hell. What had she done?

Now she had to hold herself together in the presence of a shirtless Matt with sexily mussed hair. While her heart thudded, Callie tried to drag her gaze from Matt's chest, but failed. The well-honed muscles had a dusting of hair that tapered at his waist, passing over the flat abdomen and disappearing beneath his pants.

A small smirk quirked his lips. "Are you checking out my cleavage?"

Several seconds passed before her brain could arrange the words in the right order. "You don't have man boobs."

"Good thing, too."

Time seemed to grind to a halt as they both studied each other. And then Matt stepped closer, with *goal* written all over his face, and the tension returned, ten times worse than before. But this time the air was filled with a sexual charge. Electric currents prickled just beneath her skin and spread, producing goose bumps as they went.

And her briefly returned ability to speak fled even faster than before.

"Only problem I see with this scenario?" He grabbed a fistful of fabric just beneath her fitted waist and slowly drew her closer, her pulse picking up speed with every step. "You are way overdressed."

Callie tried to protest. "The owner is—"

"Currently engrossed in a conversation with a customer about the history of Mardi Gras."

She blinked, trying to process all the input threatening to blow a fuse in her brain. Too many sparking impulses firing at once. Just the bare torso alone was enough to shove her senses into complete meltdown. But toss in the sight of all that lovely, lovely skin covering muscles and sinew and bone? The rudimentary pants clinging low on lean hips? She could just make out the top of his briefs. Blue.

Matt continued to slowly pull her forward, until her body finally met his—naked chest to, unfortunately, *not* naked chest. His eyes zeroed in on her lips, and several thoughts flashed through her brain at once.

This isn't why you're here, Callie. You need to stay focused on the job.

His mouth covered hers. And just like the focused man who'd hunted her down at the wedding reception, this man was all about the goal, as well. He tipped her head back and his lips pressed in firmly, opening Callie's mouth wide and taking his time with each retreat. Several deep, wet kisses followed. Forceful, yet unhurried. Heat and moisture and hard lips registered just before his tongue rasped against hers.

For a brief moment her mind splintered, and she moaned.

Matt gripped the fabric on the outside of her thighs, settling her legs on either side of his thighs. Unfortunately, the mounds of fabric between them prevented the satisfaction of feeling his hard body pressed against hers.

"Jesus," he muttered, arching his hip. "How the hell did people wear these bloody clothes?"

She gripped his arms, hoping to keep from melting into the floor. The fingers twisted tight in her dress hauled her that last little bit, and she had to adjust her stance to allow his leg to settle between her thighs. Then there was a skitter of pleasure up her spine from the pressure, the fabulously delicious *friction*...

My God.

She closed her eyes.

"Too bad my brother wasn't into *Space Vixens from the Planet Venus*," Matt said, nibbling his way from one side of her mouth to the other.

"Why would you say that?"

Geez, she sounded so breathless.

He dove in for another openmouthed kiss, and several mind-spinning seconds later he said, "Because their costumes were smaller. Much smaller."

Another drugging kiss consumed her, his tongue hot and demanding and doing unspeakable things to her body. His hand drifted to the small of her back to keep her pressed close. That leg pressed firmly against the part of her anatomy that desired the contact the most.

And those little rudimentary pants and thin briefs did nothing to hide the hard shaft pressed along her hip.

The sensation too fabulous to lose, she pulled herself a little higher up his leg, and the slow drag of fabric settled more firmly against the sensitive area between her thighs. Callie let out a whimper.

Good Lord. She needed to... She had to...

Matt's hands landed along her shoulder blades and began to undo those laces he'd worked so long and hard to fasten. As the back of the dress slowly fell open, cool air slid down her skin. The contact sent an illicit thrill skittering up her spine.

Surely she should be letting out some sort of protest? Where was her vow to keep her hands to herself? Where was her focus? Even more important, where was her sense of decency?

A loud laugh from somewhere in the store broke through Callie's lust-muddled brain, and they both went still. Callie silently counted to five and listened to Matt's harsh breaths before she gathered the strength to open her eyes.

Lips brushing against hers, he said, "I'm thinking we should fix our clothes."

Which totally was in contrast to the palm pressed flat against her back, holding her firmly against his chest.

"Um…yeah," she muttered against his lips, embarrassed by her less than brilliant response.

"What's on the agenda for tomorrow?" he said. "Searching out a pack of traveling circus performers to juggle flaming torches?"

Her lips smiled against his. Something about his teasing tone and his easygoing manner made the moment less awkward.

She stole a quick kiss before answering. "No," she said. "Though we do need to find someone who can transport a dragon from Colin's storage house to the park."

He pulled his head back and hiked a brow dryly. "Well, that shouldn't be hard at all."

"We're in New Orleans," Callie said. "This town

plans, produces and pulls off the Mardi Gras parade every year. There are plenty of people who can properly transport a dragon."

"So tomorrow will be about securing dragon transport?"

Callie opened her mouth to say yes and then bit her lip, remembering that her aunt had called this morning and asked for her help sorting through the stuff at the dock house. Callie had promised to drive up to Aunt Billie's place despite her suspicions the favor wasn't the real reason her aunt wanted Callie to visit.

While she was always pleased to see her favorite relative, the visit never came without a risk. But there was definitely a way to cut down on said risk. Bring backup. Provide a distraction, so to speak. Matt was the perfect person to help in that regard.

Callie eyed Matt. His hair was adorably tousled and his lips looked ruddy from their kisses. And something about his manner always put her at ease, even while revving up her body...

Talk about distractions.

"Actually," she said, "I have to head up to Clemence tomorrow. I was hoping you could ride along. I have to see my aunt Billie, and I think you should get out for an authentic taste of our cuisine and experience the bayou."

"Sightseeing wasn't really in my plans."

"But there's so much to see and this is your first trip to town. You can't come to New Orleans without sampling a little of rural Louisiana."

He tipped his head and looked down at her. Why was she holding her breath, hoping he'd say yes?

"Will there be mosquitos?" he asked.

"Big ones."

"Gators?"

"Most definitely."

"Dirt roads?"

"With potholes the size of Texas."

His lips twitched, as if fighting a smile. "Sounds enticing," he said dryly.

"On the bright side, my aunt makes the best shrimp étouffée in three counties. And she has a successful restaurant to show for it."

"Now that sounds good."

The response encouraging, Callie had to smile. "Hope you like it hot."

"Ms. LaBeau," Matt said, leaning close, his lips whispering across hers, "I like everything hot."

Chapter Four

The two-hour drive up to Clemence, located north of Baton Rouge, passed pleasantly enough. At least, as pleasant as possible given Callie remained distracted, both by Matt's presence in her car and the destination.

As usual, the closer Callie drew to her old hometown the more her stomach filled with knots. Visiting Aunt Billie always managed to be fun and painful at the same time. Hopefully, with Matt along, Callie could avoid the painful part. From the first moment her family had learned of her mistake, her aunt had been her staunchest supporter, which always made Callie feel even worse for letting her down.

Once they'd finally left Baton Rouge behind, the roads grew narrower, quieter and lined with oaks. More important, now that they were getting close to Po Boy's, her aunt's restaurant, the roads were filled with the occasional pothole.

"Man," Matt said as he steered around one. "You weren't kidding about the condition of the roads." He glanced into his rearview mirror. "That one should be named Grand Canyon, the junior."

The conversation was as good a lead-in as she'd ever get. "So what's it like where you're from?" Callie asked. She twisted in the passenger seat of her car and leaned back against the door to better study Matt as he steered her car down the road. "Where do you live again?"

"Manford, Michigan."

Which hardly answered the question burning in her brain. She hiked a brow, encouraging him to go on.

Two beats passed before he answered. "Midsize town. We have a mall, a couple of movie theatres and the hospital is decent enough. Though the emergency room isn't as big as I'd like."

Something in his tone told her that last statement represented a massive understatement.

"I thought you worked as a traveling doc," she said.

He cleared his throat. "I have a part-time job at Manford Memorial. That allows me enough free time to travel as a locums, picking up shifts in bigger cities."

"If you prefer living in a larger city, why are you living there?"

Several seconds ticked by. "It's home." He gave a shrug, the act as vague as his words.

But his voice gave him away, the lack of excitement almost palpable. Callie loved New Orleans, loved everything about the town that managed to merge quirky and a unique cultural heritage with its own brand of Southern charm, all at the same time. The city merged the concepts with a kind of easy grace that amazed her, every single time, and provided the perfect backdrop for her business. Despite the strained relationships, her family was here, too. She'd grown up in the area and couldn't imagine living anywhere else.

Matt, apparently, had little affection for his own town.

"Promise me something," she said, and he looked at her curiously. "No matter what happens, don't go to work for the Manford Chamber of Commerce doing tourist promotion, because you would really suck at the job."

Matt laughed, and she admired the strong throat, the even, white teeth. His sandy, tousled hair that begged to be ruffled, and Callie flexed her fingers against the urge to reach over and run her fingers through his hair.

In an attempt to dodge a pothole on the left, Matt steered the Toyota to the right, and the front tire hit a second pothole. He shot her a look, and Callie lifted a shoulder. "You get used to it."

He glanced at her from the corner of his eye. "You grew up out here?"

"Yep," she said. "Born right here in Clemence Parish. Spent my childhood playing in the water, fishing and catching crawfish."

"A tomboy?"

"And proud of it."

She pointed out the turns, the roads growing narrower, until finally they hit the dirt road that dead-ended into Po Boy's. There were a half dozen or so cars in the gravel parking lot, shaded by huge oaks, and Matt pulled into a spot in the front.

They exited and rounded the car. Matt came to a stop to stare up at the wooden building.

"Aunt Billie's restaurant looks…interesting."

Callie grinned at the expression on his face. The paint on the siding was peeling and cracked, the wood beneath faded to gray where exposed to the sun. The front porch held several tables and chairs, but Callie knew the customers preferred the back and the view of the river.

"Authentic," she said.

He hiked a brow. "Safe?"

She bit back a smile. "Absolutely."

They made their way up the wooden front steps. Matt's hand settled into the dip in her spine, and the heat seeped through her shirt and warmed her skin. Unfortunately, the temperature change didn't stop there. The feeling settled deeper, curling low in her stomach and spreading between her legs. Good Lord. Yesterday's dressing-room incident had clearly left an indelible impression.

They stepped into the restaurant filled with wooden tables and chairs and a few customers. As usual, Aunt Billie sensed her arrival before Callie had taken ten steps inside.

Her aunt appeared from the doorway leading into the kitchen. "Callie, hon. It's been way too long." She enveloped her in a hug before gripping Callie's arms and pulling back to give her the once-over.

Billie LaBeau loved to cook, loved to eat and she had the well-padded frame of one who did. But her generous nature dwarfed everything else in comparison. Despite the distance in the lineage, Aunt Billie took her Creole roots to heart. More important, she'd been the only relative to accept Callie's choices, without treating her life as if she'd settled for a seriously lower second best.

Not once had she looked at Callie with disappointment or thrown out little asides that alluded to how much Callie had screwed up. And while she constantly harped at Callie to visit more often, there was never any judgment in her tone.

"This is Matt Paulson," Callie said.

"'Bout time you brought a man around here again."

Billie shot her a grin. "Haven't done so since Colin. And you were eighteen years old then."

The implied *ten years ago* went unsaid and Callie fought the urge to close her eyes. Perhaps Matt's presence wouldn't be quite the protection that she'd hoped.

"Matt is a *client,*" Callie said.

Hopefully the emphasis on the word would clear up any misconceptions. Aunt Billie's only response was a raised eyebrow at Matt's hand on Callie's back, sending heat shooting up Callie's neck and flaring across her cheeks. Who needed to say anything with a facial expression like her aunt's? Matt was studying Callie, clearly amused by the conversation and the nonverbal communication.

"Welcome, Matt," Aunt Billie said. "I hope you brought your appetite."

"I never leave home without it."

Aunt Billie let out an amused snort. "That's good to hear. And Callie?" Aunt Billie returned her focus to Callie. "The family reunion is in two weeks. It's not too late to change your mind and attend."

Crap, the reunion. She'd forgotten about the annual event that she had no intention of attending, *ever.* She couldn't imagine anything worse than all the family members—those who'd been so proud she'd been accepted to Wimbly—talking about her behind her back. Mentioning her mistake again to her face. Callie had lost count of how many times she'd been told how lucky she was to be afforded the opportunity.

Many of whom now never missed an opportunity to remind her of how much she'd lost when she'd mucked it all up.

Her aunt propped a hand on her ample hip. "I'd love to have all of my family back in the same place again."

"Maybe," Callie said vaguely. "My schedule is pretty busy. I'll have to check the dates."

The look her aunt sent made her message clear. She didn't believe Callie would show up, and Billie sure as heck wouldn't pass up the opportunity to hound her more. Her suspicions about her aunt's recent call to sort through her stuff from the dock house suddenly didn't seem so paranoid. Billie hadn't suddenly been bitten by a late-summer spring-cleaning urge to clean out an old building that seldom got used anymore. She'd planned on slowly eroding away Callie's excuses.

But the thought of all her relatives looking at her as if she'd failed...

Damn it.

"Well, check them dates and try a little harder to squeeze your family into that busy schedule of yours, ya' hear?" Billie said.

"Work has been busy."

"All the more reason you need to come back for a visit," Billie said. "Let your people know how you're doing."

Callie murmured something polite and vague. Billie shot her a sharp look and then seemed to give up, letting the subject go. They spent some time catching up as Billie gave Matt a tour of the kitchen, showing him around and dolling out her blunt brand of humor as they went. Callie liked the laid-back way Matt dodged her aunt's repeated attempts to nail down the details about their relationship. Finally, her aunt seemed to realize that there would be nothing more forthcoming.

"I finally decided to send someone out to do the repairs on the dock house. The stuff inside needs to be sorted, too," Aunt Billie said. "And since you're the only one that goes out there anymore, I need to know what you want me to keep and what I can toss."

A wave of affection hit Callie, and she reached out to gently squeeze her aunt's hand. "Thanks."

She knew her aunt would have torn the thing down by now if not for her. And losing the dock house would be like losing a piece of herself.

"But first, y'all take a seat out on the deck and I'll bring you some lunch," Billie said.

Callie couldn't resist and she sent her aunt a smile. "Make sure you make Matt's shrimp étouffée extra special."

They settled at a table out back, the edge of the deck lined by the Mississippi River. Despite the rustic surroundings, Matt appeared totally at ease. She liked that he seemed comfortable no matter where he was, whether at a classy ice bar or a backwoods restaurant. They settled into easy conversation, which ended when Aunt Billie brought sweet tea and two bowls of shrimp étouffée. Callie watched with satisfaction as Matt took his first bite, eyelids stretching wide. To his credit he swallowed and appeared completely unflustered as he reached for his iced tea before taking a sip.

For some reason, she couldn't resist. Matt Paulson brought out the flirt in her.

"I thought you liked it hot," she said.

The deep, throaty chuckle sent a shocking shiver up her spine. When was the last time a man's laugh made her this...*aware?* Because that was the only word to describe the feeling vibrating just beneath the surface of her skin. Like a potential lightning bolt loomed close and the hairs on her arms lifted in anticipation, expecting the strike at any moment.

To cover, she pulled out her notebook. She still liked to handwrite her initial to-do list before entering information into her laptop later. There was something about the physical act of writing that always got her creative side going. While they ate, Callie went over where things stood for the LARP weekend.

Matt never said a word outside of answering her questions, finishing his bowl of étouffée without a complaint. By the end, sweat dotted his temple, and he reached for his iced tea regularly, but, after that first look of shock…nothing.

When he shoved his bowl back, he sent her a smile.

"Did I pass the LaBeau initiation right?"

Callie propped her elbows on the table. "You did," she said. "With flying colors, too."

A waitress refilled their iced-tea glasses and cleared their lunch dishes away. Matt took a sip of his tea, eyeing her over his glass, and an uncomfortable feeling prickled the back of her neck.

He set his glass down. "How come you refuse to come back to your family reunion?"

"I didn't refuse. I…" She pressed her lips together and slid her gaze out over the river. "I just don't have time."

"Bull," he said softly.

She ticked her gaze back to his. "It is always easy to question the judgment of others in matters of which we may be imperfectly informed.'"

Matt lifted a brow. "Mr. Darcy again?"

"No. His love interest, Elizabeth Bennet. You should read the book."

"Maybe someday," he said with a chuckle. But clearly he wasn't about to be derailed from the topic at hand. "Some people aren't lucky enough to have any family, Callie," he said, and guilt stabbed her in the gut. "Seems a waste for you to avoid yours."

She opened her mouth to defend herself, feeling uncomfortable. She couldn't formulate an intelligent response so she tried another diversionary tactic instead.

"You ready to go for a ride in my boat?" she said.

The raise of his eyebrow let her know he was on to her, but then his grin turned positively sinful. "Is that what they're calling it these days?"

The suggestion slid through her and stirred her blood, but she remained outwardly calm as she played dumb. "I don't know what you're talking about."

"I was hoping there was a hidden meaning in that question," he asked.

He leaned forward and crossed his arms on the tiny table, his face mere inches from her face. A jolt of awareness shot through her body. The proximity sent a skitter of nerves just beneath her skin.

Hazel. His eyes were hazel.

For a moment, intrigued by the discovery, she couldn't respond.

She'd thought his eyes were brown. Of course their first meeting had taken place outside at dusk, with the only lights offered those of fake kerosene lamps. At the park she hadn't gotten close enough to tell, and during the brain-meltingly hot moment in the dim fitting room she'd been distracted by that hard chest on display. But now, in the full light of day, and with them so close, she could make out the yellow and green specks mixed in with the brown.

"Nope. No hidden messages," she said. "I thought I'd show you where I used to go fishing as a kid. But I *really* want to see how the guy who prefers the city deals with a boat ride in backcountry Louisiana."

"Is this another initiation rite?"

A grin slid up her face. "Maybe," she said. "Think you can handle it?"

"I can handle anything you've got."

Fighting words if she'd ever heard them.

Her brow hiked higher. "Cocky, aren't you?"

He tipped back his head and laughed. And once again she was presented with a vision of a strong throat and even, white teeth. The laugh lines around his eyes weren't as deep as his thirty years would suggest. And Callie wondered if that meant his smile rarely made it all the way to his eyes.

"Because I'm that kind of guy, I'll let the obvious comeback for that question slide buy."

"A sign of intelligence."

"Well—" he stood up "—let's get the rest of this family hazing over with."

When they went back inside the restaurant, Aunt Billie wouldn't let him pay, of course. Callie smothered the smile as Matt wasted ten minutes trying to change her mind, without success. Callie's grin finally appeared as she watched Matt wait for Aunt Billie to return to the kitchen before he passed by their table and left enough to cover the bill plus a very generous tip. The man never came up against a problem he couldn't solve.

And what would she do if he finally turned that determination on her?

* * *

Fighting the doubt, Matt hooked his hands on his hips and stared down at the old fiberglass boat tied to the wooden dock. "You sure this thing is safe?"

"Of course it is."

Callie, loose-limbed and agile, ignored the tiny ladder fixed to the side of the deck and hopped inside the boat with the grace of a cat. Beneath her cutoffs, toned, tanned legs ended in delicate sandals. Her beautiful shoulders now on display beneath a feminine T-shirt. Opposed to Friday night's arrangement, her hair hung loose.

And, as promised, a heat wave had settled on top of the delta. The muggy temperature was stifling. Although her T-shirt was damp, her face slightly flushed, she didn't appear bothered.

Man, how did the woman handle the weather and still look so cool?

She turned and looked up at him, a smile on her lips and a challenge in her eyes. "Don't you trust me?"

His lips twitched. "Only to a certain extent."

Eyes twinkling, Callie remained silent and sent him an I-dare-you hike of her brow. After a moment's hesitation, Matt let out a light scoff and climbed down into the boat.

"Feel free to drive," she said. "I get the feeling you like to be the one steering the boat."

"Was that a metaphor?" Matt said as he sat in the driver's seat.

"Definitely."

Surprisingly, the outboard motor of the flat-bottomed boat started easily, and Matt realized that, despite being old, the boat had been carefully maintained. Given the earlier conversation with her aunt, he got the distinct feeling Callie used it more than anyone else.

Curious about why, he steered up the canal while studying the woman up front. Callie had stretched out on the bench on the bow, eyes closed and face tilted into the breeze, obviously enjoying the wind in her hair. In the bright light he could make out streaks of gold mixed with the honey-colored strands.

The towering cypress trees lining the canal blocked most of the direct light, but the lazy heat sat on them relentlessly, the air smelling of damp earth. Spanish moss hung like tinsel in a Christmas tree, adding more of an eerie mood than a festive one.

Matt settled back in his seat, surprised at the stillness of their surroundings. Other than the ripples from their boat, and the quiet purr of the small motor, nothing moved or made a sound. Several minutes passed with the boat following the serpentine path. They rounded a curve and a lake opened out before them. Ten minutes later Callie pointed Matt in the direction of a small boathouse on stilts, blending with the trees.

"Here we are."

Matt hopped up onto the porch that also served as a high dock. Beside the wooden structure a large rope hammock—looking brand-new and out of place next to the ancient building—stretched invitingly between two oak trees. After securing the boat, he reached down and pulled Callie up onto the dock.

"I hadn't planned on taking the time to sightsee while in New Orleans." And yet, here he stood in the middle of friggin' nowhere, all because he hadn't had the willpower to resist a day with Callie. "But if I had made plans, I certainly would have chosen something a little less…" He stared across the cypress-tree-lined lake and the lapping water. The endless stretch of nothing but water and trees. "Wild."

"I promise," she said, grinning up at him, "when we get back I'll take you out on the town and show you the best New Orleans has to offer, like a nice dinner out. A little dancing. And if you're really lucky, maybe even a tour of my condo. But until then—" She backed up slowly toward the edge of the dock, flipping off her sandals and slipping her watch from her wrist, leaving Matt uneasy. The light in her eyes set him on edge in ways that weren't safe to consider.

"Where are you going?" Matt asked. A thrum of anxiety curled in Matt's stomach, and he looked out at the water. "I don't think—"

"Holler when you see a gator." And with that, Callie pivoted and dove into the water.

The splash came, raining cool drops on Matt's face and shirt, and he nearly groaned at the brief relief from the heat. In her T-shirt and shorts, Callie swam toward the center of a clearing beneath the low-hanging branches of several cypress trees and turned to tread water, smiling up at him.

"You coming in?" she said. "It's the final LaBeau initiation rite."

"What the hell do I get in return for passing all these tests?"

A smile crept up her face. "A permanent spot at the family table at Po Boy's."

"If you're not going to be there, then what's the point?"

She shot him a you're-not-funny look, and he decided to let the issue slide.

"Besides," he said, "I'm not sure that's an honor the lining of my esophagus would survive."

"I told Aunt Billie to make yours extra hot."

He tipped his head as the realization hit him. "Yours wasn't as hot as mine?"

"Nope. Can't stand it spicy. I always order it mild." The playful light in her eyes was almost worth suffering through étouffée that could be used to strip paint from wood.

Almost.

"Coming in?" she asked.

He stared down at her, hands on his hips, and a smile tugged at his lips. "Promise this is the last of the La-Beau family torture?"

"Last one, I swear."

"Okay," he said.

The woman clearly felt in her element. And while he might be a bit of a fish out of water in the backwoods of Louisiana, there were still some things that he controlled. Showing the lovely Ms. LaBeau a thing or two suddenly seemed incredibly important.

And too much fun to pass up.

After the years of worry and fear and sacrifice, he suddenly felt the urge to indulge in something just for himself. A moment to be something more than just a doctor, a brother and a stand-in parent. It had been far too long since he'd had sex, and today he was going to leave his many roles behind, save one: that of a red-blooded man in the company of a beautiful woman.

He flipped open his snap. To her credit, she didn't react except for a slight flaring of her eyelids as she continued to tread water. As Callie stared up at him, he struggled to keep the amusement from his face as he slid the zipper down. He waited for her to say something. A protest. A sound of encouragement. A mocking comment. Or, at the very least, a flicker of her gaze away from him.

Nothing.

Instead, Callie kept treading water, eyes on Matt as he hooked his hands in his shorts and shoved them down, kicking them aside. His briefs clung to his hips and, for a nanosecond, he considered shucking them, too. But he wasn't prepared for the likely ending to a bout of skinny-dipping. For one split second he mentally kicked himself for not considering the need for condoms. But right now the sun beat down on his back and sweat trickled between his shoulder blades and the water looked cool. Even better, the expression on Callie's face was inviting.

He executed a shallow dive, slicing through the water, and broke the surface just two feet from where Callie continued to tread water.

Her cheeks were flushed, whether from the heat or the sight of him in nothing but briefs, he wasn't sure.

"You know," she said dryly, "I wasn't kidding before. There are gators in these waters. So you best keep all your dangly bits inside your underwear."

He laughed, secretly pleased with the first words out of her mouth. "Thanks for the warning."

Matt fought the urge to cup her neck and drag her close for another kiss. Memories of their time in the fitting room that first night flooded his mind. The taste of her mouth, the feel of her hip.

Good thing the water was fairly cool because spontaneous combustion felt like a possibility. Unfortunately, despite being a strong swimmer he couldn't figure out how to follow through on the impulse to take that mouth in the way he wanted without drowning them both. Instead, he stretched out on his back to float, biding his time until she climbed out of the water and onto the dock. In wet clothes.

Just thinking about the sight made his groin grow tight.

Pushing the thought from his mind, he stared up at the canopy of cypress trees and the sunlight peeking through the leaves, letting the peaceful scene wash over him. For the ten years since his parents had died and he'd assumed responsibility of Tommy, he'd been living life on edge. The roller-coaster ride of Tommy's addiction had worn him out, leaving him constantly braced for the next bad happening. Taking a moment to just relax was a revelation.

"This is nice," he said.

He turned his head and met Callie's face just a few feet from his, also floating.

"I love Louisiana." Her smile wrinkled her nose in a way that could only be described as cute. "Never want to live anywhere else."

What would that be like? To live where you wanted, instead of where you had to?

He'd been stuck with Manford as his home base for so long, looking after Tommy, that he couldn't imagine a life anywhere else. But nothing about his hometown appealed to him. Never had. Never would. He'd grown up there dying to get out. But when his parents had died during his third year of college, he'd had no choice but to transfer back home before his senior year. To attend medical school and complete his E.R. residency in Detroit. Commuting as much as he could.

Sleeping in the on-call room when too tired to make the drive back home.

Sometimes he wondered if his brother's life would have turned out differently had Matt been around more during Tommy's early years of college.

He hated those self-defeating thoughts.

"But as much as I love New Orleans—" Callie's hand brushed his "—every once in a while I have to get out of town and come back here. It's so…peaceful."

They continued to float for a few more minutes, and every muscle in Matt's body slowly relaxed, until he truly felt like a floater, washed up on the beach. No tension. No worries about what tomorrow would bring.

A distant rumble of thunder broke the peace and sent them swimming for shore. Matt reached the dock first, hauling himself up. He turned and leaned down to take Callie's hand, pulling her up onto the dock… and straight into his arms.

He made no pretense that his actions were an accident. He dragged her dripping body up against his, until the wet T-shirt pressed so enticingly against her breasts was plastered against his chest. His body let out a sigh of relief.

"I've been thinking about this since the dressing room," he said.

She leaned back and eyed him. "I'm guessing your thoughts didn't include a dock house and a battered deck."

"The setting is irrelevant."

Since their kisses in the costume-shop dressing room, Matt hadn't been able to think of much else besides getting Callie back in his arms. And now that he had her here, he was going to take full advantage.

He swooped in for a kiss, gathering those soft lips against his, and a tiny moan escaped Callie. The sound shot straight to his groin.

Matt pressed his hand to the back of her head and molded himself more firmly against her. Water dripped from Callie's hair, landing on his arms, and Matt was surprised the drops didn't hit his overheated skin and fizzle into vapor. The taste and the feel of Callie in his arms were just as good as he remembered. He touched his tongue to her lower lip, and she opened her mouth wide, letting him inside. But, good God, this time it wasn't enough.

Ignoring the warning voices in his head, he lifted Callie into his arms. When she wrapped her legs around his waist, her body just brushed the top of his hard shaft. This time the groan came from him.

"Callie—"

He eyed the scene and then, decision made, headed for the hammock. Callie pressed herself more firmly against Matt.

"Callie."

She wasn't helping his self-control here.

He tumbled her back onto the hammock, the action creating a gentle rocking motion, and caught his weight with his hand. He stared down into brown eyes framed with thick lashes, wet from their swim.

"I'm not prepared for this." Even as he said the words, he stretched out beside her, covering that soft body with his own. The smell of shampoo—magnolia scented, maybe?—came from her hair.

Stupid, really, to torture himself this way. He pressed his forehead to hers. "I just want to enjoy holding you for a moment." His lips tipped up at the edges. "Minus the audience on the other side of a dressing-room door."

"I figured the perv finally wanted to cop a feel."

The image of doing exactly that left Matt's chuckle sounding strained. When Callie shifted slightly beneath him, pressing more of that soft body against his, the amusement died on his lips.

"Whatever we do," he said, "we leave the clothes *on*. I don't have a condom, but I know I'd have a devil of a time focusing on the technicalities if you were naked."

Matt swiped his hand down her side, cupping her thigh, and she closed her eyes. "So the clothes stay on," she said. "Got it."

The verbal agreement spiked his pulse higher, and he pressed her mouth open again with his, finally realizing the honey-colored hair and the honey drawl matched her honey taste.

Jesus, he needed to touch her.

He unsnapped her cutoffs and flattened his palm low against her slender belly.

"Matt." She arched her back in invitation, pressing closer, her eyes still closed. "I thought we'd agreed about the clothes—"

"We did. I'm not taking them off," he said. "I just want to touch you."

He fumbled briefly at the edge of her panties, cursing softly along the way. Why the hell was he so clumsy? But the need rushing through his veins made his fingers feel too hot and too eager and too greedy to go slow.

Matt shifted and tilted his head to take more of Callie's mouth as he finally succeeded in slipping his hand beneath the elastic band, seeking out the sweet spot that would bring about the response he craved. If he couldn't take exactly what he was dying for, then he wanted to hear Callie calling his name. He knew the flush staining her cheeks now had nothing to do with the heat wave. Goose bumps peppered her skin as he slid his palm lower with a purpose.

When he reached his goal, the soft folds beneath his fingers, Callie arched against him.

"Matt." She reached for his arms, her eyes wide. "I need—"

"I know what you need."

Callie gripped his forearm and he paused, refusing to give up his position, before stroking her between her legs.

With a groan, Callie closed her eyes. "That's mighty presumptuous of you."

"At this point," he said dryly. "I don't think either of us is thinking much beyond the big O."

She sounded out of breath. "You're too goal-oriented."

"Isn't that the point of all this?"

"The point is," she said, shifting a little lower down his chest, "to enjoy the journey en route."

And then Callie's hand landed on his hard-on, and Matt sucked in a breath and froze. The images ricocheting around his head included one of him shucking her pants and sliding between her thighs. But the one that wreaked the most havoc was of Callie's face, eyes dreamy and jaw slack as he thrust hard and brought them both to a rousing finale.

"Callie. I'm not sure—"

She tunneled her hand beneath his underwear.

"You're not sure of what?" she said, and she began

to stroke him through the cotton briefs, sending a stab of pleasure down his groin and searing his skin.

The urge to roll over and pin Callie beneath him sent a small shudder down his spine.

Matt let out an undignified curse. "I'm not sure this is wise."

She smiled against his mouth and then gave his lower lip a little nip. "If you get to touch me, then I get to touch you."

Well, hell, who could argue with logic like that?

Matt had just about adjusted to the fingers stroking him through the cotton when she ran her finger across the sensitive head, pulling an embarrassing groan from his mouth.

"Hmm," she murmured. "That was fun. Let's see if I get the same response again."

Matt left her lips and ran his mouth down the curve of her breast toward the center. The wet layer of cotton and the lace beneath were frustrating, but he continued to nip, placing sucking kisses along the path from one side to the other. He flicked his tongue across the tip, the partial bud growing fuller in response, and he grinned. Her fingers on his erection fumbled a little, and her free hand gripped the short hair at the back of his neck, pulling his head up until they were face-to-face.

The wide pupils and parted mouth were a beautiful sight, right before she dove in for a soul-searing kiss that almost had him losing his focus, his fingers briefly losing their rhythm beneath her pants.

"Here's an idea," he said, his voice throatier than he would have liked. "Let's see who can stay the most focused."

Eyelids wide, she said, "Clothes stay on?"

"Deal."

Matt knew he was in trouble when Callie stopped kissing him and pulled back to look at his face. Her lips—ruddy from being consumed by his—curled into a grin and, before Matt could figure out what she had in mind, her hand slipped beneath his briefs and made contact, closing around his erection. Her soft palm encircled his hard length.

For a moment, his mind went blank and his heart flatlined.

"Callie." This time her name came out more of a groan. "I can't—"

Callie writhed against him, encouraging his fingers to get with the program again. Desperate, he used his free hand to ruck her shirt up to just beneath her breasts before he caught himself, remembering their deal.

Why'd he come up with this torture?

Matt bent forward and captured the tip of her breast with his mouth again, cursing the two layers of fabric between them. Callie's hand stroked him faster, and the need building low in his back began to increase in intensity, his movements less about teasing and more about pushing them both over the edge. And the devouring of her with his lips and teeth and tongue became as much about satisfying his need as hers.

Callie's lids went wide, her mouth partially open as she sucked in breath after breath, and her hand began to falter, the rhythm of her strokes stuttering. When she arched her back, her body giving one final shudder, she dragged her thumb directly over his sensitive tip. Matt's spine went stiff, the orgasm shooting through him, stripping the strength from his limbs.

Matt had no idea how many minutes passed before

his endorphin-soaked brain became aware of his surroundings again. A breeze gently rocked the hammock and cooled their sweat-slicked skin. The smell of sex hung in the air, and the feel of Callie's soft body pressed against Matt's lulled him into a sense of peace. In fact, he might have sworn never to move again.

"That was definitely the most fun I've ever had with my clothes on," he said, his eyes still closed. "I haven't done the third-base-only thing since high school."

"Third base. Really? Do people still use the term?"

He looked down at Callie with a grin. "Only perverts like me."

She tipped back her head and laughed, and the movement sent their slick torsos sliding against each other.

"Um…" Callie wiggled against the mess between them as a small smile crept up her face. "I think we're going to need to go for another dip in the water."

Chapter Five

The next morning, Callie leaned back in the chair in her office and stared blankly at her laptop, currently parked on her desk. She'd come to work early to get some planning done, but after the hot moment in the hammock yesterday, her mind hadn't been the same. Her *body* hadn't been the same. How could she concentrate on creating a medieval menu for a wedding reception when all she could think about was Matt?

Especially getting Matt…*naked*.

They'd driven back to the city, and the parting had been full of untapped potential. Unfortunately she'd had a meeting with a client last evening, so she couldn't invite him up to her condo. And no matter how far things had gone between the two of them, she still felt awkward asking him to come to her place once she was free. A request synonymous with asking him over for a night of sex.

Not that there was anything wrong with *that*.

After all, they were two consenting adults.

However, if her current mind frame were any indication, having Matt Paulson around would surely slow down her progress at work.

Callie set her elbow on her sleek cherrywood desk and propped her chin in her hand. Perhaps Matt was right. Maybe she should stop avoiding the extended family. Maybe if she simply started showing up to the various family functions her relatives would stop continuing to file her away under the to-be-pitied category. Avoiding the family while waiting for time to take care of the issue hadn't helped.

For God's sake, ten years surely would have cured the problem by now.

But continuing to avoid the family amounted to everyone thinking she was hiding in shame, which couldn't be further from the truth. She needed to show up, hold her head high and let everyone see that she was exactly where she wanted to be in her life, past mistakes be damned.

Callie sat up and fired off an email to her aunt, accepting the invitation to the family reunion. If she was lucky, maybe Matt would still be around and she could ask him to come with her. A little steadying presence by her side would be welcome for sure. Of course, having him around meant they could actually make it beyond the juvenile label of third base.

Unfortunately, the thought of Matt in her bed side-tracked her again.

"Callie."

Startled, she looked up. Colin stood on the other side of her desk, looking down at her with a bemused expression on his face, dark hair curling a bit just above his ears. How had he entered her office without her even hearing him? After a quick check of her watch, she realized fifteen minutes had passed by without her knowledge. Good Lord, she'd never get anything done at this rate.

"I knocked, but you didn't answer," Colin said.

"Sorry." Callie sat up and pretended to shuffle through a few files on her desk. "What have I done to warrant a visit from my favorite ex-boyfriend?"

Colin let out a huff of humor and dropped into the seat across from her. "I'd take that as a compliment if you had more exes running around."

Callie lifted a brow dryly, determined to remain unaffected by the efficiently targeted, well-meaning jab. Unfortunately, when Colin went on, remaining unaffected became impossible.

Colin crossed his arms. "The Paulson thing is turning into a bigger deal than I thought."

Oh, God.

Stunned, Callie stared at her ex, hoping to read exactly what he was talking about in his expression. But nothing in his blue eyes gave away his thoughts. Had he already guessed she was slipping quickly into a *thing*, for lack of a better word, with Matt? Callie racked her brain trying to figure out how she'd given everything away. Short of Matt leaving handprints on her body she was at a loss to explain the turn of events. Unless Colin had suddenly developed psychic powers she didn't know about.

"Uh...bigger deal?" she said.

"Yes. Like nationally televised newsworthy deal."

Television?

Matt *would* look good on a sex tape.

"Wait, *what?*" She shook her head and leaned back in her seat, trying to pry her mind out of the gutter. "I'm confused."

Clearly Colin was talking about something other than her relationship with Matt. Their sexual exploits, while hot in a kind of innocent way, were hardly the stuff of tabloids.

"The *Dungeons of Zhorg* community caught wind of the Paulson wedding," Colin said. "And there are people clamoring to come for some of the events."

Callie stared at her ex, her heart working overtime to supply enough blood to her brain. She'd only been gone for a day. One day. She'd enjoyed lunch with Matt, taken a swim and indulged in an erotic, fully clothed moment with a handsome guy. When the heck had everything become so crazy?

Being caught up in a sex-tape scandal suddenly seemed appealing in comparison.

"The LARP event was to be for the wedding guests only," Callie said.

"That was the original idea. But someone at Gamer's World got wind of the plans and now they want in on the action, too. I called and spoke with Tommy Paulson myself, and he and his fiancée are in favor of making this as big as we want, as long as Rainstorm Games foots the bill for all the extras. Our publicist is contacting the local networks and several of them are interested in running a human interest piece about Tommy and Penny's story."

Gamer's World? Networks?

Holy hell.

"Colin." Her voice came out weak. News cameras? At a wedding she'd arranged? "I only agreed to handle this wedding because the smaller scale made it doable. Money isn't the only issue here. I'm just one person, plus a part-time assistant."

And while the businesswoman in her considered the additions an opportunity of a lifetime, the woman who wanted to have time to eat and sleep over the next two months had issues with the idea. Not to mention how would she even find two minutes to see where yesterday's foray into hotness with Matt would lead? And see where the relationship would take her?

"Don't worry," he said. "I have plenty of experience with these types of events. I've launched several popular games, remember?"

"What I remember best was you arranging a zombie invasion of a wedding your wife and I planned," she said dryly.

Colin sent her an unapologetic grin.

Despite everything, she smiled. "It was an epic ending to a fabulous wedding."

Callie had gone all out in helping Colin's then-fiancée plan a spectacular Mardi Gras wedding. She'd grown pretty close to Jamie in the process. And even though Callie wished them well in their marital bliss, a little part of Callie envied them, as well. The closest Callie had ever come to anything serious had been with Colin, and their relationship ended ten years ago.

I'd take that as a compliment if you had more exes running around.

The realization suddenly made her love life seem a little pathetic. But she'd been so busy pouring all her energies into her business, determined to turn her negative into a positive that she hadn't had time for a relationship.

She hadn't lived the life of a monk. She wasn't *that* insane. Callie had dated and enjoyed herself along the way. But she'd passed on actively pursuing anything serious because she wanted to be in the right place in her life. And while she'd been building her business, her social life had lagged behind, stuck in the old days.

Hanging out with old friends was well and good, but what about making new ones?

Case in point, one of her best friend's was her ex from ten years ago.

Unfortunately, Colin seemed oblivious to her brutal personal epiphany as he went on.

"I checked out the park you chose and spoke with the people in charge," he said. "They have plenty of room and more than adequate parking."

Right. They were in the middle of discussing how her work life had just gotten hellaciously complicated. Did he have any idea what he was asking of her?

Colin went on. "I don't think we'll need that much room, but the park said they could handle up to a thousand people."

"A thousand?" she said weakly, trying to force her mind back to the concerning turn of events. Her private party wedding suddenly going public...

"Colin, that's way more work than I signed on for."

"I know you've been trying to prove to your parents how successful your business has become. I assumed you'd jump at the chance to do exactly that."

"True. But televising a wedding I've only had two months to arrange isn't exactly how I figured to pull this off."

"If anyone can do this, it's you."

"You mean if anyone is crazy enough to *try,* it's me."

"Listen, Callie—" Colin leaned forward, his blue eyes on hers "—I trust you. I know you can pull this off in a manner that will live up to the newly expanded LARP event."

I trust you.

Damn, here she was resenting the fact he'd just increased her workload by a hundred and he had the nerve to utter those words she rarely heard other than from her clients.

I trust you.

The twinge in her heart was impossible to ignore.

After her spectacular fail in college, the one person she'd directly affected the most had been Colin. She hadn't asked him to come up and bail her out. But he'd come. Because that was the kind of guy he was. And the trip had cost him greatly.

Still, he'd been the first to forgive her. The first to embrace her crazy decision to start her own business arranging themed weddings, and he even managed her website. And if that wasn't enough, he participated in the *Ex Factor* blog because it helped *her,* not him. He remained anonymous, which meant he received nothing in return, other than the satisfaction of seeing his friend succeed and her massive gratitude.

Callie stared at Colin. Obviously Colin considered the turn of events an opportunity not to be missed, for both her business and his. And Tommy and Penny appeared thrilled, as well.

"When it comes to work, no one is more focused than you, Callie."

I was until Matt Paulson landed in my life.

"Uh, thanks."

Clearly the man didn't remember how distracted she'd been when he'd arrived at her office. And all of this meant that, damn, she probably should try to tone things down with the brother of the groom. How could she give this event the proper attention while preoccupied by the potential for more with Matt Paulson?

"You know I'll give it my all," she said.

"You always do." Colin reached across her desk and gave her a friendly cuff on the arm. "I'll have my publicist coordinate things with you. And if you need any extra help, don't hesitate to holler."

She sent him a smile she didn't quite feel. "Sure."

Callie watched Colin exit her office, and the moment he disappeared Callie flopped back against her seat. The question remained, how good was she at pulling off the impossible? And how was she going to convince Matt to return to a hands-off relationship?

More important, how was she going to convince herself?

Chapter Six

"This really isn't necessary, Mr. Croft." Callie pressed the elderly man's handkerchief to the cut on her forehead, hoping the blood had stopped oozing down her face. The E.R. was packed and it was only seven-thirty in the evening. The hour they'd spent in the waiting room so far felt like the tip of the iceberg.

Callie tried again. "It was kind of you to drive me here, but I don't need to see a doctor."

A trickle of blood ran down her hand as she applied pressure to her forehead, and she cursed the timing. How could she convince the man she didn't need medical attention with her arm bringing to mind a horror flick? Served her right for being so distracted.

She'd gone to the costume shop today to rummage around and check out the crucifix she'd spied on the shelf the first day she'd visited the store. Focusing on her work hadn't come easy, especially with the dressing room in her line of sight. And then, while standing on the shelf, she'd received a call from Matt, asking her to dinner.

No wonder she'd dropped the stupid crucifix on her head.

A drop of blood landed on her thigh, and she swiped

the spot with her sleeve before the shop owner noticed. "I'm fine. Really. I can take care of this at home."

The balding man's forehead looked permanently creased with concern. "But that crucifix is heavy. You might need a CAT scan."

That crucifix was heavy, indeed. Hurt like heck on the way down, too. Reaching for the sucker on the top shelf had been a stupid plan. Maybe Matt was right. Maybe she should stick to the cheaper, less authentic, less *heavy* props from here on out. Unfortunately, that didn't solve her problem now. She kept hoping to convince the shop owner to leave, so she could leave, too. When she'd agreed to meet Matt for dinner tonight— to discuss the wedding *only,* she'd stressed to Matt— showing up bleeding wasn't exactly the professional image she'd wanted to project.

A shout from down the hallway caught the attention of the entire waiting room. A man with handcuffs was kicking and screaming and shouting profanities, being escorted by two policemen. One of the cops sported a pretty impressive bloody nose.

Callie sighed and addressed Mr. Croft. "At least go on home to your wife."

So that I can leave this E.R.

"Not until you get checked out by a doctor," Mr. Croft said.

Callie bit back the groan. She hated being forced to go with her last resort but, at this point, she had no choice. She had to call Matt anyway, because making their dinner date looked impossible at this point. And she still hadn't decided how to tell him she was putting their personal relationship, such as it was, on ice.

Callie pulled out her cell phone and placed the call, and Matt answered on the second ring.

"Hey. It's Callie." She turned in her seat to face away from where Mr. Croft was pacing and lowered her voice. "I'm sorry to bother you, but I need your help."

"Does it involve another impossible deal involving sex with our clothes on? Because I'm not sure I'm up for torturing myself tonight."

Despite everything, Callie bit back the smile and went on, "No, nothing like that. I went to Mr. Croft's shop to check out a crucifix for an *Interview with the Vampire* wedding I'm planning."

"Vampires?"

She grinned at the doubtful tone of his voice. "Set to take place at midnight. In a graveyard."

"That's just creepy."

Callie laughed. "Anyway..." She glanced at Mr. Croft, who was now speaking with the clerk again, gesturing anxiously back at Callie.

The poor man was going to have a stroke at the thought of her keeling over from head trauma.

"I reached up to grab the crucifix and managed to knock the thing down on my head." She purposefully didn't share exactly why she'd been so distracted. "And it's, um, a lot heavier than it looks."

"Are you okay?"

"I have a little cut on my forehead. But Mr. Croft is freaking out. I think he's afraid I'm going to keel over and die. He refuses to leave until I get checked out by a doctor."

She could hear the grin in Matt's voice.

"And you just happen to know one," he said.

"I hate asking you for a favor like this. But—"

"Which E.R.?"

"St. Mathews."

"I'm leaving right now."

The next half hour passed by painfully, and Callie was no closer to deciding how to handle Matt. Not only that, the waiting room looked set to explode, every seat full. A couple was arguing and several kids were crying and Callie thought she was going to lose her mind. When the double doors whooshed open and Matt entered, relief swamped Callie, even as awareness shimmied up her spine.

He strode toward her with the look she remembered from the first night they'd met. Focused and intent on solving a problem.

Matt knelt in front of Callie, and she ignored the ridiculous catch in her chest as he lifted the bandage on her forehead, examining the cut.

"How long ago did it happen?" He ran his finger gently down the edge of her tender skin, and she sucked in a breath. The scent of spicy soap hit her nose, and she took in his hair, damp and curling a bit at the edges. Clearly he'd just gotten out of the shower. And the thought of a naked Matt soaping himself made her squirm in her seat.

She'd had the pleasure of having that hard length pressed along her hip...

Mr. Croft appeared beside Callie. "Two hours ago. The crucifix is heavy. I shouldn't have kept it on the top shelf."

Matt sent Callie a conspiratorial wink before assuming a serious face again, looking up at Mr. Croft. "Was there any loss of consciousness?"

"No."

"Any vomiting or slurred speech? Have you noticed her acting or saying anything odd?"

Mr. Croft visibly relaxed a bit. "No."

Good thing the man wasn't privy to her crazy thoughts about Matt.

Matt turned back to Callie. "Feeling dizzy?"

Heck, yeah. Because you're so close, and you smell so good and—oh, my God—those hands.

The feel of his fingers and that hot hazel gaze bringing back the moment on the dock.

"No," she said instead. "No dizziness."

"I don't see a need for a CAT scan." Matt stood, keeping a reassuring hand on Callie's shoulder, and Callie fought the urge to lean into the comforting gesture. "Why don't you let me take her home, Mr. Croft? I can keep an eye on her tonight. If any concerning symptoms crop up, I can bring her back here."

Poor Mr. Croft looked incredibly earnest. Callie could tell the older man wanted to leave, but the worry just wouldn't let him go. "But what about her cut. Shouldn't she get that sutured?"

"The edges are clean." Matt pulled out something shaped like a marker from his pocket, with a clear tip. "We have a special kind of glue we use to close these kinds of lacerations. I can take care of this at home."

"You're sure?"

Matt's face adopted that perfect combination of soothing authority and self-assurance that inspired confidence. "Absolutely."

"Okay. But you'll call if something happens?"

"Of course." Matt sent Mr. Croft a smile that said, "I've got this."

Callie watched the shop owner make his way back

through the automatic doors, not allowing herself to relax until the man disappeared from sight.

She let out a sigh and turned to Matt. "*Thank* you. I thought he'd never leave."

"Guilt." His lips twisted wryly. "The damn emotion is a powerfully motivating force. And, speaking of the emotion, shouldn't you be feeling a little of the same?"

When she looked at him stupidly, he went on.

"You promised a night out on the town, showing me the best that New Orleans has to offer. To make up for the nuclear, skin-melting étouffée I had to eat at your aunt's place. I think I remember something about fine dining. Maybe a little dancing. I believe your condo was mentioned, as well."

Shoot, she'd forgotten all about that. How was she going to get out of this gracefully?

She licked her lips nervously. "Oh, well—"

"I'm only kidding." He gently pulled her to her feet. "A hot night out loses a bit of its appeal when your date is actively hemorrhaging."

"I'm not bleeding anymore." She touched the sore spot with her fingers. "At least not very much."

"How about I get you home, close up that cut and we order takeout?" He cupped her elbow, and she tried to ignore the skin-on-skin contact. "And when you start to vomit profusely, slur your words and your left pupil dilates, I'll call Mr. Croft and tell him I'm dragging you back to the E.R. for a CT scan and emergency brain surgery."

She sent him a sarcastic look.

Matt simply grinned. "Maybe next time you should wait for the proprietor to retrieve the item on the top shelf for you."

"Would you want to watch Mr. Croft crawl up a rickety old ladder?"

"Hmm," he said. "Point taken."

Another shout came up as a State Trooper hauled in a man that appeared to be flying high on something. Sirens wailed outside as an ambulance pulled up to the side ramp. Callie couldn't wait to leave the hectic scenario behind. But Matt? Well, Matt was looking around with an expression of...

Good Lord. Was that *affection*?

"You like the craziness of the E.R., don't you?" she asked.

The little boy grin he sent was adorable. "Love it."

Callie tipped her head. "Does your job in Michigan get this crazy?"

Matt's gaze slid from hers to the overflowing waiting room, the staff bustling about. The chaos in the E.R. appeared to be reaching some sort of zenith. Instead of appearing overwhelmed by the sensory input, Matt looked sorry to be leaving. A nurse came out to announce there was a three-car pileup, with several patients on the way, asking the less urgent patients to please be patient. Matt looked as if he were itching to join in the mayhem and help out.

"Manford E.R. has its moments," he said. "But never anything like this."

So if he didn't stay in Manford for the job, or because he loved the town, why didn't he move? Before she could ask, he linked his fingers with hers, and the contact did crazy things to her pulse. Ridiculous, really, after everything they'd done in the hammock. The simple feel of palm against palm should not be so stimulating.

Matt squeezed her hand lightly. "Time to take you home."

The words zipped through Callie's brain, lighting little fires in their wake. She hesitated. If Matt took her home to fix her cut and keep an eye on her, despite his previous words, the risk of a repeat in the hammock was great.

After informing the clerk to take Callie off the waiting list, they made their way out the door into the night. The air muggy and warm and, after dealing with Mr. Croft for the past hour and a half, Callie had never been so grateful to leave an air-conditioned building. Regrettably, leaving also meant she had to make up her mind how to tell Matt.

And soon.

Thirty minutes later Callie opened the door to her condominium and tried hard not to show just how torn she was by his presence. But she needed to be honest with Matt. No doubt the man expected to finish what they'd started. And, God knows, Callie longed for the same thing.

Just tell him while he cleans up your cut, Callie.

Sure, she'd just wait until he was touching her with those fabulous hands. Nothing wrong with that plan, *at all*.

Her throat tight, Callie set her purse on the foyer table and then led Matt into her kitchen. Matt came to a stop in the middle of the room, scanning the dark wood cabinets, the marble counters and the top-of-the-line kitchen appliances. Despite the small size, her upscale condo had everything she needed, including being located in the fabulous Arts District.

"Not bad for a former tomboy who used to catch crawdads," he said.

Callie smiled. "How about a drink before we get started?"

Lord knows she needed one.

"Scotch?" she asked.

"Absolutely."

Hopefully a bit of alcohol would take the edge off, so she poured two, rehearsing her lines for the conversation that was about to take place.

Handing Matt his drink, she said, "I suppose you heard about Colin and Tommy's big plans to take the DoZ weekend and go public."

Matt sighed and threaded his fingers through his hair, leaving sandy-colored spikes in his wake. "I'm sorry."

She let out a soft huff, amused. "Not your fault."

"You could have said no. Tommy and Penny were already getting what they wanted."

"Colin asked."

Matt said nothing in response, so she handed Matt his drink and he simply followed her down the hall of hardwood floors and into the bathroom containing the same dark wood cabinets and marble counters as the kitchen. The mere fact that Matt hadn't commented meant she had some explaining to do. Callie leaned her hip against the cabinet and watched Matt pull out everything he needed from his bag, totally focused on his task.

She'd experienced firsthand the chaos of the E.R. waiting room. God only knows how much worse the noise and confusion had been in back, which explained a lot about Matt's ability to focus. Obviously the man had learned to block out unnecessary stimuli, concentrating on the task in front of him. And the memory of having all that attention directed at her sent heat crawling up her back.

"I'm curious what kind of hold Colin has over you," Matt said.

"I told you before, I owe him."

"Yeah, but I considered your debt more of an 'I'm going to organize this weekend party for him' kind of obligation. Not an 'I'm going upgrade the whole shindig to a blowout publicity stop' kind of obligation."

He'd stopped, a package of gauze in his hand as he watched Callie closely.

"I'm assuming this has something to do with your college blunder," he went on.

Callie almost laughed at the benign-sounding title he'd given her mistake.

"When I got dragged to the police station, Colin made the long drive to come bail me out. Colin was livid, and I was angry because I hadn't even asked for his help. He just assumed and came." Her voice dropped a notch. "And, unfortunately, the trip wound up screwing up his finals. He…" She looked away for a moment. "He almost flunked that semester."

She took a deep breath, pushing the horrendously shameful memories away. She'd alienated herself from her parents, her boyfriend and most of her friends in one awful day. Not to mention losing the scholarship.

Coming back to New Orleans was the hardest thing she'd ever done, but she didn't regret the move for a moment.

"And now that this weekend has morphed into the party that just won't stop growing, this is a massive opportunity for Rainstorm Games," she said. "And, hence, Colin. The added publicity is also good for my business."

She took a deep breath and met Matt's gaze again, forcing the words out. "I can't pull off doing my job and sorting through—" she gestured her hand between the two of them "—this, whatever *this* is, at the same time."

A hush descended in her bathroom, and the pause felt big enough to swallow her whole. In fact, she kind of wished it would.

Matt set the gauze on the counter and stepped closer, and her awareness of him increased to distracting levels. "You're telling me that you're going to let your guilt keep you from enjoying our time together?"

"It's not guilt."

God, she hated that word. She'd spent the first few years back in New Orleans drowning in a murky sea of remorse. She'd promised herself, *promised,* she'd have nothing more to do with the emotion. But still…

Matt cocked his head and continued to say nothing, and the burn in her belly brought a frown to her mouth.

Damn.

"Okay," she said. "Maybe I do have some leftover guilt."

She hated admitting that to herself, much less to Matt. It was bad enough her parents still brought up her moment of shame, reminding her of all she'd done. She'd been struggling for years to prove to her parents she'd successfully moved on. And how disappointing to realize she'd subjected herself to the same treatment, even if unconsciously done.

Callie sighed and rubbed her forehead. There were

better ways to spend her time than to engage in end-less self-flagellation.

"From what you told me, you're partially responsi-ble for bringing him and his wife together," Matt said. "Shouldn't a happy ending release you from your debt?"

"I can't screw up this wedding and the promotional event—"

"You won't," he said, stepping so close she could see those beautiful flecks in his eyes.

"See?" Heart doing crazy somersaults in her chest, she pressed back against the cabinet. "I can't think when I'm so distracted."

He lifted a hand to her face. "First, I'll be happy to provide lessons on how to remain focused despite dis-tractions. I think the fact that I'm capable of holding this conversation with you…alone…in your condo… a bed just a room away, proves my point. Second, if I promise to let you get plenty of sleep tonight, will that convince you?"

The conflicting desires—the need to prove herself and the need to feel Matt's hands on her again—went to war in her head again. If she cut out all the bare essen-tials, she could do this. Her gaze dropped to the T-shirt stretched across Matt's chest, hugging the lean muscles beneath. How much sleep did one need, anyway?

"I think you sold me when you mentioned the les-sons," she said.

"Good." The sexy smirk on his face just about did her in, and he stepped back. "Just so we're clear, I'm going to clean up your cut and take you to bed. So if you still have a problem with that, you need to let me know now."

How could he say those words so calmly? Especially

with her pulse striving to achieve record rates? The man had stated his plans to take care of her injury and take her to bed, both declarations delivered with the same nonchalant tone as if the two activities were somehow on the same par with each other. She envied his ability to pull the coolly collected demeanor off.

She felt the need to throw him off guard, to keep him on his toes.

"Just so we're *clear*..." Now that the matter had been decided, she pulled off her bloodstained blouse and tossed the garment aside. "Not only did the corset embellish the goods, the push-up bra I wore that day on the dock made me look bigger than I really am."

Holding his gaze, she reached around her back to unfasten her bra, heart thumping hard, record rates achieved. But her pulse shot higher when Matt reached around and gripped her hand, stopping her efforts and putting about an inch of space between their torsos. She stared up at Matt, those beautiful hazel eyes boring into hers. Heat radiated from his body. Or maybe the one generating the scorching temperatures was her.

His voice low, Matt said, "There is absolutely no way I'll be able to take care of that laceration with you bare-chested. So leave the bra on." A muscle in his jaw ticked, and she had the absurd urge to ease the spot with her tongue. "At least until I'm done."

This last was delivered with a light in his eye that could melt metal.

"Nice to know I can at least warrant being labeled a distraction," she said.

"Never fear. You definitely fall into the category of a distraction. A major one. Not only did I bring the necessary equipment to clean and close up the laceration on your forehead, I brought a box of condoms, too, just in case you didn't have any here."

Her heart stopped, and then restarted with a stutter. Unfortunately, the faster rate made concentrating on the conversation difficult. She squirmed and he shot her a mock chastising look.

"You're going to have to be still," he said. "All that wiggling is…distracting."

Callie closed her lids. Best not to stare up into those hazel eyes. "Do you always have trouble focusing when closing up a woman's cut?"

"No, but they are usually dressed in more than a bra." His voice dropped an octave. "And it's never been you before."

His fingers gently traced around the bruised area briefly and she prided herself on her patience. On her ability to keep her eyes closed with that face and those dreamy eyes so close to hers. She felt his breath warm her forehead, and she gripped the counter, fighting the urge to lean up and take that fabulous mouth with hers.

She was too distracted by the memory to worry much about the sound of rustling, as if he were searching for something, but then came a brush of something soft and wet, followed by a sharp sting.

Callie's lids popped open as she sucked in a breath. "My God."

"Sorry."

An antiseptic smell drifted from the cotton ball in his hand, and he leaned in and pressed a kiss close to the wound before pulling his head back.

She stared up at those lips so close. "What are you using to clean the cut? Hydrochloric acid?"

The chuckle that followed brought a wry twist of her lips. "How did you guess?"

Callie studied Matt's face as he gently pinched the skin around the cut and applied the liquid skin adhesive. She concentrated on breathing, the sound of the air conditioner humming, anything to keep herself from rising up on tiptoe to kiss Matt, which wasn't easy. She had firsthand knowledge that he kissed like a dream. He hadn't needed much to bring her to her knees that day on the dock, just his mouth and those fabulous hands.

When he finished, he dropped his hand. "Now, be careful not to open that up until it has time to dry."

"Is that going to interfere with you taking me to bed?"

"Hell, no," he said, and then he covered her mouth with his.

At first it was just a damp press of skin against skin, his mouth slotted against hers. The heat in Callie's belly increased, seeping along her veins, and she rose up on her toes, taking more. With a groan, Matt opened his mouth, forcing Callie's open and tasting her with his tongue. He tipped his head to the right, and then to left, as if comparing how they best fit together. Heart thumping, Callie was just about to pull back and suggest moving things to the bedroom when Matt leaned down, gripped her behind the thighs and lifted her.

Callie pulled her head back. "Wait," she said with a gasp that contained both humor and desire, clutching his shoulders for balance. "What's your plan for providing lessons on how to remain focused despite distractions?"

The crooked smile on Matt's face sent anticipation and heat curling up in her stomach, and she wrapped her legs around his waist. With one hand against her bottom, he supported her weight as he pulled the box of condoms from his bag.

"No worries." He exited the bathroom, heading up the hallway and into her bedroom. He placed her on the bed, staring down at her with a heated look that sent her stomach searching for her toes. "I'll think of something."

His gaze swept down her body, the hazel eyes growing dark, and goose bumps fanned across her skin. Without a word, he pulled off her sandals and stripped her of her clothes, until all that remained were her panties and bra.

She pushed up on one elbow and reached for his shirt. "Let me help."

Matt gently pushed her back down, the crooked smile sinfully sexy. "No," he said. "Wouldn't want you to hurt yourself and pull that head wound back open."

"Then what am I supposed to—?"

Matt gripped her wrists and raised her hands over her head, curling her fingers around the wooden slats of her headboard. He leaned down and pressed a gentle kiss next to her cut.

"Your job is just to hold on and not move," he said.

A stab of desire sliced through her, heating her between the legs. "Not move?" she asked. "But how am I supposed to—"

Matt reached for the button on his shirt, and she watched, mesmerized, as he undid the row of buttons one by one and tossed the shirt aside. His eyes on hers, he reached for the front of his jeans, and Callie's heart picked up its pace. The muscles in his arms and chest rippled as he flicked open his pants and pushed everything down. Lean hips, well-muscled thighs and a heart-attack-inducing erection left Callie struggling to continue the act of breathing.

"Matt…"

The words died as he knelt at her feet, removing her bra and panties. She waited for him to kiss her. Instead, Matt picked up her leg, pressing openmouthed kisses up her shin, her thigh, and then landing on her hip bone.

"The key to keeping that incision safe," he murmured against her skin, "is to remain completely still."

She arched her back, hoping to encourage him to head south. Instead, he trailed higher until his tongue dipped in her navel, sending a skitter of sparks up her spine. He cupped her between the legs and shifted higher, his mouth moving up until it landed on a nipple.

Shock and desire shot through her limbs, and she arched her back, seeking more of that mind-blowing mouth against her skin. Matt circled the tip with his tongue, and Callie sucked in a breath. But just as she was melting at the caress, he ran his tongue down her abdomen, across her hip and landed between her legs.

Heat and pleasure blasted through her. "Oh, my God, Matt," she said, tipping her head back.

When Matt flicked his tongue against her, Callie whimpered, "Please…"

She wanted to wrap her arms around his back and pull his body down. She wanted his naked skin stretched out across the top of hers. She wanted to reach down and clutch his head, pulling him closer.

Fingers tight around the headboard, she said, "Can I let go yet?"

"Nope," he said. At least this time his voice sounded harsh, as if he were wound up tight and needed release.

Jeez, she knew how he felt.

"Not yet," he said.

He sat up on his knees, and Callie's breath escaped with a protesting sound. Palms damp against the wooden slats of the headboard, she watched Matt apply a condom, her fingernails digging into her palms. Eyes homing in on hers, he swooped up her body and buried himself deep between her legs. His pace relentless, he rocked into her.

Mind spinning, muscles straining, she struggled to keep her hold of the headboard as he moved. The intensity in his gaze and the dark, focused look on his face brought her closer to the edge. His body hard, Matt drove her higher, the muscles in his arms lengthening and bulging from his efforts.

"Matt."

"Okay."

His one-word response brought a cry of relief, and Callie wrapped her arms around his back, her legs around his hips, holding him close. Urging him on. Hanging on tight. The heat of pleasure burned hotter, brighter, until Callie was sure she'd burst into flames. Feeling out of control, she gripped his shoulders harder. The orgasm burst outward, shock waves moving through her body, and she closed her eyes, relishing the sensation, barely aware as Matt gave one final thrust, calling out her name.

Chapter Seven

The next morning, awareness came to Matt in layers, each one better than the one before. Slowly he became cognizant of a comfortable bed, of soft sheets and Callie's hair tickling his cheek, his hand resting on her hip. Her body lay lax, her breathing deep and even as she slept. For a moment he enjoyed the simple pleasure of holding a beautiful woman in his arms. A lazy morning where he had nothing he needed to do and no place he needed to be. Even better?

The potential for a repeat of last night.

He felt more relaxed than he had in a long time and not just because of the sex. Although the activities went a hell of a long way at taking the edge off the tension he'd been carrying around since he'd first laid eyes on Callie. The great sex left his body humming.

A buzzing sound caught his attention, and he peered over Callie's shoulder. His cell phone vibrated madly, inching across the nightstand in its efforts to get his attention. When it went to voice mail, his phone flashed. Five missed calls.

Damn.

Panic punched him, and he bolted upright in bed, picturing Tommy calling for help. The emergency room trying to contact him about his brother being brought in for an overdose. The police calling to deliver the tragic news...

The house was dark when Matt entered—not a peaceful stillness, but the eerie kind that filled him with dread. Suffocating. Terrifying. Anxiety crawled up his spine as he headed up the hallway and called out Tommy's name, getting no answer. He knew his brother was home because his car was in the drive.

When he spied his brother's bedroom door cracked open, Matt's steps slowed, his pulse increased and goose bumps prickled his neck, spreading throughout his limbs. His heart hammered in his chest as he slowly pushed the door open, and certainty slid into place when he saw Tommy lying on the floor, pale, as still as death.

Matt slammed his eyes shut against the memory, nausea rising in his stomach and tightening his chest. How could he have forgotten to check in with Tommy last night?

Matt fought to control his breathing, cursing under his breath, mindful of Callie sleeping next to him. He glanced down. Fortunately, she still appeared to be deep in sleep. Matt rolled out of bed and stood, reaching for the phone. As he scrolled through the missed calls, his heart continued to pound, no matter how much he told himself to calm down.

Every voice message was from Tommy, which meant he wasn't dead. At least not yet.

Relief poured through Matt, and he leaned against the wall, bracing his hands on his knees. Willing himself to friggin' get a grip.

Once he felt steadier, he padded down the hallway

and into Callie's living room. Hitting Tommy's number, Matt collapsed onto the couch and braced for the topic.

Tommy voice sounded worried. "Where the hell have you been?"

Matt rubbed his eyes and let out a self-directed scoff of ridicule.

"Sorry, Tommy. I got distracted."

Matt's mind drifted back to Callie

Yep, very distracted.

Tommy's huff sounded more amused than annoyed. "Yeah, well, when my worrywart of a big brother didn't check in like usual, I got concerned. And with every un-returned call, I thought you'd been mugged and knocked unconscious or something."

The bark of laughter held more bitterness than humor. Hopefully Tommy wouldn't notice.

"Sorry, Tommy. Long story. Wound up making a trip to the E.R. last night."

"You okay?"

"I'm fine. Just…helping out a friend."

"A friend?"

Matt ignored the implied inquiry beneath his broth-er's tone. "I'm heading back home tomorrow."

His return to Manford was long overdue.

"Good," Tommy said.

The relief in Tommy's voice had Matt sitting up right. For the first time, Matt noticed the tension underlying his brother's voice, a tension that didn't relate to his brother's worries about Matt.

"Are you, uh…?" Being a moron meant Matt's ques-tion came out incredibly lame. "Okay?" Matt finished.

Okay, of course, meaning many different things.

Are you sleeping all right?

Having trouble at work?

Using again?

Matt bit back the groan and dropped his head into his hand, phone still pressed to his ear. They'd been skirting the edges of this issue since the last time Matt had picked Tommy up from a thirty-day stint in rehab. And the two years of tiptoeing were tiresome. Because, seriously, how many ways could two men have the same conversation?

If you don't quit, you're going to wind up dead, Tommy.

I've given it up for good, Matt, I swear.

And in Tommy's defense, Matt knew his brother meant the words every time he repeated them.

Tommy's voice brought Matt back to the conversation. "No, everything's fine."

There was an awkward pause. "Good," Matt said, wondering what Tommy was *really* thinking.

"Penny and I will have a couple of steaks on the grill waiting for you when you get off the plane."

As always, Tommy managed to bring a smile to Matt's lips, despite the tension. "Sounds perfect."

Matt signed off and leaned his head back against the couch, closing his eyes. Wishing he could recapture that feel-good, peaceful moment this morning when he'd first woken up. The lingering pleasant buzz from a night of fantastic sex. The lack of the ever-present uneasiness eating away at his stomach. He was too young to feel this damn old.

The residual panic-induced adrenaline still coursed through his limbs. Normally he needed several cups of coffee before being fully awake in the morning. Today, the scare had left him supercharged, and the tension in Tommy's voice still weighed on Matt's mind.

Something had upset his little brother. And if Matt didn't get back soon and get to the bottom of whatever was going on, he might wind up dragging Tommy back to rehab again.

His gut clenched and he felt sick to his stomach.

Jesus, don't throw up.

Callie's voice broke through the unpleasant thought. "So you're heading out tomorrow?"

Matt opened his eyes and spied Callie leaning in the living-room doorway. She didn't look fully awake, with her honey-colored hair tousled and her eyes sleepy. She was in a T-shirt that just covered her bottom, her long legs bared—legs that had spent a good portion of the night wrapped around him.

Longing surged through him. The urge to pick her up and carry her back to bed was strong.

"Sorry." She pushed the hair out of her face. "I didn't mean to eavesdrop."

"No problem. And, yeah," he said. "I have several shifts I have to work this coming week."

And a brother to check in on.

Callie tipped her head. "Will you be coming back before the wedding?"

Six weeks without seeing Callie again seemed like cruel and unusual punishment. But Matt knew the tightness in his chest wouldn't ease completely with just a quick check on his brother, not with the tension he'd heard in Tommy's voice.

The playful light in Callie's eyes eased the tension until Matt had to fight a smile as he tried to sound serious. "Depends."

Clearly, she caught the underlying tease in his tone. "On what?"

"On whether or not you'll make it worth my while."

"Does a good party hold any merit?" Callie said. "I was hoping you would come to my family reunion with me. You can sit back, relax and enjoy the loaded comments bestowed upon me by some of my relatives. And if that doesn't tempt you—" her lips twisted wryly "—there'll be some great food, too. I just happen to be related to the woman who makes the best shrimp étouffée in two counties. Nice and spicy."

Matt laughed, enjoying the way Callie's dry humor eased that residual tightness in his chest. "That's not the kind of spicy I was hoping for."

Her warm gaze lit with mischief, Callie uncrossed her arms and came closer. And with each step she took every cell in Matt's body became tighter and tighter, focused on the enticing expanse of skin, the tension now of a different sort. And far more welcome.

She came to a stop in front of him. "So will you do a girl a favor and come back for a visit before the wedding?"

Matt looked up at Callie. He'd be crazy to plan a return visit when he had so much on his plate already. Two weeks of work at Manford Memorial, with a four-day stint in one of the busiest emergency rooms in Miami in between. Between travel, the need for sleep and the upcoming wedding, there wouldn't be much in the way of spare time. Adding in an unnecessary trip back to New Orleans clearly bordered on insane.

"I promise you can crash here during your stay," Callie said.

Hell, who could say no to that kind of offer?

Matt gave up, the grin creeping up his face as he

reached for Callie's thigh, pulling her into his lap. "I'll do my best to make it happen."

One week later

At ten o'clock in the evening, Matt let himself into the split-level house he'd grown up in and now shared with Tommy and Penny. Matt tossed his keys on the kitchen counter and rolled his shoulders to ease the tension of a long, boring shift in the E.R. Heading toward his side of the house, he was careful not to wake the sleeping occupants located at the other end. The arrangement had worked out better than he'd originally hoped.

One side of their shared home belonged to Tommy and Penny, providing them plenty of room for privacy. The space contained a bedroom, a family room and a guest-room-turned-gaming-room. The latter had been Tommy's childhood bedroom and, years later, served as his retreat during the worst of his getting-clean stages.

Matt had spent years tiptoeing past the room and hovering outside the closed door, watching and wondering and worrying about Tommy. Even if Tommy had moved out, there was no way Matt could ever enter the room without feeling that sick churn in his stomach, a nausea that always left him longing to vomit, just to purge himself of the feeling. During the worst times, darkness and despair had seemed embedded in every nook and cranny, oozing from the walls and carpet. The lingering echoes of those emotions still pressed in on Matt. Even now he felt the hair rise on the back of his neck every time he glanced up the hallway.

Matt lived on the other side of the house where he

had a bedroom and an office large enough to afford him some private space of his own. The kitchen and living room provided a common area in which Tommy, Penny and Matt could choose to hang out together at the end of the day. Since Matt traveled so much, he rarely spent more than a week at a time at his home base.

Clearly the current living situation wasn't a permanent solution, but for now the arrangement worked. When Penny had joined the Paulson household, Matt had offered to move into one of the nicer apartment complexes up the street. But Tommy had refused to kick Matt out of his home. With Tommy's track record, most of the decent rental properties would refuse to take him on as a tenant. Unfortunately, Penny's history ruled out even some of the shadier places in town. In truth, Matt hadn't fought the setup, mostly because the two couldn't hide much if Matt occasionally occupied the same home.

So they existed in this state of limbo, a lot like the limbo of his and Callie's relationship.

Sighing, Matt entered his bedroom and toed off his shoes. He gripped the hem of his scrub top and wearily pulled it over his head before reaching for his pants. He needed a shower, food and a good night's rest. But mostly, he needed to see Callie again.

Yesterday's sketchy night of sleep had started with dreams of her in a wet T-shirt, Matt's hands roaming freely over the thin cotton, tracing the lace of her bra. As if by magic, then he'd been stroking the bare curves of her breasts. Tasting her skin. Reaching for her shorts. And because everything came easy in a dream, suddenly she'd been naked, squirming beneath him with an endless amount of enticingly silky skin, and he'd been licking his way down her flat stomach and to her inner thigh...

He needed to get a grip.

Last week's flight back home had been delayed and he'd been stuck in the Minneapolis airport for twelve hours and, instead of catching a much-needed nap, he'd spent the entire time fantasizing about being back in Callie's bed. Not exactly the way to encourage grabbing some shut-eye on the plane, either. By the time he'd arrived home in Michigan, it was almost 3:00 a.m. and he was dead-tired, frustrated and ready to turn around and head back to New Orleans. Instead, he'd dropped into bed and tossed and turned, missing Callie even more. He'd finally fallen into an exhausted sleep and slept until nine in the morning, which meant he'd missed seeing Tommy before his brother left for work.

An anxious twist in Matt's chest had him clutching his dirty clothes, and he dumped his scrubs into the wicker hamper with more force than necessary.

At first glance, everything had seemed fine at home. Tommy looked good, Penny looked good and both appeared to be continuing on the path of the straight and narrow. Dinner that first night together had included steaks on the grill, as promised, but Tommy's behavior seemed off. The nagging feeling wasn't anything Matt could put a decisive finger on. There was a distance Matt wasn't used to, especially since they'd been living in each other's pockets for the past two years. And the tension had now been gnawing at Matt's insides for days.

Matt pondered the possible causes as he showered

and dressed in sweatpants and a T-shirt. He padded into the kitchen. Standing at the kitchen counter, he ate delicious leftover pasta, thanks to Penny, who knew how to cook. Adding her to the mix had definitely improved the cuisine in the Paulson house.

Two of his three requirements met, and with sex with Callie disappointingly out of the question, he knew sleep was still a long way off. Matt headed for his office and dropped onto the leather couch, turning on his laptop on the coffee table.

An icon popped on his screen, indicating Callie had just flipped on her computer. With her a time zone behind him, the late hour wasn't quite as bad for her as for him. He hesitated for a moment and then hit the call button.

The moment Callie's image appeared on screen, he felt his tension ease. She was sitting cross-legged on her bed, wearing pajamas. Unfortunately, the fifteen-inch screen on his laptop didn't do her beautiful eyes justice.

"This is a surprise," she said.

"A pleasant one, I hope."

"Absolutely."

He couldn't see the playful light in her gaze, but he knew of its presence because of her tone. And for a moment, all he wanted was to climb onto a plane and fly back to New Orleans where everything seemed so much easier and simpler.

And certainly a hell of a lot more fun.

"Did I interrupt anything?" he asked.

"Nothing exciting."

Files and small patches of fabric samples surrounded Callie on the bed. A silk robe clung to her shoulders but remained open in front. Matt spied a lacy tank top and what looked like a feminine pair of...

"Are those boxer shorts?" he said.

"You can take the tomboy out of the country, you know, but..." Smiling, she finished the sentence with a shrug and reached for her bedside table, picking up a glass of white wine. "At least they're hot pink and edged with lace. Besides, I haven't had to entertain company this late at night since you left."

A twinge of possessiveness flared, and Matt tamped it down and concentrated instead on the twinkle in her eyes on the monitor.

Her hair hung in a gentle loop at the nape of her neck, gathered in some sort of casual twist that managed to look comfortable and pretty and sexy, all at the same time. An empty plate on her nightstand suggested she'd just finished her dinner. Clearly she'd eaten in bed.

He wished he'd eaten in her bed, too.

Matt glanced at the files scattered on her comforter. "What are you working on?"

Her smile held more than a hint of mischievousness. "Just sitting down to compose my reply to an *Ex Factor* reader for my blog. Actually, you're the perfect person to help me with my response."

Matt let out a soft scoff. "I doubt that. I thought this was Colin's department."

Callie laughed. "He's responsible for the man's view, yes. But I wanted your thoughts before I replied."

"What's the question?"

Two seconds ticked by before she answered.

"A bride-to-be asking for advice on how to convince her future brother-in-law to walk her down the aisle," she said.

The one-two punch to his conscience came out of the blue, shocking the hell out of him.

Matt let out a groan. "You're making that up."

Callie shifted some paperwork and fabric swatches aside, settling back against her headboard with her glass of wine in hand. She stretched those toned, silky legs in front of her, bringing to mind when they'd been wrapped around his waist. The inside of his chest grew hot, heating the blood shooting through his veins.

When would he get a chance to hold her again?

He pushed the hopeless thought aside and concentrated on Callie, who was currently eyeing him over the rim of her wineglass. An expression like that meant trouble for sure.

She took a sip and carefully set her drink on the nightstand. "I had a long talk with Penny yesterday."

Of course she had.

"She was desperately trying to come up with someone to walk her down the aisle," Callie said. "And I told her she should ask you again."

Matt shifted uneasily on the couch, propping his feet on the coffee table just to the left of his laptop. Might as well get comfortable for the conversation ahead.

"Yeah?" he replied in his best noncommittal voice.

He knew Tommy was disappointed Matt hadn't told Penny he'd give her away. His brother hadn't come out and said as much, but Matt knew. The closer they drew to the date of the wedding, the tenser things had grown. Still, compared to all the other issues brewing between them, Penny's request seemed minor in comparison.

Callie's lighthearted tone was long gone. "Matt, you said yourself that I should be grateful for the family I have. That I should get over myself and go to that reunion because wasting the family I have was stupid."

His brow crinkled. "Those are *not* the words I used."

"No," she said, her chuckle drifting over the speaker. "You were definitely more tactful. But that's what you meant. And you were right. Going to the reunion is the right thing for me to do. I have a family. One that wants to see me, even if they do make the occasional callous remark." Callie sat up a touch, her brown eyes earnest, her voice soft. "You don't have that choice because your parents are dead, and that's a tragedy. But Penny doesn't have a choice, either. Her parents refuse to have anything to do with her." She paused before going on. "And that's a tragedy, too."

"I know."

Several beats passed by before Callie went on, tipping her head. "Do you not like Penny?"

He resisted the urge to bring the video chat to a close. He could sign off and close the lid to the laptop and be done with this conversation. But no matter the topic, the sight of Callie in her sexy boxer pj's was impossible to resist.

"It's not that." Matt wearily scrubbed his hand down his face. "Penny's fine."

And he meant the words, he seriously did. They weren't just a platitude he pulled out of his ass when convenient. He admired anyone who could fight an addiction and win. He knew better than most just how hard that battle could be. Penny was bright, capable and, if nothing else, she clearly loved Tommy.

"Are you against this marriage?" Callie asked.

"No." He winced at the force behind his words. He

dropped his hands into his lap, and his voice dropped several octaves, as well. "Maybe."

In response to Callie's hiked brow, Matt let out a sigh. "Yes."

Despite the harsh word, it felt good to get the sentiment off his chest. From the very moment Tommy had introduced Penny to Matt, Matt had been fighting the part of him dying to find a way to send the woman packing. He let out a soft scoff at the thought. As if he held *that* kind of power in his hands.

But the overwhelming urge had nothing to do with Penny personally and *everything* to do with the need to protect his brother, no matter what.

Matt felt like a dirtbag for admitting he didn't want Tommy and Penny to marry, but Callie's gaze remained free of judgment. And as he studied those beautiful brown eyes, relief slowly washed over him because he knew he could be absolutely, brutally honest with Callie. No matter how ugly his feelings, she wouldn't hate him for the truth.

He definitely could have used her steady presence during the worst of Tommy's addiction years.

"Tell me," she said softly.

The tight knot in his chest unwound a bit. "Jesus, Callie," he groaned out. "It's like taking the potential for disaster and multiplying the bloody thing by a hundred."

"What are you talking about?"

He dragged a hand through his damp hair, knowing he was leaving tufts sticking out in all directions. "I'm talking about Tommy relapsing and dragging Penny down with him." He scowled in an attempt to mask the all-consuming fear as he considered the alternative.

"Or vice versa. If she starts using again, how is Tommy going to resist temptation?"

Fear gripped him, and he hated himself for succumbing to the familiar emotion.

He shifted on the couch again. Now that he was on a roll, the words spilled out. "Or let's say they do manage to stay clean while they're together. What happens if the relationship tanks? Because let's face the facts here. Two former users probably aren't the most stable of sorts. How would Tommy handle the stress of a breakup and not be tempted to slip?"

Callie pursed her lips in thought as she reached for her glass and took another sip of wine. "Every relationship has the potential to tear a person down." She set her drink aside and met Matt's gaze again. "And this one is no different."

He briefly pressed his lids closed, wishing the logic helped. "I know."

But how many ran the potential to lead to something so dark? So permanent? Because nothing was more permanent than *death*.

Callie crossed her arms across her chest. "Tommy and Penny understand each other better than anyone else ever could. Yes, they could bring each other down. There's no doubt about that." She didn't sugarcoat the words, even allowing more time for them to sink deep before going on. "But I happen to believe they'll hold each other up."

He hiked a brow dryly. "Yeah, well, you arrange weddings for a living. Your favorite character is Elizabeth Bennet, a woman who conveniently managed to fall in love with a man who could save her family from destitution. A fairy tale."

"*Pride and Prejudice* is not a fairy tale."

Matt hiked a brow. "Close enough. Seriously, Callie, real life rarely works out like that." He let out a self-directed scoff. "You see happily ever after around every corner, but I get to patch people up after they beat the crap out of each other."

I get to be the lone family member left to pull my brother out of the gutter, over and over again.

"Did you have a bad shift tonight?" she asked.

Hell, yeah.

"Kind of," he said instead. Despite the topic of conversation, Matt fought a smile, his lips twitching at the memory. "The chief of staff argued with the head of E.R. about transferring a patient, a divorcing couple had a screaming match in triage and two best friends showed up because they'd beat the crap out of each other over a computer game."

Callie rolled her eyes. "The friends were guys, I'm assuming."

"Yeah. It started out as a joke and ended up fairly ugly," Matt said. "To be fair, a case of beer had been consumed, so I'm not sure you can hold them completely accountable for their stupidity."

"Of course you can hold them accountable," she said. "There's no excuse for being stupid enough to drink so much alcohol that a computer game becomes more important than a friendship."

Callie leaned forward and came closer to the screen, lying on her belly and folding her arms on the bed. The new position brought her close enough for him to see the light in her eyes. This time the spark was earnest, nothing playful about it at all.

"Penny needs you right now, Matt. She's going to be

a sister of sorts, and you owe it to your brother to start this relationship out on the right foot." A line appeared between her brows. "Don't make Penny keep paying for the same mistakes over and over again."

Callie was right. He *knew* she was right. Penny and Tommy both deserved Matt's unconditional support. But so far, he'd let fear rule his reactions. The habit would be difficult to break because the fear ran so deep that nothing short of a scalpel could cut the sucker out, and even that would take a significant piece of Matt during the process.

He'd just have to carry on with the fear firmly in place.

Matt blew out a breath and studied the woman on the screen, wishing like hell they were in the same room. "Man, I wish I could touch you right now."

A glimmer appeared in her eyes. "Tell you what," she said. "If you agree to at least have a conversation with Penny about the wedding, I'll let you watch me touch myself."

The bark of shocked amusement slipped out even as Matt's heart set up a pounding pace beneath his sternum. "Are you freaking kidding me?"

"I'm deadly serious."

He eyed Callie's cleavage, the potential blooming and bringing all sort of delicious scenarios to mind. "How many glasses of wine have you had?"

"I just had a conversation with my mother," she said dryly, "which rarely goes well. The numbing effects of two glasses of wine are about the only way I can survive our conversations. Unfortunately, that's just enough alcohol to also make me reckless—" a huge grin crept up her mouth "—but not enough to excuse me from my stupidity."

Callie dropped the robe down her shoulders and tossed it aside, leaving her lacy tank and the curve of her breasts displayed. The view on Matt's screen improved considerably.

"I'll touch mine if you'll touch yours," she said smoothly.

The libido-punching words and the seductive look on her face morphed his blood into flaming rivers of fire, licking along his limbs. He fisted his hand, fighting the groan.

He'd give anything to able to reach through the screen and pull Callie onto his lap. His mind filled with images of his time with Callie: the wet shirt plastered against firm breasts, her cheeks flushed, her mouth parted as she convulsed around his fingers in the hammock.

Even better? Callie beneath him as she'd urged him on in her bed.

On screen, she reached for the hem of her lacy tank and pulled the fabric over her head.

Callie now sat there, beautiful breasts exposed, her top dangling from her finger. "So what do you think?"

His voice hoarse, he said, "I think what they say about cameras is right."

"What do they say?" she said as she tipped her head curiously, a lock of honey-colored hair falling across her cheek.

And a bare-chested woman had no right looking so innocently adorable and sexy and sophisticated, all at the same time.

"The lens does add five pounds." A teasing grin tried

to hijack his mouth. "Specifically, 2.5 to each side. You look bigger, even without the corset."

She threw back her head and laughed, and the sound soothed away the lingering bits of his bad mood, courtesy of a shift with patients who'd brought their arguments into his E.R. Matt's muscles relaxed as the tension slipped away.

Callie scooted forward and propped her elbows on the bed, her breasts now hanging in full view of the camera. The immediate reaction of Matt's libido almost did him in, tenting his sweatpants in an embarrassing way, and he tried to discreetly ease the pressure by tugging on his waistband.

"Careful," Callie said, "or I'll hit the minimize tab on the screen, and you'll look much smaller."

A hoarse chuckle escaped. "Don't you dare."

Though God knows he had bigger worries to be concerned about, like the fact that moving air in and out of his chest suddenly felt complicated.

"I haven't been sleeping well." Her tone husky, she slowly slid a hand down her stomach. "You?"

His voice felt raw. "No."

"If you agree to talk to Penny, I'll let you watch me masturbate."

His already straining erection strained some more, and his groin grew so tight he thought he'd crack in half. Christ, every muscle was tensed and ready and willing and able, urging Matt to do exactly whatever Callie asked.

But wouldn't he be better off calling a halt to this impossible relationship now? Every interaction led him further and further down a slippery slope. He'd shown up in New Orleans to find a wedding planner and leave, but had wound up staying for two weeks. He'd left for home with the plan of returning for the wedding, and moved heaven and earth to free up some time for another trip back. Until eventually breaking things off felt impossible.

"And then I can watch you do the same," she said.

"You want me to masturbate on camera for you?"

"Why not?" she said. "We're both grown-ups. If I sign off now, what will you do?"

"Take care of this myself."

"What's a little video sexting other than a way to challenge ourselves? You know, up the ante on our third-base event on the dock."

"So now, instead of third base we're...what?" He quirked a teasing eyebrow. "Hitting zero base?"

"You wouldn't want to deprive me of the pleasure of watching, would you?"

Desire shot through his limbs, his heart slamming in his chest, and he tugged on the leg of his briefs, dying to provide a little relief.

"Why are you so intent on this little endeavor, anyway?" he asked.

"You look like you've had a crappy day."

"I did."

The arguing of the administrators had been prolonged and, as with most management types, full of a lot of hot air as both sides seemed intent on hearing themselves speak. Matt just wanted to provide appropriate care for the patient. But the scene had morphed into Matt being thrown into the mix of two men running for political office. And between the fighting friends and the divorcing couple, the evening had ended on a truly sucky note.

A little sexual release seemed a small pleasure to ask.

But part of him wondered about the point of this little, well, *exercise,* for lack of a better word. Callie lived in New Orleans. Callie *loved* New Orleans. And her business clearly thrived in a city that provided ample opportunity for themed weddings. Matt knew few couples, if any, would travel to Manford, Michigan, to fulfill their adventure wedding fantasies. And he certainly couldn't move because Tommy lived here.

The last time Matt had left his little brother for too long, Tommy had almost died....

Matt slammed his eyes closed, torn between what he wanted now and what he feared would be too hard to let go of later.

"Matt."

He opened his eyes and found Callie had shifted on her bed.

"Okay," he said. "I can't promise anything, but I'll think about having a conversation with Penny."

"That's all a girl can ask," Callie said.

A palm cupped her breast and her seeking hand finally slid beneath the front of her boxers. "I have a thing for your broad shoulders," she murmured. "I have ever since the dressing room." Her honey words rolled over him, and her thumb began to circle the tip of her breast. "I love the feel of your hard chest against mine when you move on top of me." The bud hardened and swelled, and blood *whooshed* annoyingly in his ears. He didn't want to miss even the tiniest inflection in the drawl.

Her eyes glazed over. "Picture me spread beneath you."

His chest struggled to suck in enough oxygen.

She looked like every adolescent's wet dream.

Granted, she didn't have as lush a figure as most centerfolds. But he craved the feel of her skin, her taste on his tongue and the toned legs. The gentle flare of her hips was just enough to entice a man. Her breasts were perfectly formed. As her breath came faster, the tips rose and fell faster with every breath. The hand down her panties moved faster. The fact that he couldn't see exactly what was going on was almost hotter for the secrecy.

The only thing he knew for certain was that she was ready for him. If he was in her bed right now, he could pull her beneath him and thrust deep, no foreplay needed. Good God, he closed his eyes and remembered sliding between those silken thighs and into her wet heat.

With a groan, he reached into his pants and grasped his erection. He ignored the thoughts swirling in his head as he began to stroke himself.

"Matt—" Callie's voice cracked.

"I know."

"Hurry," she said.

His hand pumped a little harder as he watched her eyes glaze over, her hips start to roll with every movement of the hand between her legs. He grew so tight he thought he'd crack.

"That's really…" Her voice trailed off. She sounded out of breath. "Hot," she drawled.

"Is *hot* the agreed upon safe word?"

"Do we need a safe word?"

"With you around, hell, yeah."

Nothing was safe with Callie around, most of all his sanity.

Even on screen he could see the flush on her cheeks

and her lips part as she began to pant for breath. And while his gaze remained locked on hers, every once in a while he saw her tick her gaze down. To watch what he was doing.

Frustrated by the constricting fabric, Matt gave up on restraint and tugged his sweatpants down to his thighs before returning his hand to his erection, his hand beginning an intense rhythm. His attention drifted between memories of Callie moving beneath him in bed and the live picture of her on screen. Sweat dotted his upper lip, and the pleasure wound tighter. He remembered the scent of her shampoo and the sounds she made as she clutched his back. Callie whimpered—even that tiny sound held a hint of the South. A second ticked by before he realized the noise had come from Callie and not just his memories.

"Oh, my God, Matt. I can't—" Callie's voice gave out.

He glanced at her, and suddenly Matt couldn't suck in the oxygen fast enough.

Matt had the overwhelming urge to lean forward and lick the computer screen, a sad substitute for the sweet taste of Callie's skin. Instead, he imagined taking her nipple into his mouth and sucking hard, picturing her writhing against him. He could almost smell the scent of sex, the feel of sweat-slicked skin against sweat-slicked skin. An electric energy pulsed in his groin, demanding to be released.

Don't you dare finish first, Paulson.

"Callie," he whispered, his voice hoarse.

The single, desperate word had the intended effect. Callie arched her back and let out a long, low moan.

Despite the soft tone, the sound slammed into Matt, and he closed his eyes, following on her heels.

Matt had no idea how much time ticked by before he could focus again. Slowly he became aware of his heaving breaths, and he lifted his head to stare at the computer screen. Callie had a dreamy look on her face and a slight smile on her lips.

"Hey," she said softly.

"Hey, yourself."

Her smile grew bigger. "Aren't you glad you agreed?"

A chuckle escaped. "Callie, hitting zero base with you is a hundred times better than hitting a home run with someone else."

Chapter Eight

Callie weaved her way through the crowded baggage terminal of the Louis Armstrong New Orleans International Airport, dodging passengers and carts loaded with luggage as she looked for Matt. Because of the location of the airport and her condo in relation to her family reunion, he'd insisted on taking a taxi to her place because picking him up would have been out of her way. And they'd be cutting the timing close enough.

She'd finally pretended to give in. But surprising him as he gathered his bags had been her plan all along. Because Matt had decided to make the trip back to New Orleans again. A special trip, just to see her. And she had every intention of making the most of the three-day weekend.

She knew how hard he'd worked to clear his schedule so he could come back for her family reunion. The effort he'd exerted on her behalf generated a lovely feel-good buzz, along with an anticipation and hope that left her alarmed at her own stupidity.

Don't expect too much, Callie.

She shoved back the warning voices in her head, promising herself not to think negative thoughts. Matt hadn't gone out of his way to steal an extra couple of days with her just so she could wallow in doubt about the future. She spied a broad back and sandy hair that curled a little at the collar, and pleasure flushed up her back.

Nope, not a chance. She intended to enjoy every second they spent together.

She grinned as she tapped one side of a very nice set of shoulders. "Excuse me, sir. Do you have the time?"

Matt turned, and, if she'd been holding out for a smile, she'd have been disappointed.

Instead of responding, he hooked his hand behind her neck and dragged her close, her body crash-landing into his. He kissed her without apology, nothing tentative or hesitant about the maneuver. Hot and hungry and brimming with heat, his hard lips moved across hers as if he'd been thinking of nothing else for the entire flight down. Perhaps since last night.

Maybe for the past two weeks.

Callie gripped his shirt and pulled him close, moaning into his mouth as she plastered her torso tighter against his. She met him turn for turn, taste for taste. Despite the crowd, she did her best to show him she'd missed him, too. His tongue rasped against hers, want and need and determination stamped in his every action. Like a gentle assault she couldn't quite fend off, not that she had any desire to do such a ridiculous thing.

When the need to inhale grew too great, Callie pulled back.

"Though my appreciation for Skype has skyrocketed, I much prefer face-to-face encounters." Matt grinned and looked down the front of her blouse, no doubt seeing the lacy cups of her push-up bra. "You hiding a watch down there?"

"Nope." She held up her wrist. "Today I'm wearing one like everybody else."

His lips quirked. "How disappointing."

"No worries," she said, mimicking his favorite phrase. "I'll make it up to you later."

"You mean after I eat lunch with the LaBeau family and start sweating cayenne pepper out of my pores?"

Callie laughed. "I can't wait." Though the thought of the entire LaBeau family being present left her nibbling on her lip in concern. All those aunts and uncles and cousins she hadn't seen in so long, swarming around her...

The day had started out cloudy and cool and stayed so for most of their two-hour drive. Fortunately, the sun finally broke through the clouds just in time for Callie to arrive at the outdoor park by the Mississippi River, Matt by her side. The crowd of LaBeaus had already gathered around the tables set up lengthwise, enough food to feed the town of New Orleans, and then some.

Callie eyed the crowd, a swell of nausea slaying the last of her appetite. "I'm thinking we should do this in small doses."

He frowned in confusion. "You mean eat?"

"No," she said. "Meet my relatives."

"If I can survive Aunt Billie's étouffée then I can definitely handle your relatives."

"Oh, they'll love you." Callie's smile felt tight. "It's me they might have a problem with."

Aunt Billie stopped by first, and Callie was grateful her aunt was so reliable. A few teasing comments later, and Callie knew she was blushing, and then a warm welcome for Matt was delivered with a hug and an offer to bring him some of her étouffée herself. Promising, of course, to bring him the milder version this time.

The next thirty minutes passed uneventfully. A few aunts and uncles and distant cousins wandered by, not to mention a few people she couldn't pin down her relationship to. Callie made the introductions and there were a few wayward comments about how long it'd been since she last came to the reunion. Several questions about her business, and one or two that were an indirect reference to her past. All in all, mostly just a whole lot of chitchat that didn't mean much. But, in some ways, meant *everything.* Slowly, her tension eased to bearable levels, and she stopped bracing every time another family member approached.

And then her parents arrived.

Callie watched her mother make her way across the grass in Callie's direction. They had the same figure, except her mother's hips reflected her love of the homemade biscuits she had perfected years ago.

"Hey, Mama."

She leaned in to kiss her mother on the cheek, even as dread curled up in her stomach and took up more than its fair share of room.

"I just heard about the weekend event you're arranging for Colin," her mother said. "A friend of mine heard about it on the radio."

Callie bit back the sigh and plastered a smile on her face. "Actually, I'm arranging the weekend for a *client,* Mama." She gestured at Matt, grateful for his steady presence at her side. "Matt Paulson hired me to help with his brother's wedding. Tommy and his fiancée met online playing one of Colin's games."

"What a lovely story," her mother said with a nod at Matt.

The way her mom eyed him made it clear she couldn't care less about the engaged couple. The brother of the groom, on the other hand...

"Callie's doing an excellent job," Matt said.

"I'm sure she is," her mother said. She turned to look at Callie. "Your little party business does seem to be doing quite well."

Your little party business...

Her mother always qualified Callie's business in such a way as to make her feelings known. As if being a themed wedding planner was okay, but only if you had no other options.

Callie's heart slipped lower in her chest as her face strained to maintain the smile, and she ignored Matt's gaze as his brows tented curiously over his eyes. He opened his mouth as if to say something, and then pressed his lips into a firm line. Apparently, in five seconds Matt had surmised the best way to deal with Callie's mother.

The proverbial biting of the tongue.

Though Callie wished she was biting his instead.

Heaven help her, not the thought to be having while holding a tricky conversation with her mother. Matt reached out and settled his hand in the small of her back, and Callie sent him a grateful look. The smile he responded with calmed her nerves and she returned the smile.

"Callie is quite bright," her mother said to Matt before turning back to Callie. "Imagine what you could have done if you'd applied the same energy to a law practice."

Her heart slipped to her toes. She knew how proud her parents had been when, in high school, she'd announced she wanted to go to law school. They'd proudly shared the news every time they'd gone back to visit their old hometown. There wasn't a single relative, distant or otherwise, that hadn't been invested in her progress at college.

And then she'd gotten arrested and lost her scholarship and...

Dear God.

Callie tried to come up with a response. "Mama—"

But that was it, because what else was there to say?

"She's the best themed wedding planner in New Orleans," Matt said smoothly.

Jeez, why was she standing here so tongue-tied? She should say something to her mother. She should defend her business, her life, her *choices*. Instead, she let Matt come to her defense.

"Of course she's the best," Callie's mother said. "But there really isn't that much competition." She tipped her head and met Matt's gaze. "Are you two dating?"

Callie's heart attempted to leap from her chest and she lightly gripped her mother's elbow. *"Mama."*

"What?" Belle LaBeau said, as if she didn't understand why Callie was so upset.

Callie shot Matt an apologetic smile. "Matt, will you excuse us for a moment please?"

The amusement twinkled in Matt's eyes. "No worries."

Callie began to drag her mother in the direction of a flat, grassy spot overlooking the river.

"Mama," Callie said, careful to keep her voice low. "What are you doing?"

"When my daughter brings a man to our family reunion, I have to assume he's more than just a client."

"Matt is—" Callie wearily swept her hair from her face. "He's not—" She dropped her hand to her side, frustrated by her inability to identify what Matt was, not only to her mother, but to herself, as well. "He's just…a friend."

Good Lord. She'd been reduced to a lying, babbling idiot.

"Does Matt live in New Orleans?" her mother asked.

The question landed like a well-placed barb in Callie's gut. What was it about mothers that gave them the ability to sniff out the painful heart of a matter in 3.3 seconds flat?

"No," Callie said, and her face felt like it would crack from the effort to keep from frowning. "He lives in Manford, Michigan."

"Never heard of it," Belle said.

"Neither had I before meeting Matt," Callie said.

"Does he have family around these parts?"

"No," Callie said, gritting her teeth.

"No ties to New Orleans at all?"

"None whatsoever, Mama."

The longer the back and forth went, the more tense Callie's spine became, until she'd thought she'd snap in half. The fact her mother was verbalizing Callie's secret concerns only made matters worse.

Thankfully, Callie's mother paused. But before Callie's tight muscles could lessen even a smidgen, Belle LaBeau opened her mouth to speak again, and Callie interrupted her.

"Is this really necessary, Mama?"

When they reached the far end of the grassy spot, Callie let go of her mother's arm.

"It's just a simple question, Callie. Surely Mr. Paulson doesn't mind? You two are either dating, or you're not." She hiked a brow. "So?"

Callie opened her mouth. "I—"

Belle LaBeau's brow shifted even higher.

"I don't know," Callie finished in a rush.

The disappointment in her mother's eyes was a familiar look. "Callie," she said with a defeated tone. "When are you going to do more than arrange *other* people's weddings and find a man of your own?"

And with that, her mother pivoted on her heel and headed back to the pack of relatives in the park. Callie stared after her.

Are you two dating?

How come she didn't have an answer to her mother's question? But there were also more important questions at hand. The wedding weekend was coming up quickly, and once the event was over, what would happen then?

Matt swung the handle with everything he had, and the ax rotated through the air and struck the wood with a solid *whump,* well outside his intended target. The small crowd gathered around the booth moaned in sympathy. Matt propped his fist on his hip, frowning at the bright red bull's-eye, the blade buried a good two feet from the outside ring.

Clearly he wouldn't be winning any awards today.

"Good thing you have other skills to recommend you, because I'm not sure you'd do so well in the Middle Ages."

At the sound of Callie's voice from behind, Matt smiled and turned to face her.

Dressed in a simple medieval barmaid dress, Callie grinned up at him. Friday had been pure chaos as the wedding guests who'd arrived early at the designated hotel had gathered for dinner at a local restaurant. Matt's time with Callie had been disappointingly limited since he'd arrived in town for the wedding, too much of Callie's days taken up with last-minute details or impromptu meetings with Penny and Tommy.

And Matt refused to be amused by the sight of Callie's and Tommy's heads bowed together, both getting excited over some ridiculous detail about the weekend. Last evening he'd caught the two of them huddled together in a corner, engaged in an earnest debate about how to set up the ax-throwing competition so as many people as possible could enjoy the view.

Unfortunately, at the time, Matt had had no idea this would be to his disadvantage.

"I think I just lost the first round," he said as he headed for Callie.

She smiled and stepped closer, closing the gap between them. "You need someone to cheer you up?"

Matt linked his fingers with hers and led Callie a few steps away, pulling her beneath the awning of a neighboring tent that wasn't quite as crowded and offered a bit of privacy. Fortunately the heat wave had ended long ago, and while the skies were clear and sunny, the cool breeze meant Matt wouldn't be needed to treat the participants for heat stroke.

A definite plus in his book.

Grateful for the rare moment alone, he leaned in to nuzzle Callie's ear, enjoying the scent. Her hair smelled of magnolias and her skin smelled like…well, like *Callie*. And how he recognized the scent after only two months, with only two actual weeks together, was beyond him.

"Cheer me up? What did you have in mind?" he said.

Callie placed her hand on his chest and leaned in close. "I'll tell you tonight if you stop by my place before heading back to the hotel."

"I could skip going back to my hotel room altogether."

"You could. However, if you spend *all* night at my place I won't be at my best tomorrow."

"So?"

He kissed his way up her neck and lightly nipped the delicate shell of her ear before stealing a hard kiss. But the simple contact felt majorly insufficient. He returned to delve deeper, tasting her tongue with his, enjoying the way she gripped the hair at his neck, as if needing the stability to stay upright.

"Just how much sleep do you need in order to pull tomorrow off, anyway?" Matt asked against her mouth.

"I'm not sure," she whispered back.

The sound of a throat clearing broke the spell.

Matt looked up and found Tommy staring at them both with the hugest grin on his face, his arm wrapped around Penny. With her black, pixie cut hair and petite frame, she looked fragile enough to break. That she'd survived what she'd done to her body never ceased to amaze Matt. Tommy was taller than Matt by an inch, but thinner by twenty pounds. At least he no longer appeared gaunt. Neither one looked as if they were nervous about the wedding tomorrow. In fact, in their medieval outfits they looked like just two of the guests enjoying the day.

Tommy's gaze shifted from Matt to Callie and then back again. "Can I steal Callie for a second, Matt?"

Matt fought like hell to pretend that heat wasn't rising up his face at his little brother catching him necking like a stupid schoolkid. Tommy looked intensely amused, if not a little shocked. Not surprising given Matt hadn't been forthcoming about his relationship with Callie. Mostly because he knew there would be questions. Questions he didn't know how to respond to.

Questions he didn't know the answer to himself.

Matt's voice came out gruffer than he'd planned. "No problem. Have at it. I'm sure you both have stuff to discuss about tomorrow."

Callie didn't look embarrassed at all. Instead, she seemed to find something in Matt's face humorous.

She reached up to plant a kiss on his lips. "I'll meet you at the LARP tent at two?"

"Sure."

Tommy and Callie instantly launched into a debate about a problem with this afternoon's schedule for the live-action role-playing as they headed in the direction of the LARP tent. Penny turned to look up at Matt, and he felt her gray gaze all the way to his medieval-approved work boots.

Wasn't dealing with a kid brother enough? Must he endure his soon-to-be sister-in-law's amusement, too?

But Penny's eyes were somber as she looked at Matt. "I want to thank you again for agreeing to walk me down the aisle."

Matt bit back a groan and shifted on his feet. He'd almost prefer being mocked for acting like a schoolkid who couldn't keep his hands to himself. When he'd decided to tell Penny he'd changed his mind, he chose to make the announcement with as little fanfare as possible. So two nights after his conversation with Callie, and the spectacular Skype call, Matt had mentioned at dinner that he'd be fine with walking Penny down the aisle, if she still wanted him to.

Tommy had looked speechless, and Penny had barely managed to let out a shocked yes before Matt had picked up his plate and concentrated on the cleanup. Too bad he didn't have any pressing activities he could bury himself in now. Somehow, he didn't think signing up for a second try at ax-throwing qualified as pressing.

Especially given his hideous lack of skills.

He swept his gaze across the field of white tents, the setting like the base encampment prior to one of the many epic battles in *The Lord of the Rings*. A crowd of people milled about in their costumes. But, unfortunately, nothing required Matt's immediate attention.

He aimed for a nonchalant shrug, hoping he pulled it off. "No biggie."

Penny let out a small laugh, but Matt got the impression that there was zero humor in the act. "It's a very big deal for me. I mean, I know I'm not exactly the girl you had in mind for Tommy."

Despite everything, Matt let out an amused scoff. "That's assuming I even gave the matter much thought. I was too busy trying to keep him alive."

He hadn't meant to let the last bit slip out.

"I know you were." She stepped forward and laid a hand on Matt's arm. "I love him, Matt. I really do."

Oh, God. How had he suddenly become the trusted

sidekick in a chick-flick movie, slated as the confidant he never wanted to be? Ever. In this life, or the next.

"I know how close you two are, and I just wanted to say…" her lips twisted, and she paused before going on "…thanks."

He cleared his throat. "Well, whether you want to be or not," he said, his voice gruffer than he'd planned, "you're part of the family now."

Tears welled in her eyes and left Matt dying to escape. Before he could figure out how to make that happen gracefully, Penny pulled him into a hug that caused the sword at his hip to jab him in the abdomen. Two of the longest seconds of his life later, Penny pulled back and reached on tiptoe to plant a kiss on Matt's cheek.

Which was nicer than he'd thought it would be, but all he really wanted was to find Callie and grab a few minutes alone. Penny shot him a beautiful smile, spun on her heel and took off.

Feeling a little lighter, he watched his soon-to-be sister-in-law thread her way through the crowd. At least the weekend weather appeared to be behaving for tomorrow's wedding. The sunny days came complete with a cool breeze and mild temperatures. Good thing, too, seeing how most of the guests were dressed for the times. No shorts or tank tops or T-shirts, just tunics and cloaks and surcoats, not to mention petticoats and peasant dresses.

He scanned the sea of colors, looking for Callie, when a hand clapped him on the back.

"Can I buy the best man a beer?"

Thwarted again.

Matt turned and hiked a brow at his kid brother. Tommy swept the brown waves of hair from his face—a nervous habit since he'd been a little kid. The sight never failed to trigger a swell of affection in Matt's heart.

"Mead," Matt said. "Callie very specifically instructed me to call it mead."

"Yeah." Tommy's brown eyes crinkled at the corners. "About Callie—"

"Beer," Matt said, fighting the scowl and hoping to put off any further questioning. Mentioning Callie's name had been tantamount to asking for his kid brother's harassment. "I'm definitely up for a beer."

Tommy shot Matt a look that screamed, "Nice try, sucker," clearly communicating that Tommy was on to his big brother's deflection technique and was only humoring him.

For now.

Matt wasn't entirely sure why he didn't want to discuss Callie with Tommy. They'd been living in each other's pockets for so long the reluctance felt strange. But something about his time in New Orleans felt too personal to discuss. A private time Matt didn't want to share with anyone.

Including his brother.

Regardless, a small knot of tension curled low in Matt's gut as they weaved their way through the crowd of people, passing the strolling minstrels on their way to the largest tent set in the middle of the field. A meeting place, of sorts, with a crowd clearly intent on reliving the feel of a medieval tavern.

Tommy found two empty stools at the end of a crudely constructed wooden table. A barmaid arrived to take their order and, as soon as she returned with two mugs of beer, the two of them were left alone with nothing but the noise around them and several years' worth of unresolved issues between them.

Sticking with the matter at hand seemed best.

"To you and Penny," Matt said, lifting his mug.

Tommy grinned and toasted Matt back. When his brother took a drink and set his beer down, the determined look on his face left Matt wishing he could go back to throwing another ax, even if it meant risking getting booed by a large crowd.

"There's something I've wanted to ask you," Tommy said.

Matt felt like a fool for not meeting his brother's eyes. "Fire away."

"What's up with you and Callie?"

Matt lifted his gaze to his brother's brown eyes—puppy eyes, their mother had called them. Funny how Matt had forgotten about that until just now. But she'd been right. Tommy had the same look that managed to look happy and sad, wise and innocent, all at the same time.

Matt shrugged. "We've decided not to label the relationship just yet."

Long-distance was the only label that fit. But the idea totally sucked. He'd been down the long-distance relationship road before. He couldn't imagine this time would end any prettier.

"But you're sleeping with her," Tommy said.

Frowning, Matt ran his thumb up his mug, staring at the trail left behind in the condensation. Not being the kind to kiss and tell left him in a bit of a quandary. He only had two choices, to either share too much or lie. And neither sat right with Matt.

Tommy let out a laugh. "Never mind. Your silence is good enough. Actually, I'm kind of relieved."

"Really?" Sleeping with Callie certainly made Matt feel better. But why the heck would Matt's relationship make *Tommy* feel better? "Why?"

A grin crept up his kid brother's face. "Because all that time you were down here in New Orleans, arranging this shindig, I felt bad that you had to be the one working out how to pull this weekend off. When a few days turned into almost two weeks…" Tommy ruffled his shaggy brown hair. "I don't have to tell you I was feeling pretty guilty."

"No worries, sport." Matt reached across the table and gave Tommy's shoulder a cuff. "You just owe me your undying allegiance for the rest of your life. Simple enough."

Matt's attempt at dodging a heavier discussion with a lighthearted response didn't work. Tommy's expression remained fixed on Matt and serious. And the look never went well for Matt.

"But before you stand up beside me tomorrow," Tommy said. "I want to say it again." Tommy leaned his elbows on the table. "I'm sorry for everything I put you through."

More than just the words, the expression on his little brother's face left Matt on edge.

Matt didn't look away, and every ounce of tease in his tone disappeared. "I know you are."

"But I also need to know that you forgive me," Tommy said.

Well, hell.

Matt sat back and stared out at the chaos beyond the tent. Forgiveness, he'd found, had been harder and harder to come by. The first relapse had been easy. The second, not so much. By the third round of rehab, forgiveness had been a huge struggle. A battle Matt had sometimes thought he wouldn't win.

But here they sat, two years later...

You can't make them keep paying for the same mistakes over and over again.

Callie was right. Even if they had been in this very spot before, and Tommy had screwed up again. And clearly Tommy needed a truthful answer and not a glib response. Maybe Tommy had put his brother through an emotional wringer, but his hard work this past twenty-four months meant he deserved nothing less than an honest answer.

That and the fact the man was set to get married tomorrow.

Matt delivered the words while staring at his mug. "I'm not gonna lie, Tommy. It hasn't been easy." He lifted his gaze to his brother. "But...come on." Matt leaned forward and folded his arms on the table. "Why would I help arrange this weekend if I still had even a trace of resentment left? All I want is for you to be happy. I mean, look around you." He gestured toward the scene that included knights, and maidens, and trolls. Matt let out a huff of humor as he looked at his kid brother. "You think I'd go to all this trouble otherwise?"

Sam's serious face didn't budge. "Yeah, you would. You *totally* would." Despite the words, a grin slowly spread across Tommy's face, bringing the same the response from Matt. "But it's good to know that's not the case."

Matt blew out a breath, and the tension in his shoulders eased. "Well, now that we have all that cleared—"

"I'm not done, Matt. I need you to lighten up a little."

"Lighten up?"

"You know what I'm talking about," Tommy said.

The noise of the tent filled the air between them, and tension curled in Matt's gut. He watched a juggler wander by, wishing he could avoid the upcoming conversation.

"Look," Tommy said, "I'm getting through this, day by day. Both Penny and I. And yeah, sure—" Tommy pushed his hair back from his face "—some days it takes all I have to make it through. But I'm clean." He stared at Matt. "I'm *clean.*"

Matt blinked back the pain, hating the words that needed to be said, even after all this time. He'd spent ten years watching Tommy, struggling to help him fight this demon that had him firmly in its grip. He'd never said the words before, because the sentiment had felt like a betrayal. But they needed to be said now.

I'm clean.

Because how many times had Matt heard those words?

Matt's words came out rough. "Yeah, I know you are, Tommy," he said. Two sharp heartbeats thumped by. "But for how long?"

Tommy barely registered a flinch on his face.

Jesus, Matt. You're such a bastard.

"You have to stop hovering, Matt," Tommy said. "I'm not a kid anymore."

"I know you're not."

Tommy went on as if Matt hadn't spoken. "Because you and I know there is no end point here. I'll always be at risk. Some days are so damn hard I want to curl up in a corner and cry." Tommy leaned closer, and Matt's chest ached so hard he thought his ribs would fracture. "I know you have this intense need to fix things. I know you see a problem and your first extinct is to swoop in, tough love and all. But you *can't* fix this for me. This is something I have to do all by myself."

"Maybe so." Matt set his mug on the wooden table with a *thump*. "But I can damn sure be around if you start to slip again."

Be around, stuck in a job where the typical day left Matt wishing he watched paint dry for a living. What was the point of this conversation? What could it possibly solve? Matt had been examining Tommy's problem from every possible angle for the past ten years. And as far as he figured, there was only one solution.

"Now if were done with the best man talk," Matt said, easing his words with a gentle pat on Tommy's back. "I've got another ax-throwing competition to lose."

Chapter Nine

Over the past ten years, Callie had sometimes wondered if she'd been fooling herself about her life. Today Callie had determined with absolutely certainty that her mistake all those years ago had been both the worst and the best turning point of her life.

If she hadn't blown that scholarship she'd probably be working for someone else right now, because that would have been the safer, easier route to take. But when her choices had been limited to only one—that one choice being whatever she could build herself from the ground up—she'd set about and done just that.

With the most important event in the history of Callie's business currently taking place right before her eyes.

The day of the Paulson-Smith wedding began just as beautifully as the day before. The grassy field was dotted with white tents that flapped in the cool breeze, providing a sharp contrast against the crystal-blue sky. A crowd of guests dressed in their best medieval fair, maidens and princesses and knights stood next to wizards and trolls. Penny's silver silk gown shimmered around her slender figure and made her look like an elegant elf.

Gorgeous.

The crowd had grown from online gaming friends to several hundred interested well-wishers. From the three news cameras mixed in with the crowd, clearly the publicity would be bigger than even Colin had guessed. With her ex, along with Penny and Tommy, set to be interviewed during the reception, the day clearly promised to be a boon for Callie's business.

So how come all she could focus on was Matt?

With about eight other things she should be checking on, Callie shaded her eyes from the sun, grinning as a chain-mail-wearing Matt walked Penny down a makeshift aisle composed of friends dressed as knights, swords drawn and creating an arch over a red carpet leading to the front of a gorgeous canopy. The sight created a happy thrum in Callie's veins. Publicity aside, the scene was the single most satisfying event in her life to date.

But Matt wearing chain mail would never cease to be Callie's favorite part. And while he protested that he was no one's knight in shining armor, she begged to differ. The smile on the bride's face, and the almost embarrassed look on Matt's, brought about a pressure in Callie's chest.

An emotion she couldn't name.

Feeling like a sappy fool, Callie grinned as she discreetly wiped the tears gathering at the corners of her eyes. Tommy looked happy. Penny positively beamed. And Matt, the man who played the largest role in ensuring this ceremony happened, looked adorably embarrassed and charmingly put out. He'd stuck by his brother and refused to give up when things got tough. And, no matter how silly Matt thought the whole affair, he'd thrown himself into making sure today took place just how Tommy and Penny wanted.

A buzzing started in her chest, creating a warmth that had nothing to do with the sun or the crowd pressing in around her.

Standing on the other side of the makeshift aisle, Colin discreetly waved at Callie and then pointed at his watch. They'd caught up earlier and planned on running through the best way to handle the news interviews set to take place after the ceremony. Which she was about twenty minutes late for.

She knew she should slip away and meet up as planned, but she couldn't force her feet to move. Callie blinked and glanced back up the aisle, unable to shift her gaze from Matt as he leaned in for Penny's kiss. Or when he stepped forward to stand by Tommy.

The buzzing grew stronger. Callie pressed her hand to her chest as the pressure became a physical ache, the realization washing over her with all the gentleness of a tidal wave.

She loved him.

The terrifying and wonderful and life-altering realization kept her rooted in place. Even as Colin managed to unobtrusively weave his way through the crowd of people craning to watch the small three-person bridal party make their way beneath the white awning covering the wooden platform—a last-minute addition ensuring the larger than expected crowd could see the ceremony.

But all Callie wanted to watch was Matt, in his chain mail and leggings and boots and the sword hanging at his side. A small grin on his face as he watched Tommy take Penny's hand and step in front of the officiant dressed as, of all things, a wizard.

And falling for the man who lived a thousand miles away felt significantly more terrifying than failing at this publicity event.

Jeez, what had she done?

A hand lightly gripped her elbow, but she didn't budge as Colin whispered in her ear.

"We were supposed to meet twenty minutes ago," he said.

"I know."

Still, she didn't move. No matter how many times she told her feet to start walking.

"What's the matter?" Colin leaned forward, his gaze landing on her face. "Good God, Callie. What's gotten into you?"

She stared up at Colin, her mind still stuck on her personal epiphany. And then she felt a drop of water hit her cheek. Concerned, Callie glanced up at the sky. Still no clouds. She touched her face and finally realized she was still crying.

Despite her ridiculously romantic ideals, she'd never cried at a wedding before. Of course, realizing she'd fallen hard for the brother of the groom was a first, too.

Concern clouded Colin's voice. "Are you okay?"

Callie didn't respond, simply watched Tommy and Penny begin to repeat their vows. And the signal that the ceremony was quickly coming to a close provided the impetus to move. With one last lingering look at Matt on stage, hands clasped behind his back, eyes fixed on his little brother, Callie turned and followed Colin silently through the throng of people to a quiet spot well away from the crowd and the ceremony.

Colin still looked at her as if she were about to go off the deep end. "Callie, are you sick?"

"No." She shook her head, hoping the motion would clear her spinning brain.

No such luck.

Colin crossed his arms, a skeptical look creeping up his face. "I know you love weddings. But this is kind of over the top, even for you."

She wiped her cheek again and found her cheek just as wet as before. Good grief, she felt as if she'd sprung a leak.

"So what's wrong?" Colin asked.

She stared up at her ex, a million responses flitting through her brain before the only one that fit came out.

"I love him."

Colin suddenly looked as though he'd prefer to be identified as the evil Zhorg and taken into custody by the crowd to be hanged by the neck until dead. And then drawn and quartered. Followed by a massive festival as the townsfolk danced while he burned, his body cremated just to be sure the deed was done.

Her ex's eyes shifted from Callie's face to the focus of her gaze, the small party standing on stage, and then back to Callie again.

Worry laced his tone. "I hope you're talking about Matt and not Tommy."

Forcing back the bubble of hysterical laughter, mostly triggered by panic, Callie rolled her eyes. "Of course I'm talking about Matt."

"Good." Colin winced. "Because falling for a man who just walked down the aisle probably wouldn't end well."

A surge of fear hit. "Matt lives in Manford, Michigan. A thousand miles away."

"I'm sure y'all can work something out."

She wished she felt so optimistic. And why hadn't she concerned herself with this detail before? Suddenly pulling off a fabulous event without losing her focus seemed a terribly stupid reason for avoiding a relationship with Matt. But this? Falling in love with a man who lived so far away? One who clearly felt responsible for his brother?

She'd only just begun to realize how complicated their relationship was.

Callie had ten years—and most of her identity—invested in Fantasy Weddings. Her business wasn't portable. She couldn't just pick up and start over again. And she loved New Orleans. Her family was here. Her friends were here.

The tension in Callie's stomach expanded.

"Hey." Colin laid his hand on Callie's shoulder. "Now's not the time to fall apart, okay?"

The concern in his face only highlighted how truly screwed she was. She wiped her cheeks and forced herself back to the matter at hand. "Of course not. I can handle this." She tried for a confidence-inspiring smile, hoping it didn't feel as weak as it felt. "Let's go talk to the news crew and figure out the best place for the interviews."

Right.

Interviews.

Medieval wedding reception.

Dungeons of Zhorg.

Callie turned her back on the end of the ceremony—and the view of Matt standing on stage—and followed

Colin in the direction of the news crews. Focusing on getting through the rest of the day appeared to be her only option.

The sun was setting as Callie forced herself to focus on the staff taking down the tents. When Matt came up beside her, she gave strict instructions to her heart to calm down. Much to her distress, her instructions went ignored when he slipped an arm around her waist.

"You okay?" he asked.

"Absolutely."

Her smile felt forced, and Callie knew Matt suspected something, but she concentrated on remaining calm so she could finish her job. During the reception, Tommy and Penny's brief interview had come out really cute, mostly because they were both so ridiculously happy. Callie had no doubt their two minutes of fame would be well received by viewers. As the maker of the video game, Colin's interview was less emotional. But Colin was more than just a geeky gamer. He excelled as the marketing guru, as well. His smooth, well-polished blurb mentioning Fantasy Weddings and the *Dungeons of Zhorg* sounded casual and didn't come across rehearsed at all.

"How much longer before I can get you alone again?" Matt murmured, a crooked smile on his face.

She discreetly fished her small pocket watch from the bodice of her princess dress, her favorite costume to date. The overdress of robin's-egg-blue split in front, forming an inverted V to showcase the design of the white satin and gold brocade pattern beneath.

And, despite the fear now curled around her spine

and setting up house, she had to laugh at the expression on Matt's face.

"I was thinking I'd like to get you out of that dress and see how you'd look in chain mail." His sex-filled smile started a thrumming vibration in her belly and spread outward. "With nothing underneath. So..." he said.

He leaned in close, sending a spike in her pulse, heat between her legs and anxiety twisting in her stomach.

"How long?" he finished.

"My assistant volunteered to oversee the cleanup," she said. "And I already spoke to the vendor who supplied the table and chairs, so I'm free to go."

Free to go.

Free to go where? Back to her place with Matt and have sex? Or free to go back to her regularly scheduled life, the one without Matt in it?

"Perfect," Matt said, steering her in the direction of the parking lot.

Swallowing hard, she glanced down at her dress and smoothed a hand down her skirt. "How did your week at Manford Memorial go?"

"As uneventful as ever," Matt replied.

She pounced on the one thing she knew for sure. Matt held no deep abiding affection for his job or his hometown. Surely that meant he'd be willing to move? No matter how much she loved him, she simply couldn't afford to start all over again.

Desperate for something to do with her hands beside reach for Matt, she picked up her skirt as she walked. "Have you ever thought about living somewhere other than Manford?"

Matt shot her a guarded look, the expression doing

little to ease her nerves. So she hurried on before she lost her courage completely.

"You know, find a new job?" she said.

"Why should I?" His steps slowed a little, making it easier to match his stride. But his tone was wary. "It's home."

Her feet fumbled, and Matt reached out briefly to steady her. Jeez, his hand on her arm wasn't helping to calm her down. But she couldn't just take him home to her bed without finding out more.

Callie opened her mouth to speak but failed at making a sound. She swallowed hard, forcing her mouth to cooperate. "But have you ever considered taking a part-time job somewhere else?" She glanced at him out of the corner of her eye. "Moving your home base?"

Matt kept his eyes firmly ahead. "Like where?"

The loaded question felt like a shotgun aimed at her heart. Was he avoiding her gaze because he wasn't sure of the direction of the conversation? Or did he know and simply wanted to avoid the topic altogether? One thing she knew for sure, she'd never know unless she asked. And sleeping with Matt now that she'd figured out she loved him would make letting him go harder in the end.

"Like here," she said. "In New Orleans."

Several seconds passed with only the sound of the gravel beneath their shoes, and Callie felt every crunch like a kick to the chest.

"I could certainly look into doing recurrent shifts as a traveling doc in their E.R.," he said.

Not exactly the answer she wanted to hear. But the response felt encouraging.

"How often could you get down this way?" she asked.

"I could pull off six, maybe seven days a month."

Six days a month? And he'd be working busy shifts. What kind of life would that be for the two of them?

Callie came to a stop and stared up at him. "That's not much time."

A small breeze kicked up, and the setting sun finally sank beneath the tops of the oak trees, casting a shadow across them both.

"Callie." With a sigh, Matt turned to face her, and she could see the conflict in his expression. "I can't leave Manford."

The words sliced through her like a sharp blade through whipped cream cheese.

"Why not?" she asked.

Matt looked out across the parking lot. Several seconds ticked by. Callie expected him to come up with something noteworthy, given the amount of time he spent formulating his response. But when the words came they were incredibly disappointing in their simplicity.

"It's my home," he said.

Callie slowly inhaled, searching for strength, before blowing out her breath in one long exhale.

"People move all the time, Matt," she said. "And it's not as if you love your job there." She waited for him to look at her again. When he kept his eyes on the park, the trees fading as dusk claimed the rest of the landscape, she went on, "I know you don't. So don't even try to pretend that you do."

"I never said I did."

She stepped closer. "So move down here." Callie longed to get some sort of a response from the man. When nothing was forthcoming, she tried again. "Make

New Orleans your home base. Tommy's married now, Matt. He's moving on with his life."

Callie died a million deaths waiting for him to respond.

"I know," he said.

Did he? Tommy seemed to be moving on with his life. But not Matt.

"Are you planning on going on the honeymoon with them?" she asked dryly.

"Jesus, of course not."

Fear and frustration made her words harder than she'd intended. "Then why not move?"

Matt strode several feet away before stopping, his back to her. He shoved his hands into his hair, leaving sandy tufts sticking up. When he finally turned to face her again, the look on his face was one she'd never seen before.

"The last time I left Tommy for too long I came home and found him unconscious on the couch." He stared off in the distance, and she knew by the look on his face he was seeing now what he'd seen back then. "He'd gone through rehab number four and had been doing well for months. But I knew right away he wasn't just sleeping. Everything was off. The room felt wrong. Tommy looked wrong. Damn, the very air in the room felt wrong. I couldn't wake up him up. And—"

His voice grew so hoarse it died out, and Callie reached out to gently wrap her fingers around his wrist, the look on his face heartbreaking.

"For two seconds I couldn't find a pulse," he said.

A chill swept up her spine and traveled out her limbs. Goose bumps pricked her arms, the hair at the back of her neck standing on end. Matt's words came out rushed.

"And suddenly all the tough love you've come to accept as necessary just doesn't matter anymore," he said.

"He's been clean for two years, Matt," she said softly.

"Which is why I started taking the occasional locums jobs in Miami and Los Angeles. But I can't be gone that long."

"I'm in love with you."

The stunned look on Matt's face would have been funny if she hadn't been hurting so much. She hadn't meant to say the words yet. And she certainly hadn't meant for them to come out the way they did. So plain. With no lead-in. Nothing, no sign from her to prepare Matt for what would follow. But maybe the simple statement would knock some sense into the man.

Callie stared at Matt, her mind spinning as she tried to make sense of the words. At first she thought his resistance simply meant he didn't feel as much for her as she felt for him. But the look on Matt's face now told her the truth. He did care about her. No telling how much, but enough that he clearly didn't want to leave. But he just couldn't let his worries about Tommy go.

Matt had suffered so much through the years, and his fear for Tommy was deeply entrenched. There'd be no reaching the man with easy words. She was going to have to be brutally, brutally honest with him to get him to see reason. He loved his brother too much, had suffered too much to let the issue go easily.

And, as hard as it was going to be, she had to fight. She deserved a chance at happiness. And Matt deserved so much more than he had in his current life.

She steeled herself against the pain she knew was sure to follow. "So that's what this is about."

Matt's expression grew guarded. When he said nothing, she went on, no matter how much it hurt him in turn. Matt couldn't be allowed to continue to sacrifice himself, not when her bluntly harsh words had a chance of getting him to see how much more he deserved out of life. "What is with you and this martyr complex?" she said.

"I don't know what you're talking about."

"Yes, you do," she said softly.

"Look, is this really necessary? I'd hoped to enjoy the rest of my time in New Orleans with you."

Anger flared, pushing the tender feelings to the back of the line. "And that will be…what? Two, maybe three days?" She forced herself to maintain his gaze. Heart thumping, she tried to keep the bitterness at bay, but his unwillingness to even consider a change hurt like hell. "I understand you want to stick around and be there for Tommy if he needs you. And I suppose you have to do what you think is right. But I can't do this anymore."

"Do what?"

"Love you. Settle for a few days here and there. I've put my life on hold and now that I've rediscovered how much life there is to live outside of work, I don't want to settle anymore."

Matt stared off into the shadows growing along the trees lining the park. A muscle in his jaw ticked, and, for the second time that day, Callie fought the tears of frustration and anger and pain that were gathering at the corners of her lids. He didn't look torn, signaling she at least had some room to convince him to change his mind. He looked resigned.

And that hurt worst of all.

"You're right," he said. "You shouldn't have to settle for whatever time I get to snatch here and there. You deserve a full-time relationship, not a part-time one. You also deserve better than to continue to endure your mother's insinuation that you've settled for less with your job. Maybe you should tell her exactly how you feel instead of letting your guilt keep you silent."

Matt unlocked her car and opened the door for her. Muscles tight, head aching, heart hurting, she gathered up her dress and slid into the driver's seat, fabric billowing around her legs. She gripped the steering wheel and willed herself to calm the heck down so she could at least say goodbye without sounding like a total wreck.

Hand on the roof her car, Matt leaned in to press his lips to hers.

"Goodbye, Callie. Thanks for making Tommy and Penny's day special."

Matt straightened up and stared down at her for three more heartbeats. And then he turned and headed across the parking lot.

Chapter Ten

One week later, Callie sat in her office and twisted off the top of her bottled water, staring at her laptop in the center of her desk. As she tried to compose a reasonable answer to her latest *Ex Factor* question, she avoided looking at the tiny camera eye centered at the top of the computer screen. And desperately tried not to remember how Matt had looked the night of their Skype sex.

She pressed her palms over her eyes. Maybe if she pushed hard enough she could force the images from her brain. Unfortunately, her brain was still filled with visions of Matt wearing nothing, long muscular legs stretched out before him. The broad shoulders and the hard chest and the flat abdomen. She loved the way his sweatpants had been slung low over his lean hips. Better still? Those sexy hands satisfying his body while she urged him on with her words. The sight of the successful conclusion would be her undoing for some time to come.

Throat dry as yesterday's leftover toast, she reached for her bottle of water and swallowed gratefully.

She might never be able to sit through a video conference again without thinking of that moment. A fact that would prove incredibly inconvenient today when she'd had a Skype session with the mother of the bride of next week's *Pride and Prejudice* wedding.

But of all the things she missed about Matt, many a sexy episode aside, she missed his smile the most. The sexy half smirk, that teasing hint of a grin. And her favorite? The smile accompanied by that spark of full-on humor in his eyes. She wished she could hang a poster on her wall with all the various looks. But that would only remind her of what was missing in her life.

And that something was Matt.

Callie slumped in her seat. The first few days after the wedding, she'd hoped that he'd call her up to say he'd rethought his position. But as one day slipped into the next, she began to wonder if she should consider moving. But leaving New Orleans, her family and her business?

She couldn't imagine life so far away from the city, the bayou of her childhood and Aunt Billie. As strained as their relationship was, she'd even miss her parents. And she'd just started reconnecting with the extended family she hadn't seen in years. She couldn't leave now.

A knock sounded on her door and a head full of brown hair poked through.

Callie sat up in surprise. "Mama."

Her mother rarely came to visit at the office. Usually it was Callie making the trip across town to see her parents.

"Hi, honey. You look…off," her mom said.

A sad smile crept up Callie's face. "I'm feeling very off."

Her mother settled into the seat across from Callie and folded her arms across her lap. She looked ready to wait until Callie explained.

"The Paulson wedding was a huge success," Callie said.

"So I heard. That's nice."

Nice.

Snippets of the event had been broadcast on two local cable channels. Tommy and Penny's brief interview had been picked up by a syndicated news channel and been aired across the country. Callie had received more business inquires in the past week than ever before. Business was booming, and Callie would probably need to hire extra help to keep up with the work.

But all she got from her mother was *nice.*

"What happened with that doctor you brought to the reunion?" her mother said.

The muscles in Callie's stomach clinched. Something in her mother's voice rubbed Callie wrong. It was the same tone she'd used the first time they discussed Callie's screwup in college. The tone that held an implied "What now?" Ten years later and her mother still expected bad news at every turn. And, as bad news went, this was the worst Callie had ever experienced.

Matt…*gone.*

And if she could blurt out the truth to Matt, there seemed no point in keeping anything from her mother now. "I'm in love with Matt Paulson."

Something flickered in her mother's eyes, but her expression didn't budge. "I figured out as much on my own."

"You did?"

"Well, I am your mother." Her mother shrugged, as if the act of giving birth to Callie somehow had provided Belle LaBeau a peephole into Callie's heart. "And it's not like you did a very good job of hiding the fact. I could tell by the way you looked at him at the reunion. When he laughed, your whole face would light up." She hesitated and then smoothed a hand down her pants. "You certainly never looked at Colin like that."

This time Callie did groan. Good God. How long before her mother let this issue go? Callie had recovered from the breakup years ago. Did her mother need therapy to get past this and move on?

"Mama, Colin and I have been over for years. He's happily married to a woman I consider a friend."

"I'm well aware of that." A soft smile appeared on her mother's face. "I happen to know the woman who planned the wedding."

In the end, Callie lost her battle with a wry grin.

"I'm not stuck on Colin," her mother went on.

The news surprised Callie, because she sure couldn't tell by her mother's action. Every single visit with her mom had ended with Colin being mentioned at some point in time.

Callie sat up straighter in her seat. "Then why are you constantly bringing him up?"

"Only because he's the last man you've brought around to visit your family. At least, he was until Matt came along."

The mention of Matt's name brought a fresh wave of pain, her heart aching. Callie shifted her focus to the window that overlooked the warehouse district of New Orleans. The day sunny and bright, but inside Callie's office felt dark.

"You're happy arranging weddings for other people, yet you haven't had a serious relationship in ages," her mother said. "What happened with Matt?"

Callie's voice sounded as hollow as she felt. "He went

back home to Michigan. And he's kind of stuck living in Manford. It's…" Callie paused trying to think of an explanation that wouldn't be an invasion of Matt's and Tommy's privacy. "It's complicated."

Her mother crossed her legs and studied Callie for a moment. And in one of those moments known horribly well by kids the world over, Callie knew her mother was about to offer advice. Whether Callie wanted it or not.

"You could move up to Michigan," she said. "Maybe even finally realize your dream of finishing college."

Callie's heart slowly slipped to her toes.

"I don't want to go back to college," Callie said.

"But that was all you talked about in high school."

"That was the dream of an eighteen-year-old who had no real idea what she wanted to do with her life," Callie said. "It was always more your dream than mine."

Her mother looked knocked flat, and a stab of guilt struck Callie again. She never meant to be quite so truthful.

"Look, Mama," Callie said. "I'm sorry you and Dad sacrificed so much to get me into a great school."

Her mother straightened her shoulders. "Your dad and I sacrificed so you could make something of yourself."

Callie dropped her head into her hands. "Mama." Callie managed not to let out a moan. Barely. She looked up again. "I love my job." She dropped her hands to her desk and met the brown gaze of her mother sitting on the other side. "This is exactly where I want to be. I'm my own boss and I have a very successful business. I appreciate all you and Dad have done for me, but—"

It was past time she told the truth and stopped letting this issue slide. She couldn't continue to remain silent.

Callie sucked in a breath and gathered her courage. "But I'm not sorry about how things turned out. I wouldn't change anything even if I *could*. If I could climb into a time capsule and undo all I'd done in college, I wouldn't." She should have spoken these words ages ago. Callie steadily held her mother's gaze. "I'm exactly where I want to be," Callie said, "doing exactly what I want to do."

The strength of the conviction in her words reminded her exactly why she couldn't drop her life and move up to Michigan. Both her mother's brows arched in surprise, and Callie let the words settle a little deeper before going on.

"This isn't my second-choice life, Mama. This is my very *best* life."

Or at least it had been until she lost Matt.

Callie pushed the crushing thought aside and concentrated on meeting her mother's gaze. "And I need—"

When Callie's voice gave out, her mother set her purse on the floor beside her chair. "What do you need?"

"I need to stop feeling like y'all are just waiting for me to screw up again."

Silence filled the room and Callie did her best not to shift her gaze away from her mother. It felt as if Callie had lived and died a thousand lives as she waited for her mother to speak.

"Okay," her mother said.

Callie blinked. *Okay?* Just like that?

"Now you need to do me a favor, Callie."

Callie fought to keep her breathing steady. "What's that?"

Her mother leaned forward, her eyes intent. "Stop

avoiding relationships. Get serious about finding someone, about sharing your *future,* with someone."

Callie's lungs stopped functioning, and she longed to take a deep breath. Problem was, she had finally gone out and gotten serious about someone.

But he was gone for good.

"Why are you still here?"

Tommy's voice echoed off the walls of the garage, and Matt turned from his task of sorting through his tools. "Excuse me?"

Matt had been banging around the garage for the past two hours, trying to pack for the move to an apartment that held little appeal, yet grateful for the mindless task of sorting through his stuff. He'd tossed the things he didn't need—a pile that wasn't as big as it should have been—and stacked the stuff yet to be packed, which was larger than need be. Boxes covered the floor of his bedroom and living room and perched on the counters in the kitchen. He couldn't seem to decide what to keep and what to throw away. So two hours ago Matt had come out to the garage, frustrated by his inability to focus, thinking that dividing the supply of tools in half would be an easier process.

He'd never had trouble focusing before. If anything, his focus had always been a problem. But with his mind stuck on missing Callie, and the impossible situation a relationship with her presented, he'd come out to sort through his problem the only way he knew how: banging the wrenches and screwdrivers and the various-size hammers around. The process offered him some satisfaction.

But zero relief.

"You heard me," his brother said.

Tommy stepped down into the garage. His wavy brown hair and brown eyes always made him look a bit like an overgrown puppy. Well, an overgrown puppy with serious issues.

His brother came to a halt beside Matt and leaned his hip against the workbench.

"How long are we going to tiptoe around this, Matt?"

Silence had been working for them so far. And Matt wasn't sure he knew how to change the status quo.

"I don't know what you're talking about," Matt said.

But he did. The dark thoughts plaguing him since he'd left New Orleans had been following him around like a black cloud hell-bent on raining down on his head, complete with lightning bolts and thunder and the foul mood.

Tommy let out a scoff. "You don't want to be here." He waved his hand to encompass their current surroundings, but Matt knew he was referencing something much bigger than a garage located in Manford, Michigan. "You want to be in New Orleans." Brown eyes gazed at Matt. "With *Callie*."

The familiar ache in his chest friggin' hurt.

"Maybe," Matt said.

Yes, his mind screamed.

Matt turned away from his brother and concentrated on repacking the tools in a manner worthy of the most diehard of obsessive compulsives. Matt knew the statistics; crystal meth addicts had one of the highest relapse rates of all the drug users.

There was no answer to this one.

Just like Tommy's addiction, this wasn't a problem Matt could fix. There was no treatment to be applied that cured the disease. Frustration burned through Matt and he randomly picked up a wrench and rubbed his finger on the cool metal.

"But my home is here," Matt said.

"It doesn't have to be."

Matt closed his eyes, his fingers curling around a Phillips head screwdriver.

"Manford doesn't have to be your home base anymore," Tommy went on. "In fact, you could take a permanent job in New Orleans. The emergency rooms there have to be busy enough to satisfy the adrenaline junky in you."

"I could," Matt said. "But I won't."

"Why not?"

Matt stared out the window at the bleak view that only appeared that way because he was in freaking *Manford.* Anxiety coiled in his stomach, and he decided to voice the words that had been bouncing around his head for years.

"Because when I walked in on you two years ago, for several seconds I thought you were dead."

The ache in his chest was all-consuming, and he met his brother's brown eyes again. They'd never discussed that day. The event had been too painful. Matt took in the way Tommy's hair flopped on his forehead, just like it had as a kid.

"And I can't bear to go through that again," Matt said.

"So what does that mean?" Tommy cocked his head. "Tough love until the day I die?"

Matt's lips twisted. "*Tough* is a pretty good word for it," he said. But as the moment lingered between them, Matt finally went on, "No matter what, you're my brother. That comes before everything else."

Tommy cleared his throat as his eyes grew suspiciously bright. "I told you before, you can't save me from myself, Matt," he said softly. And then he let out a humorless huff. "Though God knows you've tried." He rolled his head, as if releasing the tension in his neck. "You can't put your entire life on hold anymore," Tommy continued. "You have to let it go, Matt."

Anger, bright and hot, surged from his core. "What the hell?" Matt braced himself as he faced Tommy. "You're my brother, Tommy. How am I supposed to just let you go?"

"Not me," Tommy said. "The guilt."

The word slammed into Matt, leaving him gut-punched and short of breath. His ribs squeezing his heart so hard Matt was sure the pressure would crush him.

What is with you and this martyr complex?

Jesus, he'd told Callie to fully let go of the past, and here he was clinging to his. But Tommy didn't know about the thoughts he'd had…

Matt let out a self-deprecating scoff, wishing Callie was here with him with that playful spark in her eyes and her honey-tinted drawl. And the kind of nonjudgmental understanding that let a person share even the worst truths about themselves without fear.

Because how could he share that brutal news with his kid brother? He opted for the easier explanation instead.

Matt left the tool bench and headed for the stairs leading to the kitchen, dropping down to sit on the bottom step. "I should have been around more in the beginning."

"You had a medical degree you were trying to earn." Tommy took a seat beside Matt.

"But Mom and Dad were gone, and we were alone."

And God knows wading through the days, trying to figure out how to deal with Tommy and be an adult all at the same time hadn't been easy.

They sat there, side by side, and Matt tried to push the memories of the first time he'd found Tommy passed out on the floor. Of a Tommy so gaunt, so thin, his color so unhealthy that it physically hurt to look at him. Sure, Matt had been checking in by phone. But only so much information can be gleaned from the sound of a voice.

He couldn't remember the precise moment he began to have his suspicions something was off. The little niggles of doubt had always been easily rationalized away.

He's having an off week.

He's stressed.

He's just not hungry today.

Of getting the call he'd wrecked his car again, and this time not being sure Tommy was going to pull through. Perhaps the time had come to explain to Tommy exactly how much Matt didn't deserve his kid brother's devotion.

Matt stared straight ahead. He couldn't meet Tommy's eyes, not with what he was about to say.

"The third time you walked out of rehab and waded back into that mess it took everything in me not to leave." Matt closed his eyes as he remembered the turbulent thoughts from that day. Angry. Petrified. And knowing he just couldn't live this life anymore.

Tommy remained quiet beside him while silence engulfed the garage. Matt couldn't bring himself to look at his brother. The confession was hard enough to express without those wide, brown eyes staring at him. He felt like crap for sharing the thoughts with his brother. If they'd just been a fleeting thought Matt wouldn't feel so guilty. But since that day, every morning he'd woken up with the same thought.

Leave.

Get out of town.

Save yourself.

He scrubbed his face with his hands, exhausted from the mental war being waged in his head. And so friggin' sick of living his life in limbo he didn't know what to do. With every one of those thoughts came the opposing thought. Tommy was all the family Matt had. Walking away felt impossible, even during those times Matt was sure he was drowning.

"God, you have no idea just how badly I wanted to pack up and get the hell out of Dodge. Go to the farthest city that I could." He turned to meet his brother's gaze. "Because I just couldn't bear the torture of waiting around for you to finally kill yourself. Watching you waste away into someone I didn't recognize anymore."

Always braced for the next slip. The next call from the E.R. The next night Tommy didn't come home and Matt was sure that he'd overdosed, unconscious.

Or dead.

"I just couldn't stand to have my heart broken again," Matt said.

Tommy's voice sounded raw. "But you didn't go."

Matt's lips twisted at the words. They might as well be inscribed on his tombstone.

"But it's time," Tommy said. "You've got to get on with your life and stop worrying about your kid brother. Go back to Callie, Matt." Tommy's brown gaze held

Matt's hostage, and then his brother grinned. "Before you become a grumpy old man no one wants to be around anymore. Cuz, you know, you're already half-way there."

Matt slowly sucked in a breath. He'd told Callie to get over the guilt, maybe it was time he followed his own advice.

He let out a scoff. "Is this my kid brother giving me advice?"

"This is your kid brother showing you some tough love, dude, because it's my turn. You need to leave. I need you to leave." Tommy crossed his arms and leaned back against the railing. "How can I ever be sure I've made it on my own if you're always around to help me out? I've kicked the ugly addiction. Every day I'm concentrating on staying clean. I know you've tried to ease my way in the world by smoothing out the bumps along the way. Now it's time for me to handle life on my own."

Matt's chest shook with the force of the pounding beneath his ribs.

"Go back to New Orleans. Take a job there. You can visit whenever you like. This will always be your home, too." Tommy stood up, looking down at Matt. "But you belong with Callie."

Tommy climbed the last two steps and entered the kitchen, closing the door behind him. Matt stared at the door, his brother's parting words echoing in his brain.

Chapter Eleven

The waltz started, and the bride and groom headed for the center of the room, the ballroom of the Riverway plantation transformed into an eighteenth-century ball. Callie watched, holding her breath as the bridal party joined in. They'd only had two days to rehearse the dance, and certainly no time to practice in their Regency-era wedding outfits.

With the bride's dark hair upswept and adorned with baby's breath, curls pinned to her head, imagining her as Elizabeth Bennet required very little stretch of the imagination. The groom, however, wasn't quite tall enough to pull off a convincing Fitzwilliam Darcy. But the man wore the cravat and waistcoat with pride.

Callie was enjoying the results of her hard work when a voice interrupted her thoughts.

"So, will there be zombies invading this reception?"

Callie whirled and came face-to-face with Matt, and the sight sent Callie's senses soaring. In a waistcoat, white linen cravat and pantaloons, he looked unusually formal yet still good enough to eat.

"Could be a fitting end, don't you think?" he finished with an easy smile.

Callie tried to reply, her mouth parting, but no words formed.

Was he here to convince her to reconsider a long-distance relationship? Or was he here to tell her he'd changed his mind and that he was ready to let his little brother go? Maybe he was finally ready to move on from a life that including the two brothers living in a constant state of protector and the protected. Callie knew the situation had been necessary during the beginnings of Tommy's recovery days—the by-product being two men who didn't know how to simply be brothers, instead of recovering addict and responsible older brother.

Callie fisted her hand behind her back, resisting the urge to grip the lapel of Matt's coat and haul him closer. She longed to ask him the questions swirling in her brain, questions like *Why are you here?* or *Have you changed your mind?*

Or more important: *Do you love me as much as I love you?*

"No," she said. "No zombies."

"That's too bad," he said.

"Depends on who you ask."

Not the conversation she'd have predicted would take place upon seeing Matt again. Not only did she not know where to start, she was almost afraid to find out the answers. If he was here to convince her to change her mind and accept less, she just might cave.

And even as her head was telling her to be strong, her heart was breaking a little more.

"Walk with me a moment?" he asked.

Pulse picking up its pace, she said, "Sure."

Callie followed Matt out the French doors and onto the veranda, trying to convince herself to stay true to her goals.

But the past few weeks had only gotten harder, not easier, and she wasn't entirely sure she had the strength to resist a part-time relationship offer again. Not when every morning started with her missing Matt, his laugh and his dry sense of humor. And every evening ending up with her staring up at the ceiling of her room, dreaming of having him back in her bed. In her life.

But all that seemed too much to ask after two weeks of no contact.

"How did you pull off the outfit?" she asked instead.

He turned and leaned against the wrought-iron railing, the branches of the oak tree beyond lit by the light from the ballroom.

"I phoned Colin and spoke with Jamie," Matt said. "Turns out your ex's wife was very eager to help me arrange a romantic meet up with you. She insisted this would be an opportune moment. Even phoned the bride and groom to ensure I'd be welcome."

A small laugh escaped Callie. "That explains the looks they were giving me at the rehearsal dinner last night."

Matt grinned. "Beware the romantic musings of those who are about to get married. Unfortunately—" he looked down at his clothes "—everyone thought it best I blend in."

"Why are you here, other than to make the most delicious Fitzwilliam Darcy ever?"

She probably shouldn't have added in the last part.

She should be playing it cool. She should be holding her feelings closer to her chest. But she couldn't.

"I came tonight hoping to make an impression," he said.

Afraid to breathe, Callie asked, "What kind of impression?"

Matt stepped closer, instantly swamping her senses. The warm breeze ruffled his sandy hair and held a hint of magnolias, but all Callie could register was Matt's scent of fresh citrusy soap. The heat from his body. The sizzle in those hazel eyes.

His eyes never left hers. "'I have been meditating on the very great pleasure which a pair of fine eyes in the face of a pretty woman can bestow.'"

Two seconds passed before the words fully registered in her brain.

Stunned, Callie reached out and gripped the sleeve of Matt's waist coat. "You read *Pride and Prejudice?*"

A slow smile crept up his face.

"How else is a man supposed to impress a woman who arranges fantasy weddings for a living?" he asked. "Quoting Darcy seemed like a good place to start."

Too afraid to hope, Callie remained silent, her grip on his sleeve growing tight.

"I just got started on the paperwork to obtain privileges at St. Matthews Hospital," Matt went on. "Turns out they have a need for a few more E.R. docs."

Heart hammering, she had to ask, "For locums work?"

"Nope," he said. "Full-time. Well, 80 percent time, anyway. Because that will leave me some room to do an occasional locums shift up in Manford."

Afraid to burst the budding hope in her heart, Callie hiked an eyebrow, and Matt smiled.

"Only one week every three months or so. That will give me plenty of time to visit my brother and his wife." His lips twitched, as if holding back a smile. "Especially now that I'm going to be an uncle."

The last was delivered so nonchalantly that several seconds passed before the news registered.

Callie let out an embarrassing whoop and launched herself into Matt's arms. He folded his arms around her, and she realized her feet were still dangling off the ground. But she didn't care. She basked in the feel of his embrace and the ever-growing realization that finally, *finally*, Matt was in New Orleans for keeps. Matt appeared in no hurry to let her down. Callie had no desire to ever let him let her go.

She buried her face in his neck and inhaled, enjoying the smell of warm skin and the feel of Matt's arms around her again. "What changed your mind?"

"Well," he said, his voice rumbling though his chest to hers. "You said you wanted me here. Tommy wanted me here. And I wanted to be here. Ultimately not being here seemed kind of stupid."

"I love your logic."

"I figured you would."

Matt set her back on her feet, but kept his arms wrapped firmly around her back, her chest pressed against his hard torso.

She looked up at him. "Did Tommy have to beat you off with a stick?"

"No." Matt's hazel eyes grew serious, and he gazed through the French doors at the couples now waltzing across the floor. "He used his own brand of tough love on me. And he agreed with your assessment. That I was good at the tough love while he was using, but I sucked after he'd quit."

"Remind me to send Tommy a huge present every year on his birthday."

"Yeah? Well, he told me he planned to send you a gift every month for getting me out of his hair. And it wasn't only logic that brought me back."

"No?"

"Yeah, there was also this little issue of me falling in love with you."

Tears gathered the corners of her eyes, and she blinked, forcing them back. How would she maintain the professional demeanor with tears in her eyes? Matt swept a strand of hair from her cheek, his fingers taking their time, and then cupped her face.

"I'm sorry it took me a while to get my head on straight," he said. "I didn't mean to make things so hard on you."

She sniffed and sent him a watery smile. "'You must learn some of my philosophy. Think only of the past as its remembrance gives you pleasure.'"

"Ah," Matt said, his lips twitching. "I love that line. And I admire Elizabeth Bennet and her practical approach to life." He eyed the front of her dress. "But I have to confess, the clothing of her era leaves a lot to be desired. Though you look beautiful, this isn't my favorite costume."

"Yeah, the A-line style doesn't exactly flatter the figure. Don't worry," she said, grinning up at Matt. "They aren't as flat as they look in this dress."

With a crooked smile, Matt leaned in and nuzzled her neck. "No worries," he said. "I'm thinking that admiring your occasional kooky attire will keep me happily entertained for the rest of my life."

* * * * *

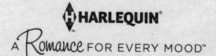

♦ HARLEQUIN®

SPECIAL EDITION

Life, Love and Family

Coming in July 2014

THE BACHELOR'S BRIGHTON VALLEY BRIDE

by *USA TODAY* bestselling author

Judy Duarte

Clayton Jenkins is going undercover…in his own business. The tech whiz wants to find out why his flagship store is failing, so he disguises himself as an employee and gets to work. But even a genius can't program every step of his life—like falling for single mom Megan Adams and her young daughter! What's a billionaire to do?

Don't miss the latest edition of the *Return to Brighton Valley* miniseries!

Look for **THE DADDY SECRET,**
already available from the **Return to Brighton Valley** miniseries by Judy Duarte!

Available wherever books and ebooks are sold!

www.Harlequin.com

HSE65825

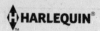

Becoming The Prince's Wife
by
Rebecca Winters

A forbidden love...with a prince!
Attorney Carolena Baretti has learned to keep her cards
close to her chest. But when a chance encounter with the
handsome crown prince ignites a fiery attraction, Carolena
finds that he may just be the one man she can trust....

Crown prince Valentino finds himself increasingly
distracted from his duty by the mesmerizing gaze of
beautiful commoner Carolena. But Valentino knows he is
playing with fire...to be with Carolena he would have to
sacrifice *everything*—including his right to the throne....

Torn between love and obligation...

Don't miss the second edition of the
Princes of Europe duet, available
June 2014 from Harlequin Romance
wherever books and ebooks are sold.